DEADLY STRAITS

D0107919

A Thriller By
R. E. McDermott

Published by R.E. McDermott

Copyright © 2011 by R.E. McDermott

ISBN: 978-0-9837417-0-1

For more information about the author, please visit
www.remcdermott.com

Layout by Guido Henkel, **www.guidohenkel.com**

For Andrea

"Whosoever commands the sea commands the trade;
Whosoever commands the trade of the world commands the
riches of the world,
and consequently the world itself."

—Sir Walter Raleigh, October 1618

CHAPTER ONE

Offices of Phoenix Shipping
London
10 May

Alex Kairouz turned from the screen and swiveled in his chair to bend over his wastebasket, barely in time. He vomited as his nausea crested, then slumped head down and sobbing over the basket. A hand appeared, holding a tissue.

"Wipe your bloody face, Kairouz," Braun said.

Alex did as ordered.

Braun continued.

"Mr. Farley, please be good enough to refocus our pupil on the task at hand."

Alex tensed against the pain as he was jerked upright by his thick hair and spun around to once again face the computer screen. He closed his eyes to blot out the horrific sight and tried to put his hands to his ears to escape the tortured screams from the speakers, but Farley was quicker, grabbing his wrists from behind and forcing them down.

"Open your bloody eyes and cooperate, Kairouz," said Braun, "unless you want a ringside seat at a live performance."

Alex looked not at the screen but at Braun.

"Why are you doing this? What do you want? If it's money—"

Braun moved his face inches from Alex's.

"In due time, Kairouz, all in due time." Braun lowered his voice to a whisper. "But for now, you need to finish our little lesson. I assure you, it gets much, much more amusing."

M/T *Western Star*
Eastern Holding Anchorage
Singapore
15 May

Dugan moved through the humid darkness of the ship's ballast tank, avoiding pockets of mud. At the ladder he wiped his face on a damp sleeve and turned at muttered Russian curses to shine his flashlight on the corpulent chief mate struggling through an access hole. The man's coveralls, like Dugan's own, were sweat soaked and rust streaked. The Russian pulled through the access hole with a grunt and joined Dugan at the ladder. Sweat rolled down his stubbled cheeks as he fixed Dugan with a hopeful look.

"We go up?" he asked.

Dugan nodded and the Russian started up the long ladder, intent on escaping the tank before Dugan had a change of heart. Dugan played his flashlight over wasted steel one last time, grimacing at the predictable result of poor maintenance, then followed the Russian up the ladder.

He emerged on the main deck at the tail end of a tropical thundershower so common to Singapore. His coveralls were already plastered to his skin by sweat, and the cool rain felt good. But the relief wouldn't last. The rain was slackening, and steam from the deck showed the negligible effect of the brief shower on the hot steel. Two Filipino seamen stood nearby in yellow slickers, looking like small boys dressed in their fathers' clothing. One handed Dugan a wad of rags as the second held open a garbage bag. Dugan wiped his boots and tossed the rags in the bag, then started aft for the deckhouse.

He showered and changed before heading for the gangway, stopping along the way to slip the steward a few dollars for cleaning his room. The grateful Filipino tried to carry his bag, and, when waved away, ran in front, holding doors as an embarrassed Dugan made his way to the main deck. Overtipped again, thought Dugan, making his way down the sloping accommodation ladder to the launch.

He ducked into the launch's cabin and settled in for the ride ashore. Three dogs in six weeks. He didn't look forward to telling Alex Kairouz he'd wasted his money inspecting another rust bucket.

***

An hour later, Dugan settled into an easy chair in his hotel room. He opened an overpriced beer from the minibar, then checked the time. Start of business in London. May as well give Alex a bit of time to get his day started before breaking the bad news. Dugan picked up the remote and thumbed on the television to Sky News. The screen filled with images of a raging refinery fire in Bandar Abbas, Iran. Must be a big one to make international news, he thought.

***

Alex Kairouz sat at his desk, trembling, his eyes squeezed shut and face buried in his hands. He shuddered and shook his head, as if trying to physically cast out the images burned into his brain. Finally he opened his eyes to stare at a photo of his younger self—black hair and eyes in an olive face, and white even teeth, set in a smile of pure joy as he gazed at a pink bundle in the arms of a beautiful woman. He jerked at the buzz of the intercom, then struggled to compose himself.

"Yes, Mrs. Coutts?" he said into the intercom.

"Mr. Dugan on line one, sir."

Thomas! Panic gripped him. Thomas knew him too well. He might sense something wrong, and Braun said if anyone knew—

"Mr. Kairouz, are you there?"

"Yes, yes, Mrs. Coutts. Thank you."

Alex steeled himself and mashed the flashing button.

"Thomas," he said with forced cheerfulness, "how's the ship?"

"Junk."

"Damn."

"What'd you expect, Alex? Good tonnage is making money. Anything for sale now is garbage. You know how it works. You built your own fleet at rock-bottom prices in down markets."

Alex sighed. "I know, but I need more ships and I keep hoping. Oh well, send me an invoice." He paused, more focused now, as he glanced at a notepad on his desk. "And Thomas, I need a favor."

"Name it."

"*Asian Trader* is due into the shipyard there in two days, and McGinty was hospitalized yesterday with appendicitis. Can you cover the ship until I can get another superintendent out to relieve you?"

"How long?"

"Ten days, two weeks max," Alex said.

Dugan sighed. "Yeah, all right. But I may have to break away for a day. I got a call from Military Sealift Command this morning. They want me to inspect a little coaster for them sometime in the next few days. I can't ignore my other clients, even though sometimes it seems I'm on your payroll full-time—"

7

"Since you brought that up—"

"Christ, Alex. Not again."

"Look, Thomas, we're all getting older. I mean, you're what, fifty now—"

"Forty-seven my next birthday."

"OK, forty-seven. But you can't crawl through ships forever. And it's a waste of talent. Plenty of fellows can identify problems. I need someone here to solve them."

"OK, OK. I'll think about it. How's that sound?"

"Like what you always say to shut me up."

"Is it working?" Dugan asked.

"All right, Thomas. I give up. For now. But we'll talk again."

Dugan changed the subject.

"How's Cassie?"

"Ah…she's…"

"What's wrong?" asked Dugan.

"Sorry, my mind was just wandering a bit, I'm afraid. Cassie's fine, just fine. Looking more like her mother every day. And Mrs. Farnsworth says she's making remarkable progress, considering."

"And how is the Dragon Lady?" Dugan asked.

"Really, Thomas, I think you two would get on if you gave it a chance."

"I don't think I'm the one who needs that advice, Alex."

"Well, if you were around more and Mrs. Farnsworth got to know you, I'm sure she would warm to you," Alex said.

Dugan laughed. "Yeah, like that's going to happen."

Alex sighed. "You're probably right. At any rate, I'll have Mrs. Coutts e-mail you the repair specifications for *Asian Trader* straightaway. Can you get up to the yard in Sembawang tomorrow morning and begin preparations for her arrival?"

"Will do, pal," Dugan said. "I'll call you after she arrives and I get things started."

Alex thanked Dugan and hung up. He'd maintained a good front with Dugan, and, for that matter, everyone else. But it was draining. The everyday minutia of running his company he'd so enjoyed just a few days ago seemed pointless now—there'd likely be no Phoenix Shipping when this bastard Braun was finished. But that didn't matter. Only Cassie's safety mattered. His eyes went back to the photo of his once-complete family, and he shuddered anew as the images from Braun's video flashed through his memory.

Ali Reza Motaki, president of the Islamic Republic of Iran, stood at the window, gazing out at the well-manicured grounds. He tensed as his back spasmed. Even in the comfort of the presidential jet, the long flight from Tehran to Caracas had taken its toll. He massaged his lower back and stretched to his full five foot five.

"And is this Kairouz controllable?" asked a voice behind him.

Motaki turned to the speaker, President Hector Diaz Rodriguez of the Bolivarian Republic of Venezuela.

"He is devoted to his daughter," replied Motaki. "He will do anything to keep her from harm. Don't worry my friend, Braun has it well in hand."

Rodriguez smiled. "And what do you think of Braun? Is he not everything I promised?"

"He seems…competent."

Rodriguez's smile faded. "You seem less than enthusiastic."

"I am cautious, as you should be. Acting against the Great Satan is one thing. Duping China and Russia simultaneously is another. We cannot afford mistakes," Motaki said.

"But what choice do we have?" Rodriguez asked. "For all their fine words of friendship, neither the Russians nor the Chinese have acceded to our requests. If we must maneuver them into doing the right thing, so be it."

Motaki shrugged. "I doubt the Russians and Chinese would view it as mere maneuvering."

Rodriguez nodded as Motaki moved from the window to settle down in an easy chair across from the Venezuelan.

"And now it is even more critical that we succeed," Motaki continued. "The damage at the Bandar Abbas refinery is worse than reported in the media. Iran will have to import even more of our domestic fuel requirements, just as the Americans are pressing the UN for tighter sanctions. It is strangling our economy, just as your own lack of access to Asian markets for Venezuelan crude cripples your own."

"That's true," Rodriguez said. "And to be honest, I am concerned we're using only one company. We are putting all our eggs in one basket, as the *yanquis* say."

Motaki shook his head. "No, Braun is right about that. With widely separated attacks, the plan is complicated. Braun's selection of Phoenix was astute—a single company with ships trading worldwide, controlled by one

9

man without outside directors. Control Kairouz, control Phoenix, no questions asked."

Rodriguez nodded. "So we proceed. When will Braun confirm the strike date?"

"I got an encrypted message this morning through the usual channels," Motaki said. "July fourth looks promising. Perhaps we can, as they say, rain on the Americans' parade."

"Excellent." Rodriguez rubbed his hands together. "That will allow me to include some sympathetic remarks in my speech on our own Independence Day on July fifth. Perhaps I can even get an early start in laying these terrible deeds at the feet of the Americans."

Motaki smiled and nodded. And, perhaps in so doing, become the sacrificial lamb should things go awry, he thought.

CHAPTER TWO

Jan Pieter DeVries scratched his bare belly and looked down from the bridge wing. He wore dirty khaki shorts and a wrinkled shirt hanging open from missing buttons, and was shod in flip-flops. A dark tan and tangle of long brown hair made the thirty-year-old look more like an itinerant fisherman than a captain and ship owner, but M/V *Alicia* was his free and clear.

At just over two hundred feet, fifteen hundred tons deadweight, and a shallow draft, she was a trim little ship. She'd been well maintained in prior years, when she was named *Indies Trader* and operated by his stiff-necked family back in Holland. She'd been a "parting gift" of sorts—a convenient way for the family DeVries to prune one of their less desirable branches. It was a parting that suited Jan Pieter as well. Even with no maintenance, *Indies Trader* could trade years before cargo surveyors questioned her seaworthiness—longer in remote ports of Asia, far from the disapproving oversight of the family DeVries. She was perfect for his plan—just as he'd promised a broker named Willem Van Dijk.

He renamed the ship *Alicia*, after a girl whose last name he'd forgotten but whose sexual appetites and flexibility were vivid memories. He moved his first cargo for Van Dijk and never looked back. The broker handled everything, and each voyage included clandestine calls at remote anchorages where illicit goods changed hands, with revenue split between the partners.

As crewmen left on vacation, Van Dijk arranged Indonesian replacements, among the first a competent chief mate named Ali Sheibani. Soon Sheibani was running the ship, and DeVries became a pampered passenger, spending little time on the ship in port and sea passages in his cabin, listening to music through state-of-the-art headphones, smoking dope, and reviewing his burgeoning account balances. M/V *Alicia* had perhaps five years of life left, assuming breakdown maintenance, then he would scrap her and retire a rich man.

But first he must satisfy the US Navy. He peered down into the open cargo hold, where Sheibani escorted three men, two in blue coveralls and a third in white. A blue-clad figure looked up and DeVries nodded, receiving a return wave before the man lowered his gaze and turned to speak to his companions. The other men laughed. At least they were in a good mood.

***

Dugan watched as Petty Officer First Class Doug Broussard US Navy, returned the Dutch captain's nod with a wave.

"Captain Flip-Flop reached the bridge," Broussard said. "So much for his participation."

Dugan and the third man in his party, Chief Petty Officer Ricardo "Ricky" Vega, USN, laughed.

"Probably just as well," Vega said, nodding to a small man in coveralls talking to a crewman nearby. "The chief mate there seems to be running the show."

Broussard nodded. "Yeah, he seems OK. But I wish his English was better." He leaned closer. "But what about the ship?"

Vega shrugged and turned to Dugan.

"What about it, Mr. Dugan?" Vega asked. "You're the expert."

Dugan shook his head and looked around. "She's not quite in the crapper yet, but she's on the way down. Give Flip-Flop up there a few years and you'll be wearing snowshoes to keep from crashing through the frigging deck." He paused. "Tell me again why we're inspecting this greyhound of the seas."

Vega grimaced. "Mainly because we got no choice. We got a SEACAT exercise scheduled off Phang-Nga, and our boats and gear got off-loaded here in Singapore by mistake, instead of up in Thailand. If we don't pre-position the boats so the Royal Thai Navy guys get some hands-on with us prior to the exercise, it's gonna be a cluster fuck. We can't run up under our own power, 'cause the Malaysians and Indonesians have a hard-on about unescorted foreign gunboats in territorial waters." Vega paused. "*Alicia* here is all that's available that can meet our time frame."

Vega looked around the cargo hold again and shook his head. "Thing is," he continued, "she falls outside our normal chartering criteria. That's why MSC wanted a third party to give her a clean bill of health before we take her."

"So basically," Dugan said, "the MSC chartering pukes want someone to blame if the fucking thing sinks."

Vega grinned. "Pretty much, yeah."

Dugan sighed and looked pensive. "OK, look," he said, "her inspections are current, and the firefighting equipment was serviced last month. We're talking a two-day run in good weather and sheltered water, never out of sight of land, with a dozen ports of refuge. She's not the Queen Mary, but I guess she'll do."

Dugan finished as Sheibani, the chief mate, approached. "You like ship, yes? You want us fix something? You tell me, no problem."

"We'll need some pad eyes welded to the deck for securing gear. You have chalk we could use to mark the locations?" Dugan pantomimed marking.

"You wait," Sheibani said, palms outward in the universal sign for "wait" as he shouted up to a crewman on main deck who scurried away.

As they waited, Broussard pointed at the booms. "Those look way too small, Chief."

Vega turned to Sheibani. "Your booms. How many tons?"

"Three tons," Sheibani said. "Both booms same. Three tons."

Vega nodded. "The boats with cradles weigh twenty tons. We'll need shore cranes at both ends."

"No problem here in Singapore," Broussard said. "I'll get on the horn to Phang-Nga."

Sheibani looked up at a shout and stretched with easy grace to catch a piece of chalk sailing down from main deck. He turned. "You show. I mark."

Dugan unfolded a sketch, and they started through the hold.

**

Chief Mate Ali Sheibani, AKA Major Ali Sheibani, Iranian Revolutionary Guard Corps Navy, seconded to Qods Brigade for the work of Allah, praised be His Name, in Southeast Asia, watched the infidels' launch depart as he attempted to ignore the nervous captain beside him.

"This is too risky, Sheibani," DeVries repeated.

Sheibani sneered. "A bit late to develop an interest," he said in perfect English.

DeVries bristled. "I'm the captain and owner. I'll cancel the charter."

"Try, DeVries, and both your captaincy and your ownership will come to an unpleasant end." Sheibani glanced at nearby seamen. "You might, with a little help, fall into the hold. A tragic, but not infrequent, occurrence. Go now. Go play your music and smoke your dope."

He turned his back, and Captain DeVries, master after God of M/V *Alicia*, slunk away.

SEMBAWANG MARINE TERMINAL
SINGAPORE
22 MAY

Dugan stood on *Alicia*'s main deck and glanced at his watch. Balancing two clients simultaneously was always a challenge, but he had a bit of time before Alex's ship was high and dry and the shipyard was only five minutes away. He looked down into the hold through the open hatch, watching as the second boat landed beside her already-secured twin. Longshoremen swarmed, unshackling the slings and securing the boat. Dugan nodded approval as Broussard supervised the process.

"Sweet boats, Chief," Dugan said to Chief Petty Officer Vega, who stood beside him. He pointed to a steel container secured aft of the boats. "Firepower in the container?"

"Can't have a gunboat without guns," Vega said.

"Isn't that risky?" Dugan asked. "I mean, with all these people involved."

Vega shook his head. "We couldn't keep this quiet, anyway. We figure to let everyone see her leave with our guys riding shotgun. The raggedy-ass pirates in the strait like softer targets. We've hidden tracking transponders in each of the boats with a backup on the ship, and Broussard will report in every six hours."

Dugan nodded and extended his hand. "OK. It looks like everything's in hand here. I have one of Phoenix Shipping's tankers going on drydock this morning, and she should be almost dry, so I'll head back to the yard. When will *Alicia* sail?"

Vega took Dugan's hand. "At this rate, they'll finish by midnight and sail at first light." He grinned. "Presuming they can drag Captain Flip-Flop out of whatever whorehouse he's in."

Dugan laughed. "OK. I'll stop by tomorrow morning and see she gets off all right. It's on my way to the yard, anyway."

"See you then," Vega said.

Neither noticed a crewman squatting behind a winch, pretending to grease it.

Third Mate Ronald Carlito Medina of the Phoenix Shipping tanker M/T *Asian Trader* pushed his way down the narrow gangway, ignoring the protests of oncoming workers as he squeezed past. He paused on the wing wall of the drydock, captivated by the controlled chaos unfolding far below. Mist filled the air as workers blasted the hull with high-pressure water, and he watched the American Dugan race into the bottom of the dry dock, the shipyard repair manager in tow. Dugan stopped and pointed up at the hull as his voice cut through the din of machinery, demanding more manpower. The yardman responded with that patient Asian nod indicating not agreement but "Yes, I see your lips moving." Medina smiled as he turned to move down the stairs to sea level and dry land beyond.

Dodging bicycles, trucks, and forklifts, he made his way to the main gate and a cab for the Sembawang MRT station, and minutes later sat in a train car, backpack between his feet as he leaned back and dozed. He could have been a student or civil servant on his day off—anything but a Jihadist intent on Paradise. But then little was as it seemed.

He was born to a Christian father and Muslim mother, and official records listed him as Roman Catholic but orphaned in his infancy, he was adopted by his Muslim grandparents. A fiercely proud man, his grandfather called him Saful Islam, or Sword of Islam, and set about bringing the boy up properly, intent on erasing the stain on the family name left by his daughter's marriage to an infidel.

At the age of twelve, and with his grandfather's blessing, young Medina joined the Abu Sayyaf freedom fighters in the service of Allah, where his non-Moro appearance and official identity were considered gifts from Allah to blind the infidels' eyes. He was a resource, and a valuable one, and the leaders of Abu Sayyaf reckoned he would be more valuable still if he had a legitimate cover to roam the world. When the time was right, Ronald Carlito Medina entered the Davao Merchant Marine Academy.

***

Medina started awake as the train jerked to a stop in Novena station. He dashed off the train and up the escalator into Novena Mall, past chain stores and fast-food outlets to settle at a terminal in an Internet café. The meeting with his contact the previous day had been troubling, providing a mission but few resources. And the American Dugan's almost constant presence aboard *Asian Trader* was another unanticipated complication. But Allah would provide. He moved the mouse and clicked on a link for the website of the Panama Canal Authority.

CHAPTER THREE

Sembawang Marine Terminal
Singapore
22 May

Dugan stood on the dock and watched as Sheibani, the chief mate, manned *Alicia*'s bridge wing and spoke into a walkie-talkie, and the crew took in mooring lines in response. They got to a certain point and stopped.

"What the fuck's going on?" asked Chief Petty Officer Vega beside him. "They singled up lines fore and aft and then just stopped, and the friggin' gangway's still down."

In answer to his question, a cab raced onto the dock and skidded to a stop near the gangway. A disheveled Captain Flip-Flop exited the cab, shoved a wad of money through the driver's-side window, and lurched up the gangway in an unsteady trot. He reached the top to derisive cheers from the crew and disappeared into the deck house, as the crew set about taking in the gangway.

"Christ if that doesn't look like standard operating procedure," Vega said as he watched the crew take in the final lines.

"Yeah, I'd have to agree that doesn't look like it was unexpected," Dugan said as they watched a tug warp *Alicia* away from the dock.

"Well," Vega said, "thank God it's only two days and that the chief mate seems to have his shit together."

Dugan nodded silent agreement as he stood beside the navy man and watched *Alicia* move into the channel. One ship away and one to go, he thought as his mind drifted to *Asian Trader* sitting on drydock less than a mile away. That was a strange one. *Asian Trader* had been in the yard over a week and Alex Kairouz hadn't called once. Alex was a hands-on guy, and though Dugan knew he had Alex's complete trust, he also knew Alex was incapable of staying aloof from the myriad details of his business. At least he had been that way.

"I guess that's it then," said Vega beside him, pulling Dugan back to the present. "Thanks for the help, Mr. Dugan." Vega extended his hand.

"My pleasure, Chief," Dugan said, as he shook Vega's hand. "I guess I'd better get on over to the yard and see what latest crisis is brewing on *Asian Trader*.

M/V *ALICIA*
NORTHBOUND, STRAITS OF MALACCA
23 MAY

Broussard looked out from the bridge wing over the waters of the strait and suppressed a yawn. His attempt at sleep off watch had yielded catnaps between sweaty awakenings, as the decrepit air conditioning of the four-man cabin he shared with his team had labored in vain. The sun was low now, so maybe nightfall would lessen the strain on the antiquated cooling system. Perhaps Hopkins and Santiago, now off watch, would have better luck sleeping than he and Washington had.

He'd just begun his second six-hour watch, but he was already sweating. The body armor was hot, and he was restrained from shedding it only by Chief Vega's graphic description of what he would do to anyone who did. Broussard's single concession to comfort was his helmet strapped to his web gear instead of on his head.

"How do you copy?" asked Washington's voice in Broussard's ear, as his subordinate checked in from his position on the stern.

"Five by five," Broussard said.

He looked up as Sheibani approached with his ever-present smile. Nice little guy, he thought, though he talked like an Asian in a crappy TV movie.

"Mr. Broussard," Sheibani said, "you sleep very good, yes? Cabin OK?"

"Just fine," Broussard lied, "thanks for your hospitality."

"Good," Sheibani said, squinting into the distance. "What that?"

Broussard followed Sheibani's gaze and said over his shoulder, "I don't—"

A light burst behind Broussard's eyes as he dropped, equipment clattering. Sheibani pocketed the sap and knelt to bind the American's wrists before rising to move away, his smile now genuine.

***

Broussard awoke to a throbbing head, the scuffed blue tile of the officers' lounge cool on his cheek and filling his vision. He was gagged and bound hand and foot, the night sky through the portholes telling him the sun had set.

"Ah, Broussard," said a strangely familiar voice, "you decided to rejoin us."

He ignored his pounding head and twisted to look up, then tried to twist away as Sheibani pried his eye wide with thumb and forefinger and a bright light obliterated his vision. He squirmed as Sheibani repeated the process on the other eye.

"Good," Sheibani said. "Pupils equal and reactive. I feared a concussion. I don't normally use nonlethal force. It was a learning experience."

Broussard's curse emerged as an irritated grunt through the tape covering his mouth.

"Patience, Broussard," Sheibani said. "I want to hear what you have to say, but first you must listen."

He barked orders and two crewmen manhandled Broussard into a chair. Hands bound behind, he balanced on the edge of the seat, feet pressed to the deck. Hopkins and Santiago perched nearby, similarly restrained. All were barefoot and stripped to their utility trousers. Broussard's hope surged at Washington's absence then died as quickly.

"While you napped," Sheibani said, "Washington and I chatted."

Sheibani nodded and his subordinates stepped into the passageway and dragged in a plastic-wrapped bundle, leaving it in front of the three Americans and throwing back the plastic. Washington was face up, blood pooled in empty eye sockets. The severed fingers of one hand, his genitals, and his eyeballs were piled in the center of his massive chest. Ebony skin was flayed in wide strips and blood wept from raw flesh to pool on the plastic. Broussard screwed his eyes shut and fought rising vomit. Hopkins did the same, but Santiago made strangling noises, vomit pulsing from his nose. Sheibani ripped the tape from Santiago's mouth as the sailor retched on the corpse and then coughed wetly before managing a ragged breath.

**

Washington had told Sheibani nothing. He had, in fact, spit in Sheibani's face, sending the Iranian into a rage that ended in Washington's death. Sheibani regretted his loss of control, but, after some thought, decided Washington would serve him in death as he'd refused to in life. As horrible as the mutilations to the big man's body appeared, they occurred when he was beyond feeling pain.

"I suspected," Sheibani lied, "there were tracking devices. Washington provided the locations, maintaining to the end there were three. But I'm a suspicious fellow. I could question each of you, but that would be tedious.

Instead, Broussard, I will question you. You don't know which locations Washington divulged, so you must reveal them all. If you refuse, I kill your colleagues and resort to more painful techniques. Understood?"

Broussard glared.

Sheibani sighed. "I see you need convincing."

He drew a pistol and shot Santiago in the head. The man fell, twitching across Washington's corpse, blood pumping out in a widening circle as Broussard's screams were muffled by the tape and his attempts to stand thwarted by Sheibani's underlings. Hopkins stared down in shock, attempting to move his feet out of the spreading blood pool.

Sheibani ripped the tape off Broussard's mouth. "Now! The locations!"

Broussard tried to spit in Sheibani's face, but his lips were still glued shut from the adhesive, and spit leaked down his chin. Sheibani laughed and put his gun to Hopkins's head.

"Wait," Broussard croaked, forcing his lips apart.

Sheibani prodded Hopkins's head. "The locations!"

"In each boat," Broussard gasped, "behind the fire extinguishers, and one in the forward storeroom."

Sheibani smiled as one of his underlings rushed out. Only then did Broussard understand.

"You didn't know."

"I knew the number, not the locations," Sheibani said, grinning. "You saved us a great deal of time and may be of further use. Cooperate and you two live. Fail to do so and Washington's death will seem merciful. Consider that as you wait."

* * *

Sheibani left the room and moved up the stairway to the bridge. He passed the captain's cabin and saw DeVries through the open door, sprawled on his bunk with his headphones, in a funk of blue smoke. He sneered and climbed the last flight to the bridge.

On the bridge wing, he watched in the moonlight as a Zodiac inflatable matched *Alicia*'s speed and moved alongside. Lines were passed as a rope ladder dropped from main deck, and the transponders were transferred. He confirmed everything was going to plan and rushed back down to the lounge, where two men stood guard.

"Listen well, Broussard," Sheibani said, producing a small recording device.

Sheibani pushed a button and Broussard's voice came from the speaker, giving an earlier position report.

"You two," Sheibani said, "will be placed in a small boat and report in as expected. If you try anything, Hopkins will be killed and you will be taken to a secure location, where it will take you a long, long time to die. Understand?"

Broussard nodded and Sheibani continued.

"Your previous reports were identical. Keep them so. My men have memorized these recordings, both words and tone. If you deviate in the slightest, they terminate the call and shoot Hopkins." Sheibani smiled. "And you will envy him."

The crewmen's smirks confirmed their command of English.

Using the Americans to buy a bit more time was a calculated risk. If his men had to disconnect, and could do so cleanly, Singapore would suspect technical problems, given that the Zodiac was on *Alicia*'s agreed course. But even if Broussard managed a warning, Sheibani's men would have plenty of time to kill the Americans and dump their bodies and the transponders before disappearing into the mangrove swamps along the Malaysian coast. And *Alicia* would be well concealed before the Americans even mounted a search.

First the stick, thought Sheibani, now the carrot.

"We don't need you, Broussard, but if your help buys us a bit of time, I will spare you both. You will be hostages, eligible for exchange in time. Will you cooperate?"

Broussard nodded.

"Excellent," Sheibani said as he ordered his men to get the Americans to the boat.

Minutes later, Sheibani stood on the bridge as the Zodiac maintained *Alicia*'s original course and speed, and *Alicia* inched to port. When the separation was sufficient, he set a new course and increased speed for his hideout, eight hours away.

***

Broussard lay on the plywood floorboard as the boat bounced along. They were still bound, their arms in front and their ankles bound more loosely, changed to allow them to inch down the rope ladder into the boat. He faced Hopkins, dumped there after the midnight call, when his resolve to warn Singapore had melted at the sight of the gun to Hopkins's head. After that, the terrorists had relaxed, dumping the hostages on the floorboards, not bothering to retape Broussard's mouth. He whispered to Hopkins in the moonlight.

"Donny, can you hear me?"

Hopkins nodded.

"Donny, you know they're gonna kill us, right?"

Another nod.

"I'm warning Singapore on the next call. You with me?"

Hopkins stared at Broussard. He nodded.

"We got one shot," Broussard said, and he whispered his desperate plan.

Broussard's ears rang from a slap. "No talking," screamed the closest hijacker, rolling Broussard so that his back was to Hopkins and taping his mouth. Something hard dug into Broussard's thigh, and he smiled beneath the tape moments later as he slipped bound hands beneath his leg and felt the shape of his small folding Ka-Bar knife through the fabric. Tiny in the cavernous pocket, his captors had missed the knife. He adjusted his plan.

***

The outboard stopped, and Broussard was dragged upright and the tape ripped away. The two *Alicia* crewmen flanked him as opposite the two hijackers that had arrived in the Zodiac held Hopkins up, a gun to his head. The Americans sat across from each other, their bound feet flat on the plywood floorboard as they leaned back against the inflation tubes forming the boat's sides. One of Broussard's captors punched speaker mode on the sat phone and dialed Singapore, nodding to Broussard as the duty officer answered.

"*Alicia*—" began Broussard as Hopkins shot bound hands up to deflect the gun and jammed bound feet down to propel himself straight up, breaking the terrorists' holds as he flew backward over the side. As anticipated, the men hesitated to fire with Singapore listening, and a heartbeat after Hopkins's escape, Broussard duplicated his move, screaming "Mayday, terrorists" as he flopped overboard.

The original plan had been to escape in the darkness, with death by gunshot or drowning the likely outcome. The knife changed things.

Broussard stroked downward with bound hands, ignoring muffled shouts and gunfire. At ten feet he fumbled for the knife, forcing himself calm as he put it between his teeth and opened it with his hands. Blade open, he grabbed the knife in both bound hands and slashed the ankle binding to kick for the surface, the knife point extended above him.

The Zodiac was a dark shadow on the moonlit surface, and he kicked for the starboard tube. Just before impact, he lowered his hands, then thrust upward, relying on momentum and arm strength to pierce the tough skin. A maelstrom of bubbles erupted.

The boat listed to starboard as panicked terrorists rushed to stare at the roiling water. Broussard moved under the port bow, farthest from the disturbance, to break the surface with his face, sucking in sweet air. The men were shouting as he floated, hidden by darkness and the overhang of the inflation tube. He submerged again and clenched the knife handle between his teeth, sawing his wrist binding against the blade. With his hands free, he surfaced, unsure of his next move.

The list worsened as the men argued. Broussard had decided to puncture another air chamber when he heard splashes as the terrorists dumped the transponders, followed by the rumble of the awakening outboard. He dove deep, surfacing as the outboard faded to the east, and called out to Hopkins.

"Here. I'm hit bad," came a weak reply.

"Hang on, and keep talking," Broussard shouted, swimming toward the voice. He arrived as his friend slipped below the surface, and he dove, groping until he grabbed an arm. He kicked them to the surface and gulped air as he made out Hopkins's face in the moonlight, tape dangling from a cheek. Hopkins coughed.

"C'mon, buddy. You can make it. Hang in there."

"I'm all sh…shot up," Hopkins said, "… got a full clip into m…me."

"Knock that shit off, Hopkins. You gotta make it, or Vega will kill me," Broussard said.

Hopkins rewarded him with a feeble smile before he closed his eyes and spoke no more.

Broussard ran hands over Hopkins's body, confirming by touch the accuracy of Hopkins's diagnosis, as he struggled to apply pressure to more wounds than he had hands. The lightening sky found them bobbing in a circle of bloodstained water as Hopkins stared through lifeless eyes. Near exhaustion, Broussard checked for a pulse one last time, then blinked back tears of anger and grief as he closed Hopkins's eyes and let his friend sink.

***

An hour later aboard a Super Lynx helicopter of the Royal Malaysian Navy, vectored to the last-known coordinates of the *Alicia* by the Singapore Operations Center, Broussard looked over the straits. Sheibani's smirking face rose unbidden.

"Keep smilin', asshole," he said, "payback's gonna be hell."

CHAPTER FOUR

Christ. What an ugly building. Dugan walked up the rise to the embassy entrance. Singaporean civilian guards confirmed his identity and business, and he moved through a metal detector and bombproof doors, past a Marine guard to passport services. Minutes later, he stood in a windowless conference room as Jesse Ward appeared, trailed by a younger man.

Dugan hadn't seen Ward in person in some time. The man's wiry black hair was thinner and flecked with gray now, and his dark face lined. Intellect still sparkled behind the soft brown eyes, but in khakis and a rumpled blue blazer, he looked ordinary and forgettable. The perfect look for an intelligence agent.

"Good to see you, Tom," Ward said, pumping Dugan's hand as he nodded toward his companion. "This is my boss, Larry Gardner."

Quite a contrast, thought Dugan, shaking Gardner's hand. Gardner was much younger, with a flawless tan, movie-star looks, and black blow-dried hair. His suit had never graced a store rack, high-end or otherwise, and his silk tie sported a perfect knot. The cuff of his snowy dress shirt protruded from his jacket to reveal monogrammed initials, and a gold Rolex advertised resources beyond a government salary. He looked like a lawyer. Dugan disliked him on sight.

"OK, what gives?" Dugan asked as they sat. "It must be important to get you all the way from Langley to Singapore."

Ward opened his mouth, but Gardner cut him off.

"What's your relationship with Phoenix Shipping, Dugan?" he asked.

Dugan shot Ward a questioning look, then shrugged. "Alex Kairouz is my biggest client and a good friend. I'm taking one of his ships through yard period up in Sembawang right now." He paused. "Why? What's this all about?"

"Would it surprise you to know Kairouz has links to terrorists?"

Dugan's face registered surprise before his eyes narrowed in anger.

"Alex Kairouz? Terrorists? Bullshit. He hates those Muslim fanatics."

"Who said anything about Muslims, Dugan?"

Dugan glared at Gardner. "It was a wild guess. The IRA and the Popular Front for the Liberation of Kansas haven't blown anyone up lately."

Gardner colored and opened a folder, pretending to study the contents. "He's given you a lot of money."

"He hasn't 'given' me a damn thing. He paid me for services rendered."

"Perhaps," Gardner said, "but your association, and other things, put you under a cloud. Ward here speaks well of you, but until we're sure where your loyalty lies—"

"Where my loyalty lies?" Dugan interrupted, looking first at Ward, then refocusing on Gardner. "You know, if I were sensitive, this would hurt my feelings."

"Look, Dugan," Gardner said, "lose the attitude. Your duty as an American citi—"

"Mr. Gardner. Larry. May I call you Larry?" Dugan asked, continuing without waiting for a response. "Larry, I assure you, I will cooperate."

Gardner flashed Ward a smug smile.

"However," Dugan went on, "cooperation is about relationships. For example, the bond Agent Ward and I enjoy. But Larry, I don't feel that same chemistry here. I'm sure it's my fault, but I think I should continue with one of your associates." He paused. "Is Moe or Curly Joe available?"

Gardner's smile faded. "You son of a bitch," he said, rising to stalk out, then slamming the door behind him.

Ward shook his head. "You could get me canned, Tom."

"Nah. Even the government needs a few competent people around. Why don't you buy me dinner while you brief me on my duty as a loyal American?"

Ward nodded.

"Great. See you in the lobby of Trader's at eight. And grab a nap. You look like shit."

"Thanks," Ward said.

"Seriously," Dugan said. "If you drop dead, I might have to deal with that asshole."

***

Ward drained his mug. Crab shells overflowed a plate, surrounded by mostly empty dishes of fried noodles and other Singaporean delicacies. Dugan lifted a pitcher of Tiger beer and raised his eyebrows, but Ward declined. Dugan refilled his own mug and looked around. They sat alone on the roof terrace of the restaurant, above the bustle of open-air eateries that lined Boat Quay. Access via a cramped spiral staircase made service difficult, but Dugan's status as an old customer and generous tipper allowed secluded dining.

"Secure enough for you?" Dugan asked.

Ward nodded.

"So tell me, Jesse, how'd you end up with that asshole as your boss?"

Ward shrugged. "The agency occasionally buys in to the 'nutty management theory of the week,' in this case, 'leadership candidates' rotating through supervisory positions. Ops is usually exempted, but not this time. Gardner's our first. I got him because maritime terrorism isn't as sexy as falling planes."

"Surely everyone sees through him. He's got the personality of a dose of clap."

"He can be slick when he wants to, and he's connected. He has political aspirations." Ward grinned. "Maybe you shit on a future president."

Dugan shuddered. "God help us."

"Anyway, I'll handle him."

"Handle him while we do what exactly?" Dugan asked.

Ward looked Dugan straight in the eye. "Tom, I need you to accept Kairouz's offer."

Dugan looked puzzled. "How did…"

Then he understood. "Son of a bitch. You bugging my phone?"

Ward didn't blink. "Of course you're bugged. And so am I, and so is everyone else. You might not have read it, but you signed that waiver a long, long time ago. Way back when you agreed to keep your eyes and ears open and to take some pictures for us now and again. How could it be otherwise? There's too much at stake not to monitor ourselves."

After a long moment, Dugan nodded. "All right, point taken. That doesn't mean I like it. So what's the deal with Phoenix? Oh yeah, and what the hell did Gardner mean when he said my association with Alex 'and other things' put me under a cloud. What other things?"

"You inspected a ship for MSC last week," Ward said.

Dugan nodded. "The *Alicia*, but how's that relevant?"

"She was hijacked en route to Thailand."

"Hijacked? No way," Dugan said. "What about the navy protective detail?"

"Three dead," Ward said. "The only survivor was the team leader, a young petty officer named Broussard. He managed to get off a warning and was picked up floating in the strait by the Malaysians."

Dugan grew quiet. "I met him," he said at last. "Seemed like a nice kid."

Ward only nodded, and Dugan continued. "But I still don't see what that has to do with Phoenix...or me."

"MSC chartered the ship through Willem Van Djik in Rotterdam," Ward said. "Van Djik was told about the job by a call from someone at Phoenix. He was under surveillance by the Dutch for unrelated smuggling issues. The phone conversation itself was secure, but they heard his side through bugs in his office and traced the source to Phoenix in London. They only put two and two together after the hijacking.

"Thing is," Ward continued, "MSC chartered *Alicia* because she was the only available tonnage, and that was no accident. Backtracking it, Van Djik spent a lot of money chartering other suitable tonnage though a variety of fronts just to take the other ships out of play."

Ward looked Dugan in the eye. "People don't jack gunboats to water ski, Tom, and you're tied to this from both ends. There's your connection to Phoenix and the fact that you inspected the ship before she was hijacked and knew the cargo—"

"Along with about a thousand other people," Dugan said.

Ward held up his hands. "I'm not saying I think you're involved, Tom, but it is a coincidence, and folks in my business don't much like coincidences. I've known you a long time, but for someone like Gardner, you look a lot like a suspect. I'm sticking my neck out here bringing you in. To be honest, I probably wouldn't, except for our long relationship and the fact that, with your relationship with Kairouz, you're our best shot at getting inside Phoenix quickly."

"Jesse, I'm not trained for this."

"Mainly you'll be helping us place a British agent," Ward said.

Dugan hesitated, toying with the idea of telling Ward about Alex Kairouz's recent strange behavior. No, he thought, best leave that for now. "I just don't feel right spying on Alex," Dugan said instead.

"What's better for Kairouz? Having you there or a stranger?"

Dugan grew quiet. "All right, I'll do it," he finally said.

"Good. Assuming you accept the possibility Kairouz is guilty."

"Like you accept the possibility that I'm guilty?" Dugan asked.

Ward changed the subject.

"Tell me what you remember about *Alicia.*"

Dugan shrugged. "Not much to remember. She's a little one-hatch coaster owned by her skipper, a Dutch guy who's running her into the ground. Chief mate's name is Ali something—Sheboni, I think. He seems to be running the show."

"Sheibani," corrected Ward. "According to Broussard, Sheibani orchestrated the hijacking and murdered three of Broussard's guys in the process. Two at point-blank range in cold blood."

Dugan's face hardened. "That little fucking puke. Do you have any leads?"

Ward shook his head.

"We had the strait blanketed by satellite coverage within hours of the news, with no sighting. *Alicia* couldn't have cleared the strait by then. We're assuming she's on the Indonesian side, and given her last-known position and maximum speed, she could be anywhere along two hundred miles of coastline—a thousand miles, counting islands and inlets. Hundreds of good hiding places."

Dugan nodded. "I see the problem. You can't really even rule out too many places due to water depth. As I recall, *Alicia* draws fourteen feet fully loaded. That's fifteen hundred tons. Those boats and associated gear totaled less than fifty. She can get pretty light."

"That's right," Ward said. "But the real priority is recovering the boats, and we don't figure the hijackers will waste any time getting them off *Alicia.* The boats alone will be much easier to hide and move through the mangrove swamps."

"There's your answer," Dugan said.

Ward looked confused, and Dugan continued. "*Alicia*'s gear can't handle the boats. They need a crane. And shore cranes need strong docks, and big floating cranes are few and far between."

Two Days Earlier
M/V *Alicia*
Indonesian Coast

Sheibani moved from bridge wing to bridge wing as he calmly issued helm orders, conning *Alicia* up the shallow, twisting passage through the mangrove swamp in the moonlight and on a rising tide. He had his best man on the helm, and he'd lightened *Alicia* to seven feet. The rest of the crew manned the rails with powerful handheld lights and called warnings of obstacles.

With the propeller and rudder only partially submerged, the ship handled poorly, but each time he grounded in the soft mud, he waited for the tide to lift her, then backed off to continue his cautious transit. He regretted no one would know of *Alicia's* final resting place and appreciate his skill, but duping the infidels was satisfaction enough.

As the sky lightened in the east, he spotted his objective ahead in the predawn: a crumbling concrete dock by a pool of still water. Trees rose from gaping cracks in the dock, some a foot in diameter with tops higher than *Alicia's* deckhouse, and thick limbs spread over the water. Sheibani shouted a warning, and the crew scurried into the deckhouse as he retreated to the wheelhouse and increased speed. He pushed the helmsman aside and took the wheel himself to slam *Alicia's* port side toward the dock, her momentum forcing her superstructure, booms, and masts through the foliage. Stout limbs snapped like cannon shots and fell across the deck as the little ship slowed abruptly. *Alicia* listed slightly to starboard as she fought her way through the obstacle, then Sheibani heard the screech of steel on concrete. He killed the engine and *Alicia* shuddered to a stop.

Seconds later, Sheibani stood on the starboard bridge wing, watching as his crew boiled from the deckhouse and went about their prearranged tasks. Some climbed to the dock and began passing mooring lines, while others fired up chain saws and began clearing the deck of broken limbs, tossing the debris over the offshore side of the ship. In minutes, the ship was secured, overhanging limbs shielding most of the vessel. The camouflage netting would do the rest.

He'd first come to this place on a dirt bike, guided by an old man who'd worked here long ago. All that remained was a crumbling dock and dilapidated Quonset hut, its rusted sides covered in vines, the open end a black cave in the greenery. Convincing the International Development Fund to finance a port miles from deep water must have been difficult, even years ago, but the developers had been well connected. They slapped down a dock and dredged a thirty-five-foot-deep hole along it to collect a hefty progress payment. Months later, when a survey party found the site abandoned and overgrown and the deepwater channel into the dock to exist only on paper, the government feigned outrage, the IDF shrugged, and everyone forgot the site until Allah guided Sheibani to it thirty years later. He'd used the site as a smuggling depot for three years, anchoring *Alicia* in deep water miles away and approaching by Zodiac. Both the ship and this place had served his needs well, but it was time to move on.

Sheibani nodded to himself as he moved through the hold, pleased at the progress. He watched as men swarmed the boats, removing the securing straps and lashing heavy vinyl tarps over the cockpit openings before sealing the boats completely with industrial stretch wrap. Soon they would be as buoyant and unsinkable as corks.

In the aft end of the hold, men emptied the weapons container, hoisting its contents over the main deck to the crumbling concrete dock, while forward, the chief engineer squatted on the deck, cutting through plating. The hissing torch changed pitch, and a neat circle of steel tumbled into the water of the ballast tank below, hot edges belching steam. Sheibani glanced up through the hatch at patches of blue sky through overhanging tree limbs and camouflage netting, then moved to the ladder, reviewing preparations as he climbed to the main deck. All that remained was rigging a web of wires around the hold, tight between the pad eyes at the bottom of the hold and the top of the hatch, to corral the boats directly under the open hatch. God willing, he could sink his prison at dawn. He would not miss *Alicia* or the heat or the Indonesian monkeys.

***

The sky was lightening as Sheibani stood with the crew on the dock. *Alicia* was below the dock now, and a short, steep gangway led down to main deck. The camouflage netting was gone and the hatch open to the sky as the chief engineer climbed the gangway.

"It is done, Major," he said. "She's down past her marks with the bow a bit deeper. I've started flooding the cargo hold through the broached ballast tanks. The water will run to the forward end and speed the sinking of the bow. The engine space aft will flood last. By the time the water shorts out the pumps, she will be free-flooding." He paused. "God willing, she will settle straight down."

Sheibani nodded and watched. Water rose in the hold, and the boats floated free, rising as the ship sank beneath them. Then *Alicia*'s deck went under, and water poured over the hatch coaming, cascading down on the boats from all sides like a waterfall. The boats bounced and bobbed under the torrents, and within seconds *Alicia* fell out from under them with a great bubbling swirl. A relieved grin split the chief engineer's face as the boats bobbed to the surface unharmed, and a spontaneous shout of *"Allahu Akbar"* rose from the throats of *Alicia*'s former crewmen.

***

The tile was cool on DeVries's cheek as he lay trussed hand and foot. His head throbbed from the beating, and he felt the deck tilt beneath him as the hull moaned under unfamiliar stresses. The lights winked out and he closed his eyes and wished for an end to the bad dream, opening them as water wet his cheek. He flopped about in the deepening flood, cursing ships and the sea and his stiff-necked family. In the end, his grave was marked by a section of the bridge deck and the tops of the masts and king posts, rusted brown and blending with the surrounding jungle, the only sign that Captain Jan Pieter DeVries, master after God of the good ship *Alicia*, had gone down with his vessel.

CHAPTER FIVE

US EMBASSY
SINGAPORE
27 MAY

Dugan sat in the same conference room, waiting. When Ward appeared, Dugan raised his eyebrows. "Where's the Boy Wonder?"

"Gardner flew back to Langley this morning," Ward said. "Management conference."

Dugan snorted, then continued. "Any news on *Alicia*?"

Ward shook his head. "Negative. The Indonesians are being their usual noncooperative selves, but we have our own assets on the ground tracking down every available crane. And we've tasked the satellites to collect imagery of every dock capable of supporting a large crane and every anchorage deep enough to support a floating crane. We still got bubkes."

"Crap."

Ward shrugged. "It's still our best lead. Obviously they've found a hiding spot, but, sooner or later, they'll have to come to a crane or a crane has to come to them. Intelligence is a game of patience, Tom."

Ward changed the subject. "You call Kairouz yet?"

"Since you're bugging my calls, you know the answer to that."

"Make the call."

"So," Dugan asked, "what happened to 'intelligence is a game of patience'?"

Ward scowled.

"Don't get your bowels in an uproar. My relief arrived last night, and I showed him around *Asian Trader* and gave him my turnover this morning. Alex will be expecting a call. I was just waiting until it seemed natural."

"No time like the present," Ward said.

Dugan sighed and pulled out his cell phone.

OFFICES OF PHOENIX SHIPPING
LONDON

Alex's stomach boiled from too much coffee, even at this early hour, and he was tense and irritable from lack of sleep. Nothing had been the same since Braun's arrival with his thug Farley. He eyed his overflowing in-box. His productivity had suffered as well, and he'd instructed Mrs. Coutts to hold all calls while he attempted to clear the backlog.

He looked over, annoyed, as the intercom buzzed.

"Yes, Mrs. Coutts?"

"I'm sorry to disturb you, sir, but Mr. Dugan is on line one."

He smiled despite the tension. Trust Dugan to charm his way past Mrs. Coutts. He mashed the flashing button.

"Thomas. How are you? Did Guido arrive?"

"I'm fine, Alex," Dugan said. "I picked him up at Changi airport last night, and we walked the ship together this morning. She's off the dry dock now and should shift to the ExxonMobil refinery to load sometime next week. Guido's got it."

"Excellent, Thomas, and thank you for helping me out in a bind."

"No problem, Alex, but there's something else I want to discuss. I think I'm ready to take you up on your offer and come to work for you full-time."

Alex sat stunned. Thomas couldn't come. Not now. If he sensed something wrong and went to the authorities—

"Alex, are you there?"

"Yes, yes, Thomas. I'm just…surprised. Why the change of heart after all these years? Are you serious? What about your consulting practice?"

"Serious as a heart attack," Dugan said. "As to why, I guess you've finally convinced me I should spend more time behind a desk. And since you're seventy percent of my billings anyway, I'm not concerned about the practice. If it doesn't pan out, we'll just go back to the way it was. You know money's not an issue for me anyway, thanks to Katy's financial wizardry."

"What about Katy?" Alex asked. "Won't she be upset if you move to London?"

Dugan laughed. "Let's face it, Alex, I'm traveling most of the time anyway, and just because my kid sister lets me crash in her pool house between trips, doesn't mean I'll be missed that much. I'll still get back home for holidays, which is about as much as they see me now, anyway." Dugan paused. "But what's with all the objections? You trying to talk me out of something you've spent ten years talking me into?"

"No, no, not at all. It's just unexpected, and the timing is a bit…awkward. You see, I just hired a fellow as director of operations," Alex lied on the fly, "with the understanding that he'll eventually move into a newly created general-manager slot. I had no idea you'd reconsider, but if I bring you on now as general manager, he'll take it as bad faith."

"I see your problem, Alex. How about this? I don't mind competing for the GM spot, so why don't you hire me for a trial period as this guy's equal, say director of engineering. Then after a while, you decide who's the best fit. If I later decide to leave, you have this new guy in place. If we decide I should continue, you'll have a choice. It will be no hardship for me to resign later if necessary."

The logic was unassailable. Alex stalled again.

"You've really caught me by surprise, Thomas. May I call you back?"

"Sure, Alex," Dugan said, "take your time."

"Fine, Thomas. Talk to you soon."

Alex Kairouz disconnected and buried his face in his hands.

***

"Captain Braun, Mr. Kairouz is not to be disturbed," Mrs. Coutts said.

Braun stood in Alex's door, hand on the knob as he glared back over his shoulder.

Mrs. Coutts gave Alex a look of helpless apology.

"It's fine, Mrs. Coutts," Alex said.

She nodded and retreated to her desk.

Braun shut the door and moved to Alex's favorite armchair.

"You should sack that old bitch, Kairouz, and get someone easier on the eyes," he said, pointing to the sofa. "But come sit. I don't have all day."

Alex stood, stiff with rage. "I'm cooperating, Braun, so don't abuse my staff. Clear?"

"That's *Captain* Braun, and you're *not* cooperating, or that old hag wouldn't interfere. She'll have an accident if she isn't careful. Is *that* clear? Now sit," Braun said, pointing again.

Defeated, Alex complied.

"Now," Braun said, "who is this American?"

"Thomas Dugan, a consultant and friend. I'll get rid of him."

"Won't that arouse curiosity, given his rather logical offer?"

"Perhaps," conceded Alex, "but I can hold him off. Long enough for you to finish whatever this business is and be gone."

Braun shook his head. "I think not. I don't want some curious Yank starting to ask questions. Better to keep him close and watch him. Besides, he may prove useful."

"I'll just get rid of him," Alex repeated.

"On the contrary," Braun said, his voice hardening, "offer him the job, effective immediately."

"No. Best keep him away."

Braun sighed. "How tiresome."

He rose from the chair to snatch Cassie's photo from the desk and toss it into Alex's lap. Alex set the picture on the end table and glared.

"Time for a reminder, Kairouz? Must we review the videos?" Braun paused. "Then again, she does look like your dead wife. Perhaps you've already begun her education. Bedding the retard are you, Kairouz? Perhaps I can help. Have her broken in by a dozen big fellows while you watch. Sound appealing?" Braun laughed and awaited the expected response.

Alex charged, but Braun was younger, fit, and well trained. In seconds, Alex was face down, his right arm twisted behind him, as Braun ground his face into the carpet.

"I grow tired of these lessons, Kairouz. The next time you cross me, Farley will rape the retard in front of you as a down payment. Understand?"

Alex nodded and Braun released him. "Good. Now phone Dugan." He sneered. "After you pull yourself together, of course. You're pathetic."

Alex heard Braun leave as he lay unmoving, and tears of impotent rage stained the carpet.

US EMBASSY
SINGAPORE

"That's great, Alex," Dugan said into the cell phone. "I'll e-mail Mrs. Coutts my flight information. I assume I can stay at your place as usual until I find a place of my own?"

"Of course, Thomas," Alex said. "Cassie will be excited when I tell her."

"I look forward to seeing you all. Bye now," Dugan said and hung up.

He sat silent for a moment until Ward spoke.

"So what do you make of that, Tom?"

"I honestly don't know," Dugan said. "He...he has been acting a bit strange lately, and he definitely seems a bit less enthusiastic than I anticipated."

"Yeah, something's up, all right," Ward said.

Dugan didn't respond.

"Having second thoughts?" Ward asked.

"I don't know if I can do this, Jesse. I may have taken a few photos and snooped around for you a bit, but I'm not a spy, and I sure as hell can't learn to be one in twenty-four hours."

"Don't worry. The Brits will backstop you. MI5 is putting together a team now."

"I sure hope you know what you're talking about, pal," Dugan said.

OFFICES OF PHOENIX SHIPPING
LONDON

Karl Enrique Braun, freelance "problem solver," formerly of the East German Ministry for State Security (Stasi), returned to his spacious new office, the former home of three disgruntled ship superintendents now displaced to the cubicle farm. He was sated from an excellent lunch, courtesy of his new Phoenix Shipping credit card, and he smiled at the sign on the door: Captain Braun—Director of Operations. The "captain" was a nice touch and as real as his name, after all. He'd been many people in service to the state. When the end had come, he'd forecast it a bit more clearly than his former colleagues and arrived in Havana hours after the wall fell. The Cuban Ministry of the Interior (MININT) was a Stasi clone and always in need of talent, especially talent with fluent Spanish and Cuban roots. He touched his face. The Cubans had excellent plastic surgeons.

His Nordic good looks and native fluency in a half a dozen languages provided the Cubans an asset of incalculable value, and he parlayed that to his own advantage. He'd become a "consultant" and then a free agent, protected by the Cubans in exchange for sharing intelligence. Capitalist by default now, he worked for anyone with his fee, from drug lords to African dictators. His best clients to date were Latin American demagogues, champions of a failed model, buying the votes of the dispossessed with promises no economy could make real, especially not the bungled economics of the neo-socialism.

Braun smiled again. No client had been as malleable and oblivious to fees as that idiot Rodriguez in Venezuela. It would be a shame to lose the cash flow should it prove necessary to sacrifice him as damage control. Then again, the Iranian had proven to be more than generous and deserved his fire wall. Braun was looking forward to a very comfortable retirement.

He settled in behind his desk and contemplated the latest turn of events. He didn't like this American lodging with Kairouz, but it was apparently an arrangement of long standing; best to keep to routine. Besides, Kairouz was thoroughly cowed, and this Dugan was one more American he could throw into the mix to make things all the more believable.

Willingly to the slaughter. Braun could hardly believe his good fortune.

CHAPTER SIX

Mohammad Borqei stood, balled fists in his back as he stretched to ease the stiffness of the old shrapnel wound. American shrapnel, for the Great Satan had been generous in aid to Saddam when the madman had been murdering Iranians. Borqei swallowed his anger. He moved from the window to his desk and picked up the message from Tehran.

A wistful smile crossed his bearded face at thoughts of Iran, a home he'd never see again. It had taken years to craft his "legend" as a moderate, advancing viewpoints he despised in mosques across Tehran, enduring the hostility of colleagues, and finally imprisonment for seditious acts. Then he'd "escaped" to the US via Canada, and the foolish Americans had tugged the Trojan horse through the gate.

He'd settled in Dearborn, with its large Muslim community, joining interfaith groups and preaching tolerance. When the Imam of the House of Islamic Knowledge died in a car crash, he was the logical choice to assume leadership of the community's preeminent mosque. Able to count Islamic voters, the local congressman fast-tracked Borqei's citizenship application and stood smiling as he took the oath. Indeed, Borqei's public "assimilation" was so convincing that it undermined his mission. His inner circle of the faithful was small and resistant to all efforts at expansion.

For, despite cynicism about American ideals as preached and practiced, the Muslims of Dearborn were optimistic. Conflicts with their "real" American neighbors were frequent but waged with words during meetings, not by stone-throwing mobs or suicide bombers. Each grudging compromise was a small victory, as their sons played American football and ate *halal* pizza, and they built new lives, much better than those they'd left behind.

Borqei had faced the paradox. His need for "assimilated" Americans would never be met by American-born Muslims, who were corrupted beyond redemption. Hezbollah had come to his aid, trolling teeming refugee camps for orphans. While they trained in Iran, Borqei prepared the ground, helping the faithful of his inner circle get citizenship, allowing them in turn to use the Child Citizenship Act to adopt "foreign-born children," all graduates of Hezbollah training. They arrived, committed to serving Islam by becoming ever more American in appearance. He had a dozen now, and the first was the finest.

Yousif Nassir Hamad, or "Joe" Hamad, was finishing college, with honors, on a US Navy ROTC scholarship. Fluent in Arabic, he was courted heavily, and Borqei had been helping him review his options, deciding just where in the navy he could best serve Islam. Now it had been decided for them. Borqei gazed at the message with distaste.

KAIROUZ RESIDENCE
LONDON
28 MAY

"No!" Cassie glared defiance, flopping the hair bow on the table. "This dorky uniform is bad enough. Please, Papa, tell her I don't have to wear it."

Alex studied the bow over his cup, remembering Cassie's delight when Mrs. Farnsworth first made it. As Cassie, at age fifteen, struggled between her physical and mental ages, conflicts had become frequent—difficult for Cassie, but harder still on Mrs. Farnsworth.

"Cassie, the bow makes you even prettier," he said.

"I hate it, I hate it," Cassie spoke into her cereal, pouting.

"Cassie," Mrs. Farnsworth said, "a proper young lady does not pout. People respond to courtesy, not petulance or angry demands. Would you like to ask me again, young lady?"

Alex stiffened. The proper-young-lady campaign was difficult for him, but Mrs. Farnsworth was insistent that repeated challenge strengthened Cassie's abilities. He accepted the theory but was incapable of causing Cassie discomfort. He bit his tongue and left correction to Mrs. Farnsworth, thankful she was made of sterner stuff.

"Please, Mrs. Farnsworth, must I wear it?" Cassie asked, barely audible.

"Not if you don't wish to," Mrs. Farnsworth said. "Now go up and tidy your hair. It's almost time to go."

"Oh thank you, thank you," Cassie cried, rushing to the door. She stopped midstride and turned. "Oh. I almost forgot. When will Uncle Thomas be here, Papa?"

Alex smiled. "He arrives this evening, Cassie. He'll have dinner with us."

"Cool," Cassie said, then bolted for the door.

"Don't...." Mrs. Farnsworth said at Cassie's retreating back, "... run."

Alex chuckled as Cassie disappeared. "A bit late, I'm afraid."

Mrs. Farnsworth smiled. "She's coming along nicely."

"You expected that?"

The housekeeper nodded. "Self-assertion. Notice how she tried to play us against each other? A good sign."

Alex deferred to her judgment. She'd cared for Cassie since infancy, and the shelves of her bedroom overflowed with books on development, special needs, and remedial teaching techniques. Many nights he saw her through the open doorway, pouring over arcane tomes.

He sighed. "I have mixed emotions at seeing innocence replaced by manipulation."

"Loss of innocence is inevitable, sir, if she's to achieve independence. We won't be around forever."

Alex nodded as they sipped coffee in silence. Mrs. Farnsworth seemed uneasy, on the verge of speaking several times, then studying her coffee.

"The coffee isn't that interesting. Speak your mind, Mrs. Farnsworth. If it's about Thomas—"

Mrs. Farnsworth shook her head. "I resigned myself to your friendship with the boorish Mr. Dugan some time ago. It's this Farley I'm concerned with. He's not working out, sir."

Alex stiffened. "Go on."

"I can't understand why, without notice, you engaged him as our driver, replacing Daniel after years of loyal service. I've managed to keep Daniel busy with other tasks, but he feels wronged. He may leave us."

"You're quite right, Mrs. Farnsworth, and I do apologize. The need arose suddenly and for reasons I can't discuss, but I've handled it badly."

"'Need,' sir? What need? Farley's reckless and unsavory in the extreme, hanging about the kitchen, offending Mrs. Hogan with crude humor, and calling Daniel an 'old kike' to his face." She lowered her voice. "And he ogles Cassie with undisguised lust. The lout must go."

Alex tried to speak several times before succeeding.

"He'll leave soon," he said. "Until then, make sure Cassie is never alone with him."

"Did you understand what I said, sir?"

"Perfectly," Alex said through tight lips, "but I can't discharge him yet. He's a bodyguard. There have been...kidnap threats against Cassie."

"Good Lord. From whom? Have you notified the police?"

"Anonymous e-mail threats," Alex lied, reciting the story Braun invented. "The police are investigating. I hired Farley at their recommendation."

Mrs. Farnsworth digested the news but focused on the imminent threat.

"Understood, sir. But I still don't trust Farley. We must replace him."

"Impossible," Alex said.

"But surely the agency you engaged—"

"God damn it, woman!" he said, red-faced. "I'll thank you to stop meddling and do as you're told!" He glared at her, then seemed to deflate as he sat, elbows on the table and face buried in his hands, as if hiding from his own outburst.

Mrs. Farnsworth sat shocked until Alex spoke again, his head down, avoiding her eyes.

"That was unthinkable. Please forgive me, Mrs. Farnsworth. I'm overwrought with concern about Cassie."

She stiffened. "As am I, sir. Will that be all?"

"I'll hire another car and use Daniel to run errands around the office. That will salve his feelings and spare him contact with Farley."

She rose. "Whatever you decide, sir. I must check on Cassie."

Alex called her name as she reached the door, and she turned.

"About your...suspicions. Please watch Cassie closely."

"I always do, sir. I always do," she said softly.

***

Alex smiled as he watched Dugan rub his stomach in mock distress.

"It's clear I'll have to find my own place quickly, Mrs. Hogan," Dugan said to the cook. "If I stay here too long, I'll be needing a new wardrobe."

The cook beamed as she poured coffee. "Sure, and it was nothing fancy, Mr. Dugan," she said, retreating to the kitchen.

Another Dugan conquest, thought Alex. Thomas had even managed to defrost Mrs. Farnsworth a bit this evening. He noticed the housekeeper's approving glance as Cassie chatted happily with their house guest.

"Cassie, you have homework, so say good night," Mrs. Farnsworth said.

"Please, please, may I do it in the morning?" Cassie pleaded.

"No, dear. I'm sure your father and Mr. Dugan have matters to discuss."

"Oh, all right," Cassie said, standing to hug Dugan. "I'm so glad you're here, Uncle Thomas."

"Me too, Cassie," Dugan said. "We'll talk tomorrow after school. Daniel will be driving you home before you know it."

"Not Daniel, Farley," Cassie said.

"We've a new driver," explained Mrs. Farnsworth, her distaste obvious.

"And he's really creepy, Uncle Thomas," Cassie said. "But Papa says he'll go away."

Dugan looked at Alex, confused.

"I'll explain later, Thomas," Alex said. "Now Cassie, where's my kiss?"

Cassie hugged Alex and pecked his cheek as Mrs. Farnsworth stood.

"Will that be all, sir?" the housekeeper asked.

Alex smiled and nodded, hoping to hide the sudden tension, but the look on Dugan's face signaled he'd been unsuccessful.

"So, what's up?" Dugan asked, after Cassie and Mrs. Farnsworth left.

Alex hesitated, then lowered his voice. "There have been kidnapping threats against prominent families."

"You've been threatened?"

"Not directly," Alex lied, "but I was concerned. I engaged Farley as a bodyguard. Turns out he's not the most personable chap."

"But why's Mrs. Farnsworth upset?"

Alex sighed. "I didn't consult her. You know how proprietary she is regarding Cassie. Farley being a lout made things worse."

"I see," Dugan said, but the look on his face said he didn't see at all. Tactfully, he changed the subject.

"Fill me in on the work situation," Dugan said. "What about this other guy? How do you envision the work split?"

"His name is Braun, Captain Karl Braun," Alex said. "He's director of operations—scheduling, crewing, fuel purchases, payroll, that sort of thing. You'll be technical director—maintenance, yard repairs, and so on. We'll play it by ear on overlaps."

"Sounds fine," Dugan said. "I'm eager to start."

Alex hesitated. "There's really no rush, Thomas. Why don't you work half days a few weeks to settle in, hunt for a flat, and get your feet on the ground?"

"I want to earn my keep."

"Of course, of course," Alex said, "but it's a marathon, not a sprint."

"OK...I guess," Dugan said. "Easy does it" was not Alex Kairouz's style at all.

"It's settled then," Alex said, rising. "Join me for a nightcap?"

Dugan yawned. "No thanks. I'm jet-lagged as hell. See you in the morning."

***

Two hours later, Dugan lay awake in the dark, mulling Alex's strange behavior. From what he knew, Alex failing to involve Mrs. Farnsworth in any matter related to Cassie was unthinkable. However, even if he had, Dugan didn't think Mrs. Farnsworth would nurse a grudge when Cassie's safety was concerned. Something was definitely not right.

PENTHOUSE, PLAZA ON THE THAMES
LONDON
28 MAYBE

"How is it you're livin' like a fuckin' Saudi prince, and I'm in a bloody closet over a garage?" Ian Farley asked, glaring from the sofa. At six foot and two hundred pounds, he looked like a muscle-bound skinhead, full of quiet menace. If he would only stay quiet.

Braun took a sip of brandy, then held the snifter to his nose, savoring the aroma as the liquid slid down his throat. He looked from the dancing fire to the glass wall of the huge living room with its view of Parliament across the Thames. Rain on the glass refracted the lights to dazzling effect. Cuban weather was better, but he couldn't enjoy the finer things in the worker's paradise, and Braun was making the most of London. At Kairouz's expense, of course. He looked at Farley and sighed. No more than his due, given the fools he had to endure.

"Because, Farley, your cover is a servant. You live in servant quarters."

Farley started to speak, but Braun's look chilled him.

"And don't leave the girl's proximity again, unless she's at school or else-where your presence would be suspicious. Understand?"

"Yeah, yeah, I got it."

Braun sipped again and studied Farley over the rim of his glass. For all his faults, Farley had the necessary skills—and he was expendable. The rest of the operation was equally lean, his only other operative a techno-geek eager to keep past work for foreign governments secret. Blackmail wasn't Joel Sutton's only incentive. Braun had dismissed the IT staff and contracted Sutton at a huge fee, again with Kairouz's money.

Sutton had bugged Kairouz's office and phones—office, home, and mobile—and now controlled the company computers. Braun monitored the work phones in real time and other phones via recording. He'd avoided bugging Kairouz's home; the daily chatter would be tedious to sort through and reveal little. Dugan's presence might change that.

"With Dugan around, spend time in the house," Braun said. "Keep your ears open."

"For what?" Farley asked.

"Signs Dugan is suspicious, of course." Idiot.

"Not so easy, guv. That bloody Irish bitch hates me. She'd poison me tea given the chance, and that snooty cunt Farnsworth stares holes in me. I ain't exactly Mr. Invisible."

Braun sighed. "All right. Do the best you can."

"OK." Farley rose to go. "When do I get a go at the retard? Remember our deal."

"Keep it in your pants, Farley. I'll tell you when. And you can't damage the goods. She'll bring a fortune in the Middle East. The wogs love blonds."

Farley leered. "I'll be a regular bleedin' Sir Galahad. She'll be cryin' when she has to leave me, she will."

CHAPTER SEVEN

OFFICES OF PHOENIX SHIPPING
1 JUNE

"How many more?" Dugan asked into the intercom.

"Just one, sir," Mrs. Coutts said. "A Ms. Anna Walsh in ten minutes."

"Send her straight in, please," Dugan said.

He was worried. Had he missed a signal? Ward had told him he'd recognize the agent when she appeared and just to "follow her lead," whatever that meant. If the last applicant wasn't the agent, Dugan had screwed the pooch big time.

He looked out the big windows at the Thames just across Albert Embankment and wondered again at Alex's insistence he use his office. Strange, given Alex's resistance to hiring a new secretary and his irritation when Dugan pressed the point.

***

Braun sat in his office across the hall multitasking, checking schedules and listening with one ear. The interviews were in Kairouz's office at his insistence. He wanted a feel for the American, and it was far easier to move Dugan than to bug his temporary office in the conference room. He was pleased Dugan demanded a secretary. The more he fixated on such details, the less time to meddle. And perhaps he'd hire something one might actually want to get a leg over. Braun had shelved his own plan for a playmate with regret. Someone close by was a liability unless they were in on the operation, and he didn't want to expand the team. He smiled. Maybe Dugan would help him out.

***

"Come in, Ms. Walsh," Dugan said, leading the final job seeker to the sofa.

She was five four with shoulder-length auburn hair, green eyes, a freckled nose, and looked much younger than the thirty-eight years on her resume. A well-tailored wool skirt stopped above the knee, accentuating legs encased in dark silk. The neckline of her designer blouse was revealing, and she exuded sexuality.

She smiled. "My updated CV," she said, handing Dugan several pages.

He settled in his chair as he read the note attached.

We may be under audio or video surveillance. Follow my lead. Must convey impression I am a tart you are hiring for looks. Conclude by hiring me on the spot.

Dugan nodded. "Ah, well, Ms. Walsh. Tell me about yourself."

Her recitation was captivating. At typing speed, she crossed and uncrossed her legs; at spreadsheets and software, she leaned in and smiled. By then he was beyond listening. He only belatedly realized her lips had stopped moving.

"Yes... very impressive, Ms. Walsh," he said, befuddled, turning a page to stall.

"Pardon my digression, Mr. Dugan," she said, "but your office is beautiful."

"Actually, I'm borrowing it from the managing director while mine is completed."

"Well, it's lovely. And the sofa so comfy." She smiled. "Will you have one like it?"

"Why don't I hire you and you can make sure I do?"

"I'd love to," she said, "depending on salary, of course. The range indicated is below expectations, I'm afraid. Might there be flexibility?"

"We could go a bit higher," Dugan said. "How's 10 percent sound?"

"I suppose I could start there until you're satisfied with my... services." She smiled. "Then I'll expect a 25 percent increase."

Dugan stood and extended his hand. "Welcome aboard, Ms. Walsh."

Anna rose, moving closer as she took his hand. "Anna, please."

"All right, Anna. Let's get the ball rolling."

***

Mrs. Coutts gave Anna a withering look before turning to Dugan.

"And when is she to start, sir?" she asked, ice in her voice.

"Tomorrow if possible," Dugan said. "We'll put her on outfitting my new office."

Mrs. Coutts looked as if she'd been slapped.

"Under your supervision, of course," Dugan added, but the damage was done.

"Very good, sir. Come along, Ms. Walsh," Mrs. Coutts said, moving into the hallway as Anna hurried after.

Dugan watched them disappear and wondered how to patch things up with Mrs. Coutts.

***

Braun stood in his doorway and watched Anna's retreating backside. Bloody well perfect. And more than enough to distract Dugan. And when Dugan was out of the way, he'd double the slut's salary if she was accommodating. It was only Kairouz's money, after all.

M/T *ASIAN TRADER*
SEMBAWANG SHIPYARD, SINGAPORE
1 JUNE

Medina leaned on the rail, mentally hurrying his shipmates down the steep gangway in their "goin' ashore" clothes. The ship floated at a wet berth now, the main deck high above the dock, her tanks mostly empty. The second mate smiled and waved up at Medina, then said something to the man beside him, who shook his head and laughed, undoubtedly at a joke at Medina's expense. Let them laugh, thought Medina; the last laugh would be his.

He'd volunteered for night watches, citing his desire to explore Singapore by day. He spent those days in internet cafés and, as plans evolved, the electronics shops of Sim Lim Tower, returning to nap each afternoon in preparation for evenings alone on board. Or almost alone. The yard night shift was populated by the sick, the lame, and the lazy—they topped the gangway in search of a sleeping place, never to be seen again except as man-hours on the yard invoice. It had been dicey at first when the American Dugan was around. He'd had an unfortunate tendency to show up at all hours, checking on progress. But with the yard period almost over and the little Italian in charge, things were more predictable on the night watch.

Medina entered the deckhouse, climbed the stairs to the bridge deck, then began a slow deck-by-deck descent, walking each passageway to ensure everyone was ashore. He continued into the engine room, where he found yard workers dozing in scattered corners, and then walked the main deck from bow to stern, finding no one. Satisfied, he went to his cabin and locked the door behind him before rooting in his wardrobe locker.

He placed two items on his bed, and then sat in his desk chair and looked at them, still amazed that he'd been expected to strike a mighty blow with such meager weapons. An ancient Makarov pistol with a single clip and a martyr's vest, now disassembled, were his entire arsenal. His contact had given him the things, said "Allah will guide you," and left, leaving Medina uncertain and trembling at the prospect of failure.

He smiled now, thinking of his initial doubt, for Allah had been generous in His guidance. Had not Allah given him the interest in electronics years before, and had He not opened Medina's eyes to the canal's weak point? And did not the Holy Quran tell of David slaying Goliath with a single stone?

Medina unlocked a desk drawer and pulled out two plastic-wrapped bundles, the last two of twelve to be placed. Each was the size of a cigarette pack, and a length of antenna wire extended from each. They contained plastique, scavenged from his martyr's vest, and each held a detonator, a tiny remote-ignition circuit of his own devising, a nine-volt battery to power it all, and a small but powerful magnet. Their destructive force was minimal, but each would produce a significant flash, and that was all he needed.

Medina's mouth was dry. Tomorrow the ship shifted to the refinery loading berth. He had made great progress since Dugan's departure, but he had to finish tonight. He slipped a charge in each front pocket, donned a fanny pack, and went down to the main deck.

The yard was quiet save distant shouts and welding flashes from the dry docks, but Medina felt exposed in the glare of deck lights. He breathed deep and forced himself to an unhurried walk, up the deck to the vent for number one port ballast tank. Near the vent, he scanned the deck, then pulled a spool of wire and cutters from his fanny pack. He fed the fine wire into the vent pipe slowly to prevent kinks, and when an ample length dangled into the tank below, clipped the wire and bent the free end under the vent opening and wrapped it securely around a bolt head, almost invisible.

He moved to the manhole and stared down into the black void. They'd removed the temporary lights. He pulled an elastic headband from the fanny pack and donned it, slipping a small flashlight into it like a headlamp to free his hands and light his way down the ladder. He left the ladder at the uppermost horizontal stringer plate and moved forward through the tank, one of twelve forming the double hull between the cargo tanks and the sea, counting the frames forming the ship's ribs as he went. When he reckoned himself in position, he looked up and smiled as his light illuminated the vent opening near the shipside, the fine wire he'd placed dangling out, almost invisible.

Structural members marched up the outer hull like widely spaced shelves or rungs of a giant ladder, and Medina climbed, stretching and straining to pull himself up to the underside of the main deck. At the uppermost member, he clung one-handed, his feet on the next member down as he reached toward the ship's side with a charge. He gave a relieved grunt as the magnet sucked the charge to the steel, and then examined the placement. It sat on the uppermost member, like a box at the back of a high shelf, invisible unless someone scaled the structure as Medina had.

He groped under the vent and pulled the dangling wire to the charge antenna and twisted the two together, locking them with a tiny wire nut with trembling fingers. Sweat stung his eyes and soaked his coveralls, and he wiped his eyes with the back of his free hand to study his work in the beam of his little light. Perfect, he thought, and began to inch his way down.

Clang. The sharp ring of steel on steel sent Medina's heart into his throat, and he clung motionless, listening as more noise indicated activity on the main deck above him. He recovered and continued his descent, faster now. Back on the horizontal stringer, he moved aft toward the ladder with no clear plan. Should he go up? He still had to drill and plug a tiny hole near the top of the common bulkhead between this tank and the adjacent cargo tank. But what was happening on main deck? What if they were bolting the manhole? No one knew he was here. He'd be trapped until he starved to death or drowned when they flooded the ballast tank.

Medina took a deep breath and controlled his fear. His hand fell on the fanny pack, and he felt the small cordless drill through the fabric. He gathered his resolve and moved across the tank to the cargo-tank bulkhead.

Twenty minutes later, Medina eased his head out of the manhole and surveyed the main deck. Whoever had been there was gone, and he pulled himself from the manhole and stood on deck. His legs ached from climbing, but he felt the weight of the remaining charge in his pocket and pressed on. A half hour later, he exited the last ballast tank, sweating and dirty but exultant. He entered the deckhouse and went to the Cargo Control Room, where he walked to a control panel labeled "Mariner Tek—Model BT 6000—Ballast-Tank Gas-Detection System."

He extracted a pair of needle-nose pliers and a spool of wire from this fanny pack, then secured the power to the panel and opened it. This was the easy part. He'd studied the schematic in the technical manual for days and knew it cold. His fingers flew as he wired in jumpers, then arranged them within the existing wiring so that nothing looked amiss. He stepped back and admired his handiwork before closing the panel and powering up the system.

Green lights glowed, showing all ballast tanks safe and gas-free. He smiled again, knowing those lights would stay green, regardless of conditions in the tanks. He powered down the system and hummed a little tune as he climbed to his cabin for a shower.

Offices of Phoenix Shipping Ltd.
London
3 June

Dugan wrinkled his nose at the faint smell of fresh paint and watched through the door as Anna scooped up folders from her own desk and maneuvered around a ladder in the outer office. Over Alex's objections, Dugan was working full days, even though his new office was a work in progress. Conversion of the storeroom to office space was all but complete, and throughout the process, Anna deferred to Mrs. Coutts completely. She'd managed to assuage the older woman's antipathy by following suggestions to the letter, including counsel as to proper dress. Unfortunately, Anna's sensuality defeated even Mrs. Coutts's wardrobe hints. The elderly secretary concluded the poor child was destined to look a tart, with no help for it.

"Last of the lot, Tom," Anna said, dumping folders on his desk.

"Thanks," Dugan said. "Computers?"

Anna sighed. "I've been on to Sutton four times today."

"OK. Keep on him," Dugan said.

As Anna left, Dugan stole a glance at her well-shaped backside before forcing himself back to work. He opened the folder on top of the stack to find a note.

Dugan, ask me to dinner tonight. We must talk.

Dugan pocketed the note. About time. Ward said contact would be through Anna. So far, there hadn't been any. He felt isolated, and for the first time, ill at ease in Alex's presence.

He pressed the intercom.

"Yes, Tom," Anna said.

"Can you stay late? I may need you to pull more files for me. I'll make it up with dinner. You pick the place."

She laughed. "Quite the best offer I've had all day. Bring your gold card."

"No problem. Thanks," Dugan said, picking up the phone to call Alex.

"Yes, Thomas," Alex answered, looking at his caller ID.

"Alex, I'm working over. Please give Mrs. Hogan my regrets."

Alex paused. "I've things to do as well. She'll put something back for us."

"Alex, that's not necessary. I've made—"

"No problem, Thomas. I'll just call home—"

"Alex. I have other plans."

A silence grew. "Very well," Alex said at last. "I'll see you tomorrow then."

Dugan hung up, troubled by his friend's behavior. He sighed and returned to the file he was studying.

***

"It's seven," Anna said from the doorway. "Starving me is nonproductive. I'm more agreeable on a full stomach."

Dugan stood and walked to the door. "Sorry. Lost track. You picked a place?"

Anna nodded and gathered her things. As they walked out, she pointed to light leaking beneath a door. "Captain Braun's working late."

Dugan shrugged. "He's always here when I leave."

***

About bloody time, thought Braun, irritated at Kairouz's failure to control Dugan. Not that he was too concerned. Working late was an obvious ploy to have a go at the slut. Took him long enough. Braun smiled. If they became lovers, bugging her flat might be worthwhile.

***

Anna listened as Dugan talked. After deflecting his attempts to discuss business with a quick hand squeeze and almost imperceptible head shake, she'd hung on to his every word. She deserved an Oscar. Despite knowing it was an act, he was enjoying himself.

"Dessert?" the waiter asked.

Dugan gave Anna a quizzical look.

"I'm stuffed," she said. "How about coffee at my place?"

Dugan asked for the check.

In the cab, Anna crawled onto his lap and kissed him, keeping at it all the way to her building. Dugan exited the cab, unable to hide his arousal from the smirking cabby, as Anna pulled him into the lobby for a smoldering kiss and kept at it in the elevator, kissing his neck and giggling. She dragged him to her door and fumbled with the key before pushing him in, lips on his, and closing the door behind them with her foot. Then she stopped.

"Sit." She pointed to a sofa as she threw the bolt, then moved to a chair.

Dugan stood in the entryway, his confusion complete.

"Surely you knew that wasn't genuine," she said.

He glanced down. "Part of me was hopeful."

Her face turned cold. "Yes, well, hope springs eternal. Sit."

Dugan complied. "OK. What now?"

She softened. "First, I'm sorry if I overdid it. We don't yet know how closely we're being watched. I was unsure you could fake it. So I aroused you."

"Superbly," Dugan said.

Anna colored. "Understand, Mr. Dugan, I'm happily married. I will deal with you professionally and expect no less."

"Married? Really?" Dugan said. "Must be tough."

"That's none of your business."

"You're right. Sorry," he said. "Let's just consider this, for the purposes of our cover only, our first spat and put it behind us?"

She ignored the sarcasm. "Tonight we set our cover. We can speak freely here. This place will be swept daily. Assume you're under surveillance elsewhere, for sure at the office."

"Are you sure?" Dugan asked.

"We put an undercover on the janitorial staff to do a sweep. Our offices and Kairouz's are bugged. From Braun's office."

"So Braun's running things. And he's bugging Alex, so Alex isn't involved."

"He's involved. Maybe he's using Braun to create deniability."

"I can't believe Alex is a willing party to terrorism."

Anna was noncommittal. "We'll see. Anyway, this is where we communicate. As lovers, it'll be natural to come here evenings or even to sneak off for afternoon trysts. We'll raise eyebrows but not suspicions."

"But won't whoever it is just bug this place?"

"We'll handle that. I'll tell you about it if and when necessary."

Dugan bristled. "Do let me know when I'm deemed trustworthy."

"Tom, we compartmentalize. You needn't be so touchy."

He considered that. "Yeah, I understand. Sorry I overreacted. Let's put the hostility behind us and go back to being Tom and Anna."

"Fine by me. Provided you stop being so damned cheeky."

Dugan smiled. "But that's my most endearing quality."

She shook her head and moved to the kitchen to brew coffee. When she returned, they settled down to discuss strategy.

"This is going to be harder than I thought," Dugan said. "I must admit Alex is behaving strangely. Like he's going out of his way to minimize my office time. We arrive late every day, then he has me out the door at the dot of five. Totally out of character for him; the guy's a workaholic. Braun must be coercing him somehow, maybe through threats to Cassie."

Anna looked skeptical. "I've seen Kairouz's file. He isn't someone easily intimidated. After his entire family was killed in the Lebanese civil war, he came to London as a penniless teen with no prospects and managed to build a major shipping company from scratch. Now he's wealthy and connected. If he's being threatened, why wouldn't he turn to the authorities?"

"I don't know. But Alex Kairouz is no terrorist."

Anna sighed. "Let's start with what we do know. This Farley arrived on the scene right after Braun's employment. We can assume he's a player, and the computer guy is in on it for sure. Word among the clerical staff is that Braun dismissed the IT people and brought Sutton on right after he joined the company. I suspect Hell will freeze over before we get any sort of reliable computer access."

"The biggest problem," Dugan said, "is how to snoop without raising suspicion if we're caught. If Braun's somehow squeezing Alex, he's pretty damn smart. We don't want to put his guard up."

Anna smiled. "We just need a believable motive. You have one made-to-order."

Dugan looked confused.

"Think about it," Anna said. "You and Braun are rivals. We style our snooping as an attempt to uncover some incompetence or malfeasance on Braun's part, so you can undermine him with Alex. Even if we're caught, it will look like corporate politics."

Dugan nodded, impressed. "Pretty sharp."

Anna smiled at the compliment and spent the next half hour briefing Dugan on how they would develop their cover relationship. At midnight, she let him out.

"Must keep up appearances," she whispered at the doorway, sending him off with a smoldering kiss.

***

Braun slumped in the driver's seat. He'd just decided the Yank was making a night of it when Dugan exited the building and turned up the walk. I overestimated him, thought Braun. When he's gone, I'm sure the bitch will enjoy having a real man.

CHAPTER EIGHT

The chief mate tensed at the console, focused on the rising level in the last cargo tank.

"Stop," he barked into his radio, commanding the terminal to stop pumping. The load was complete, and at a nod from the chief mate, Medina left to check the drafts.

It was a relieved Medina that rushed down the gangway. They'd taken minimal ballast for the short transit to the refinery; water hadn't even risen to his plugs. The ballast tanks were empty now, and the plugs had held as powerful fans pushed inert gas into the empty cargo tanks, displacing oxygen-rich air before gasoline surged into the tanks.

He'd been terrified that the gas pressure—slight though it was—would unseat the shredded bits of Styrofoam cup he'd packed into the tiny holes. He'd paced the deck, alert to telltale whiffs from ballast-tank vents or the loud keening of gas whistling through an unplugged hole.

But they all held, praise be to Allah, high on the bulkheads, submerged now under a foot of gasoline on the cargo-tank side. It wouldn't take long for the cargo to dissolve them.

But it would be long enough.

Braun smiled. Sutton had hacked backdoor access to several porn sites, making tracking his communications like looking for a needle in several thousand haystacks. Only the logic of the method had convinced Motaki to disregard his revulsion at accessing the sites. Braun's smile widened. Perhaps this might expand the Iranian's horizons a bit.

He opened an encrypted file. Motaki had done well. The Chechens looked European, and below each picture was age, height, weight, and hair and eye color. Braun printed the pictures and erased the file before typing the Web address of the Baltic Maritime Job Exchange, to begin his search for unemployed ex-Eastern Bloc mariners resembling the Chechens.

ANNA WALSH'S APARTMENT BUILDING
8 JUNE

Joel Sutton, dressed in a British Telcom uniform and with toolbox in hand, rang Anna Walsh's doorbell. Showing his face was a risk, but he'd confirmed Dugan and the bitch were at work, and no one else would know him. When no one answered, he picked the lock and went to work.

He hid transmitters in the phones and throughout the small apartment and a tiny receiver on a high closet shelf, tapped into a spare circuit in the existing phone wiring. Satisfied, he left things as he'd found them and rode the elevator to the lobby, leaving his toolbox there as he went to the van. He returned with a heavy shopping bag, its handles biting into his hand, to collect his toolbox and ride the elevator to the basement.

The telephone box was well marked and he set to work, stepping back twenty minutes later to survey the results. Concealed under a stack of boxes and connected to the panel by a hidden wire sat a lead-lined wooden box with a near-invisible antenna wire run to a high window. The box was soundproof, with a speaker inside echoing any sound from the apartment. Inches away was a cell phone, voice activated to dial at any sound. There was no connection between the devices but sound waves, eliminating a trace. The outgoing cell signal was detectable, but isolating it would be difficult. Difficult became impossible as the audio was relayed through two identical boxes, both hidden far away in high-cell-traffic areas.

All the phones were untraceable, purchased for cash, and modified with long-life batteries. Each box held enough plastic explosive and white phosphorus to destroy the contents and anyone opening them without first calling the phone inside and entering a disarming code.

Sutton dialed Anna Walsh's number on another throwaway phone and let her voice mail greeting play without responding. In the basement of the Iranian embassy, another cell phone disconnected after Anna's words were recorded, and a technician phoned his superior. His superior walked to a window of his second-floor office and smoothed his hair with his right hand in full view of another man standing across the street pretending to read a newspaper. The man walked to a public phone and dialed a number from memory.

"Hello," Sutton said.

"I'm sorry. I was ringing George McGregor. I misdialed," the man said and hung up.

Sutton disconnected and reached for his toolbox. Surveillance was established for whoever the hell was running it. He left the building to ditch the van.

OFFICES OF PHOENIX SHIPPING

Dugan cursed as his monitor went black for the third time. He checked his watch. Might as well pack it in. Ever since he and Anna had begun their "affair," they'd stayed late every night to establish a pattern of being in the office after hours. They left together every evening, and twice Dugan slept on her sofa, arriving the next morning in the same clothes—a fact noted by office gossips. What Dugan had failed to anticipate was the impact of his relationship with Anna on his other relationships.

Mrs. Coutts registered disapproval in every icy glance, addressing him with cold formality, while Anna was somehow transformed in Mrs. Coutts's view into a poor innocent led astray by her lustful boss, a sexual predator. It got worse. Daniel, the driver, shared the gossip with Mrs. Hogan, the cook, who, certain he was wrong, passed it on to Mrs. Farnsworth. After admonishing Mrs. Hogan on the evils of gossip, Mrs. Farnsworth phoned Mrs. Coutts so that she might find the source of the malicious rumor and squash it, only to learn the rumor was true.

Mrs. Farnsworth, never one of Dugan's fans, now addressed him, when she spoke at all, as if he was only slightly less unpleasant than something she couldn't get off her shoe sole. Mrs. Hogan registered disapproval in her own way. His eggs this morning had been rubber, served with black toast and orange juice with a half-inch layer of seeds in the bottom of the glass.

The only female in the house who still liked him was Cassie, but she was in bed when he got home now, and his first morning absence had not gone unnoticed. Her inquisition the following morning had been curtailed only by a "proper young lady is not nosy" dictum from Mrs. Farnsworth, accompanied by an icy stare at Dugan.

It had come to a head on the ride in this morning, with Alex's repeated throat clearing.

"You better spit it out before you get a sore throat, Alex," Dugan said.

"It's... awkward, Thomas. Your involvement with this Walsh woman is upsetting the household."

"Agreed," Dugan said, "but I'll be damned if I know why. My private life's my own."

"True, Thomas. But the ladies"—Alex smiled—"except Mrs. Farnsworth, of course, all held you in high regard. I'm sure they didn't think you a monk, but assumed you would choose a more... appropriate partner. Hiring a woman for her looks just to bed her is just so... unsavory."

"Anna's a damn good secretary."

"Indeed," Alex said, "a fortunate accident according to Mrs. Coutts."

"How about you, Alex? Do you share the ladies' opinion?"

Silence answered.

"That's the pot and the kettle, old friend," Dugan said. "Kathleen was your secretary."

He regretted the words immediately. Alex purpled.

"Don't you dare imply my marriage was the product of some cheap office dalliance. Kathleen worked for me for years before we dated. I am your friend, but if you ever, ever repeat that, I will be no longer. Is that clear?"

"That was a cheap shot, Alex. I'm sorry. I guess I'm just confused by everyone's reaction. I certainly don't want to upset your household. Should I move out?"

"Perhaps that's best," Alex said, still angry. "But where? In with Miss Walsh?"

"That's my business, Alex," Dugan said, and they'd ridden the rest of the trip in silence.

**

And now I'm homeless in London, thought Dugan as Anna popped her head in the door.

"How about dinner?" she asked.

"I'm with you," Dugan said, standing to leave. "We've weighty matters to discuss."

"Oh?"

Dugan smiled. "How'd you like a roommate?"

***

Perfect, thought Braun as Dugan and Anna left. The timing on Sutton's visit had been spot on, and if the Yank moved in, perhaps they'd spend more time in the apartment, and he could off-load some of the surveillance. A celebration was in order. A nice dinner courtesy of Kairouz and some entertainment. He dialed his cell as he left the office.

"Send me the little brunette at ten," he said into the phone. "I forget her name."

"Yvette," a voice said, "and the price is triple. You bloody near killed her last time. I couldn't work her for days. I expect payment for lost time."

"No problem," Braun said. "Make sure she brings the toys."

He hung up and hailed a cab, smiling as he settled in the seat—things were going well.

***

Dugan and Anna stepped out into a beautiful evening, pleasantly full and mellow from wine. He'd recounted his trouble with Alex over dinner as Anna feigned delight at the prospect of cohabitation. Dugan played along, though less than eager to exchange a good bed for a lumpy sofa. Anna clung to him now, head against his shoulder as he started to hail a cab.

"No, don't," she said. "It's lovely. Let's walk."

Foot traffic was light, but as they reached Anna's building, a short, bald man, head down and phone to his ear, rushed down the steps to collide with Anna, moving on without slowing. Dugan glared after him.

"Easy, Tarzan," Anna said, a restraining hand on Dugan's arm. "I'm fine. Let it go."

Anna tugged Dugan's arm and they moved inside.

In the safe haven of the apartment, Dugan relaxed, but before he spoke, Anna clamped a hand over his mouth.

"I think I'll shower. Care to wash my back, Tiger?" she asked.

"Sounds delightful," Dugan said, nodding as she removed her hand.

He stood in the bathroom in mute confusion as Anna arranged the showerhead so the water drummed loud against the plastic curtain. She removed her shoes and motioned him to do the same, then led him on tiptoe through the small kitchen and out the back door of the apartment. There were two

58

apartments per floor, all with front entrances served by the residents' elevator and rear entrances with a common service elevator. As she closed her own door, a tall man in a rumpled suit beckoned from the open back door of the next apartment. Anna entered the apartment with Dugan in tow and followed the man into the living room.

The tall man grinned. "And how is our Phoenix Shipping slut?"

"Sod off, Harry," Anna said. "Lou back yet?"

"Any minute," Harry said as a key rattled in the front door and Lou entered.

"You're the guy who ran into us," Dugan said, still confused.

"Guilty," Lou said. "I had to let Anna know about the bugs."

Anna nodded at the new arrival. "Tom, this is Lou Chesterton and"—she indicated the tall man—"Harry Albright. My colleagues in the Anti-Terrorism Unit."

Dugan shook hands as she continued. "Who wired us?" she asked.

"Sutton," Lou said. "Professional job. Multiple booby-trapped relays. Untraceable."

"Christ," Dugan said, "there goes our time outside the fish bowl."

"Welcome to our world, Yank," Lou said, turning to Anna. "Shower running?"

"Less than five minutes, but we don't have long." She turned to Harry. "Cover audio?"

Harry smiled. "Some of the finest sex sounds the Internet has to offer."

"Voices?" she asked.

"Not a problem," Harry said. "Talk is minimal and a bit... repetitive. I distorted it, and you can put on music to help mask it. It'll do for tonight."

"What's after the sex sounds?" Anna asked.

"Snoring in an endless loop. To buy time for you two to come back and do some recordings for alternative sound feeds."

"I don't snore," Dugan said.

"Actually, you do. Like a bloody train," Anna said. "At least on my sofa."

"Actually, you both do. At least on my recording," Harry said as Dugan smirked.

"Right," Lou said, "we best get to it. Harry, get Anna the portable CD player while she briefs Mr. Dugan here."

Minutes later, they crept into Anna's apartment. She turned off the water and gave a sensuous moan as she placed the CD player by the bedside phone. Dugan, per instructions, grunted sexual sounds, looking so self-conscious Anna was hard-pressed not to laugh. She put music on her sound system and started the sex sound track on the portable player. Satisfied, they slipped out the back door and into the other apartment.

CHAPTER NINE

Braun read the decrypted message and cursed. He pulled the sat phone from a drawer. The encryption algorithm was unbreakable, and calls were routed through random and changing links, but still, he preferred to minimize voice contact. He sighed; anxiety was to be expected, he supposed, when one dealt with amateurs. He dialed. In Tehran, an identical phone rang.

"Yes," Motaki answered.

"I got your message," Braun said. "All is proceeding. *Asian Trader* sailed from Singapore on schedule, and I chartered a VLCC named *China Star* to the Iranian National Oil Company. She must depart Kharg Island no later than 21 June to arrive in the Malacca Straits as *Asian Trader* reaches Panama. Please ensure there are no loading delays in Iran."

Braun had learned that giving his principals some simple task within their control always had a calming influence.

"I will see to it," Motaki said. "But what about Panama? I'm concerned we do not have sufficient control. Rodriguez might be a problem if his pet project goes awry."

"Our man on *Asian Trader* has minimal resources. It is not a problem."

"All right," Motaki said. "And this man Richards?"

"On standby pay. He knows nothing yet. I'll move him to Jakarta when the time is right."

"So, the sideshows move ahead. What of the main attack?"

"The Chechens are at the training facility. They can't become experts, but they will learn enough to serve our purposes."

"Their Russian is better than their English," Motaki said. "I still think a facility in Eastern Europe would have been better."

"Chechen-accented Russian," Braun replied. "Chechen seamen are rare, Mr. President. Here in UK their accents are unrecognizable, and if they say something that reveals them to be other than seamen, it can be covered as language misunderstanding."

"And what of these men whose identities you've stolen? What if one of them should make an inconvenient appearance?"

Braun smiled. "Those men are being well paid to stay home. I employed them for fictitious ships under construction in China and put them on full pay to stand by, ready to fly at moment's notice. The seamen get paid for nothing, and the agency gets their commission. All courtesy of Kairouz. Everyone is happy."

"Very well," Motaki said, his acknowledgment grudging, "and the last ship?"

"I have several options, but it's too early to—"

"Mr. Braun, need I remind you—"

"You need remind me of nothing, Mr. President, but the main attack is the most difficult. Runs from Black Sea ports to the target are short, with no chance to manipulate arrival time. Additionally, the ports involved are not the most efficient, and there may be lengthy delays. There are many things that can go wrong," Braun said. "With respect, sir, too many cooks spoil the broth. Please leave this to me."

"Very well," Motaki said, "but keep me informed."

"Of course."

ANNA WALSH'S APARTMENT BUILDING
1915 HOURS LOCAL TIME
9 JUNE

Dugan sat with the Brits in the apartment next to Anna's. Dugan and Anna had returned there the first night, to work with Harry recording scripts for additional cover audio, including, to their discomfort and Harry's amusement, breathless sexual audio. Anna had colored and pointed a smirking Harry from the room as she moaned "Yes, yes, yes," into the mike.

Dugan had been skeptical.

"How do you turn a few hours into days of fake audio?" he'd asked.

"Bloody magic, Yank, and the wizardry of British intelligence," Harry had replied. "But we don't need 'days.' You spend nights there, and most of that sleeping. Sex will occupy some time and Internet tracks laced with your recordings will work there." Harry had shrugged. "That leaves hours, and conversation varies little day to day. Our lads have software to assemble daily dialogues, then they review and tweak it. Mornings, you'll need to mind what you say, but we'll craft evening dialogues for you to play at Anna's while you stay here. We'll add sex as it seems to fit, and that will be that."

And so it had. To his delight, Dugan traded Anna's lumpy sofa for the bed in the surveillance apartment, creeping into her place each morning to begin the daily charade. The surveillance apartment became their center of operations, a meeting place by day, and a refuge where Dugan and Anna could escape the bugs for a while each evening while the fake audio ran.

***

"I smell a rat," Dugan said, holding up a copy of the daily ship-position report.

"What do you mean, Yank?" Lou asked.

Dugan tapped the page. "This ship. The *China Star*. She's a VLCC Phoenix chartered from a competitor, then subchartered to the Iranian National Oil Company. I can't see any way we can make money on that sort of deal at prevailing rates."

Harry looked confused. "A vee bloody what?"

"Sorry," Dugan said. "VLCC is short for 'very large crude carrier.' Supertanker to you."

"But what's it mean?" Anna asked.

Dugan shrugged. "Maybe nothing, but it might be a lead. At any rate, it's the only thing I've been able to turn up so far. If I can get a look at the charter agreement, I might be able to make some other connections."

"Can you get at it?" Anna asked.

Dugan shook his head. "That's another thing that makes me suspicious. There's neither a copy of the agreement on the server nor is it in the hardcopy files. I could just ask for it, but if I'm right, that might set off all sorts of alarms."

"So how are you going to get it?"

"I've got an idea," Dugan said.

HEAD HILL TRAINING CENTER
SOUTHAMPTON, HAMPSHIRE, UK
11 JUNE

Khassan Basaev's monitor flashed a congratulatory message and a prompt to move to the next training module. He yawned and arched into a stretch, rubbing his blue eyes before he reached out of habit to stroke a nonexistent beard. He grimaced at his unfamiliar reflection in the monitor and hoped he looked "European" enough. His three companions were also freshly barbered, with lighter lower faces stark against tanned necks and foreheads, a difference fading under application of the sunlamp. All the men's hair was light, blond to brown, and they looked Nordic rather than the mujahideen they were.

"Ah. Another milestone," Shamil whispered in Russian from his seat next to Basaev. "Quite impressive for a mountain peasant."

Basaev gave a brief smile as Aslan and Doku chuckled. "Joke as you will, Shamil," Basaev said, "but don't forget our mission."

"I never do," Shamil said, serious now, as all the men turned back to their terminals.

Basaev looked around the computer training lab, empty on a Saturday except for the four men. The instructor had been surprised at Basaev's request to use the training facility on the weekend for review, declining an opportunity to relax in town with the rest of the class after a grueling week of instruction. The Chechens had no desire to mix with the other—mostly British and Western European—students. Basaev's men were known collectively as "the Russians" by the others, an insult not normally tolerated. Now it comforted him. The infidels couldn't tell a Chechen from an Eskimo.

Shamil's joke aside, they were no peasants, but university graduates, fluent in several languages. They'd met in university in Grozny a lifetime ago, before Russian aggression drove them to the Cause of Allah and Free Chechnya. They escaped the city just before the Russians encircled it, fleeing to a mountain village, where weeks had grown to months and then years as their war ground to a fitful stalemate, neither side capable of victory. In time, they were ignored, and if it was not victory, it was better than living under the Russian heel. The village became home, and they started families. Life had been simple but full.

So much so that Paradise for Basaev was not a place of willing virgins but a vision of his village. A place to hold his wife, as she whispered he would be a father once more, as he watched his toddler move around a modest hut. A place gone forever when the guns of a helicopter gunship tore his family into bloody refuse, identifiable only by shreds of clothing.

He'd been away at the time, leading a dozen others on a routine patrol. They returned to bury their dead and move into hiding, asking Allah only for Russians to kill, a wish come true as Russians arrived in force to crush the holdouts. It became a long, hard war of attrition, and they killed many Russians, but there were always more. Iranian agents were frequent guests in his mountain hideaway, asking nothing in return for their aid. Until last month.

"We are not seamen," Basaev had protested, "and why strike our Muslim brothers? Killing Russians is pleasing in the sight of Allah."

"You do the work of Allah," the Iranian said, "but there are tasks more urgent. We can teach you the skills required but cannot make our other brothers look European."

"And the Faithful who die?"

"Most casualties will be infidel tourists, and the Faithful who die will be gathered into Heaven. And ask yourself this, Basaev: are those that whore themselves to gawking tourists really our brothers? Are the governments that fawn on the Americans in return for military aid really true Muslims? When was the last time you saw a Saudi or Egyptian or a Turk or anyone but an Iranian in these mountains, bringing you guns and ammunition and medicine?" The Iranian had paused. "You should reflect upon who stands by your side during your darkest hour."

Basaev had conceded the point but continued to resist. "We know how to kill Russians and should continue until Allah calls us to Paradise."

"Look around you," the Iranian said. "Four left. And in these mountains, groups of two or four or seven fight on, growing fewer as the Russians grow stronger, financed by the sale of oil. If, God willing, you sell your lives for a hundred Russians each, there will be four hundred infidels in Hell. A drop in the ocean. Take my offer and slay infidel tourists by the thousands and bring down the Russian economy. Think, my brother."

"I have," Basaev said, "and it is clear to me this will raise oil prices and enrich Iran."

The Iranian smiled. "The better to support world Jihad," he said.

In the end, Basaev had acquiesced, and now he slipped into silent prayer, asking for Allah's favor, for he thought himself a godly man and sought divine approval often. The self-deception was so complete he never understood he'd converted to a more elemental faith, kneeling among the bloody remains of his family at the altar of vengeance. His religion was the destruction of all things Russian.

Basaev pulled himself back to the present and clicked his mouse to bring up the next module, "Cargoes and Possible Ignition Sources."

Dugan got off the elevator and walked through the deserted offices, illuminated by the morning sun filtering through hallway windows. He left the overhead lights off and made his way past the cubicle farm to an office marked CHARTERING. He looked around nervously, then opened the door and entered, turning to ease the door closed.

"May I help you, Mr. Dugan?"

Dugan spun to see Abdul Ibrahim sitting at his desk with a perplexed expression. Even on a Saturday, the little Pakistani wore a well-tailored suit and a perfectly knotted silk tie.

"Uh… Mr. Ibrahim. Forgive me for not knocking. I didn't know you were here. I was uh… just going to leave a note on your desk to call me. I would have messaged you, but I'm having some problem with my e-mail."

Ibrahim smiled and gestured to a chair. "No apology necessary. Please. Sit and tell me how I may be of service."

Dugan took the chair, his mind racing. Shit.

"I'm just curious," he said. "I saw a VLCC on the position report… *China Star*, I think her name is. I noticed she was subchartered to lift a cargo to Japan. I figure if rates are good enough to charter in, then subcharter on that route, I should check it out. If that trade picks up, it means I can get our ships positioned in the Far East much more cheaply for repairs. That will really help our maintenance budget."

Christ, thought Dugan, pretty smooth. That even sounded believable to me.

Ibrahim looked uncomfortable. "I have only a vague recollection of the details, but I will look into it and get back with you Monday, if that's all right."

He'd hit a nerve. Dugan started to back off, then realized that any damage was already done. He may as well find out what he could. In for a penny, in for a pound.

"You're head of chartering," Dugan said. "This is a big-money deal that went down three days ago."

Ibrahim was sweating. "I… I…"

"Mr. Ibrahim," Dugan said, "I've known you almost ten years and know you're honest. If you've somehow caught up in something illegal—"

Ibrahim shook his head. "Not me," he said, lowering his voice. "Braun put together the charters. I went to Mr. Kairouz, but—"

He stopped and looked around, then lowered his voice further. "I will not speak of it here. But I know you are Mr. Kairouz's friend, and something is very, very wrong. I will tell you what I know. Meet me near the entrance to Vauxhall tube station in one hour."

Dugan nodded and rose to leave. He opened the door quietly and looked around before slipping out and down the corridor to his own office. He closed his office door just as the elevator doors opened down the hall.

***

Braun stepped off the elevator and swiveled toward the quiet click of Dugan's office door closing. What the bloody hell was Dugan doing here?

VAUXHALL TUBE STATION
LONDON

Braun watched Dugan and Ibrahim from a distance as they stood on the platform, staring straight ahead as they pretended to be disinterested strangers waiting for a train. He couldn't see their faces but noted tension in their postures. They were obviously conversing. Amateurs.

Braun mulled the possibilities. Dugan's fumbling attempts to catch him in some malfeasance or incompetent action were apparent and concerned him not at all. Nor did Ibrahim know anything except the barest financial essentials of the *China Star* deal, and Braun had arranged those to look like a kickback scheme. So even if Dugan learned of *China Star*, he couldn't go to the authorities without implicating his friend Kairouz.

Braun considered killing them both, just to be sure, but dismissed the idea. Two dead executives from the same company were bound to attract unwanted attention. But there was the problem of perception. He'd promised Kairouz that if he couldn't control the little Pakistani, the man would die, along with his family. Braun hated breaking promises. Kairouz had to understand Braun was a man of his word. Otherwise, when things got really challenging, Kairouz might feel insufficiently motivated.

It was a conundrum, and he now regretted the specificity of his threat. Killing the Paki and his entire family would be far too sensational and sure to attract media attention. Braun sighed. How tedious. He continued to mull things over as he waited until the men boarded separate trains. He had no need to follow. He knew where Ibrahim lived.

ANNA WALSH'S APARTMENT BUILDING
1615 HOURS LOCAL TIME
11 JUNE

"He's really stressed out," Dugan said. "Apparently Braun handled the charters of *China Star* personally. The first Ibrahim learned of it was when the ship appeared on the position report. Like me, he thought it looked hinky and started asking questions." Dugan paused. "That's when it got interesting. He went to Braun, who blew up. When he failed to get satisfaction there, he approached Alex, who told him if he didn't back off, he'd be fired."

"More proof of Kairouz's involvement," Lou said, "but what's Ibrahim make of it?"

"He doesn't know what to think," Dugan said. "On the surface it looks like some sort of kickback deal. His main fear is personal. He believes Braun has somehow forced Alex to enter a shady deal, and he's afraid that he will somehow become the fall guy if the deal goes sour. He's pretty conflicted. He's worked for Alex a long time and knows he's scrupulously honest. On the other hand, Alex seems to be deferring to Braun completely, and Ibrahim thinks he's screwed no matter what he does. I guess that's why he opened up to me so easily."

"You're sure no one saw you?" Harry asked.

"I can't see how," Dugan said. "We left the office separately and met off site."

"Still," Anna said, "I wish you had consulted us before the meet."

"No time," Dugan said, "Ibrahim seemed to be in a talkative mood, and I didn't want to give him time to think about it."

"Well, your instincts were probably right on that," Anna said.

"I guess that's it then," Lou said. "*China Star*'s not even at the load port yet, so I doubt there's an immediate threat. We'll just keep an eye on it and see what develops. Is there anything else, Anna?"

Anna shook her head, and Harry and Lou stood up. Anna followed them to the door. Just as they reached the door, Lou turned. "By the way, good work, Tom," he said.

Dugan nodded as Anna let the pair out and locked the door behind them.

"Let me second that," Anna said as she returned. "It was good work."

Dugan sighed. "Something's obviously up with Alex, but I know he's a victim."

"Given the evidence, Tom, I can't understand your certainty."

"I just am," Dugan said. "I know him."

"You seem unlikely friends, really."

"How so?"

"Well, you're just… different, that's all. Alex is so… so 'European' I guess is the word. Tactful, multilingual, almost courtly, and…" Anna stopped.

"And I'm what…" Dugan deadpanned. "Blunt? Monolingual? Abrasive?"

"Tom, please, I didn't—"

Dugan grinned. "How 'bout 'American'… will that sum it up?"

Relieved, she smiled. "Quite nicely, you bloody annoying Yank. But seriously, whatever do you and Alex Kairouz have in common?"

"Dead wives," he said softly and looked away.

He lapsed into silence, and she thought he'd said all he intended. Then he went on.

"Years ago, Alex hired me to inspect a ship. He liked my work and became a regular client. Later I was working a short project in his office that got delayed. I tried to extend my hotel, but they were booked, as were most hotels in London, so Alex invited me home."

Dugan smiled. "Cassie was just a toddler. Mrs. Hogan served a great meal, and after Mrs. Farnsworth took Cassie to bed, Alex and I had brandy and coffee." He smiled again. "Mostly brandy. That's when he told me his wife had died of cancer two years earlier. His wounds were raw, and it was obvious he was burying his grief in work and raising Cassie."

"The more we drank, the more we opened up. My wife had been dead awhile, but it all came back." He paused. "Because I had suppressed it too. My kid sister was a rock after Ginny's death, but some things I couldn't share even with her, but Alex and I connected. We drank and talked and vented. About good things and bad and things we missed most. We got shitfaced and maudlin and toasted lost loves, and sober and hungover and finally"—Dugan gave a sheepish smile—"embarrassed by our behavior. We never spoke of it again. But I know Alex Kairouz, and Alex Kairouz is no terrorist."

Anna nodded, understanding and intrigued.

"Will you tell me about Ginny?"

She was afraid she'd offended him, but slowly his face softened.

"The love of my life," he said with a wistful smile. "Her name was Virginia."

"How'd you meet?"

Dugan chuckled. "I ran into her. Literally. I bashed my old pickup into her brand-new Mustang convertible in a parking lot."

"You met in a car crash?" Anna asked, incredulous.

"More like a fender bender. She was livid. The first words she ever said to me were 'Why don't you watch where the hell you're going, you big jerk?'"

Anna smiled. "Not a terribly auspicious beginning."

"Oh, but it was. There she was, green eyes flashing and the wind in her red hair, ready to kick my ass, all five foot two inches of her, the most beautiful woman I'd ever seen. She calmed down and we traded contact info, and then she called the next day. She was having trouble with the insurance because the accident happened on a private lot with no police report. I told her just to get her car fixed and I would pay for it, provided she let me buy her dinner to apologize. Long story short, we married a year later."

"What did she do?" Anna asked.

"She was a teacher. First grade. She loved kids," Dugan said.

"Did she die of cancer too?"

"Accident," Dugan said. His face clouded, and he looked away. Anna moved closer and took his hand.

"I'm sorry," she said, "it was wrong of me to pry."

"No. It's OK," he said, turning back to her. "I want to tell you, though I don't know why. It's just… difficult to get out." She squeezed his hand, and he went on. "We were both off for the summer when I was offered some relief-chief work. Since the only way to a permanent chief-engineer job was to start as relief, I jumped at it. We postponed a planned trip, and I went back to sea.

"It was a container ship on a North Europe run. Sat phones were new, and the ship didn't have one. I called Ginny from pay phones on the dock in US ports, but in Europe then you had to go to the phone company or a hotel to call the US. I couldn't always get away from the ship, but I did call from our last European port with our ETA in New York so she could meet us, and we could spend a few hours together before the next trip."

Dugan paused. "When I called, she told me she had a surprise for me in New York, but I couldn't drag it out of her. Then we just talked about everything and nothing, like you do when you're in love, just feeling connected. She was talking about visiting her sister in upstate New York when we got cut off. I kept trying back but kept getting a German recording. I got through a half hour later, but there was no answer, and I had to get back to the ship.

"We hit a storm coming back, lost some containers overboard and took minor damage. We were delayed, but I knew Ginny would call the company for an updated ETA before she left home. When we docked, the Coast Guard and a crowd of insurance surveyors boarded to inspect the damage.

When the crowd cleared and I hadn't seen Ginny, I grabbed my coffee can of quarters and headed for the pay phone. I got no answer at home, so I called Ginny's sister." Dugan paused. "That's when I found out.

"We had a renovated apartment, hardwood floors and rugs everywhere, all sizes. Ginny loved the damned things. She slipped on one and smashed her head on the coffee table. When she didn't show up and her sister couldn't reach her, she called the police. They found Ginny.

"Ginny wasn't great with administrative details. Her sister was still listed as next of kin, and she didn't know how to reach me or when I'd return. After the autopsy, she went ahead with the funeral. Ginny was buried the day before I arrived. I didn't even get to say good-bye."

Anna squeezed his hand and nodded, not trusting herself to speak, as Dugan went on.

"I know now her sister did the best she could, but I wasn't rational. I said terrible things to her. I apologized later, but scars remain. I don't hear from her."

"Oh Tom, I'm—"

He ignored her, as if having started, he couldn't stop.

"My shipmates found me crying on the dock. The first thing I remember is my sister, Katy, packing up my stuff. She took me home and moved in and commuted to school. I drank. She tried to help, but she was a college kid with no idea how to handle a morose, nutty drunk. I got it in my head Ginny was murdered. I needed a target for my hate, I guess. I went down and demanded a copy of the autopsy report."

Dugan took a ragged breath as a tear leaked from his eye. "It took a bottle of Wild Turkey to get through it, but I found Ginny's surprise. She was pregnant."

"Oh God. Tom, I'm so sorry."

"I was in a drunken rage, still convinced someone had killed her. I read it all again and again—date, time, and cause of death—until I understood. Until I found the bastard." He turned, his anguish unbearable, as he revealed a dark secret he'd shared with no one, not even Alex, in twenty years.

"It was me," he whispered. "I killed them."

Anna sat entranced as it poured out. His realization that Ginny died near the time of their last call. His image of Ginny irritated at the disconnection. Of an impatient wait for a callback and a slip on the rug as she rushed to answer.

"If I hadn't kept trying," he said, "Ginny and our baby would be alive."

Anna sat, unsure how to respond, but knowing grief, survivor's guilt, and failure to share these terrible thoughts had solidified this horrible notion. No words could heal this. She hugged him awkwardly as he hid his face in her shoulder, ashamed of his horrible secret.

After a while, he lifted his head. "Sorry," he said with an embarrassed smile.

She kissed him tenderly, and he tensed. She stood and tugged him to his feet.

"Anna, wait."

She placed a finger on his lips and pulled him toward the bedroom. Sex was slow and tender as they explored each other with the wonder of new lovers, mingled with an inexplicable familiarity. Afterward, Anna lay in the crook of his arm as she toyed with his chest hair.

"A penny for your thoughts?"

"I'm wondering why women always ask that after sex."

He jumped as she jerked his chest hair. "Ouch. That hurt, damn it."

"Serves you right for spoiling the moment."

Dugan hugged her close. "Lady, it would take a lot more than that to spoil this moment."

They lapsed into silence, each thinking their own thoughts.

"Ah… actually," Dugan said, "I may spoil it. What about Mr. Walsh?"

"Who?" She raised her head, confused.

"You know. Your husband."

Anna began to laugh. "My God, Dugan. You are a bloody Boy Scout, aren't you? Ex-husband, Tom. I'm long since divorced."

"But you said—"

"Cast as a slut," she said, "I needed to discourage you. Actually, I was pleasantly surprised I wasn't forced to use a knee to the groin."

"So what happened?" Dugan asked.

"Not much to tell. We met in school, both studying forensic accounting. You know, finding people 'cooking the books' as you Yanks say. We married, and I joined MI5 and David went to a private firm. After training, I joined a firm supplying temps, basically a front to place me in companies under investigation. In time," she continued, "my job seemed to upset David. I guess it was emasculating, like he was a stodgy accountant and I was a spy. He hinted and then demanded I quit, but I quite liked my job."

She sighed. "Perhaps I was selfish. I might have dealt better with his inse-curity, but I didn't. He grew cold and had frequent—and open—affairs, as if advertising he was a stud. We divorced, and last I heard, he was married for the third time and living in the Midlands."

"Is the offer of a penny for my thoughts still open?"

"Sure."

Dugan hugged her tight. "David was a fucking idiot."

Anna smiled into his chest.

"I've often thought so myself," she said.

CHAPTER TEN

Braun sat in Alex Kairouz's favorite chair and watched over steepled fingers. Alex sat on the sofa, ashen faced and trembling as he digested the news. Ibrahim's body was found in an alley, throat slashed and wallet missing. Metro Police considered it a random street crime, as did the media. There was a small story on an inside page of *The Daily Telegraph* and a thirty-second mention on the morning news shows. Braun was pleased.

"Quit sniveling, Kairouz," Braun said. "It's your own bloody fault."

"M... my fault. You basta—"

"Of course it's your fault," Braun said. "Didn't I warn you what would happen if you didn't control Ibrahim? As a matter of fact, please note I spared his wife and children. For now. I'll remedy that if you don't quit whining and get back in the game."

"What do you want?"

"Your renewed participation. Does it surprise you to know your friend Dugan has been snooping about? He and Ibrahim became fast friends, unfortunately for Ibrahim. Dugan is out of control, and I'm holding you responsible for putting him back in the box."

"I warned you this would happen," Alex said. "How can I possibly control Thomas?"

"To start, get closer to him," Braun said. "Play on his friendship and find a way to keep him ignorant and out of the picture. You're a clever fellow. I'm sure you'll come up with something. I don't care how you do it, but contain him."

"And if I can't?"

"Then Mr. Dugan and the family Ibrahim will all meet with accidents. Are we clear?"

Alex gave a stiff nod, and Braun rose and walked out.

He was pleased with his solution. Delegation was the mark of a good manager, and surely Kairouz could control Dugan for a week or two. After that, it wouldn't matter.

Anna awakened and lifted her head from Dugan's chest to peer at the lighted alarm clock. Dugan stirred, his soft snoring interrupted as he shifted in his sleep. Anna smiled down at his sleeping face, barely visible in the light of the clock. She had never before mixed her professional and personal lives. She knew she should regret it. She didn't.

She shook his shoulder.

"Wh... time is it?" Dugan's voice was thick with sleep.

"Ten thirty. Almost bedtime."

He smiled. "Again?"

Anna poked him in the ribs. "*Separate* bedtimes, I mean. Come on. Get up. We need to go over a few things before I go back my place."

Dugan pulled her close. "What's wrong with staying right here? We seem to communicate just fine."

Anna laughed and pulled away. "You're too easily distracted. Up."

Dugan sighed and sat up to grope for his boxer shorts.

"I'm gonna grab a beer. Get you anything?"

"Just a glass of wine," Anna said. "I'll be out after I visit the loo."

***

Anna came in, wrapped in a silk robe, and joined him on the sofa. Dugan was staring at his beer bottle, lost in thought.

"It's not your fault, you know," she said.

He shook his head. "Yeah, it is. Ibrahim trusted me, and it got him killed. I should have left it to you guys."

"Tom, you have no idea what tipped Braun off or even if Braun killed him. It could have been a common robbery/homicide, just like it appears."

"You don't really believe that?"

Anna sighed. "Actually I don't, but what I do believe is that you can't second-guess yourself in this business. Otherwise you'll go loopy."

"'Loopy'?"

Anna smiled. "I believe that's 'nuts' in Yank speak."

"I'm not too far from that now," Dugan said, "and Alex is closer. Did you see him when he came into my office today?"

"He looked horrible," Anna agreed. "What did you two talk about?"

"Ibrahim mostly," Dugan said. "Alex is really taking it hard, but in a crazy sort of way, he's more like the old Alex. He asked us to dinner on Wednesday. I put him off until we could discuss it. What do you think?"

"We should go. Reestablishing closer contact can only help."

"Yeah, well, it's likely to be strained," Dugan said. "Apparently all the ladies of the house except Cassie are convinced I'm a lecherous toad."

Anna smiled. "Just shows what remarkable instincts they have."

KAIROUZ RESIDENCE
15 JUNE

"Oh. I'm ever so sorry, Mrs. Hogan," Gillian Farnsworth said as she bumped into Mrs. Hogan bustling out of the pantry.

The cook smiled. "No harm done. Did you see Cassie safe to school?"

Mrs. Farnsworth shook her head. "Barely. That Farley is a menace."

"Aye, he's a bad 'un. I'd like to poison his bloody tea and bury him in the back garden."

Mrs. Farnsworth smiled at the image of portly Mrs. Hogan dragging Farley across the lawn; thoughts of Farley rarely brought a smile. His hulking presence upset their routine, and his driving was deliberately reckless, provoking tirades from Gillian to which he responded with insincere "Sorry, ma'ams" and smirks in the mirror.

The women fell quiet as Farley came in the back door.

"Hello, luv," he said to the cook, ignoring Mrs. Farnsworth. "How 'bout a cuppa?"

"You've a kitchen in your quarters, Farley. Take your tea there," Mrs. Farnsworth said.

"Well, ain't we all high and mighty? The old kike took his tea here."

"You aren't Daniel," Mrs. Farnsworth said. "And do not call him that. It's not teatime, in any event. Stop loafing. Wash the car."

"I did it yesterday," Farley said.

"Then do it again."

He glared at her, barely under control, and a chill ran through her before he slammed out. She felt Mrs. Hogan's arm on her shoulders.

"Don't you worry, dearie," the cook said. "He lays a hand to you or Cassie, I'll gut 'im like a pig, I will." She held open a capacious apron pocket to display the handle of a kitchen knife. Suddenly, burying Farley in the lawn didn't seem so far-fetched.

Mrs. Farnsworth smiled. "An appealing thought, Mrs. Hogan, but if you're arrested, where ever would we find a cook as good?"

"Hah. Nowhere, that's where, me girl."

"Right you are." Mrs. Farnsworth composed herself. "Now, where were we?"

"Oh, I almost forgot. Mr. Kairouz rang to—"

"He did? Is anything wrong? He's been very upset about Mr. Ibrahim."

"Aye, that he has," Mrs. Hogan said, "but he seemed a bit better just now. In fact, he rang to tell me we'll have guests tonight."

"Who?"

Mrs. Hogan made a face. "Mr. Dugan and his tart."

"Her name is Anna Walsh, Mrs. Hogan, and Alice Coutts tells me she's a lovely girl."

"Aye," the cook said, "and what else do you call a 'girl' fancyin' a rich gent old enough to be her father? She's a tart, right enough." She sighed. "But it's him that's the letdown. Men. Even the best of 'em thinks with the wee head down below. Mr. Kairouz excepted, o'course."

Mrs. Farnsworth stifled a smile. "Mr. Dugan isn't quite old enough to have sired Ms. Walsh. Do try to keep an open mind."

"Oh, aye. I'll give the little tart every benefit of the doubt, I will."

Hiding her amusement, Mrs. Farnsworth moved down the hall to sit in her tiny office under the stairs. She'd turned the former closet into a neat and efficient workspace, with a small desk and chair. A corkboard was covered with schedules and "to do" lists, and an under-desk computer fed a flat monitor and keyboard. A photo collage of Cassie filled the opposite wall.

As always, the photos brought a smile, one that faded a bit at her tired reflection in the monitor. She had fine features and soft brown eyes, but her hair was as much salt as pepper now, and there were lines that hadn't existed even weeks ago. Not that she cared. Physical beauty had only brought her pain. Her plain, matronly image and the "proper" world she created was a safe haven, not only for her, but for Cassie as well.

She smiled at the photos again. Cassie—her great treasure—bequeathed by a dying woman who had seen through her lies and trusted her anyway. A woman who squeezed her hands and extracted a promise. A promise Gillian fully intended to keep. Progress was uneven and success unsure, but Cassie would have a good life. Gillian would see to it.

TWENTY-SEVEN YEARS EARLIER
HER MAJESTY'S PRISON HOLLOWAY
NORTH LONDON

When the prison gates clanged shut behind Daisy Tatum, she was terrified. Not of freedom, but of failure and slipping back into her old life. She was twenty-two and had never had a job or a bank account or a credit card. She'd taken every course prison offered but knew it wasn't the same. A charity had gotten her a job, but she'd never waited tables.

The first day was bad. She mixed up every order and dropped a tray. But the café owner, an ex-con himself, was patient. Two weeks later she walked home to her tiny apartment, her first ever paycheck in her pocket. She was unlocking the door when strong arms encircled her.

"Hullo, luv. Don't we look smart? A regular stunner," Tommy's beery breath wafted over her as he pushed her inside into the tiny kitchenette.

"Right hurtful it was, you not comin' round to see dear ole Dad. But I kept tabs on ya. She's busy, I sez to me self, so I'll just pop round and see her." He glared. "So 'ere I am."

Daisy stared, mute, tears streaking her cheeks.

"There, there now," Tommy said. "No need to carry on, though I'm a bit misty me self. Prison suited you, I see. You ain't near the washed-out hag you was. Do a fair business among the lads what fancies older birds, I'll wager. Matter of fact, we'll have our own little family reunion in a bit, but first you can say hello to an old friend."

He put the drug paraphernalia on the kitchen bar, and Daisy's terror turned to rage as he ignored her to melt heroin in a spoon, humming a tune to himself, her own aspirations irrelevant. Memories came flooding back: the nightmare of being strapped spread-eagle on a filthy mattress when Tommy sold her virginity to a fat pedophile with halitosis; of turning tricks for "special clients" in the back of Tommy's "gentleman's club" until she looked old enough to be put on the streets. She remembered rebellion and attempted escapes and beatings. And more beatings when she failed to make enough or to induce miscarriages or just because Tommy bloody well felt like it. Beatings until all the fight was out of her and the pain dissolved into a dull blur of the drugs, Tommy's "little pick-me-ups" to keep her ambulatory and producing. She remembered his sneer when he visited her in jail to tell her she was worth neither bail nor a lawyer and to warn her to keep her bloody mouth shut and do the time.

Tommy's tune ended abruptly as the kitchen knife entered his chest to the hilt, propelled by 120 pounds of hatred fueled by thirteen years of rage. He died surprised, unable to believe his kindness was so unappreciated.

Daisy panicked. She gathered her meager belongings and fled, stopping to make a call from a pay phone. A short bus ride later, she sat on Gloria's sofa.

***

"Served the bastard right," Gloria said, "but Daisy's history. We have to reinvent you. And you can't stay here, luv. They know we were cell mates. This is the first place they'll look. But not to worry. Auntie Gloria's on top of it."

Gloria found Daisy a place to hide with a trusted friend of a friend and reappeared two weeks later, in disguise and carrying a shopping bag.

"Sorry, luv," she said, hugging Daisy. "The coppers were all over me for a while, but I think they've given up. Just to be safe, I came here by tube and transferred a half-dozen times." She grinned and led Daisy to the sofa. "I wanted to deliver your new life in person."

Daisy looked on, confused, as Gloria fished a newspaper from the shopping bag. She saw a photo of a woman resembling herself above a story titled "War Widow Dead in Car Crash."

"Wh… what is this?" Daisy asked.

"Your new life, luv," Gloria said. "Gillian Farnsworth, age twenty-four. Died three weeks ago in a crash. Widow of Leading Seaman John Farnsworth, Royal Navy. Poor sod. Died in the Falklands when the Argies sank his ship. No kids and both John and Gillian are only children of dead parents." Gloria smiled. "It's bloody perfect."

"I… I don't know Gloria. How can I—"

"Daisy. Luv," Gloria said. "We couldn't ask for more. Widow of some poor enlisted sod blown up by an Argie bomb. Anyone asks, you tear up. It's too painful to discuss. It's perfect."

"But… but how can I pretend? I don't know anyth—"

"You don't pretend, luv," Gloria said, "you become."

She pulled a thick file from her bag.

"It's all here. Parents' names, important dates, schools, teachers, everything. With that mind of yours, in two weeks you'll know Gillian better than she knew herself."

"But surely there's a record of her death."

Gloria nodded. "In Oxford, where she died in a crash while passing through, and which is not at all cross-referenced to Reading, where she was born and lived her whole life. Only a search at Oxford will turn up Gillian's death certificate, but someone would need to know first, that she was dead, and second, that she died in Oxford. But no one is likely to be looking. She has no family, and all her friends live in Reading. If they should cross your path in London at some point, they'll just assume it's a coincidence. Many people share names."

"But how will I live? I'm not even a very good waitress, and I'm sure she worked at something I couldn't possibly do."

Gloria smiled. "Perfect again. She worked as a nanny to a family that returned to the US just before her death. She was between jobs. I phoned the American family, pretending to be a prospective employer. They didn't know of her death and gave a glowing reference."

"I don't even know what a nanny does."

"She wipes noses and bums and says 'there, there' a lot," Gloria said. "You'll pick it up. We'll position you with an arriving American family. They'll likely be clueless and over-the-top with the whole idea of having a 'real British' nanny. That'll give you a chance to get Kings Cross out of your speech. Most of the Yanks can't seem to tell a Yorkshireman from an Aussie anyway. Anyone who isn't North American sounds like Sir Lawrence Olivier to them." Gloria patted her hand. "You'll do fine, luv."

And so she had, finding she'd a real aptitude for the work. She worked for a succession of families, receiving glowing references from them all. Twelve years later, there was no better nanny in London than Gillian Farnsworth.

Kathleen Kairouz had hired her on the spot, and Gillian soon fell in love with the gentle woman and flawed child. When Kathleen was diagnosed with cancer, Gillian took on Kathleen's care without a second thought but began to have misgivings. She'd grown to love Cassie and worried about the impact on the child if she were found out and arrested.

She found Alex Kairouz in his study one evening, staring into the fire. He looked up and motioned her to a chair across from his desk.

"How is she?"

"Resting comfortably. They increased her dosage. I hope she'll have an easy night."

Alex nodded as Gillian went on. "Mr. Kairouz, when Mrs. Kairouz… no longer needs me, I will be tendering notice."

"But why, Mrs. Farnsworth? Cassie needs you. I need you. If it's money—"

"No, no, sir. That's not it at all. There are… things. Personal reasons I can't discuss."

Alex persisted. "You can't just leave us in our hour of greatest need. Please, tell me what's wrong. We can work something out."

"I can't say, sir. But I will stay until you've found someone."

Alex stared at her a long moment and then nodded, almost to himself, as if he'd made a decision. He unlocked a drawer and handed her a file.

"Does it concern this?"

The file held a photo of Daisy Tatum stapled to her arrest report. There was a copy of her prison record, an article about Tommy Tatum's death, and a copy of Gillian Farnsworth's death certificate.

"When did you know?" she whispered.

"The second week," Alex said. "Kathleen was supposed to wait for the report before hiring." He smiled. "I didn't sack you because she wouldn't have it. She's an uncanny judge of people, you know. I often included her in business dinners for her opinion of potential clients or associates. She's never wrong.

"Anyway," he continued, "she made me reread the damned report line by line as she stood at my shoulder, pointing out you were victim, not villain. So I didn't turn you in. A decision for which I'm most thankful." He held out his hand, and she returned the folder.

"But I won't compel you to stay, though our need is great." He paused. "I'm not without connections. Two months ago, the body of a street person was fished from the Thames, a drowning victim. Her fingerprints were a match to Daisy Tatum, allowing the police to close that file." He paused again. "I also understand that when the records office in Oxford moved last month, several death certificates were misfiled. Just simple clerical errors, but I doubt Gillian Farnsworth's death certificate will be located in a hundred years."

He walked to the fireplace and tossed the file into the flames. "So Daisy Tatum is dead and Gillian Farnsworth very much alive. You've a place in my home as long as you wish, but the decision is yours. The file burning brightly is, I assure you, the only copy."

Tears streaked her face as she watched her past disappear up the chimney.

"Thank you, sir. I should like very much to stay."

"Then so you shall, Gillian. Welcome home."

Kathleen passed ten days later. The death hung over the household, but Gillian refused to let Alex bury himself in work. "The child has lost her mother and shouldn't lose her father as well," she said, insisting he spend an hour with Cassie each morning and evening. He soon cherished his time with the laughing child and spent most of his free time with her.

Cassie was their salvation and their bond.

CHAPTER ELEVEN

"You're sure the house isn't bugged?" Dugan asked for the third time.

"Swept it myself after Anna alerted us to the dinner," Harry said. "Showed up this afternoon as a meter reader while the cook was at market and the Farnsworth woman and driver were collecting the girl at school. I had time alone in the house. Things are unchanged; phone taps to a recorder in Farley's quarters but no bugs in the house. Makes sense. Cuts out a lot of idle household chatter."

"Not that it matters, Tom," Lou said. "If Kairouz is under duress, he'll assume he's being monitored and say nothing. And if he's a player, which seems likely, he'll lie. The best you can hope for this evening is a return to a closer relationship that we can use to watch him for slipups. You may not like that, but it's a fact."

Dugan said nothing, frustrated he'd convinced no one of Alex's innocence. His only partial convert was Anna, and her support was tepid at best.

"Tom. We best go if we're to reach Alex's by half seven," Anna said.

Kairouz Residence

Dugan and Anna arrived shortly after Mrs. Farnsworth and Cassie had reached home from choir practice. Cassie was still in her school uniform. She hugged Dugan and smiled at Anna.

"You're beautiful," Cassie said, her sincerity evident.

Anna was in a dark skirt and white silk blouse with lace at neck and wrists, simple but stunning. She blushed. "Why thank you, Cassie, you're quite lovely yourself."

"I look like my mom. She died, but I have pictures. Want to see them? They're in my room." Cassie took Anna's hand.

"Dinner's almost ready, Cassie," Mrs. Farnsworth said.

Cassie sighed. "Oh OK," she said, releasing Anna's hand. "After dinner, OK?"

Anna smiled. "I shall look forward to it, Cassie."

Cassie insisted on sitting between Anna and Dugan, and dinner conversation was unforced, as Cassie chattered and Anna listened with unfeigned interest. Mrs. Farnsworth said little, but watched with grudging approval. By meal's end, even Mrs. Hogan was smiling, serving coffee and nodding. During dessert, Anna gave Cassie's hand an affectionate squeeze, but as she withdrew her own hand, the lace at her cuff tangled in Cassie's charm bracelet and separated with an audible rip.

"Oh dear," Anna said, inspecting the dangling lace with an embarrassed laugh.

"I'm really sorry," Cassie said, "it was an accident."

"My fault entirely," Anna said. "No harm done. I'll get it mended."

"I can do it," Cassie said, folding up the edge of her jumper to reveal a needle wrapped with thread stuck into the underside of the hem.

"A proper young lady," she intoned in an unintended but accurate mimic of Mrs. Farnsworth, "prepares for any eventuality."

Anna looked confused.

"At one time," Mrs. Farnsworth explained, "young ladies always kept needles and thread near at hand. It seemed practical."

"Yes," Cassie said, "and that's not all—"

"Cassie," Mrs. Farnsworth said, "Ms. Walsh may wish to have it mended elsewhere."

"Oh no," Anna said. "I accept with thanks, Cassie. Then perhaps I can see the photos."

"OK," Cassie said. "We can go up now, and you can take your blouse off while I mend it. I don't want to stick you. That hurts."

"Excellent idea," Mrs. Farnsworth said, rising. "I'll get Ms. Walsh a robe."

Alex smiled. "Seems we're to be left on our own, Thomas. Join me in the study?"

"Thought you'd never ask."

Minutes later, they sat in the study, brandy in hand. Dugan watched Alex over the rim of his glass. Alex looked older, much older. The gray at his temples spread through his black mane now, and dark-circled eyes topped pale, hollow cheeks. Dugan was reminded of those "before and after" pictures of past US presidents.

"I haven't enjoyed a meal or the company as much in some time," Alex said. "Thank you for joining us. And Thomas, I'm sorry for my earlier behavior. Anna is wonderful." He smiled. "Cassie obviously likes her, and she has her mother's sense of people. So if Anna passed muster with Cassie, defrosted Mrs. Coutts, and in one evening charmed both Mrs. Hogan and Mrs. Farnsworth, she is exemplary indeed. I toast your good fortune." He raised his glass.

Dugan smiled and raised his own glass.

"Thomas, I've been thinking. We have a number of dry-dockings scheduled next year. We could save a great deal of money if we confined them to a single yard and negotiated a volume discount. I think it would be a good idea if you spent a week or two touring the Far East yards and discussing it with them." Alex smiled over his brandy glass. "Anna wouldn't have much to do while you were away. You could take her along. Make it a bit of a holiday."

Son of a bitch, thought Dugan. He's trying to get rid of me.

"Good idea," Dugan said, trying to sound casual, "we'll probably have most of our ships in the Far East trade if the *China Star* deal is any indication of market trends."

Alex stiffened. "Whatever do you mean, Thomas?"

"Ibrahim mentioned the *China Star* deal to me. He seemed concerned, actually."

"*China Star* is just some deal of Braun's. I don't really know the details."

"The Alex Kairouz I know could recite every word of every charter agreement from memory," Dugan said. "C'mon, Alex. What's goin' on?"

"Just drop it, Thomas. Please." Alex's eyes darted about the room.

Lou was right, Dugan thought, Alex thinks we're bugged. A catch-22. He needed Alex to confide in him, but the man would never do so if he thought he was monitored. Dugan considered his half-formed plan and decided to take a risk.

"You can speak freely, Alex," he said. "We're not being bugged."

"What? What do you mean?" Alex asked.

"I know something's wrong, so I hired an investigator," Dugan lied. "He came in at night and swept the office. I know Braun is bugging our offices and phones. He swept your house today. Phones are bugged but not the house. Talk to me, Alex."

Alex buried his face in his hands. Dugan waited for Alex to unburden himself or, if he was wrong, explode into angry denial. Either way, Dugan's lie cast him as a concerned friend, not a covert agent. But when Alex looked up, his face held neither relief nor anger but terror.

"Thomas. What have you done?" Tears ran down ashen, stubbled cheeks.

"What do you mean, Alex? What's wrong?"

"Cassie," Alex said, "he'll... wait, I'll show you."

He stood and locked the study door before moving a laptop from his desk to the low table beside Dugan. The computer booted as Alex opened his case and thrust a CD at Dugan.

"Look at it," Alex ordered, and Dugan slid the disk into the computer.

The clip began with a narrator, a woman speaking French as she walked the streets of a Third World village to a rude hut. Inside, a young girl was held spread-eagle by a group of women. One produced a knife and began to cut at the girl's genitals, in full view of the camera and explaining as she performed the butchery. Even with the volume turned down, the girl's screams carried through the narration. The screen morphed to a new scene: large, dirty men sodomizing a blond girl of no more than six. Dugan slapped the computer closed and swallowed hard to keep Mrs. Hogan's meal from ending up in the wastebasket.

"Good God, Alex, where did you get that filth?"

"Braun," Alex said. "He says it will all happen to Cassie if I disobey. You watched seconds, but it's over an hour and gets worse, much worse. I'm forced to watch it regularly."

"But surely you contacted the police?"

Alex nodded. "I pretended to go along with Braun, then phoned Scotland Yard. I was on hold when a live video of Cassie walking up the school steps filled my computer screen, filmed through a sniper scope with crosshairs on her head. The message was clear. I hung up. Braun called at once, warning me not to try it again."

He paused. "Even then, I didn't give up, but I realized I couldn't alert the police until Cassie was safe. I knew my phones were tapped, so while dining with a customer that night, I excused myself to visit the loo and ducked into the restaurant office to use the phone. I called a contact at the security firm I use and set up a meeting in St. James Park the following day at two. Time was short, so I told the man I would provide details at the meeting.

"I assumed Braun couldn't watch everyone, so I intended to send written details to the park via Daniel, with instructions for a bodyguard and safe house. I would string Braun along until the security people whisked Cassie to safety. I never got that far. Braun rang the next morning and said he'd 'taken the liberty' of canceling my appointment. He said he wouldn't do anything to Cassie immediately to lessen her hostage value, but if I continued my efforts, Mrs. Farnsworth would have a fatal accident."

"But… but how did he find out about the park?" Dugan asked.

"He either anticipated whom I might call and bugged them or bugged the phones of my usual restaurants; there aren't many. I only know he blocked me everywhere. I was terrified."

"Wasn't the guy you contacted suspicious at the cancellation?"

Alex shook his head. "He rang to confirm an e-mail cancellation Braun sent in my name. I confirmed and apologized. He probed a bit, but had no reason to suspect duress."

"So," Alex continued, "I hired Braun and Farley. Braun forces me to watch the video weekly. 'Motivational sessions' he calls them. He stands over my shoulder as I watch, detailing additional things Cassie will face if I resist in any way. I had a session this afternoon."

Dugan sat stunned. It was a wonder Alex wasn't dead of a heart attack.

"What does he want, Alex?"

"Not money. I tried to buy him off. He needs the company for something."

"What's he done so far?" Dugan asked.

"I haven't a clue," Alex said. "He made me sign blank contracts and give him carte blanche on all accounts. For the most part it seems to be business as usual, but he's doing things at the margins in my name, and perhaps yours. *China Star* is a case in point. When Ibrahim got curious, Braun told me that unless I kept him quiet, he would kill the man and his entire family. I had to threaten to sack poor Ibrahim and order him to refer inquiries to Braun.

"He's dangerous, Thomas, and very, very good. Your investigator may already be dead and Braun listening to our every word." He paused. "Initially I feared you'd endangered Cassie, but I realize now nothing's changed. Braun still needs me, and she's his guarantee. But if Braun is listening, you'll be dead by morning. And if your efforts have somehow escaped his attention, you should go. Take my offer to visit the yards and keep going. You can't help us, Thomas. I have to see it through and hope Braun spares Cassie. Save yourself and tell no one so Cassie isn't endangered further."

Dugan realized any promise to safeguard Cassie would seem unbelievable to Alex. If Alex Kairouz, with all his connections, had been unable to do so, what chance did Dugan have alone? And Alex thought Braun was listening, despite Dugan's assurances. Suddenly Dugan realized Alex was playing to the bugs, assuring Braun of continued cooperation while, if there were no bugs, warning Dugan to escape. Alex might be cowed, but his brain was working.

The revelation was more disquieting than encouraging. Alex was stretched to the breaking point, and Dugan was concerned for his health, mental and physical. He had to let his friend know the situation wasn't hopeless, and he would never have a better opportunity.

"Alex, I know Braun isn't listening because the house was swept with much better equipment than is available commercially. I'm working with US and British intelligence."

Alex listened as Dugan explained and assured him Cassie would be protected. They stood and Alex hugged Dugan with a ferocity born of relief. For the first time in months, Alex Kairouz did not feel he was alone, staring into a black abyss.

And Dugan wondered how to tell the others about the newest member of the team.

CHAPTER TWELVE

Constrained by the driver's presence, Anna was quiet during the cab ride as Dugan pondered a way to break the news. He hadn't found one by the time they walked into the apartment.

"So, how'd it go?" Lou asked.

"Well, I think," Anna said, turning to Dugan. "Tom, did you learn anything from Alex?"

He tried to ease into it. "We discussed *China Star*. He thinks—"

"Bloody hell, Dugan," Lou said. "How did that come up? You weren't supposed to—"

Anna waved Lou to silence and gestured for Dugan to continue. He took a deep breath and made a clean breast of it, finishing to dead silence.

"Bloody unbelievable," Lou said. "You revealed an operation to a prime suspect."

"He's a victim," Dugan said. "How much evidence do you need?"

"More than a bloody fairy tale," Lou said.

"Bullshit. He made up a story complete with video, then waited weeks to present it? No way. We can use him, and I decided to enlist him."

Anna exploded. "YOU decided! On whose bloody authority? I'm lead agent, not you. You might have at least discussed it before charging in on a white horse to save the bloody day."

"Things were happening fast," Dugan said. "I wasn't sure I'd have another chance. Maybe I should have discussed it first, but what's done is done."

"Yes, Tom. Maybe you should have," Anna said, ice in her voice.

"Actually," Harry said, "we can verify Kairouz's story. Phone records will confirm calls to Scotland Yard and from the security firm, and we can question the security firm under the Official Secrets Act. If that checks out, I doubt it's a fairy tale. British Telcom has a night shift. We can confirm the calls straightaway."

Dugan shot Harry a grateful look.

"Do it," Anna said, and Harry dialed. Moments later, he hung up and nodded.

"Phone records corroborate Kairouz's story," Harry said.

"OK," Anna said, "we'll deal with the security firm tomorrow. Perhaps this can be salvaged. But we have to tell Ward." She gave Dugan a withering look. "I believe that will be your job, Tom."

Dugan gave a resigned nod, pushed a preset on his sat phone, and set it on the coffee table in speaker mode.

***

Five time zones away, Ward's phone trilled as he worked late. He saw Dugan's number on the display.

"Hold one, Tom," he said into his own sat phone as he reached for the office phone.

Gardner wanted in on field agents' calls, but in reality, disturbing him after hours incurred his wrath. Ward protected himself by leaving voice mail on Gardner's office number to verify attempted contact. Gardner was seldom there after hours, so Ward preferred to talk with field agents then just to avoid his boss's interference.

"Gardner," came the answer. Shit, Ward thought.

"Yes, Larry," Ward said, "I've got Dugan. You want in?"

"Damn. Yeah, OK. Come down here." Gardner hung up without awaiting a reply.

Ward told Dugan he'd call him right back and went down the hall to Gardner's office. Gardner was in a tux.

"Don't you look spiffy," Ward said.

"I'm due at the symphony with the Gunthers in twenty minutes. This better be good."

Ward understood. Image enhancement. Senator Gunther chaired the Senate Intelligence Committee, and Gardner would spin a tale of having to stop by the office to handle a problem. The indispensable man.

Gardner pointed at the conference table. "Use the speakerphone," he said.

"Hello, Tom," Ward said as Dugan answered, "Larry Gardner is with me on speaker."

Dugan paused. "Hello, Jesse. Hello, Larry. I have—"

"Cut to the chase, Dugan," Gardner said. "I'm running late."

Dugan hadn't expected Gardner. He led with *China Star* again, stalling.

"We have suspicious activity on a ship named *China Star*, now loading at Kharg—"

"Where?" Gardner asked.

"Kharg Island, Iran," Ward said. "Go ahead, Tom."

"If there's anything to it," Dugan continued, "the mostly likely target would be the Malacca Strait near Singapore."

"When does she sail?" Ward asked, scribbling.

"Unknown," Dugan said. "I'll keep on it, but you might initiate satellite surveillance—"

"Just worry about your end, Dugan," Gardner said. "What else? Or did you call just to alert us to a ship which 'might' be suspect and may be days away from leaving port?"

There was a long pause, then Dugan spoke in a rush, as if eager to finish his recitation of the events of the last few hours before he was interrupted. He needn't have worried; both Ward and Gardner were shocked speechless. Gardner recovered first.

"YOU FUCKING DID WHAT?" Gardner screamed, launching an abusive tirade punctuated with a list of Dugan's violations of the Patriot Act. Then he turned on Ward.

"God damn you, Ward, where the hell is that limey cunt you had sitting on this idiot?"

Dugan interrupted before Ward could respond.

"Look, Larry, calm down," Dugan said. "I've explained that Alex Kairouz is not—"

"That's not your call, asshole. Leave that to the intelligence professionals."

Dugan lost it. "'Intelligence professional'? And that would be you? You couldn't track a fucking elephant through ten feet of snow."

The Brits regarded their shoes in the sudden silence.

"You're done, asshole," Gardner's voice whispered through the speaker. "You've killed the operation. I'll have the Brits arrest you. You and Kairouz can be cell mates in Gitmo."

"Actually, Mr. Gardner," Anna said, "the operation is far from compromised."

"Who's that?" Gardner demanded. "Damn it, Ward, this line was supposed to be secure."

"We're perfectly secure," Anna said. "I'm Agent Anna Walsh, AKA the 'limey cunt.'"

Oh shit, can this get any worse, Ward thought as Gardner gaped at the phone.

"I do not intend to end this operation," Anna continued, "and expect your continued support. Of course, we're recording now as standard procedure, as, I'm sure, are you. Should you proceed with action against Mr. Dugan, I will ask for an official review, including this conversation. Dugan's remarks were intemperate, but he was provoked, and your language was equally foul. On that subject, while I admire your ability to malign my nationality, gender, and character in the space of two words, your terminology was most objectionable. I believe our superiors will agree, should it come to that. So let's just move on, shall we?"

"Yes, of course," Gardner said. "Uh... what do you propose?"

"We'll work out a way to communicate with Kairouz, and I'll detail assets to shadow the girl and her nanny and to intercede if necessary," Anna said.

"Why? You might tip off Braun."

"Risks are minimal. It will reassure Kairouz, and it's the right thing to do," she said.

"Still, it seems a waste of assets," Gardner said.

"British assets, protecting British subjects, at the discretion of Her Majesty's representative. That would be me," Anna said.

"Uh, OK, your call. Anything else?"

"No," Anna replied, "unless you or Agent Ward have anything."

"No," Gardner said, disconnecting without looking at Ward, who had a great deal to add but nothing he wanted to say in front of Gardner.

***

"That was amazing, Anna. Thank you," Dugan said.

"Yes, well, everything's relative," she said. "This Gardner twit infuriated me even more than you, something I scarcely thought possible twenty minutes ago."

Harry grinned. "I dunno, I think the Yank redeemed himself. I rather enjoyed the 'ten feet of snow' bit. I woulda loved to have seen the wanker's face."

The men laughed as Anna struggled to suppress a smile.

CIA Headquarters
Langley, Virginia

"How in hell did you let this get so out of control, Ward? Dugan just blew the whole operation, just to protect his raghead buddy. He's dirty. Get the finance guys on this: bank accounts, e-mails, phone records, foreign-held companies, the lot."

"We've had Dugan's complete financials for years," Ward said. "He doesn't need money. I share your concern about his actions, but if Walsh and her team are comfortable, we have to respect that. Besides, if Dugan wanted to scuttle us, he'd do it quietly."

"Just because he's fooled the crumpet munchers doesn't mean he's not a traitor."

"OK, OK, I know you're upset, but try to calm down. Go enjoy your evening."

The reminder of the social engagement worked as intended. Nothing was more important to Gardner than a chance to rub shoulders with the power elite.

Gardner nodded and rose. As they walked out and Gardner locked his door, Ward got in a subtle dig.

"Enjoy the ballet with Congressman Gaynor," he said.

"It's the symphony with Senator Gunther," Gardner said.

Ward shrugged. "Whatever."

Gardner stalked off, appalled at Ward's ignorance. No wonder he was still an agent.

Minutes later, Ward sat at his computer, requesting a flyover of Kharg Island, Iran, with a specific request for updates on the *China Star*. He'd refrained from mentioning satellite coverage to Gardner, fearing the man might object because it was Dugan's idea. If you didn't ask, no one could say no.

CHAPTER THIRTEEN

M/T *Asian Trader*
South China Sea
Bound for Panama
16 June

Medina jogged down the deck, his routine well established after two weeks at sea. The afternoon sun was warm on his back as he moved along the deck and dropped to do push-ups near a ballast-tank vent. His exercise attracted no notice now other than jokes about his sanity. It was the perfect way to keep check on events unfolding unseen below the deck at his feet.

The gasoline had eaten through the Styrofoam by now, he was sure of it. In his mind's eye, he envisioned the gasoline weeping down the bulkheads of the empty ballast tanks, evaporating in the process. As the sun warmed the deck each day, the expanding air in the empty tanks whispered out the vents, and at night, sea water rushing past the outer hull cooled the air and reversed the process, sucking in oxygen-rich sea air. Fumes would escape each day, but most would remain, slowly filling each tank from the bottom up as it "breathed" through each cycle, mixing its contents into explosive vapor.

He put his nose near the deck as he did push-ups and smelled the faint odor wafting from the nearest vent to lie invisible along the deck before being swept away by a breeze. He smiled. The tanks were ripening and chances of discovery slight as the wind dissipated the fumes. His plan would work, *inshallah*.

Sterling Academy
Westminster, London
17 June

The car lurched to a stop, and Farley watched Gillian Farnsworth's face in the mirror, disappointed that she was ignoring his provocation. She got out and went into the school, returning with a glum-looking Cassie in tow.

"Take us to the doctor's and wait," she said. "We should be out by half two."

Farley grunted and shot off with squealing tires, pondering the change in the woman over the last two days. She'd never hidden her disdain or hesitated to challenge him, but always with an undercurrent of fear, despite her brave words. She was different now, more confident. A subtle change, felt rather than spoken. Should he tell Braun? He dismissed the notion, sure he'd get a scornful response.

He curbed the tires in the waiting area of the doctor's building, bringing the car to a rocking halt. The housekeeper ignored it as she exited the car, hurrying Cassie along with her. She'll get hers, he thought as they bustled into the building. Maybe he'd make the old bitch watch while he shagged the retard. Now wouldn't that be sweet.

***

"Why do I have to get a jab?" Cassie whined as the elevator opened on the third floor.

"It's a flu shot," Mrs. Farnsworth lied. "Now out you go."

They were expected and led to an exam room, where a nurse took Cassie's vital signs and directed Mrs. Farnsworth to the doctor's office. Anna Walsh sat across from the doctor. She motioned Mrs. Farnsworth to an empty chair.

"Doctor," Anna said, "might I speak to Mrs. Farnsworth alone?"

He smiled. "Certainly. I'll check on Cassie."

"You do know what's going on?" Anna asked as the doctor left.

"I know you're MI5. Mr. Kairouz told me. I assume you'll take Cassie to safety."

"It's not that simple," Anna said. "Removing Cassie makes it obvious Alex is cooperating, but we don't have enough evidence to hold either Braun or Farley. You would all likely still be targets." She leaned closer and lowered her voice. "We have to play this out, making the best of the hand dealt us. Here's what we're going to do…."

TEHRAN, IRAN
17 JUNE

Motaki was anxious. Gasoline shortages ate at his support like a cancer. Former allies grew distant, rumors abounded, and even Imam Rahmani was under pressure. How ironic, he thought, that he had been so successful in importing material for his nuclear program, only to be undone by something as prosaic as gasoline. But, God willing, that would soon change. The intercom buzzed.

"Yes, Ahmad?"

"Sorry to disturb you, sir, but President Rodriguez is calling."

He sighed a thanks.

"Mr. President. Nice to hear from you."

"Good day, my friend," Rodriguez said, "are you well?"

Motaki curbed his impatience. "Yes, thank you. How may I help you?"

"It's about the… our project. I've heard no reports and—"

Camel shit for brains, thought Motaki. Not on an open line.

"Yes, the petrol shipments," Motaki said. "I will arrange an update via secure means."

"All right… fine," Rodriguez said. "It's just I've heard little and—"

"Never a bother, my friend," he said as he silently cursed Braun. "Anything more?"

"No. No. Thank you," Rodriguez said before saying a polite good-bye.

Motaki frowned as he tapped out a terse message on his computer.

OFFICES OF PHOENIX SHIPPING
LONDON
17 JUNE

Braun returned from lunch to find a telltale spam message. He downloaded a video clip from the porn site and decrypted the embedded message.

CONTACTED BY OUR FRIEND. UPDATE HIM TO PREVENT REPETITION.

That bloody Venezuelan. Like Motaki, Rodriguez had a secure sat phone, but to preclude overuse, Braun first locked it into receive-only mode. Anticipating problems, Braun also allowed Rodriguez backdoor access to a single porn site, used by him alone to isolate him from the real operation. He'd still been a pest, deluging Braun with frequent inane messages and suggestions to the point the German no longer even downloaded them. The idiot must have contacted Motaki on a landline. He'd underestimated the Venezuelan's stupidity.

CARACAS, VENEZUELA
17 JUNE

Rodriguez answered the sat phone on the sixth ring.

"Mr. President," Braun said, "forgive me. I was awaiting updates before reporting."

"You do well to remember who is in charge, Braun. Now report."

Braun stifled a laugh. "Yes, sir. *China Star* arrived at Kharg, and our Chechen friends—"

"Yes, yes," Rodriguez said, "what of Panama?"

"*Asian Trader* is en route from Singapore. All is according to plan."

"Remember," Rodriguez said. "Minor damage. And we must not be implicated."

"Don't worry, sir. Our man can kill himself and those around him, but little more. And even if he survives, he knows nothing."

"Are we still on schedule for July 4?"

"Yes, Mr. President," Braun said. "Is there anything more, sir?"

"No. That is sufficient, Karl, but do not fail to keep me informed."

"You may rest assured I will, sir."

"Thank you, Karl. That will be all."

Braun shook his head and hung up. Bloody pompous fool.

CIA HEADQUARTERS
LANGLEY, VIRGINIA
17 JUNE

"Caught any bad guys today?" asked a familiar voice.

Ward chuckled into the phone. Mike Hill worked for NSA, tasked with global electronic snooping. "Not yet, Mike, but the day's young. Whatcha got?"

"You know that London site the Brits are monitoring and sharing intel on with us?"

"Yeah, Phoenix Shipping. What about it?"

"Well, we also have ongoing surveillance on that nut job in Caracas," Hill said, "and El Presidente received a scrambled sat phone call this morning from guess where?"

"Phoenix Shipping?"

"Bingo, brother. The Brits had the outgoing, too, but not the Caracas end. We aided our cousins who were pathetically grateful, though they covered it with British reserve—"

Ward grinned. "OK, OK, Hill. I get the picture."

"Jeez, nerds are never appreciated. Anyway, the bad news is we couldn't unscramble it."

"Well, even the connection is a breakthrough," Ward said.

"Ah, but our legerdemain continues," Hill said. "Earlier El Presidente called Iran, rather stupidly in the clear. We recorded one President Motaki shitting his pants at the mention of a 'project,' and El Presidente's failure to be updated on same. Motaki says not to worry, and presto, El Presidente gets a call from London." Hill paused. "A reasonable man might conclude a connection between Iran and Venezuela running through Phoenix Shipping."

"Outstanding," Ward said. "When next we meet, my friend, drinks are on me."

"Don't be cheap. You have an expense account. I want dinner."

"Done," Ward said.

CHAPTER FOURTEEN

"It's been a friggin' week since Jesse made the Iran/Venezuela link," Dugan said, "and we've still got squat."

Anna shrugged. "That's not surprising. Braun's smart, and we probably got a bit lucky on the *China Star* thing. With increased electronic surveillance here and in Caracas and Tehran, something will break soon."

"Yeah," Dugan said, "but until then, all we have is *China Star*, and only suspicions at that. I wish there was some way we could be sure."

"But we have some time there as well, Yank," Harry said. "She just sailed. She'll be in the middle of the ocean for a while, out of harm's way."

Dugan nodded, then seemed to think of something. He opened up his briefcase and pulled out his laptop to punch at the keyboard. He brought up the Searates.com Web site and began entering information.

"Shit," Dugan said.

"What is it?" Anna asked.

"At her current speed, *China Star* should be in the middle of the Straits of Malacca on the Fourth of July. Now what are the odds of that?"

Steven "Bo" Richards slouched in a chair with his feet on an ottoman, clad in boxer shorts and nursing a hangover. He'd woken at noon and roused the whore to deal with his morning erection before shoving her into the hall, throwing money after her and slamming the door as she struggled into her clothes. He drained the beer and dropped the bottle on the carpet before scratching his stomach. The bed lay in tangled disarray, and a cart held the remains of a room-service breakfast. The room needed tidying, an event deferred by the Do Not Disturb sign on the doorknob outside.

He checked the time and stood to slip on a pair of jeans and pull on a tee shirt. He was tying his shoes when he heard a knock.

***

Sheibani stared at the *Do Not Disturb* sign, calming himself. The scum inside was a thug of the Great Satan, and Sheibani longed to kill him sight unseen. But the deception required Americans, and Richards's citizenship and record were documented. He forced a smile as the door opened a crack.

"Yeah?"

"Mr. Richards, I am Ali. May I come in?"

Richards opened the door and stood aside, nodding toward the sitting area. Sheibani entered and took a seat with his back to the wall as Richards settled across from him.

"Your accommodations are to your liking?" Sheibani asked.

"Yeah, yeah, everything's fine," Richards said. "What's the job?"

How American. Sheibani struggled with anger.

"In a week or so," Sheibani said, "a ship named *China Star* will transit the Malacca Straits, escorted by a security force comprised of private contractors and US Navy personnel. Or rather, men disguised as US Navy personnel. You will lead that force."

"Why me?" Richards asked. "I'm no sailor, and the pay is far beyond anything offered for a straight security job."

"In good time, Mr. Richards. For the moment let's just say—"

"You plan to sink the ship and block the strait," Richards guessed.

Sheibani once again swallowed his ire. "On the contrary. We will avoid blocking the strait, while appearing to attempt just that. We will ground in Indonesian waters and escape."

"Won't that be obvious to the crew?"

"The crew will be dealt with," Sheibani said.

Richards nodded. " Resources? How many in our team? Weapons?"

"The makeup and armament of the team will be as you require; in fact, I want you to recruit some of the team. The goal is deception. We will be joined by a young Arab-American naval officer."

"So why do you need me?"

"Insurance," Sheibani said. "Survivors will report an attack led by Americans."

"But you have an American."

Sheibani shook his head. "The ship is Liberian flag, but the senior officers are American. We will present them with an unusual situation. We must gain control fast, before they have a chance to think too much about it. Our young mujahideen is untested, and he looks like the Arab-American he is. They will likely be less suspicious of a countryman who shares their ethnicity."

Richards smirked. "So I'm your token white man."

Sheibani nodded. "I suppose you could say that. Questions?"

Richards shook his head. "No questions," he said, then smiled. "But seeing as how I'm such a valuable commodity, I think we need to renegotiate."

Sheibani suppressed a smile. So predictable. He feigned resistance and then yielded to Richards's exorbitant demand. After all, he'd never live to collect the money.

M/T *CHINA STAR*
STRAIT OF HORMUZ
23 JUNE

"Make your course one seven five," said Captain Dan Holt of the VLCC M/T *China Star* over his shoulder as he squinted out at the ship traffic.

"One seven five, aye," the helmsman repeated, then a moment later, "Steady on one seven five, sir."

Holt watched as the Strait of Hormuz widened and ships spread out in the increased sea room. He walked over to study the radar.

"OK, put her on the mike," he said to the helmsman.

"Aye, sir. Steering one seven five. Transferring control to the mike," the sailor said, switching control to the autopilot, or "Iron Mike," and watching the gyrocompass repeater a moment before he stepped away from the wheel.

"OK, Ortega," Holt said to the second mate, "call me if necessary. And don't let me catch you with your nose glued to the radar. Visibility's good, so use the radar to confirm a bearing or distance, not as a substitute for your goddamned eyes."

"Yes, Captain," Ortega said.

"OK. You have the conn. Helm's on the mike, steering one seven five."

"I have the conn, sir. Helm's on autopilot, steering one seven five," Ortega said.

Holt gave a curt nod and strode out the door, down the single flight to his office. He settled into his chair and glanced at a printed e-mail before reaching for the phone.

"Engine Room. Chief speaking," Jon Anderson said.

"Chief, can you come up?"

"OK," Anderson said. "I'm buttoning up the transfer pump. Give me a minute."

Ten minutes later the chief stood at Holt's door in oil-stained coveralls and carrying a clean piece of cardboard. He slipped off dirty work shoes to avoid staining the carpet and moved to the sofa in stockinged feet, placing the cardboard down to protect the fabric before sitting.

"Jesus H. Christ," Holt said, "aren't you friggin' engineers ever clean?"

Anderson grinned. "Some of us work for a living instead of sitting on our ass. You said come, so here I am. Want me to leave?"

Jon Anderson was one of Captain Daniel Holt's very few friends, a relationship rooted in mutual respect and the fact that Anderson took no crap from Holt.

"No, God damn it," grumbled Holt as he sat. "Coffee?"

"Nah. I've had my quota." Anderson smiled as the ship rolled. "God it's good to be out of there and back at sea."

"That's for sure," Holt said. "I'm just surprised they didn't give us a big ration of shit when they boarded and found Americans aboard. I can't say I was happy to be there."

Anderson shrugged. "Maybe we had a guardian angel. Anyway, what's up?"

Holt handed Anderson the e-mail and waited while he read it.

"What the hell is Maritime Protection Services?"

"Just what it says," Holt said. "Hired guns to protect us through the Malacca Straits."

Anderson looked skeptical. "Are we talking gunmen running all over the ship?"

"I don't think so. I think they just shadow us in a boat."

"Still sounds hinky," Anderson said. "I'll bet they know jack about tanker safety. We get all sorts of training about no matches, cigarette lighters, no spark-producing equipment, et cetera, et cetera, and now we're supposed to be OK with a bunch of trigger-happy assholes circling the ship with machine guns?"

"I agree," the captain said, "but the charterer hired them, and our owner agreed, so that's that. As long as they keep their distance, it should be all right."

"Yeah, well, like you say, there's nothing we can do about it." Anderson grinned. "Besides, I bet somebody's getting a kickback. They'll get an invoice for a hundred grand, and we'll be escorted by an old guy in a canoe with one tooth and a pellet gun."

Holt laughed. "I wouldn't doubt that for a minute."

CHAPTER FIFTEEN

Gardner glared at Ward. "No. And stop beating a dead horse, Ward. The answer was no two days ago, and it's still no."

"We should notify MALSINDO," Ward persisted, using the acronym for the alliance of Malaysia, Singapore, and Indonesia policing the Malacca Strait.

"And tell them what? Your boy Dugan and his terrorist buddy have a gut feeling?"

"Listen, Larry—"

"No, YOU listen, Ward. Me, chief. You, Indian. Understand?"

Ward bit back a sharp reply. "At least let's notify our own guys."

"Ward. It's a goddamned VLCC," Gardner said. "It will check into the traffic system, so I see no need to cry wolf and look stupid. You've screwed this up enough, so let's just lie low and avoid embarrassment."

Great, Ward thought, all this asshole is worried about is image. There was a huge difference in the scrutiny *China Star* would get if the authorities suspected trouble.

"Look, Larry. You have to understand—"

"No, YOU look. I haven't handed you your ass for your boy Dugan fucking things up by the numbers, but if you mention *China Star* to Singapore, I will HAVE YOUR ASS! Clear?"

Ward managed an angry nod.

"Fine. We're done. I'm invited to a congressional prayer breakfast, and I'm late."

Ward stifled an impulse to suggest Gardner pray for some fucking brains and stalked to his own office. After a moment of indecision, he glanced at his watch and called London.

***

"The bloody wanker," Lou Chesterton said. "So what now?"

"I follow orders and hope you'll do the same, but I know you Brits are blabbermouths."

"Yes, we are a loose-lipped lot," Lou said. "Why, given that the British High Commission is next door to your embassy, I suspect our Singapore lads gossip over the fence like old hens."

"No doubt," Ward said. "However, I hope if they do somehow hear about *China Star*, that they keep their efforts low-key. My ass is hanging out here a bit, Lou."

"Understood," Lou said. "I'm sure things will work out."

M/T *ASIAN TRADER*
PACIFIC OCEAN BOUND FOR PANAMA
26 JUNE

Medina frowned. The sun had pounded the deck for a week, and the steel deck grew hotter each day. He wore gloves now for push-ups, and even the wind rebelled, veering astern and matching their speed to leave the deck becalmed. He watched a nearby thunderhead and willed it closer, with its promise of cooling rain and concealing wind.

His eyes moved toward the bow as the bosun descended from the forecastle with a grease gun. He knew fumes were thick on deck just aft of the raised forecastle and watched the bosun for a reaction. Sure enough, upon reaching the deck, the man tilted his head, and Medina saw cognition in his eyes. The sailor squatted and sniffed at a tank vent. He rose to find Medina beside him.

"We have a bulkhead leak. We must tell the chief mate," the bosun said, starting aft.

"Wait," Medina said. "I smelled it before on the starboard side too. Let's check it out before we get everyone excited."

Unwilling to appear an alarmist while a green third mate remained calm, the bosun followed Medina under the centerline pipe rack, out of sight of the bridge watch high above.

Medina stopped under the pipes. "There's the problem," he said, pointing to a rising stem valve, the spiral threads of its stem protruding vertically from its center.

The bosun scoffed. "How can that be the problem?"

"Look closely," Medina said.

The bosun hid his amusement as he bent low over the irrelevant valve. Junior officers became senior officers and were to be humored. He was about to straighten when strong hands on the back of his head slammed his face toward the valve, and he lost his balance, adding to his downward momentum. His last memory was the tip of the valve stem rushing toward him and a searing pain as it mangled his left eye and pushed into his brain.

Medina kept his full weight on the bosun's head until the flailing stopped. He removed the man's shoe and dabbed the sole with grease from the man's grease gun, then pressed the shoe to the deck, simulating a slip in grease. He put the shoe back on the bosun's foot and laced it.

A freshening wind cooled Medina's face as he ran aft for help. A cooling rain was washing the bosun's blood into the sea by the time he returned with that help two minutes later.

OFFICES OF PHOENIX SHIPPING
LONDON
28 JUNE

"Why does anyone have to go?" Braun demanded. "For that matter, why even have a damned inquiry? The captain logged it as an accident."

Alex gritted his teeth. "Because it's the law, Braun. Whenever—"

"Captain Braun."

"All right. Captain Braun. Whenever there's a death at sea, international law requires an inquiry at the next port of call with a company representative in attendance."

"Well, I'm sure as hell not letting you go, and I'm not going." Braun smiled. "Wait a minute. Send Dugan."

"I don't think—"

"Didn't Dugan take *Asian Trader* through the yard in Singapore just last month?"

"He started her through, yes," Alex said. "But I don't think—"

"I don't care what you think, Kairouz. He knows the ship. He's available. Send him. Now get out."

Alex stiffened and left Braun's office as the German reflected on how often adversity is opportunity in disguise. He was a bit concerned that the accident might draw unnecessary attention to *Asian Trader*, but that effort was a sideshow anyway. He was sure the expendable lunatic there would manage to kill himself in spectacular fashion. Now, with luck, Dugan would be there to take the fall after it happened. Braun hummed a little tune as he brought up the Web site of the National Bank of the Caymans and opened a new account in Dugan's name.

ANNA WALSH'S APARTMENT BUILDING
2135 HOURS LOCAL TIME
28 JUNE

Dugan and Anna's team sat around the coffee table in the surveillance apartment, his sat phone open in speaker mode on the table.

"Braun's adamant," Dugan said. "Alex called me into his office and told me I was going to Panama. We carried on a conversation for Braun's benefit while we scribbled notes back and forth. I made the expected excuses—said it was Braun's job, I was too busy, et cetera, and Alex made a show of forcing me."

"But why is Braun so keen for you to go?" Anna asked.

Dugan shrugged. "After the *China Star* deal, I guess he wants me out of the way."

"It makes sense," Ward's voice from the speaker said. "He isn't likely to allow Alex out of his control, and Tom knows the ship. I don't think we should read too much into this."

"I agree with Ward," Lou said. "He has *China Star* under satellite coverage, and we still have Anna in the office to keep an eye on things. If Dugan pushes back at this point, it may make Braun suspicious."

Anna nodded. "OK, let's keep Braun happy then. Between *China Star* and the Caracas intercept, we're finally getting somewhere. We don't want to upset him now."

"I'll pack a bag," Dugan said.

CHAPTER SIXTEEN

Borqei stared at the message, sighed, and dialed the phone. He had a conversation in Farsi, including code words. An hour later, Yousif's adoptive mother went to her doctor, who admitted her to his private clinic and called her clergyman, Borqei, of course. Borqei informed the navy that Ensign Hamad's mother was gravely ill, along with the doctor's number for verification. In hours, Hamad was on a plane from San Diego, with connections in Los Angeles.

***

In a toilet stall in LAX, a man slipped Yousif an envelope under the divider. He opened it to find a ticket to Jakarta, a forged passport, and a wallet holding cash, a driver's license, and credit cards. The hand reappeared under the divider, and Yousif passed over his own boarding pass and ID. His seat on the plane to Detroit would be occupied by a man looking very much like him. It wouldn't do for the airline to record him as a no show.

An hour later, Yousif sat in the international terminal, in civilian clothes with boarding pass in hand, baffled at his trip to Indonesia but trusting Imam Borqei.

Sheibani stood with Richards, watching in the growing light as his men spread netting over the boats moored fifty meters away under overhanging limbs. A good staging point, he thought, where the Andaman Sea narrowed into the Malacca Strait. Sheibani felt secure in Aceh Province. Holy Jihad had strong support here, where Islam first arrived in Indonesia.

"Is the cover sufficient?"

Richards nodded. "Between the trees and net, they'll be invisible to the satellites."

"And you have everything you need?"

Richards grinned. "Enough C4 to blow 'em and enough clay to fool your bomber boys."

"Do not ridicule them," Sheibani snapped. Deceiving brave men was regrettable. He hoped they would be welcomed in Paradise, and he would not allow them to be mocked by this infidel.

"I leave tomorrow to collect our American in Jakarta," Sheibani said. "You must finish before we return tomorrow night."

"What? Why? We got four days."

"The others will not understand, but this man may. Finish and cover it."

"Shit," Richards said.

Sheibani left Richards to his work, and the next morning as he got into his SUV, the American had the material stacked next to the boats.

"Gonna be broilin' under that camo net," the American said.

"Just make sure you finish before I return."

Sheibani left Richards cursing, as he drove off down the jungle track, the American soon forgotten. Success was only a matter of degree. Even if they failed to dupe China into believing the attack was an American ruse to justify seizing control of the strait, the attack alone was enough to raise oil prices and divert suspicion from Iran. Sheibani smiled and mulled his plans for "spontaneous" street demonstrations once American treachery was discovered.

JUDICIAL INVESTIGATIVE DIRECTORY HQ
PANAMA CITY, PANAMA
1 JULY

The chair groaned as Lieutenant Manuel Reyes reached for a file.

"One day, Manny," Sergeant Juan Perez said, "your fat ass is gonna hit the floor."

"You're just jealous, shrimp," Reyes said, with some truth. At six four and powerfully built, Reyes towered over his diminutive partner. Perez stifled a reply as Captain Luna approached and handed Reyes a folder.

"What's this?" Reyes asked.

"You boys are taking a little boat trip," Luna said. "Fatality on a tanker."

"Shit. Why us? Why not those SMN assholes?" Perez asked, referring to the Servicio Maritimo Nacional. "Wait. Let me guess. She arrives on a weekend."

"You know the drill, Perez," Luna said. "Suspected foul play comes here."

"Foul play?" Perez asked, interested now.

"Looks like it," Reyes said, looking up from the file. "You read this, Captain?"

Luna nodded. "No witness except the guy that reported the accident. Victim a skilled seaman in good health. Good weather. Yeah, it warrants a look."

Reyes continued, "Says he fell on a valve stem that pierced his brain through the eye."

"No way," Perez said. "With his hands free? I can see a broken arm or jaw, or even losing an eye. But the thing couldn't go into his brain unless he came straight down on it with force. Sounds like he had help."

Reyes and Luna nodded.

"Any bad blood between the victim and the witness?" Perez asked.

"Nothing in the file," Luna said. "Her agent will update you on the ETA. Keep me posted." He grinned. "Perez has time to stock up on seasick pills."

Reyes smiled. His partner's aversion to anything that floated was a department joke. Perez got violently ill, even riding a launch in the smooth water of the harbor. Reyes decided to let him stew for a bit before volunteering to work the case solo. Served him right for that fat-ass remark.

"This'll screw up the weekend for sure," Perez muttered at Luna's retreating back.

"I hope not," Reyes said, nodding at a framed photo of his eight-year-old twins in soccer uniforms. "The boys have a game this weekend, and I don't want to miss it."

OFFICES OF PHOENIX SHIPPING
2 JULY

Braun smiled as he read. He was managing message traffic for both *Asian Trader* and *China Star* now, sending or modifying messages in Dugan's name. The ruse wouldn't work long, but the attacks were imminent. *Asian Trader* had increased speed per "Dugan's" earlier orders, with a new ETA of 0100 hours on July 4, ready to start canal transit at first light. The ship would arrive a full twenty-four hours before anyone else in the office had a clue it had reached Panama.

He accessed the Panama Canal Authority webpage auctioning transit slots, signing in as Dugan. Bidding for the July 4 slot was heavy. He doubled the current bid and grinned as no challenger emerged. The slot secured, he pulled up an outgoing message he'd intercepted and held, asking the agent to arrange a hotel and airport pickup for Dugan. He added orders to advise the authorities that *Asian Trader* had transit priority and to request the inquiry be postponed until after transit. Braun hit send and leaned back, satisfied.

Dugan would arrive after the attack—in time to be detained. An investigation would reveal Dugan's Cayman Island account, owned through a series of fronts, with recent transactions totaling a million dollars from sources with known terrorist links. The money had stayed in the account just minutes before Braun whisked it away, causing it to vanish through another series of skillful transfers. A frame was one thing, but a million dollars was not something he abandoned lightly.

Things were progressing, despite a few hiccups. *China Star* and *Asian Trader* were on schedule, and the Chechens were in position for the final act. He could hardly ask for more.

PARIS, FRANCE
2 JULY

Basaev paced the room. He was impatient, as they all were. They'd been in the seedy transient hotel a week, keeping to themselves as they studied their course notes and identity documents, preparing to board the ship as a riding repair crew. Their weapons waited in the load port, concealed among the tools to be loaded aboard for the "riding crew" to use during the voyage. They would take the first flight from Paris to the load port as soon as they received word the ship had moved to the loading berth. They would board the ship just before sailing, when they would receive less scrutiny.

Allah make it soon, prayed Basaev.

CHAPTER SEVENTEEN

M/T *CHINA STAR*
ANDAMAN SEA
EAST OF BANDA ACEH, INDONESIA
3 JULY

Holt peered into the predawn gloom as *China Star* crept along at dead slow. He muttered and moved to the radar, his escort's late arrival just the latest irritation. He still chafed at the peremptory e-mail from this Dugan, ordering him to board the "escort team leader" for a "pre-transit conference." And his own company hadn't backed his protest.

The VHF squawked. "*China Star*, this is MPS team leader. Do you copy, over?"

"I copy, MPS," the captain said. "I have two targets to starboard. Is that you, over?"

"Affirmative, *China Star*. Five minutes out. Are you rigged for boarding, over?"

"Starboard side. I'll light it up." He walked over and threw a breaker, and floodlights bathed the boarding area and the adjacent sea in a circle of light.

"Thank you, *China Star*. I have a visual on the ladder. See you in five, out."

"Bonifacio," Holt barked. "Make yourself useful. Go meet our guest and escort him to the bridge." Third Mate Bonifacio scurried out, cursing the curiosity that led him to hang around after he was relieved.

Holt heard the engines now, a growing roar that subsided as the boats cut speed, one paralleling the ship as the second moved crab-like into the light to the pilot ladder. I'll be damned, he thought, looking at the flag. US Navy. Then he cursed as not one but six black-clad figures scrambled aboard. He waited until an agitated Bonifacio arrived with visitors in tow.

Holt looked at the group. "You seemed to have lost a few, Bonifacio."

"Captain, I told them—"

"Not his fault, Captain. We deployed," said the leader of the group, an American.

Before Holt could respond, the man extended his hand.

"I'm Bo Richards, MPS." He nodded at a second man. "This is Ensign Hamad, US Navy."

Holt shook their hands, glancing at a third man who hung back, gripping his weapon.

"By helping private firms," Richards said, "the US can protect the strait without upsetting local governments."

"Riding around under the Stars and Stripes isn't low profile," Holt said, not buying it. "What the hell is going on here?" he asked just as the phone rang.

The second mate held up the phone. "It's the chief," he said. Holt took the phone.

"Three GI Joe-lookin' assholes are in my engine control room. What the hell's goin' on, Cap?" Anderson demanded.

"Hold one, Chief," he said, looking at Richards. "The chief engineer's none too pleased with your 'deployment,' nor am I. So just get back in your little boats and follow us."

"Apologies, Captain," Richards said. "We'll do it any way you want. However, we do need a meeting with you and the chief before we leave."

Holt hesitated. "Fine," he said at last. He spoke into the phone. "Chief, can you come up to the D Deck conference room?" He nodded at the response and hung up.

"Mr. Ortega, you have the conn," he said to the second mate. "Course is one two five. Steering is on hand."

Holt listened to the man's confirmation before turning to the third mate. "Mr. Bonifacio, get some rest, but first ask the steward to bring coffee to the conference room."

Holt led the group down to the conference room, swallowing his irritation at the belated realization that the third man, the silent one, had remained on the bridge. Jon Anderson joined them in the conference room, fit to be tied. As before, Richards diverted the engineer with introductions as the smiling steward arrived with coffee. As the steward served, Anderson sank into a chair beside the captain as Richards closed the door.

Without warning, Richards slammed the steward down on the table and with one fluid movement pulled a silenced sidearm and fired twice into the man's face. Holt and Anderson watched horrified as the steward's blood and brains pooled on the table. They looked up to see Richards's steady smile and dead, dead eyes.

"Now gentlemen," Richards said, "let's discuss our little cruise, shall we?"

M/T *CHINA STAR*
MALACCA STRAIT
DUE WEST OF PORT KLANG, MALAYSIA
LOCAL TIME 4 JULY

Richards watched the bridge crew in the glow of console instrument lights. With a gun at their heads and the dead steward in front of them, the senior officers had been understandably cooperative. Most of the crew was now captive in the crew lounge. The gear had been brought aboard, and the gunboats ran dark, hugging the ship's starboard side, their return masked by the huge ship's own radar signature.

The captain was on the bridge, along with Second Mate Ortega, Third Mate Bonifacio and Urbano, the helmsman, all dead tired, allowed no rest in over twenty-four hours. Richards, Yousif, and Sheibani shared guard duty, two at a time with the third napping as needed. The three hijackers in the engine room followed the same two-watching-one-resting pattern, guarding Anderson and First Engineer Benjamin Santos. By design, only the seamen on watch knew the hijackers' numbers, and ignorant of the odds, the others captive in the crew lounge would be less inclined toward heroics.

Not that it mattered. The thick lounge windows were all but unbreakable, and the handles of the lounge doors were lashed to the storm rail in the passageway, precluding worries of hidden keys. The steward's body dumped in the lounge and a warning the doors were booby-trapped further discouraged resistance, enhanced by the cook's report of grenade-festooned doors when he returned under guard with sandwiches, water, and buckets for "sanitary needs."

***

Holt squinted at the radar through watery eyes, his stomach boiling from endless coffee.

"Southbound VLCC," squawked the VHF, "this is Klang VTS. Report. Over."

He felt the gun at the back of his head.

"OK, nice and businesslike," Richards said.

"Jesse," Mike Hill said, "two calls in two weeks. People will talk."

Ward chuckled. "Whadda ya got, Mike?"

"You know that boat we been tracking? *China Star*?"

Ward sat up, interested. "Yeah."

"Well, she picked up admirers. Two Malaysian boats as escorts."

Christ, that was fast, thought Ward. "Malaysians? You sure?"

"Not positive," Hill said, "but the two guys in each boat are Asian, and they're flying red-white-and-blue flags. A stern wind is keeping the flags limp, but they're red-and-white striped. That means US or Malaysia. I know it's not us, so it must be them. The boats look a lot like our Dauntless 34s, but that's a pretty common design."

"Two guys per boat is a bit light. Our crews are bigger."

"Lemme look again. Shit, there's a ladder rigged. They're on board. I should have caught that."

"Actually, I'm relieved," Ward said. "We passed a back-channel warning to the locals but got no response. Any other friendlies in the area if they need help?"

"There's a CARAT exercise on to the south," Hill said, using the acronym for the Cooperation Afloat Readiness and Training exercise. "A multinational cluster fuck. Us, Singapore, Malaysia, and Indonesia. I'd hate to lead that parade."

Ward laughed. "Sounds like everything's OK. Thanks for the update."

"No sweat, pal," Hill said and hung up.

***

For all his relief that his backdoor warning had paid off, Ward couldn't shake an uneasy feeling. He was in the supermarket two hours later, shopping for his Fourth of July cookout, when it hit him. He rushed through the checkout to his car and began punching numbers into his sat phone, praying his gut feeling was wrong.

M/T *CHINA STAR*
MALACCA STRAIT
WEST OF PORT DICKSON, MALAYSIA
LOCAL TIME 4 JULY

Sheibani moved through the chart-room curtains onto the darkened bridge.

"We're close," he whispered. "Best deal with the excess crew as they sleep."

"It'll make the others more difficult," Richards protested.

"They will hear nothing in the engine room," Sheibani said, "and we tell these their shipmates tried to escape, and a few were injured by booby traps, and the rest gave up after warning shots. It will calm them long enough. Soon we'll be in Indonesian waters and no longer need them. Any fool can ground a ship."

"OK. Will you do it?"

"Yes. I will take Yousif."

"No," Richards said. "That leaves me too thin here."

"You do well to remember who is really in charge, Richards."

The comment hung in the air until Richards broke the silence.

"All right," he whispered, "but go quietly and hurry back."

Sheibani smiled in the dark as he moved away. He'd included Yousif as an afterthought to salve his pangs of conscience. He would not let the young man die without dipping his sword in the blood of the infidel.

***

Sheibani peeked in a window. Men slept sprawled on sofas and armchairs or the deck. Three insomniacs played cards in the light of a lamp. He moved back and targeted the window, nodding for Yousif to take another. They opened fire, stitching holes around the edge of the thick glass before directing fire into the center, sending a maelstrom of shards inward, followed by grenades as they ducked low. Sheibani rushed to the window after the explosions, unmoved by the carnage, firing at anything that twitched. He looked over at Yousif bent over a puddle of vomit.

"Control yourself and rejoice in the blood of infidels. Come, a few still squirm. We will toss in two grenades each and finish it."

Yousif shook his head, mute.

"Beard of the Prophet, you are a woman. I will finish alone. Go."

Yousif stumbled up the stairs to the bridge as explosions sounded behind him. Sheibani arrived on the bridge moments later to find Yousif trembling in the dark, wiping vomit from his chin. Sheibani's foul mood was tempered by the ease with which his captives accepted his tale of attempted escape. If they noticed the patterns of shots and explosions didn't match the story, it hadn't registered. A comforting lie was more palatable than a terrifying truth.

***

Sheibani erred in thinking his act went unnoticed below. Engineers are attuned to sound and vibration, for unexpected noises invariably herald problems. In the control room, Anderson and Santos felt the shocks through their feet, though their guards were oblivious.

Anderson paced in front of the control console. Unlike Holt, preoccupied with conning the ship, his automated engine room allowed him time to think. With Americans among them, he figured the hijackers nonsuicidal. He was partially right; Yousif and the men in the boats were eager martyrs, while Richards and Sheibani planned escape. The three guards in the engine room were also unenthusiastic martyrs, Burmese mercenaries hired by Richards.

No one seemed intent on destruction; they had neither stopped the inert-gas system nor ventilated the cargo tanks into the explosive range. They were either intentionally leaving the ship in a safe condition or were inept. They didn't seem inept.

Anderson didn't figure he and Santos were there by accident. Their captors anticipated a possible need for a senior engineer, and while they might kill one to coerce the other, if either escaped, the other likely wouldn't be killed. But he sensed they were nearing some climax, perhaps connected to the shocks he'd felt. Time was getting short.

He watched the guards out of the corner of his eye. The engineers were accustomed to long periods in the windowless control room and at least had the distraction of monitoring the main engine and engineering plant. Their guards had no mental stimulation whatsoever, and being confined in a box had taken its toll. They were noticeably less alert than they had been when the ordeal started over twenty-four hours before. Anderson took a chance.

***

Santos watched as Anderson turned toward him and repeatedly arched his eyebrows to get his attention. He stared silently as Anderson looked at the CO2 alarm on the bulkhead then pointed at him with a finger shielded by his body. Santos grew more puzzled as Anderson then looked pointedly toward a rack of emergency-escape masks used for tank entry and discreetly pointed to himself. The chief obviously had a plan, but what? He was still trying to piece it together when Anderson turned to the senior of the three guards.

"I'm hungry," he said. "We're not going to escape aft, so how about bringing down more sandwiches before I find another way out of here?"

The hijacker looked confused. "You no talk."

"Santos can go with one of your guys," Anderson pressed. "They can leave and shut that door tight." He pointed to the door leading to the deckhouse stairs.

"No. No eat. Shut up now."

Suddenly, Santos understood, but the hijacker wasn't cooperating. Anderson turned back to the console, disappointment on his face, but Santos was elated. He caught Anderson's eye and nodded. He'd plotted his own escape for hours. The only thing stopping him had been his fear of retaliation against Anderson. Now it seemed the chief had a plan of his own.

***

"Toilet." Santos hugged his stomach and moved toward the door.

The nearest hijacker leveled his weapon. "You stop."

Santos moaned. "Must go toilet."

The man spoke and the others laughed, obviously at Santos's expense. The head man nodded, and the underling escorted Santos out the door to the engine-room toilet and the deckhouse stairs beyond. As the control-room door shut behind them, Santos hurried across the narrow vestibule to the toilet. He tried to close the toilet door, but as expected, his captor shook his head, so Santos shrugged down his coveralls and sat, glaring out at the man. Minutes later, he pulled up his coveralls and moved to the small sink, his back to the hijacker. He turned on the water and extracted a fistful of powdered hand soap from a container on the sink, his actions hidden by his body. He murmured a prayer and turned off the water.

Surprise was complete as soap flew into the guard's face. His weapon hung slack as he jammed fists to burning eyes. In one fluid motion, Santos plucked a pen from his pocket and drove it into the man's throat. Blood covered Santos as he grabbed the man's wrists and pinned him against the bulkhead, praying no sounds of the struggle reached the control room. The man gasped and bled out, powerful spurts soaking Santos's face and front. It took an eternity before the flow dwindled, and a stench filled the space, signaling loss of sphincter control. He let the body slide down the bulkhead and stood trembling, willing the face from his memory.

Santos cleaned himself as best he could with paper towels from the toilet. A mop from the cleaning-gear locker became his improvised lock, jammed across the narrow passageway between the outward-opening control-room door and the opposite bulkhead, its tangled head compressed tight against the door just above the knob. He grabbed the hijacker's gun and hurried up the stairs.

USS *Hermitage* (LSD-56)
Malacca Strait
North of Riau Island, Indonesia

Captain Jack Leary, USN, sat in his ready room with the sat phone at his ear.

"Captain Leary, this is Jim Brice from the embassy in Singapore. I'm conferencing in Jesse Ward from Langley. We need your help. Go ahead, Jesse."

Leary listened. When Ward finished, Jim Brice spoke.

"Port Klang has nothing unaccounted for near *China Star*, and they didn't send out any escorts," he said.

"Are they following up?" Ward asked.

Brice sighed. "I suspect they'll drag their feet until she's out of their waters."

"That's not gonna hack it," Leary said. "Any threat needs to be handled before the passage narrows at Phillip's Strait. But what can *we* do about it?"

"Can you check it out?" Ward asked.

"I'm running a multinational effort planned for months. I can't just head north."

Ward persisted, "Maybe one vessel—"

"Look, Ward," Leary said, "I can't go into territorial waters without consulting my counterparts. And they'll request instructions, and we'll get no decision until the tanker is in flames or safe and halfway to Japan. See my problem here?"

Ward sighed. "Yes, I do, Captain, but what *can* we do?"

After a long silence, Leary replied. "I guess we take a risk. I can get a chopper over her without being too obvious. If there's a problem, we close, and if that ends well, we call it a multinational effort and all take a bow. If not… well, I never wanted to be an admiral anyway."

"Thanks, Captain," he said. "By the way, is that sailor from the hijacking with you?"

"Broussard? Yeah, he's one of our referees."

"Might be a good idea if he was on that chopper."

M/T *China Star*
Malacca Strait

"Where the hell have you been?" Richards demanded.

"Preparing our escape," Sheibani said. "Allah smiles on the prepared."

"Good," nodded Richards, mollified. "How much longer?"

"We turn into the western channel now and ground off Rupat Island in an hour, maybe a bit longer. I will reduce speed. I don't want to ground hard enough to breach both the outer and inner hulls." He smiled. "It is difficult to swim in crude oil."

Richards returned the smile, heartened by mention of escape. Sheibani moved to where Ortega stood near the helmsman.

"Make your course one seven oh," Sheibani said.

Holt stepped in from the wing just as the second mate protested. "The western channel is too shallow. We cannot!"

Sheibani shot Ortega in the head, and Holt recoiled as wet bits of brain hit his face and slid from his chin to fall beside Ortega's twitching corpse.

"One seven oh," Sheibani repeated, and the terrified helmsman spun the wheel.

"Half ahead," Sheibani said.

Bonifacio stood on the far side of the bridge, waiting, but the captain stood frozen, staring down at Ortega's body, barely visible in the predawn light. Bonifacio raced to the console.

"Half ahead, aye, sir," he shouted.

Such a pity, Sheibani thought. Just when I get these monkeys trained I have to kill them.

***

Anderson stole a glance at the clock, willing Santos to hurry.

The head man said something, and his underling started for the door. Anderson's mind raced, desperate to buy Santos time, when unexpected motion caused him to grab the console storm rail as the ship turned.

The head man reached the console just as the engine control changed to half ahead.

"What you do?"

Clueless, thought Anderson, looking past the head man to the second man, halfway to the door, unsure what to do given the new development.

"I do nothing," Anderson said. "We don't control here. Bridge do." He pointed to the phone. "You talk friends. They tell you."

The hijacker picked up the phone, and when he hung up, Anderson launched into a stream of technobabble.

"OK, OK. You shut up now." The hijacker stuck the gun in Anderson's face, Santos forgotten for the moment. Anderson sneaked a look at the time. Damn it, Ben, what's taking so long?

***

Santos stood in the CO2 room, racked with indecision. Was he really meant to trigger the CO2? He had a gun now. Should he try to rescue Anderson? He felt the ship turn and slow and decided to trust his instincts. He crossed himself, pulled the release, and raced aft.

***

"What you do?" the senior terrorist demanded, gun to Anderson's chest.

"Not me. Bridge do," Anderson screamed over the alarm. "Big mistake. Someone started gas to put out engine-room fire. Gas comes in twenty seconds!" He pointed to the raucous alarm and the large red sign beneath it.

DANGER—CO2 RELEASE—WHEN ALARM SOUNDS VACATE IMMEDIATELY.

The head man reached for the phone.

"No time! We stay, we die!" Anderson moved toward the engine-room door.

The head man dropped the phone and leveled his gun. "Stop," he ordered, as the other hijacker struggled with the most obvious exit, the door leading to the deckhouse.

"No," Anderson lied, pointing to the blocked door, "that door locks automatically to keep people out of engine room. Don't worry about your friend. He'll escape with Santos. We must go this way." Anderson pointed through the control-room window to a large sign stenciled on the engine room bulkhead, reading EMERGENCY ESCAPE ROUTE, with an arrow pointed down.

The underling rushed to Anderson's side, and an argument broke out between the hijackers. Anderson grabbed three masks from the rack, keeping one and setting the others on the deck to allay the men's suspicions. The men didn't notice that the two he'd set out for them came from a shelf of discharged masks, awaiting recharge.

Anderson slung the mask around his neck and fled into the engine room, with the men on his heels, juggling masks and guns. He raced down the steep stairs sideways in a controlled fall, right hand gripping the rail behind as he steadied himself with his left on the opposite handrail in front, feet hitting every third step. It was an acquired skill, and he was soon well ahead, increasing his lead on each flight of stairs as he spiraled downward. The hijackers could do nothing to stop him, for they dared not kill their guide out of the maze.

He planned to lead them to the emergency escape trunk, sure that when they saw the vertical ladder out, they'd push past him in their panic. When they were on the ladder, he planned to fade back into the engine room and escape by a different route with his mask. The hijackers wouldn't know Santos had locked the hatch until they were at a dead end, on top of the ladder, with no escape.

The warning horns continued their plaintive wail as Anderson reached the lower engine room and rushed aft beside the giant turning shaft. He hadn't figured on such a lead. They would be suspicious if he stopped now. He decided to lie on the deck at the foot of the ladder, feigning a pulled muscle. He stepped into the escape trunk and looked up.

To a square of black sky and stars. Shit. Ben hadn't closed the hatch.

OK, change of plans. He'd try to make it out and lock the hatch down behind himself. He started up the long ladder at breakneck speed as the alarm horns began to fade. Halfway up, the CO_2 began to roar through distribution nozzles, and he looked down. The expanding gas sucked heat from the humid space, condensing moisture in the air. His terrified pursuers emerged from the thick white fog, climbing toward him for all they were worth.

***

Santos stood on the main deck looking at the hatch. Was he really meant to close it? What else could the chief have meant by the "not going to escape aft" clue? But what if he misunderstood and cut off the chief's escape? But no, the clue could mean nothing else. Santos grabbed the cantilevered counterweight that held the heavy cover open just as the horns stopped wailing below. He hesitated. One quick look, then he'd close it for sure.

He peeked over the hatch coaming to see Anderson climbing fast with the hijackers right behind, all eyes on the ladder and none looking up. Santos braced himself and waited until Anderson began to emerge.

"Jump, boss," he yelled as he hooked his arm under Anderson's and heaved, their combined strength sending Anderson over the hatch coaming to land in a heap. Santos pulled up on the counterweight with all his strength, and the heavy cover crashed shut. He slapped one of the threaded dogs in place and spun the wing nut to screw it down tight. No one else was coming out.

Below, the junior hijacker was in the lead, and he balanced himself on the ladder and loosed a burst up at the hatch cover in spite of his boss's screams of protests. The protests died quickly, as did the men, as ricochets caromed through the close confines of the steel escape trunk.

The shots were faint outside, swallowed by the myriad sounds of a ship underway.

"What now, Chief?" Santos asked, helping Anderson to his feet.

"Damned if I know, Ben," Anderson gasped.

CHAPTER EIGHTEEN

M/T *CHINA STAR*
MALACCA STRAIT
NORTH OF RUPAT ISLAND, INDONESIA

"*China Star*, *China Star*. You are out of the main channel. Repor—"

"Change," Sheibani said into the mike, twisting the knob to a new channel. He keyed the mike rapidly and nodded at responding clicks from the boats, confirming compliance via a prearranged code.

"Too late to stop us, and their babbling might disrupt contact with the boats," he said as Richards nodded. An unfamiliar alarm shrieked and they looked across the bridge to where Holt stood at a flashing panel.

"What are you doing?" Richards said as he rushed over, gun raised.

Holt seemed beyond caring, as if being forced to dump Ortega's body overboard had erased any illusions of survival.

"I'm trying to silence this friggin' alarm if you'll get the fuck out of the way."

Surprised, Richards complied. "What is it?" he asked, lowering his gun.

"CO2 release. Probably a false alarm."

Sheibani frowned. He was reaching for the phone when the ship blacked out. He heard the distant muted roar of the emergency generator.

"Main-engine trip!" Bonifacio cried.

In the engine room, the generator engines had coughed to a halt as the CO2 rose to the level of the generator flat and the engines sucked in CO2. With no power, safety devices shut down the main engine and everything else, and the remotely located emergency generator sprang to life automatically to power limited emergency services.

Richards leveled his gun. "False alarm, my ass. Fix this. Now. Or you're dead."

"There's no fast fix, you ignorant asshole," Holt said. "The CO2 has to be purged. That means resetting dampers and starting fans. Takes time."

"So how do you do that?" Richards asked.

Holt smirked. "I call the chief engineer."

Richards knocked him to the deck.

"Enough!" Sheibani yelled as Bonifacio helped Holt.

Sheibani started to call the engine control room, then realized the futility of that action. Anyone still there would be dead.

"Yousif," he said, "go down and check. Cautiously. If you have difficulty breathing, return at once."

Yousif nodded and left as Sheibani moved to the chart and stepped off the distance with dividers. By the time Yousif returned, Sheibani was reassured. They were near Indonesian waters, and momentum would take them there.

"Gas," Yousif said, breathless from his climb. "I got halfway down but saw the body of one our men. The control-room door is jammed close with a mop."

"The man's gun?"

Yousif shook his head. "Gone."

Sheibani nodded. "Yousif, watch these three. Richards, join me on the wing."

"This is bad," Richards said when they were alone.

The Iranian shrugged. "She will ground with or without us. The VHF is on the emergency circuit, so we can communicate with the boats. If the Burmese died, it saves us killing them, and if any survived, they will report being led by an American. If the engineers are alive and armed, they will hide in a defensive position and wait for help."

"But they know what went on."

"They were in a windowless box and know nothing," Sheibani said. "There are many hiding places, and time is short. And they are armed. Why risk being shot? We leave them."

"OK. Let's finish these guys, blow the boats, and get the hell out of here."

"A half hour more," Sheibani said, smiling at the lightening sky. "The farther we drift, the shorter our swim."

***

Anderson studied his blood-covered subordinate in the growing light.

"Christ, Ben, are you hurt?"

"Not... not mine," Santos said, suddenly drained. He looked down, as if seeing the gore for the first time, then bent and retched, as Anderson stood near, unsure what to do.

Santos straightened, wiping his mouth on a sleeve.

"We got a gun," he said, retrieving it from the deck and thrusting it at Anderson.

Anderson accepted the unfamiliar weapon.

"What now, boss?" Santos asked again.

"A drifting VLCC will bring help," Anderson said. "There's three hijackers left aboard for sure, and even with a few more from the boats, they lack manpower to rig a tanker this size with enough charges to sink it, and they can't use the cargo because we're still inert. With a dead ship, the pumps are down, so they can't even jettison cargo. And they seem like pirates, not terrorists, so why don't they just clean out the safe and haul ass?"

Santos nodded as if equally baffled.

"Let's assume the worst," Anderson said. "If the murdering assholes aren't gone before help arrives, the hostages become bargaining chips. If we can free at least some of them, they can scatter and hide." He looked at the sky. "Let's move before full light."

Santos nodded and trailed Anderson around the machinery casing, into the deckhouse and the glow of emergency lighting. Anderson eased the stairwell fire door open and peeked up the first flight to the A Deck landing and started up. A putrid smell washed over them as they left the stairwell on A Deck.

"Christ," Anderson whispered, "smells like somebody shit in a meat market."

Santos's face contorted, and he rushed forward, stopping short at the rope lashing the lounge door and the sight of grenades hung from the door frame. The metal door was peppered with dents, as if attacked inside by hundreds of screwdrivers. Scattered fragments had penetrated to smash into the steel bulkhead across the hall and fall mangled to the deck. Stench wafted from the holes.

"We have to go in, Ben," Anderson said softly. "Some might live."

Santos untied the rope as his boss studied the grenades. Pins in place. Window dressing. Anderson was careful nonetheless as he pulled the grenades from their magnetic clips and set them aside.

The battered door refused to budge, and Anderson leaned into it. It yielded suddenly, with a wet sucking sound, as the partial torso blocking it slid away, and Anderson pitched forward on his hands and knees. Gore squished between his fingers and soaked the legs of his coveralls as he stared at body parts in a horrifying jumble. The reek of open bowels was overpowering. He tried to rise and slipped, then scrambled backward on his hands and knees through the gore to draw himself up against the far bulkhead of the passageway, fighting down vomit and wiping his hands furiously on his coveralls.

Santos stared into the room. After a moment, he crossed himself and closed the door before sliding down the bulkhead to sit opposite Anderson.

"No one alive there, boss," he said quietly.

"They mean to kill us all, Ben. I have to try to help whoever's left, but we only have one gun. Hide, Ben. Survive to testify against these bastards."

Santos shook his head. "In that room," he said, "are two cousins and my sister's husband, and others from my town. What will I say to their families? That I hid only so I could live to testify? Who will believe it? I would not be alive, boss. Only waiting to die. We go together."

USS *HERMITAGE* (LSD-56)

Chief Petty Officer Ricky Vega passed the backpacks to Broussard and scrambled aboard the SH-60 Sea Hawk as the younger man stowed them.

"Welcome to Malacca Air," said the pilot into his helmet mike. "I do believe this is the earliest I've ever seen boat people vertical and ambulatory." He grinned over his shoulder.

Vega grinned back. "Fuck you... sir."

"I see rising in time to actually put in a day's work has made you cranky, Chief Vega."

Vega just grinned. He waited until they were well clear of *Hermitage* before speaking.

"So what's up, sir? They told me to get Broussard here ASAP. I decided to tag along."

"Milk run," the pilot said. "Gotta eyeball some gunboats shadowing a tanker."

Broussard and Vega exchanged looks.

"How are you armed?" Vega asked.

The pilot laughed. "In the middle of a multinational exercise? Not a chance. It's not great PR to kill your allies while you're training 'em."

Vega moved his backpack so his Beretta M9 was in reach. Broussard did the same. Neither had gone unarmed since the *Alicia* incident. Another "milk run."

"Got it on the scope yet?" the pilot asked.

"Christ, yes," said the copilot. "She's huge. Be over her in twenty."

M/T *CHINA STAR*
0618 HOURS LOCAL TIME
4 JULY

The boats were visible now and Rupat Island a dark slash ahead. Sheibani looked into the wheelhouse at the captives, wondering which would foul themselves when the boats exploded. It would be amusing when they found themselves unharmed. Like killing them twice. And Yousif. He would be denied even the illusion of martyrdom and understand before he died just how he had been used.

"Chopper." Richards pointed.

"Sooner than expected," Sheibani said, unconcerned. "Very well. Let us end it."

He smiled on his way to the VHF. "We'll soon be in Paradise, Yousif. *Allahu Akbar!*"

"*Allahu Akbar!*" Yousif parroted with a nervous grin.

Sheibani keyed the mike, and the roar of engines split the air as the boats rocketed away. Five hundred yards out and they turned, and the crews shouted encouragement to each other before speeding at *China Star*, rooster tails behind them.

***

"Boats moving away," the pilot said, swinging the chopper to frame the boats in the open side door. As Vega and Broussard watched, the boats turned, their crews shouting and gesturing before the sea behind the boats boiled and the boats shot forward.

"Those are our boats!" Broussard screamed into his mike. "They're gonna ram the tanker! Suicide bombers!"

"Get closer," Vega said. "Put us right on their asses and keep them in the door."

"Roger that," the pilot said as he descended and closed on the boats sideways. Vega and Broussard left their seats and gripped grab rails as they opened fire.

Firing pistols from an unstable platform at a bobbing target was a long shot. They hoped to get lucky. They didn't. The boats separated, making it impossible to target both, and the second man in each boat manned a .50-caliber machine gun. The pilot turned to present a minimal target and fled.

Broussard and Vega watched fireballs erupt at the ship's side, followed by booming thunderclaps as water and debris rained down. They awaited secondary blasts that never came.

***

Sheibani and Richards emerged from behind the drawn curtains of the chart room, where they'd sheltered against the possibility of flying glass. Sheibani walked toward a confused Yousif as Richards stepped out on the wing.

"Just burn marks on the hull and debris in the water," Richards said as he returned. "The chopper's hovering a mile off, probably reporting. Let's go."

"In good time," Sheibani said and smiled at Yousif.

"I… I don't understand," Yousif said. "Why didn't we explode?"

Sheibani shrugged. "Our brothers' sacrifice was a regrettable but necessary subterfuge."

"You had men martyr themselves for… some sort of… of trick?"

"Just so," Sheibani said. "Now, as far as you are concerned—"

"For Christ's sake," Richards said. "If you wanna give speeches, run for Congress." He shot Yousif in the face.

"I told you no head shots!" Sheibani yelled, looking down at Yousif's ruined face.

"So they ID him with DNA and fingerprints," Richards said. "He's wearing armor, genius. Should I have shot him in the foot and waited for gangrene? Let's finish and go."

"Very well," Sheibani said. "Since you're so eager, you do the honors."

Without hesitation, Richards shot Urbano in the head, but as he turned the gun on Bonifacio, Holt shoved the third mate, and Richards's burst went wide, shredding the man's ear and shoulder. As Bonifacio fell, Holt charged, aiming a left-handed haymaker at Richards while deflecting the gun with his right hand. Richards slipped the punch and it glanced off his head. Unable to raise his gun, he fired a burst across Holt's thighs and twisted like a matador as the captain's momentum carried him wounded to the deck.

Richards scrambled backward and felt his ear, cursing as his hand came away bloody.

"Why the hell didn't you shoot him?" he demanded over his shoulder.

"I assumed you could kill unarmed men. Now if you're done mucking about, we can—"

Sheibani jerked at an explosion to port.

***

The chopper hovered, with orders from *Hermitage* to "continue at discretion," which the pilot figured meant he was screwed no matter what.

"Whadda ya think, Chief?" he asked. "Not much damage."

"I concur, sir," Vega said.

"Get closer," Broussard urged. "We need to know what we're facing."

"Listen, Rambo," said the pilot, "our entire arsenal is your unauthorized peashooters."

"C'mon, Lieutenant," Broussard said. "The .50s are gone, and they're not likely to take us down with small arms. We can get closer."

"*We* aren't flying this bird, sailor. That would be *me*."

"The orders *are* to continue surveillance, sir," Vega said. "Can't see much from here."

"Shit. All right, we'll circle fast, then dart out of range."

He tilted the chopper toward *China Star*.

M/T *China Star*

Anderson waited to dash up the exterior stairway to the starboard bridge wing. The sea was littered with debris, and he stood parsing this latest development. They had one gun, limited ammunition, and grenades taken from the lounge. A search of the workshops had yielded no weapons but led to the discovery that inspired their plan. They'd found scuba gear and two underwater scooters on the starboard side of main deck.

The plan was to get between the hijackers and the hostages and leave the escape path clear. They had crept to D Deck, one level below the bridge, and Anderson waited on the starboard exterior stairs for Santos to creep through the deckhouse and toss a grenade overboard to port as a diversion. With the hijackers focused on the port side, Anderson hoped to rush onto the bridge from starboard and get between the hostages and hijackers, keeping them at bay until Santos joined him. He hoped that, faced with resistance, the hijackers would run.

But the explosion of the boats confused things, and Anderson crouched against the side of the house, unsure. He flinched at gunfire above. God damn it, they were killin' 'em. He rushed up the stairs just as an explosion sounded from the far side of the ship.

***

Sheibani rushed to the port wing. Richards glanced at the unmoving men, then backed after him. "What's going on?" he demanded over his shoulder.

He reached the port door just as Anderson charged in from starboard, firing. Outside, Sheibani dived aft for cover. Richards began to return fire just as a poorly aimed bullet from Anderson caromed off a window frame into his armor with stinging force. He backed outside through the door and ducked down beside Sheibani.

***

All for nothing, Anderson thought as he took cover. The bastards killed everyone.

"Christ," Holt growled. "You couldn't hit a bull in the ass with a fucking bass fiddle."

Relief washed over Anderson. "You OK, Dan?" he asked over his shoulder.

"Of course I'm not OK, you dumb ass," Holt snarled. "The son of a bitch shot me." He went on with a catch in his voice. "And they killed the others."

Anderson fired at movement, striking the doorway near where he'd aimed, just as Santos burst through the starboard door and dropped down beside Bonifacio.

"Boney is alive," Santos said. "Not too much blood. I think he will live."

The third mate groaned as Santos dragged him to cover.

"Thank God," Holt said from behind the steering stand, crawling to retrieve Yousif's gun and then forward to help Anderson.

"Ben," Anderson said, "encourage them to leave with one of those grenades."

***

131

"Fuck this," Richards said. "Like you said, let's leave them and get out of here."

"That was the engineers. The bridge crew heard things. And may live, thanks to you."

They bickered. Sheibani was considering shooting Richards himself when a grenade clanged down beside them on a crazy bouncing path, past them and over the edge of the deck to explode below on top of the lifeboat.

"Beard of the Prophet," Sheibani said, "how I wish we'd kept some grenades."

"Uh… I have one," Richards said, groping in a side pocket.

Allah deliver me, Sheibani thought.

"Then throw it, you idiot. And make sure to pull the pin."

Sheibani raised his head at a sound as the chopper loomed toward them.

"Our toothless friends are coming to watch, Richards. Please don't disappoint."

***

The chopper was running in fast from starboard when the pilot pulled up at muzzle flashes inside the wheelhouse. Something exploded on the far side of the ship, and a large armed man in bloody coveralls bolted up the starboard stairs and into the wheelhouse. More shooting.

"Folks aren't playing nicely," the pilot said.

"Good guys and bad guys, but who's who?" Broussard asked as a small man dashed up the stairs and into the wheelhouse.

"Company coveralls," Vega said. "Must be crew. Bad guys must be to port."

The pilot circled far to the port, in time to see a grenade explode on top of the lifeboat. Broussard trained binoculars on black-clad figures crouched just aft of the open bridge door. One looked up.

"Sheibani!" Broussard screamed. "That murdering bastard! Get us closer!" He loaded a full clip as Vega did the same.

The pilot slowed and studied the weapons in the hands of the terrorists.

"Lieutenant," Vega said, "that scumbag killed three of my men. Skinned one of 'em alive. We can't hover with our thumb up our ass and do nothing… sir!"

"Roger that, Chief," the pilot said as he slipped the chopper sideways at the ship.

"OK, junior," Vega said, sitting on the deck with feet toward the door, "let's improve our odds." He rolled on his side and raised his knees, the Beretta between them in a two-handed grip, pointing out the door. "Squeeze your knees together for support," he said, and Broussard copied. "We'll be stable and smaller targets. Course, if they drill us, we'll be singing soprano."

"Lieutenant," Vega continued, "keep us a little high so we don't take friendly fire from inside and vice versa, and angled down a bit so we can see the targets."

"Roger that, Chief. Good hunting."

Broussard was trying not to think about a bullet in the balls.

"Target left," Vega said, indicating he would take Richards.

"Sheibani is mine," Broussard confirmed.

"Let's do it, junior," Vega said.

***

A bullet ricocheted beside Sheibani and whined away. He aimed at the black square of the chopper door but saw nothing except an indistinct mass near the bottom of the square.

"Hurry, fool," he said. "We must kill them and get inside."

Richards rose to his knees, the door to his left. To minimize exposure, he would throw left-handed. He flinched as a bullet whined off a bulkhead, pulled the pin, and twisted to his left.

***

Vega knew the range was absurd. They were shooting downward, so they didn't have to worry too much about the bullets dropping over the ridiculous distance, but all they could really do was put rounds in the general vicinity and hope. He shot economically nonetheless, adjusting as the pilot closed the range. He was thankful his target was not returning fire until he saw the man draw back to throw. In a heartbeat, Vega evaluated the situation and emptied the clip as fast as he could pull the trigger.

None of Vega's fusillade struck his target directly, but a ricochet clipped the man's ankle midway through his throw. He jerked and released the grenade prematurely. It sailed forward over the wind dodger, tumbled to the main deck far below, and bounced over the side to explode harmlessly. Broussard, hearing Vega's fire and deluged by ejected casings, also changed to rapid fire.

***

"I'm outta here," Richards said as bullets struck around them. He rose to a crouch and limped aft. Sheibani moved in concurrence, passing him to rush ahead down the stairs and into the shelter of the deckhouse.

***

Anderson's joy at the retreat was brief.

"The Chartroom door," he shouted and rushed through the curtains with Santos.

Santos held the door open and stood aside, giving Anderson a clear shot at anyone topping the stairs. They tensed as a door opened below, followed by hurried footfalls descending the stairs, away from them.

"They're running," Anderson whispered. "It's over, Ben."

"Not yet, boss," Santos said, plunging through the door.

***

The stairs were solid plate, and Santos knew a blast at one level would be contained. At D Deck he tossed a grenade, banking it like a billiard ball off the bulkhead of the next landing down, so it bounced down the stairs after the fleeing hijackers.

"For Paco and Juni," he said his cousins' names as he ducked back and covered his ears.

***

Sheibani heard the clatter and leapt the last steps to the B Deck landing, grabbing the handrail to slingshot around the landing and continue his plunge, feet hitting every third step. He was well out of the kill zone when the grenade detonated at limping Richards's back.

His ears rang as he resumed his downward rush, thankful he'd delayed killing Richards. He'd planned to leave the American's body on the bridge, his gambit of preparing two sets of escape equipment a ruse. But Allah had preserved the American as a shield. He pushed Richards from his mind. He had to get out of the stairwell. One more deck to go.

***

Santos hit the landing fast, slipping in Richards's slimy remains and crashing to his knees. He tossed the grenade from his knees, banking it once again off the lower-landing bulkhead. "For Victor," he invoked his brother-in-law's

134

name before ducking back. He covered his ears just as he heard the main-deck fire door open. Missed him, he thought, as he awaited the blast.

***

The main-deck fire door slammed behind Sheibani as he ran down the passageway and clamped hands over his ears just before the blast. After the blast, he straightened, training his gun on the fire door. "Come out, come out, my foolish friend," he whispered.

The engineer threw open the fire door, then ducked back to the safety of the stairwell as bullets bit through the metal cladding of the door as it swung closed. Sheibani cursed himself for falling for the ruse and reflected. If the monkey had grenades left he would have tossed one, and if armed, he couldn't fire without exposing himself. Sheibani watched the door and stripped off his armor one-handed, dumping it on the deck while backing toward the starboard door. Outside, he closed the heavy steel watertight door behind him, twisting the handle of a closing dog with a solid clunk as the door seated, then jamming all six dogs to delay pursuit. He grinned as he donned the scuba gear. The chopper still hovered to port, and the monkey trembled in the stairwell, no doubt pleased at slaying the idiot Richards. They would still be searching the ship when he was halfway ashore.

***

Santos slipped back up the stairs to retrieve the dead hijacker's gun. When he returned to main-deck level, he heard a door slam and the dogs of a watertight door being engaged. He threw the fire door open for a look, darting his head out near the deck, where it wouldn't be expected. Seeing no threat, he moved into the passageway, not to starboard after Sheibani but to port, to exit the house on the opposite side and circle astern, aft of the machinery casing. He moved deliberately, in no hurry now.

***

Sheibani laughed aloud as he hefted the sea scooter by its handles, its weight pressed against his thighs as he lugged it to the ship's side. Five feet from the rail, his world went black.

***

The booby traps were Santos's idea. Anderson had lifted each sea scooter as Santos used duct tape from the bosun's shop to tape a grenade in the recess just in front of the propeller cowling. He left the grenade handle pointing downward, held against the deck by the weight of the unit, and then taped the grenade handle to the deck so it wouldn't fly off and alert the terrorists when they lifted the units. Finally, he had pulled the pins.

Santos waited out of sight. He feared the booby traps would be seen and had pressed the hijackers hard down the stairwell to keep them distracted. If the remaining man did disarm the trap, Santos intended to charge forward as he splashed into the water and rain the remaining grenades down on him.

Santos flinched at the explosion and then raced past the blackened remains of the sea scooter to where Sheibani lay unmoving. His upper body was intact, shielded by the heavy body of the scooter, but both legs were severed above the knees. Bright arterial blood pumped from the stumps and puddled on the deck. Sheibani groaned.

Santos squatted, bringing his face close.

"Can you hear, you fatherless son of a whore?" Santos asked.

Sheibani nodded.

"Then know this is for the men you murdered today." Santos spit in Sheibani's face.

The Iranian looked up with a mocking grin as spittle ran down his cheek.

"And this," Santos whispered, rising and unzipping, "is from their families. Do you think Allah will gather you into Paradise reeking of piss?"

Sheibani's smile vanished as urine stung his eyes.

***

Santos sat in bloody coveralls, staring at the body, hugging his knees, and crying. Tears of mourning for his family, friends, and shipmates. Tears of release from terror. But mainly tears of relief that when the mothers and fathers and women and children of his shipmates mourned their men, they would know their men had been avenged, and that Benjamin Honesto Santos had not hidden like a frightened rabbit, waiting to testify.

***

The chopper hovered, its occupants staring down at the sobbing man. They had arrived in time to watch in shocked silence as the scene played out below them.

"Who the hell is that guy?" the pilot asked.

"I don't know his name yet," Broussard said, "but he's my new best friend."

"Amen to that," Vega said.

CHAPTER NINETEEN

CIA Headquarters
Langley, Virginia
Local Time 4 July

Ward pulled into his parking spot. Traffic before daylight on a holiday had been almost nonexistent, but he knew that would change. If he didn't get home ahead of the jam sure to follow the Fourth of July parade, his ass would be in a crack. He smiled as he got out and headed into the building; after twenty years of long hours and blown holidays, the "I'm busy saving the world" excuse no longer cut much ice with Dee Dee.

Brice had few details when he'd called earlier. He'd promised Ward an e-mail update as soon as he learned more. True to his word, Ward found an e-mail waiting. Christ. Twenty-four dead seamen. Four survivors. Two wounded. Ten dead bad guys, but no one to interrogate. None of it made sense. Ward picked up the phone.

"Jim Brice."

"Jim. Jesse Ward."

"I've been expecting your call," Brice said. "It's confusing as hell, isn't it?"

"I'll say. It looks like it was over before we got there," Ward said.

"Essentially it was," Brice said. "The bad guys murdered most of the crew, and the four survivors took out the bad guys with an able assist from our surveillance chopper."

"Political fallout?"

"I think we dodged a bullet," Brice said. "Captain Leary was masterful. He planted the seed with his Indonesian counterpart on the exercise that Jakarta was unlikely to throw bouquets to anyone who got them involved. Simultaneously, he got the Singaporeans to convince the Malaysians it would be a coup if they saved the day. When the Indonesian waffled about *China Star*'s position, the Malaysian promptly agreed she was in Malaysian waters and accepted Leary's offer of choppers for a boarding party of Malaysian marines. Leary then arranged a tow to the anchorage off Jurong, where the Singaporeans will fend off the press and sequester survivors."

Ward smiled. "Good for him. I guess he's still in the running for an admiral's star then. But tell me, how is it two explosive-laden boats blow up against a loaded tanker and only leave a dent and scratch the paint?"

"Only way we can figure," Brice said, "is that the boats held shape charges directed back on the boats themselves, away from the ship. We'll know more when forensics gets through with the pieces of the boats we salvaged."

"Strange."

"That's not the half of it, Jesse. What I didn't put in the report, because I just found out, was the composition of the assault team."

"Go on."

"Three Burmese rent-a-thugs," Brice said, "and four Indonesian villagers longing for Paradise. It's the remaining three that are interesting. One was the ex–chief mate off *Alicia* and the guy that masterminded the hijacking of the boats. Broussard and Vega ID'd him, but we have no idea who he really is. Then there's a rogue American named Richards: ex–US Army, ex–private-security contractor, in our files as a known bad actor. We used him on some low-level stuff a time or two, but he was way too volatile and unstable. He was cut off the company Christmas-card list some time ago." Brice hesitated.

"You're one short," Ward prompted.

"Yeah, the last guy could be a problem. Yousif Nassir Hamad AKA Joe Hamad, Ensign USNR. The cream of the latest crop of NROTC graduates, allegedly on compassionate leave in Dearborn, Michigan."

"Oh shit," Ward said.

"Shit is right. This kid's the poster child for Arab-American assimilation. The navy was ready to put his picture on recruiting posters." Brice paused. "Like I said. A problem."

"You got a solution?" Ward asked.

"We're working on it."

"Need any help?" Ward asked.

"We're good. But we'd like the body to stay 'unidentified' a while. Do what you can to make sure no one at Langley gets hot to trot to run down the identities of every single assailant. I need a little breathing room here."

"Done," Ward said and wished Brice luck.

***

Three hours later, Ward was still at his desk, trying to piece together the strange parts of the puzzle. Should he call Gardner? He didn't look forward to that conversation. Ward smiled. Screw it. He'd been right about *China Star*, so Gardner couldn't come down too hard. And since his boss was going to be pissed anyway, he might as well combine the chewing out for disobeying orders along with one for failing to keep Gardner informed. Two transgressions for the price of one.

Ward glanced at the time and shut down his computer. He might have time to get home and spend the afternoon hosting his holiday cookout before he got an irate call from Gardner. That would get Dee Dee off his back, at least.

Ward was locking his door when Gardner appeared.

"Where the hell do you think you're going?"

"Home," Ward said.

"Not before we talk. I'll call you in when I'm ready." Gardner stomped off without waiting for a reply.

Ward glared at Gardner's back.

***

As it turned out, Gardner did get a call—from the deputy director of the CIA. The Old Man received a morning briefing report 365 days a year. In a slight nod toward relaxation, on holidays he delayed perusing the report until after a late breakfast and most of a pot of coffee, but when something attracted the Old Man's interest, he inquired. *China Star* qualified.

Blindsided, Gardner had panicked at mention of *China Star*, weighing his options. Just before he threw Ward under the bus, the Old Man offered a gruff "well done."

"Just doing our job, sir," Gardner had replied before a polite good-bye.

He was enraged at Ward's disobedience, all the more so since the man had apparently been right. His first instinct was to pick up the phone, but he quickly had second thoughts. If he could get into the office and ahead of Ward on the information curve, maybe he could paint Ward as out of touch and not doing his job. He might not be able to openly punish the man for disobeying orders, but there was more than one way to skin a cat.

Gardner's plan had fallen apart when he found Ward in the office. His only outlet for petty retribution was to keep Ward waiting as he skimmed the intel from Singapore and simmered. After a cursory review, he decided to kill a bit more time by checking his e-mail, and his eyes were drawn to a flashing "high priority" icon. As he read the message, his frown morphed into a smile. He printed the e-mail and punched his speed dial.

"Ward. Get in here."

***

Ward controlled his anger as Gardner waved him to a chair.

"So, you were right," Gardner said. "I guess even a blind pig finds the odd acorn."

You're welcome, asshole, Ward thought.

"But don't go getting too smug"—Gardner shoved a paper across the desk—"because your instincts about Dugan are a bit further off the mark."

Ward studied the printout detailing transfer of a million dollars through several accounts with terrorist associations into and out of a new Cayman Island account, held by a series of dummy corporations and trusts that led back to Thomas Dugan.

"Dugan's under financial surveillance?"

"You're god damned right," Gardner said.

"Larry, we've had his financials forever. Dugan's not for sale, and if he was, it'd take a lot more than this. This is chump change."

Gardner scoffed. "So someone wasted a million bucks to set up your buddy?"

"Not really. The money's gone. What's that tell you?"

"That Dugan's smart. He made it disappear."

"Yet dumb enough to leave a trail in the first place? I don't think so, Larry."

"Whatever. Dugan and Kairouz are still our prime suspects. Clear?"

"Crystal," Ward said.

"Good. Get out." Gardner shut down his computer as Ward rose.

"Wait a minute," Gardner said. "Where's your pal now? I don't want him to disappear."

Ward stifled his anger and looked at his watch. "He's on his way to Panama. He's not going to disappear."

"Whatever. At least the asshole is out of the way for a while." Gardner also checked the time. "I'll be at the parade," Gardner said. "Senator Gunther invited me to sit with him on the reviewing stand. Call me if there are any developments."

Ward nodded and walked down the hall, dreaming of putting a bullet into Gardner's head.

CHAPTER TWENTY

Reyes hung up the phone. Something was very strange. *Asian Trader* hadn't delayed on the Pacific side even long enough to off-load the dead seaman's body. A death at sea was traumatic for all concerned, and usually the company involved was eager to land the remains and put the event behind them. The ship's agent had also seemed surprised, saying only that he was following orders from a Señor Dugan that nothing should prevent the ship from meeting her priority transit slot.

Given the accelerated transit, Reyes had expected pushback when he told the agent that since *Asian Trader* wouldn't anchor at Cristobal until early evening, the inquiry would start the following morning in daylight. The agent had seemed unconcerned, allowing that was expected, and in any event, Señor Dugan himself would attend the inquiry and was not arriving until later this evening.

Now why would an owner pay dearly for early transit and then so easily accept delay? He had many questions for this Señor Dugan. But that was tomorrow.

He looked at the stack in his in-box and sighed. He'd actually been looking forward to getting out of the office for a while. He glanced at the time and considered calling Maria to meet him for lunch later. Then he remembered. She was helping with the field trip to the locks today. He smiled as he remembered the twins' excited chatter at breakfast about seeing the big ships.

His smile faded as he looked back at the in-box. He sighed again and picked up a file.

OBSERVATION DECK
MIRAFLORES LOCKS VISITOR CENTER
PANAMA

"*Aiee! Miguelito. Cuidado.*" Maria Reyes grabbed her son. "No climbing. That means you too, Paco," she added to his brother about to join his twin on the rail.

"*Si, Mama,*" said the boys in sullen unison before the ship in the lock recaptured their attention. Maria smiled and stepped back where she could keep an eye on all the children.

The passengers on the big white ship waved back at the excited children until the vessel moved away toward Pedro Miguel, replaced by a container ship, stacked high with colored boxes. With a mother's eye, Maria noticed the onset of boredom as here and there children began to act out. She grabbed a boy racing by, hugging him close.

"Is this Alejandro I have captured, running when he knows not to do so?"

"*No, señora,*" the boy said with an impish grin.

"You are not Alejandro? You look just like him. Well, if you see him, please remind him not to run."

"*Si, señora,*" said not-Alejandro.

"Good." She released him with a playful swat. "Behave yourself and earn a treat."

As not-Alejandro spread news of treats, Maria glanced at Señora Fuentes, who mimed eating. Maria nodded and herded the children toward the stairs. She hoped they liked her cookies. She knew two of them would. She smiled as she watched her sons, little copies of their father. If Manny returned from Cristobal early, she thought, they might work on their little "project." A daughter would be nice this time.

M/T *ASIAN TRADER*
APPROACHING PEDRO MIGUEL LOCK
PANAMA

The detonator felt heavy in Medina's pocket as *Asian Trader* stood second in line at Pedro Miguel Lock, ships stretched behind her through Miraflores back to the Pacific. He watched the gates close on the leader, a tanker whose bright paint marked her as fresh from the builder's yard, and glared at the American flag hanging limp above the name M/T *Luther Hurd* painted on her stern.

The captain relayed an engine order from the pilot, and Medina moved the joystick, inching *Asian Trader*'s port side along the center guide wall projecting from between the double locks. Heaving lines flew to drag aboard wires to attach the ship to the mechanical "mules" that would pull her through the lock, and Medina watched the *Luther Hurd* complete her vertical journey and inch from the lock ahead of them toward Gaillard Cut and Gatun Lake beyond.

Allah had been generous since the bosun's death, cooling the deck with daily showers, but today the sun hammered the steel, and Medina worried about fumes. His target was Gatun Locks across Gatun Lake, where even a blast failing to breach the lock could destroy several ships and plug the locks with scrap. His secondary target was here at Pedro Miguel, which like the upper lock at Gatun, held back the lake. Destruction of either would drain the lake and destroy the canal, with catastrophic secondary damage. Allah guide me, Medina prayed as the ship inched forward amid clanging bells, the mules tugging her into the lock.

CRUISE SHIP *STELLAR SPIRIT*

The second mate of *Stellar Spirit* stood among the passengers lining the rail as a tanker crept into the east lock and his own ship prepared to enter the west. Mingling was required of the ship's officers, not a chore on "fun runs" with willing young females eager for romance, but deadly dull on canal runs populated by oldsters and honeymooners who surfaced only for meals. The newly wed and the nearly dead, he thought, looking over gray heads to the gates closing behind *Asian Trader* as he debated slipping away.

M/T *ASIAN TRADER*
IN PEDRO MIGUEL LOCK, PANAMA

In the end, Medina's decision was made for him.

"Bridge, this is the bow," squawked the radio. "I smell strong gasoline fumes, repeat, strong gasoline fumes on deck. Over."

Medina pulled his gun and was moving even before the control pilot keyed his radio to respond, rushing to the port bridge wing to shoot both the control pilot and captain in the head before returning to the wheelhouse to meet the confused assisting control pilot coming in from the starboard wing. He ended the man's confusion with a bullet. The terrified helmsman fled the wheelhouse, down the outside stairs. Medina didn't bother to chase him. He was calm now as he returned to the starboard wing, sure that when the people of his grandfather's village spoke now, it would be of Saful, Sword of Islam, not Faatina, Whore of the Infidel.

"Allahuuuuu Akbaaaaar!" he screamed as he thumbed the remote.

***

The blast was beyond imagination, amplified by Medina's design. Twelve blasts actually, grouped in pairs and separated by milliseconds, starting aft to build into a directional force, battering the gates that held the lake at bay.

The canal's designers were no strangers to redundancy, and the locks had double, massively overdesigned gates, the twin leaves of each mitered pair meeting in a point upstream so the weight of water pressed them closed as a lock drained. A good design, but unequal to a blast of near nuclear strength. The gates crumpled like tinfoil and ripped free, their useless remains undulating in the rushing torrent, impeded only by the debris from *Asian Trader*.

Constrained by the lock walls and the incompressible water beneath the ship, the blast forced an escape upward, ripping the entire cargo-tank section free of the ballast tanks and tossing it into the air to crash down at an angle, one end landing on *Asian Trader's* bow and the other on *Stellar Spirit* as the passenger ship nosed into the western lock. Checked at either end but unsupported in the middle, the cargo section split like an overripe fruit, ruptured tanks gushing tons of gasoline into the torrent now rushing through the open lock.

In the lock, watertight integrity vanished from *Asian Trader's* battered remains as the forward collision bulkhead collapsed into the forepeak tank, and her after pump-room machinery was driven through the engine-room bulkhead. She sank, pushed by the torrent as she settled but restrained by remnants of the outer hull blasted tight against the lock walls. The steel screamed like a living thing as it yielded, a huge friction brake holding the mass upright as it settled to the lock floor.

The end of the ruptured cargo block resting on *Asian Trader's* bow dropped as the bow sank beneath it until the middle of the cargo block rested on the wall separating the locks. There the section teetered, the high end on *Stellar Spirit*, the middle on the wall between the locks, and the low end dangling unsupported over the ruined lock, as spilled gasoline ignited, turning the entire scene into a maelstrom and sucking air from passengers still alive deep in the cruise ship. The flames rushed southward on the flood, a fiery wall of death moving toward Miraflores, Balboa, and the wide Pacific beyond.

"Christ. What was that?" asked Captain Vince Blake as he hung on the windowsill and stared out through the cracked glass of the bridge windows. The pilot shook his head and raced to the wing, Blake on his heels. Blake could see men down on *Luther Hurd*'s bow, some beginning to stir. He moved to the back of the bridge wing and saw a similar scene on the stern.

"Everyone's down," Blake said, "will you take the conn while I organize help?"

"Do it," the pilot said, moving to the opposite wing as Blake raced to the phone.

"Engine Room. Chief," Jim Milam answered.

"You OK down there, Chief?"

"I think so. What happened, Cap?"

"Explosion ashore. The mate's down on the bow, and I can't see the second. We're in the cut, and I can't leave the bridge. Can you—"

"We're on it," Milam said.

"Thanks, Jim," Blake said, hanging up to join the pilot on the starboard wing.

He followed the pilot's gaze ashore, confused.

"We've slowed down?"

The pilot shook his head. "There's a current," he said, pointing at eddies and flotsam moving along the bank.

Oh shit, Blake thought.

"Full ahead," the pilot said.

"Full ahead," Blake relayed the order to the third mate at the joystick.

The pilot stared ahead, fear in his eyes.

MIRAFLORES LOCKS VISITOR CENTER

Maria pushed herself up from the sun-heated tiles, relief washing over her at the sight of her sons nearby, stunned and crying but unhurt. Señora Fuentes's timing had been fortunate, placing them in the patio area behind the building before the blast. The teacher herself was less so. She lay on the tile in a growing circle of blood, the back of her head smashed on the corner of a concrete bench. Maria fought down panic and crossed herself before closing the teacher's sightless eyes.

The other mothers had recovered and were calming the terrified children, dabbing at scrapes with napkins wet with bottled water. Outside their sheltered corner, the ground was dotted with bodies and sparkled with broken glass. A big blond man staggered onto the bridge wing of the ship in the lock and peered upstream.

Suddenly, Maria stood in water and the man screamed, pointing as she splashed from her corner to look. Water poured over the lock gate. What didn't fall into the lock fanned out in shallow waves, lapping at buildings to slosh back and fall into the lock from the sides. Mule wires moaned as the ship rose, operators dead or unconscious, unable to slack the wires. One by one, the mules were pulled from their tracks and overturned. Upstream, beyond the colored boxes of a container ship, she saw a yellow blur.

"Fire!" the blond man screamed. "Go inside! High! Away from the windows!"

Maria called to Isobel and Juanita, and the three mothers started the group up the outside steps to the observation deck, Maria clutching her boys' hands as she brought up the rear, counting heads. The first level was littered with bodies and glass crunched underfoot as the mothers ignored scattered moans and herded their charges upward. They had to save the children.

The children were all crying by the time they reached the next level. Maria could feel the heat.

"No time to go higher," she shouted, trying a door. "We must get inside!"

The door was locked. The building was controlled access with entrance from the ground floor only. Doors relocked behind people as they exited to the observation decks at each level.

"The toilets," she yelled, and the women herded the children toward three doors near the end of the observation deck.

"There is no room," Maria said as the other mothers divided the children between the two small restrooms. "I will put my boys in the janitor's closet."

Isobel nodded as the door closed, and Maria was left alone with her sons. She dragged them to the tiny closet, faint with relief to find a janitor's sink filling the small space. She lifted her boys into the big sink and turned on the cold water, stilling their protests with slaps.

"Listen to me," she said. "Do not turn the water off. Keep your heads under and only stick your noses out. Understand?"

"Don't leave, *Mama*," Paco pleaded.

"If I stay, we cannot close the door. I'll be fine with the others," she lied. "Remember I love you, *hijos*," she added softly.

"*Si, Mama*," the boys sobbed as she closed the door.

God, protect my sons, she prayed, moving through the heat.

"Your boys aren't here," Juanita said as Maria pushed in. "They must be in the other toilet with Isobel."

Maria forced a smile and prayed God would forgive her for putting her own children in a more sheltered location. "Yes, but there's no more room there," she lied. "I'm your new roommate."

Juanita nodded as Maria fished out her cell phone—to find it dead. An image flashed of Manny chiding her for not keeping her battery charged. Oh *Mi Amor*, she thought, I hope you know what a wonderful life you have given me.

"Do you have your cell?" she asked Juanita.

Juanita shook her head. "I left my purse in the excitement."

Maria nodded as the roar and heat increased.

"Oh Maria, what can we do?" Juanita asked.

"It's in God's hands, Juanita," Maria said. "We should pray."

Juanita nodded, unable to speak, as Maria turned to the children.

"Children, we will talk to God. Please hold hands and help each other be brave."

They joined hands as she prayed. "*Padre nuestro que estas en el cielo, santificado...*"

CNN CENTER
ATLANTA, GEORGIA

The blast enlivened a slow news day in the US with newsrooms on holiday staffing. In moments, a CNN staffer discovered the Internet camera feed from the Canal Authority, with real-time photos of ships in transit. Five minutes later, he dreamed of a bonus as he e-mailed photos of the final feed of the Centennial Bridge camera: one of a man on the bridge of the M/T *Asian Trader*, mouth open in a shout, a gun in one hand and a remote in the other; the second showed the explosion. The photos were aired in two minutes flat, and within five, all the networks had them. Talking heads speculated, and executives screamed at people to get some goddamned facts or to make them up if necessary.

PEDRO MIGUEL LOCK
PANAMA

Breach of an upper lock was an event long feared, for the canal's designers had respect for the forces of God and nature, an outlook validated just months before the canal's opening when the "unsinkable" Titanic plunged to the bottom. But fears faded with decades of safe operation until they seemed as quaint as high button shoes. Gone were safety chains to restrain runaway ships, removed in 1980 in admission that ships were now so big as to make them useless. Eliminated earlier were the emergency dams meant to seal a breach; removed in the fifties after years of disuse. Only the double gates had survived, now blasted to scrap; for what design could anticipate the deluded fanaticism of *Jihad*?

***

The chopper hovered above Pedro Miguel as Juan Antonio Rojas, administrator of the Autoridad del Canal de Panama, watched gasoline drain from wrecked tanks, not a gush now but gurgling belches as air bubbled up to break vacuums. Each burp flared, but the gas burned near the source now, with only scattered islands of flame floating southward.

"It's burning out," he said into his mike.

"I pray you're right," said Pedro Calderon, ACP operations manager, from the seat behind Rojas.

"How fast are we losing the lake?" Rojas asked.

"Hard to say," Calderon said. "I'll know more after the next depth reading, but the lake was already low. If that plug fails…" He pointed at the wreckage partially blocking the lock.

As if in response, gasoline gushed anew from the ruined tanks, sending up a fireball and disturbing a precarious balance. For the ruptured tanks had not disgorged their contents evenly, and most of the gasoline remaining in the mangled mass was trapped in the lower, unsupported end. As the last of the cargo drained from the higher end, the cargo block pivoted on the central lock wall like a huge seesaw, the lighter end rising from *Stellar Spirit* as the lower end dipped toward the waters of the lock. The upper end of the cargo block was inches off the cruise ship when the fire-weakened steel buckled in the middle, dropping the higher end back down across *Stellar Spirit* as the lower end plunged into the lock. Water rose behind the new obstacle, forcing it down the lock and tearing it free of the remaining wreckage ashore. At the moment of separation, the portion of the cargo block in the lock shifted, filling the lock wall to wall as it slammed into the face of the ruined deckhouse.

***

The men in the chopper watched helplessly as the cargo section hit the deckhouse and shifted it several feet, then in grateful amazement as the water compacted the mass. Water gushed through in a dozen places and ran over the top inches deep on either side of the deckhouse, but the debris was damming the flood more effectively than before.

"*Gracias a Dios*," Rojas whispered. "It holds."

"*Y Jesus y Jose y Maria*," Calderon added as he crossed himself.

"Move over Miraflores," Rojas ordered the pilot, and in moments they were there.

Water swirled over the locks and down the slope a foot deep, carrying pools of burning gasoline, the flames dancing over the new rapids and around overturned mules on the lock walls as if they were rocks in a river roaring out of Hell. The operations building and visitors center smoldered, and a blackened container ship bobbed in a lock, surging against the gates astern in great hollow booms. But even as they watched, the flow ebbed and soon barely overtopped the complex.

"Get men here by chopper," Rojas ordered. "If we crack open the lock valves, we can drain off the water upstream from below the surface and contain floating gasoline north of Miraflores."

As Calderon spoke into his radio, Rojas looked southward. Gasoline burned in places, and nearby was a burning hulk, her bow hard aground, the first ship to meet the flames south of Miraflores. Faced with certain death, the pilot had warned those behind and bought them time by swinging his ship across the canal like a gate, slowing the flames and preventing his ship from drifting down on Balboa like a flaming battering ram.

Nor was that pilot the only hero, Rojas thought, squinting downstream where the busy docks were unharmed. After the pilots had turned their ships, they released their tugs to speed seaward under ships' power. The masters of the freed tugs had taken initiative, nosing into the bank at strategic points and using their propeller wash to divert the fire from the docks at Balboa, La Boca, and Rodman across the harbor.

"A crew is on the way, *jefe*," Calderon said. "I should return to the operations center."

"One stop more," Rojas said. "Gatun Locks," he said to the pilot.

"So, old friend," Rojas said as they flew north, "how long will the miracle hold?"

Calderon shrugged. "An hour... or a year. It's in God's hands."

Rojas nodded and fell silent until they hovered over Gatun Locks.

"I ordered everything out of the lake," Calderon said. "Seven client vessels came up from Cristobal before the attack. We will send them back down to Cristobal, along with the one northbound vessel that reached the lake. Eight ships total."

"Priorities?"

"Two tankers and three container ships all laden and with no way to reduce their drafts will go first. Then two passenger ships, with a tanker in ballast last. We'll get the deep-loaded vessels over the sill of the upper lock while we still have water. We'll lighten the others in the lake if necessary."

"The ballasted tanker is the new American ship?"

"*Si*. Her maiden voyage."

"Is that her?" Rojas pointed.

"*Si*," Calderon said, and Rojas motioned the pilot to circle the anchorage.

"So, Pedro. Who, do you think, was *El Señor Luther Hurd*?"

"No idea, *jefe*," Calderon said.

"Nor do I," Rojas said, "but perhaps we can make him famous. Leave the *yanqui* in the lake. I have an idea."

CHAPTER TWENTY-ONE

The photos on Ward's monitor seemed as unreal now as when they'd flashed on TV, prompting his return to work. Gardner had called to vent outrage Ward hadn't notified him immediately, hanging up as soon as he learned what little Ward knew. Ward knew little more now, hours later. The focus now was on Panama, but the spotlight would swing his way soon enough; and the spotlight was a bad place for a spook with no answers. He lifted the phone.

"Carlucci."

"Frank, Jesse Ward."

"Well," said Frank Carlucci, Panama Station Chief, "one of three people at HQ who hasn't called, besides the janitor and the snack-bar lady. How may I disappoint you?"

"That bad, huh?"

Carlucci sighed. "You don't wanna know."

"Yeah, I do. Can you update me?"

"Jesus H. Christ. Didn't that pompous asshole you work for fill you in? I spent twenty minutes answering his dumb-ass questions. Don't you people talk?"

"Gardner? When?"

"Over two hours ago," Carlucci said.

Ward stopped, embarrassed.

"Ah... I'm sorry, Frank. Could you..."

Carlucci relented. "OK, Jesse. The short version: Five ships toast, one a cruise ship, everyone dead. All three Pacific locks out of commission, with all ACP personnel dead. A hundred visitors at a visitors center, including a school group, all presumed dead. A bunch of American expats missing from a barbecue at Pedro Miguel Boat Club. Hospitals swamped with related casualties. The death toll is a guess. Pedro Miguel lock is breached but partially plugged by debris, and they're losing the lake. A total disaster."

"Shit," Ward said. "OK. I'm on the way. Keep Dugan with you when he arrives."

"Who?"

Christ. Gardner didn't tell him. Ward summarized the operation.

Carlucci exploded. "You knew about this and didn't warn us!"

"No, we didn't know. Look, Frank, it's a long story. I'll explain when I arrive."

"I hope you know what you're doin' here, Jesse."

Yeah, me too, Ward thought.

MIRAFLORES PALACE
CARACAS, VENEZUELA

Rodriguez awoke, savoring the silk sheets and Eva's skin as she lay atop him, tense and unmoving. He slapped the teenager's butt, laughing as she flinched.

"You let me oversleep. I should imprison you for treason." He chuckled as she leaped up, trembling.

He was still smiling minutes later as he entered his spacious outer office, gesturing to his secretary for coffee before nodding to his waiting chief of staff, who followed Rodriguez into his private office.

"What news?" Rodriguez asked, thumbing the TV remote.

"Excellency, there have been… developments…"

Rodriguez shushed him and raised the volume as scenes of devastation filled the screen.

"…over five thousand dead, including passengers of a cruise ship. Photos obtained by CNN show the attacker moments before the blast." A photo of a man with upraised arms appeared. "…unconfirmed reports of a link to a similar attempt yesterday near Singapore…"

"This is a disaster! Why was I not informed immediately?" Rodriguez screamed.

"Forgive me, Excellency. But I have strict orders not to disturb your… *siestas.*"

"Could you not see this was an exception, imbecile?"

"I was not sure—"

"Out! Everyone out!" Rodriguez screamed as his coffee arrived, and his terrified secretary fled with the chief of staff, clutching the undelivered coffee.

His mind raced. If he was exposed, who knew what the Americans or Chinese might do. The Chinese might even be the greater threat, since any retaliation would likely be blamed on the Americans. He took the sat phone from a drawer, his single link to Braun. He smiled as his rage subsided and summoned his chief of staff.

"Come in, Geraldo," Rodriguez said agreeably as the man returned, still shaking.

"Destroy this phone within the hour and incinerate the debris. Also, due to the tragedy, our own Independence Day celebration tomorrow will be muted. Cancel the fireworks and other events. I will speak of our shared sorrow and announce the money saved will be added to our Panamanian Relief Fund."

"But Excellency, the money is spent. There will be no savings."

"Nor is there a relief fund, you idiot." Rodriguez shook his head at the man's inability to grasp the nuance of diplomacy.

OFFICES OF PHOENIX SHIPPING

"Hello," Basaev said in Paris.

"It's a go. Good luck," Braun said.

"Understood," Basaev said and hung up.

Braun was improvising in response to the unexpected. *China Star* was in Singapore, and coverage was limited while Panama dominated the news. Blow-dried anchormen had descended on the isthmus and hired every available helicopter at exorbitant rates, screaming "cover-up" at the Panamanian authorities' fruitless efforts to restrict air traffic over the canal. But things weren't all negative. The Black Sea vessel had berthed at last, allowing him to unleash Basaev. He just needed to wind things up while his luck still held.

He studied a CD, a dialogue pieced together from recordings of Rodriguez, Dugan, and Kairouz, with Rodriguez detailing the attacks and the others agreeing. Initially he'd been concerned with the focus on Panama, for Rodriguez talked of little else and he had to use what he had, but the unexpected severity of the Panamanian attack strengthened the ruse. The recording would be more credible still when Kairouz confirmed it, on pain of unspeakable horrors to befall Cassie. Things were coming together despite the unexpected.

He tapped out a message to Motaki.

RECENT EVENTS NO PROBLEM. FINAL PHASE INITIATED. TIDYING UP.

He encrypted the message and piggybacked it on to the porn-site video, then lingered on the site, aroused. He hated to celebrate alone. Perhaps sweet little Yvette had recovered.

PRESIDENTIAL RESIDENCE
TEHRAN, IRAN
0130 HOURS LOCAL TIME
5 JULY

Motaki stared at the monitor, bleary-eyed. US markets were closed for the holiday, and it was after market hours in Europe and Asia, but from Toronto to Sao Paulo gold and oil spiked. The panic was sure to roil Asian markets at the open. But where was Sheibani, and why was there no coverage of *China Star*? And more to the point, would the unintended disaster in Panama heighten global security and jeopardize the final strike?

He calmed himself. Everything was Allah's will. Panama was necessary to recruit Rodriguez, who provided Braun, who so cleverly blinded the infidels to Iran's role. Motaki slipped a hardware key into a port to allow access to his office e-mail. He expected the spam message but rose to ensure none of his sleeping family stirred before accessing the porn site.

He read Braun's message with relief. Soon now, he thought, glancing at the time. He wouldn't wait up for the Asian markets. He needed his rest.

HOSPITAL DEL NIÑOS
PANAMA CITY, PANAMA

Doctors scurried by, heads bent in urgent exchanges, struggling with disaster beyond even the worst postulated by planners of never-held emergency drills. Reyes reentered the room he'd fled when Miguelito had stirred and cried for Maria. Telling the boys terrified him because first he must accept it

154

himself, abandoning the lies he'd told himself when he couldn't reach her. But truth lay nearby in a makeshift morgue.

He met the sad gazes of his parents and in-laws. One grandmother sat at each bedside, holding the boys' hands as the men stood nearby quiet in their grief. Reyes's mother rose and took his face between her hands.

"You should rest, *hijo*. We will call if the little ones wake."

Reyes shook his head. "There is no rest for me, *Mama*."

"I know, *hijo*, I know. But you need this time to grieve. The boys need your strength."

Reyes folded her in a hug, then nodded and left. He was near the visitors lounge, crowded with people glued to a TV, when he heard his name.

"Manuel," Maria's father said, hurrying after him. "Do you know yet who did this?"

He shook his head. "No. I left the office when—"

He stared past his father-in-law and charged into the lounge to the TV.

"...confirmed the explosion of the M/T *Asian Trader* was the work of a suicide bomber, as shown in this photo obtained by CNN. At present, no group has claimed responsi—"

Reyes stared. After the blast, the search for his family had taken precedence. Only now did he hear the familiar name. He ran for the stairs.

BEIJING, PEOPLE'S REPUBLIC OF CHINA

President Zhang Wei waited until the steward poured tea and bowed from the room.

"So, gentlemen. What of these attacks?"

"They seem linked," Premier Wang Fei said.

"But motives are unclear," added Li Gang, Minister for State Security. "Malacca alone could be a US ruse to justify increased US Navy presence in the strait, but Panama makes no sense in that context."

Wang nodded. "We must consider it. Your instructions, Mr. President?"

"Tread cautiously," Zhang said. "Offer Panama our help while assuring the US our help is based on mutual interest and not to exert influence. The lie will be recognized, but reducing the burden on US taxpayers will make it palatable. Simultaneously, signal our resolve to protect our own interests in the Malacca Straits by rotating our new destroyers through to visit our friends in Myanmar on a regular basis."

"At once, Mr. President," Wang said. "Further thoughts?"

"Just one," Zhang said. "Not so very long ago, our Venezuelan friend petitioned us to lend financial support to a second canal in Nicaragua. As I recall, one of his main arguments was that it would reduce our vulnerability to trade disruption at Panama." He paused. "President Rodriguez was quite prescient, it seems."

"Almost clairvoyant," Wang agreed.

"Explore that," President Zhang said.

GARDNER RESIDENCE
ALEXANDRIA, VIRGINIA

Gardner cursed the Panamanians. He was on hold. Christ, what a day. He was at post-parade drinks at the Gunthers' when the news hit. He'd immediately called the DDCI and volunteered to "coordinate intelligence." That had backfired. Ward had been useless, and that territorial asshole Carlucci in Panama was worse. First he copped an attitude, and then tried a brush-off.

Gardner had soldiered on, working from home to dress up what little he knew into some semblance of a briefing. Then after all that, the Old Man rejected his offer of a personal Power Point presentation, insisting on a phone report—a mediocre recitation at best, and one it seemed the DDCI had already heard.

"Thanks, son," the Old Man said when he finished. "What's Ward's ETA in Panama?"

Carlucci had sandbagged him, obviously with Ward in on it. Blindsided, he'd played along. "This evening, sir. I'll call back with an updated ETA."

"Unnecessary. Just inform me of anything significant."

He'd found himself listening to a dial tone.

Ward left without so much as a "by-your-leave," and everyone knew but him. And Ward was apparently still unconvinced Dugan was dirty, even after finding the offshore account and the ship he was babysitting in Singapore blew up. Just how many "coincidences" was Ward going to swallow? And now the insubordinate bastard wasn't answering his phone.

Gardner fumed for hours, racking his brain for ways to reestablish control. He had to be careful though. Dugan's involvement was a problem. He'd documented his own suspicions of Dugan by initiating the financial probe, but he hadn't overridden Ward about involving Dugan in the first place, so he wasn't completely in the clear. It could get even messier if Ward continued to insist on the traitor's innocence. What was required was a clear, unambiguous confession, sooner rather than later.

Inspiration came after his third Glenfiddich. All it took was a word to the Panamanians. When Dugan confessed, Gardner's doubts were on record. If he didn't—well, Gardner could hardly be held responsible for the excesses of foreign police.

He smiled and poured another scotch, thinking pleasant thoughts as he waited.

***

Like everyone in Panama, Sergeant Juan Perez was working late, trying to wrest order from the chaos. He looked down at the flashing button on his phone, surprised at the gringo's persistence. He'd classified this Gardner as an asshole about ten seconds into the first call and lapsed into Spanish before hanging up. When multiple hang-ups failed to discourage him, Perez put him on "perpetual hold." True, it tied up one of his lines, but he had three and could only talk on one at a time anyway.

Perez looked up as Captain Luna emerged from his office, pointed at his watch, and mimed eating. Perez nodded and stood, giving his phone one last look before leaving. Perhaps the gringo asshole would give up before he returned from dinner.

***

Reyes waited outside until Captain Luna and Juan Perez left for dinner. He wanted no awkward condolences and feared he might be sent home. The squad room fell quiet as he entered, warning his colleagues away with body language and a grim face.

As he sat, he noticed the blinking "hold" light on one of the lines he shared with Perez.

"*Teniente Reyes. Quien habla?*"

"You speak English?" a voice blurted, obviously startled.

"Yes, I speak English. This is Lieutenant Reyes. Who is this?"

"Gardner, Lieutenant. Lawrence Gardner. I'm with the Central Intelligence Agency in Washington. I have confidential information regarding the *Asian Trader* situation."

Reyes bristled. Not a "situation," gringo. Murder. Who was this drunken asshole?

"Information, *señor*?"

"A man named Thomas Dugan arrives there this evening. You should question him."

Reyes sat bolt upright.

"Interesting, *señor*," he said. "This implies advanced knowledge of the attack, yet we had no warning from the CIA." His words held unmistakable menace.

"We knew nothing of the attack," Gardner sputtered, "but Dugan works for us. I mean he's supposed to, but I... that is, some of us... feel he's been turned. A great deal of money recently appeared in his offshore account, and he supervised repairs to *Asian Trader* in Singapore last month."

Gardner lowered his voice. "Please understand. Not everyone agrees with me. I'm warning you as a brother in arms. I appreciate your discretion."

"I will treat you as a confidential informant," Reyes lied.

"Thank you," Gardner said, relief in his voice.

"On the contrary, *señor*, thank you."

Reyes hung up without waiting for a response and thumbed through his notebook for Dugan's flight number and arrival time.

CHAPTER TWENTY-TWO

IBERIA AIRLINES FLIGHT 6307
APPROACHING PANAMA CITY, PANAMA
2125 HOURS LOCAL TIME
4 JULY

Lights brightened and Dugan stirred, trying to focus on the announcement.

"…attack. The airport is closed. We are cleared to refuel and will depart for Miami, where agents will meet us. Nonresidents attempting to deplane here will be reboarded."

A stewardess knelt beside him. "*Señor Dugan?*"

He nodded.

"You are to deplane. You will be met."

Met by whom, he wondered minutes later in the immigration line.

"*Señor Dugan,*" a big man said, taking Dugan's passport. "Come with me please."

"What's this about?" Dugan asked as he complied.

The man slammed Dugan against a wall and cuffed him, before dragging him toward an exit. A man approached, speaking unaccented Spanish.

"*Teniente Reyes.* I'll take Mr. Dugan now. Thank you."

"Regrettably, *Señor Carlucci*, he is under arrest," the big man said. "Unless, of course, he has immunity?"

He smiled at Carlucci's head shake.

"Then I will wish you good evening," he said.

JUDICIAL INVESTIGATIVE DIRECTORY HQ
PANAMA CITY, PANAMA

Reyes towed Dugan inside, rushing between glass walls through which could be seen rows of occupied desks. A small man gave a puzzled wave as Reyes shook his head and hurried by, hustling Dugan downstairs to an unmarked door. Dugan found himself in a concrete cube. Pipes crisscrossed the ceiling and cast odd shadows. The walls and floor were stained, as was a battered wooden table. Reyes shoved him into the single chair.

"Look," Dugan said, half turning, "I think there's some misunderstanding—"

Reyes slapped the back of his head.

"Yes, *Señor Dugan*. You misunderstand. You are here to answer questions. Clear?"

Dugan nodded.

"Good," Reyes said. "Tell me of *Asian Trader*."

"I'm here to attend an inquiry aboard. I was to board her at the Pacific anchorage. Why? Was she damaged in the attack?"

Reyes's eyes narrowed. "Why do you say that?"

"The pilot announced an attack. You asked about the ship. Seems logical."

Reyes changed tacks.

"Why did you buy a priority transit slot?" he asked.

"I… I don't know what you're talking about," Dugan said.

Reyes slammed Dugan's face into the table and raised him by his hair.

"Enough lies," Reyes whispered. "The truth. Or you will not leave here alive."

Blood ran down Dugan's face as he turned to Reyes with a cross-eyed stare.

"Fuck you, asshole."

Under the circumstances, an ill-considered remark.

***

"*Digame*," Luna said.

"*Capitán Luna*. Frank Carlucci."

"What can I do for you, *Señor Carlucci*?" Luna asked.

"Tell me what you know about Thomas Dugan."

"Not much. *Señor Dugan* was to attend an inquiry on *Asian Trader*," Luna said. "Reyes was to meet with him tomorrow, but now..." He paused. "You know of Reyes's loss?"

"What loss?" asked Carlucci.

"Maria died today at Miraflores, and his boys were hurt. He is with them at the hospital."

"*Capitán*," Carlucci said, "Reyes arrested Dugan at the airport less than an hour ago."

"You are misinformed," Luna said.

"I saw him myself," Carlucci said, "there is no mistake."

"I will get back to you," Luna said, hanging up to rush into the squad room.

"Perez," he said. "Where's Reyes?"

Perez looked uncomfortable.

"God damn it, Juan! Tell me!"

"With a gringo," Perez said. "In the Hole, I think."

Luna ran with Perez on his heels. They found Dugan lying on the concrete, Reyes above him, fists clenched, red faced with rage.

"Manny! No!" yelled Luna as they wrestled him away.

"Juan," Luna ordered as he knelt beside Dugan, "get Manny out. Call a doctor."

He touched Dugan's face. Dugan winced and cracked an eye.

"Is he gone?" Dugan asked weakly, relieved when Luna nodded.

"Lie still," Luna said. "A doctor is coming."

"He's not so fuckin' tough," Dugan croaked. "I was beat up worse than this by three guys outside a bar in Naples."

M/T *LUTHER HURD*
GATUN LAKE ANCHORAGE, PANAMA

"Seize my ship," Captain Vince Blake said. "That's piracy, by God."

"Goddamned right," agreed Chief Engineer Jim Milam, glaring defiance.

Rojas looked at Calderon and nodded. Calderon dialed his cell phone as Rojas turned back to the American captain.

"*Capitán Blake*," he said, "to be clear, this was approved by your president."

"Ray Hanley?" Blake asked, unable to picture the irascible president of Hanley Trading and Transportation parting with his brand-new ship.

"I refer," Rojas said, "to the president of your country. You will, of course, need to confirm this. We have your embassy on the phone."

Rojas nodded to Calderon, who passed Blake the phone. Blake put the phone to his ear and listened, thunderstruck, grunting an affirmation before hanging up and looking at the chief engineer.

"Son of a bitch. It's true, Jim," Blake said. "The president approved this."

"And I voted for that asshole," Milam muttered.

It was a done deal, thanks to Rojas's preparation. He'd briefed the Panamanian president promptly, and when the inevitable phone call from the American president had come, asking "how can we help," the answer had been "give us *Luther Hurd*." The interests of one shipowner paled beside potential loss of the canal.

Blake took one last shot.

"But surely you have other ways to block the lock?"

Calderon shook his head. "Our temporary caisson gates are in Balboa. Even if we could somehow get them up into the lake, the damaged gates are obstructing placement. But a tanker just upstream of the damaged lock will work. We will ballast her until she grounds and build an earthen dam against her upstream side. Your ship is the ideal size, empty and clean. No danger from pollution or fire and explosion."

"Hanley will do well," Rojas added. "Above market rate during use, and a return to service at our expense plus five years revenue, guaranteed."

Blake sighed. "When do we start?"

Rojas look flustered. "I'm sorry; I was unclear. There is nothing to start. We will remove the crew and place the ship with tugs."

"You've discussed this with your pilots?" Blake asked.

"We've moved dead ships before," Calderon said.

"Smaller vessels," Blake said, "in still water with mules. We barely fit the lock; there'll be current, no mules, and little room for tugs to maneuver. You'll need the engine."

"And you'll need the plant up to ballast her down once in place," Milam said.

"We'll find a way, gentlemen," Rojas said. "There are seamen among our employees."

"Look, pal," Milam said, "nobody's gonna learn this ship in a few hours."

"The chief's right," Blake agreed. "We'll ask for volunteers. We won't need many."

The room grew quiet. "You would do this?" Rojas asked.

Blake shrugged. "We're your only shot."

TOCUMEN INTERNATIONAL AIRPORT
PANAMA CITY, PANAMA

"Long day," Ward said, shaking Carlucci's hand.

"Not over, I'm afraid," Carlucci said. "Let's talk while we walk."

Ward followed him away from the Gulfstream toward his car.

"Dugan was arrested on arrival. I couldn't spring him and smelled a rat because a cop named Reyes drove off with him solo." He paused. "I called his boss, who said Reyes wasn't working because his wife died in the attack and his kids are in the hospital. I filled him in, and he hung up and called back five minutes ago saying Dugan had an 'accident' but is OK. Translation—he got there before Reyes killed Dugan."

Carlucci continued as they got in his car.

"We're headed there now. I expect Dugan's a bit worse for wear."

Ward groaned. "Jesus H. Christ. Does it get any worse?"

"Yeah, it does," Carlucci said. "Seems Reyes got a 'confidential' call from that asshole Gardner that Dugan was dirty and hinting he should be questioned aggressively."

"That stupid son of a bitch," Ward said.

"My sentiments exactly," Carlucci said.

JUDICIAL INVESTIGATIVE DIRECTORY HQ
PANAMA CITY, PANAMA

The Americans sat across the table from Luna, Reyes, and Perez.

"You can see Dugan," Luna repeated, "when you explain your failure to warn us."

Damn Gardner, Ward thought, trying again.

"Captain, we didn't know. Just let us see Dugan, and I'll tell—"

"No," Luna said. "Tell us now. Or we resume questioning Dugan. File your protest. We will know everything before it works through channels."

Ward sighed and nodded at Carlucci, who addressed Luna in Spanish.

"*Capitán*. We have your word this remains confidential?"

Luna nodded. "Juan," he said to Perez, "go turn off the recorder."

He turned back to Carlucci. "Is that sufficient, *Señor Carlucci*, or would you like to accompany *Sargento Perez*?"

"Your word is more than sufficient, *Capitán*," Carlucci said as Perez left the room.

Luna nodded his thanks, and Ward began the briefing, including Dugan's role in the operation.

"So," he concluded minutes later, "we thought this trip to Panama was a ruse to get Dugan out of the way. We didn't suspect the attack."

"I am confused," Reyes said. "You do not deny the truth of the information provided by Gardner—the money in Dugan's offshore account and the fact Dugan was involved with *Asian Trader* just before she departed Singapore for Panama. And yet you seemed convinced of Dugan's innocence. Why?"

"Because," Ward said, "I've known him for over ten years and know he would never do this. And even if I'm wrong about that, I know he is far too smart to leave such obvious evidence to be found. Also, Lieutenant, ask yourself this: If you were Dugan and you *had* committed this heinous act, would you board a plane for Panama and land in the middle of the chaos? Only God and good fortune are holding the lake back. If things had gone a bit differently, Dugan could have deplaned in Tocumen just in time to be washed into the Pacific."

Reyes and Luna nodded. After a long pause, Luna spoke.

"Very well, gentlemen," he said. "You can see Dugan. Beyond that, I promise nothing."

"Captain Luna," Ward said, "as devastating as this attack was, I don't think it is the final objective. Braun is still in place in London, and that tells me he has more attacks planned. I need to go there, and I need Dugan. His expertise may be vital in preventing another attack."

Luna looked Ward in the eye.

"Agent Ward," he said, "my concern is bringing the murdering bastards that did this to justice. I am not yet convinced *Señor Dugan* is not one of them, despite your assurances. He will remain our guest for the time being."

M/T *Luther Hurd*
Gatun Lake Anchorage, Panama
0120 Hours Local Time
5 July

Blake sat at the loading computer in the Cargo Control Room, cursing.

Milam turned from the window. "The magic box giving you trouble, Cap?" he asked.

Blake sighed. "No, but it's anybody's guess how much water we'll have on the way in. I go in too deep and we ground before we get there. Go in light and risk getting sucked into the lock before we can get her down."

"We need to get her down fast, all right," Milam agreed.

"But how?" Blake asked. "We'll need water in the cargo tanks, and the emergency storm ballast crossover's way too slow."

Milam looked thoughtful. "How 'bout some new connections."

"Breach the bulkheads?"

Milam nodded. "I got two cutting rigs. We can drop the water level in the ballast tanks enough to get into the top of the tanks, and the cargo tanks aren't inert yet, so that's no problem. The First and I can cut holes between each ballast tank and the adjacent cargo tank, then drop into the cargo tanks and open holes between them. We'll make her one great big cargo tank. Open the sea valves and throw on the all ballast pumps, and you're done."

Blake frowned at the notion of intentionally destroying the watertight integrity of his brand-new ship. "But I won't be able to control draft and trim en route," he said.

"Yeah, you will," Milam said. "We'll cut the ballast-tank bulkheads up high. The ballast tanks won't spill into the cargo tanks until they're almost full. Trim her any way you want, then overflow the ballast tanks into the cargo tanks when we're in position."

Blake sighed. "Do it," he said.

Milam moved for the door but stopped as he glanced out the window.

"We got company," he said to Blake.

Blake moved to the window. "God damn it," he said. "What are they doing back? Anyone the hospital released was supposed to go to a hotel."

Second Mate Lynda Arnett was walking up the deck, trailed by three crewmen and a sheepish looking Pedro Calderon. Arnett's right hand was in a cast, and the three men following her sported a variety of bandages. She entered the Cargo Control Room moments later with Calderon as the three sailors waited in the passageway, out of sight but within earshot.

"Arnett," Blake said, "you OK? How're the others?"

"I'm OK. A broken wrist is all. Chief Mate's got a concussion, and the bosun's leg is broken. Alvarez, Green, and Thornton are with me—minor injuries."

Blake's face hardened. "Why are you here?"

"It's all over the news. We came to help."

Blake looked a question at Calderon.

"Panic was rising," Calderon said. "We released the plan to calm things a bit."

Blake turned back to Arnett. "But I told that goddamned agent—"

Calderon interrupted. "*Señorita* Arnett can be quite... persuasive. She threatened to remove certain anatomical features to which the agent is very attached should he fail to provide transport. She was very convincing. I authorized the boat, hoping you might reason with her."

Blake and Milam smiled as Arnett reddened.

"I appreciate this, Lynda," Blake said, "but we got it covered."

"The chief mate's down and the third mate's green. I'm staying."

"God damn it, woman," Blake said, "you got a busted arm, for Christ's sake."

"Wrist," she corrected, "and what's this 'god damn it, woman' shit? Pissant chivalry? Or discrimination? Put me off and I'll sue your freakin' socks off."

Chief Steward Dave Jergens spoke from the doorway, breaking the tension.

"Lynda," he said, "Cookie put supper back. Y'all come on in, and I'll warm it up." He inclined his head to include the three sailors in the passageway.

Blake shot Jergens a grateful look.

"Thanks, Dave," he said. "Go on, Lynda. Go eat. I'll think about it, OK?"

She left with a stiff-necked nod. Jergens stood aside to let her pass but hung back.

"Something else, Dave?" Blake asked.

"Cap," Jergens said, "my guys want to help, too. We'll handle lines or... something."

"Christ on a crutch—" Blake caught himself.

"Look, Dave," Blake said, "I appreciate it, I really do, but you can't stay."

"Ain't right, Cap'n," Jergens said. "We got as much right as anybody to help."

Blake stalled. "OK. OK. I'll get back to you. All right?"

Jergens nodded and left. When he was out of earshot, Blake turned to Milam.

"Did I just hear the chief steward volunteer to work on deck?"

"Same with the engine gang," Milam said, "right down to the wiper. They're all ready to whip my ass if I even suggest puttin' them off."

"Christ, what's goin' on?" Blake asked.

"Maybe it's understandable," Milam said. "Remember how you felt on 9/11?"

Blake grew quiet.

"Stunned, outraged, but mostly helpless," he said finally.

"I figure everyone did," Milam said. "Now we *can* do something. Nobody wants to be left out. We should let them help."

"I can't risk their lives unnecessarily," Blake said.

"Just let 'em contribute. They can haul gas cylinders, pull hoses, rig lights, whatever, then ride until just before the lock."

"Might work, and it's better than a mutiny," Blake said, turning to Calderon.

"Can you arrange a launch to remove nonessential crew before the lock?" he asked.

"*Por supuesto, Capitán,*" Calderon said, "it would be my honor."

"Thank you, *señor,*" Blake said, turning back to grin at Milam.

"What the hell you waiting for?" he said. "You got holes to cut. And I have to convince Arnett to disembark with the rest."

"Glad I got the easy part," Milam said, heading for the door.

JUDICIAL INVESTIGATIVE DIRECTORY HQ
PANAMA CITY, PANAMA

Dugan kept moving so he didn't stiffen up. The old doctor had been thorough and seemed competent, though his English was limited.

"Is OK. I see much worse," he'd said, leaving as Perez arrived with rice, beans, and strong, sweet coffee. Despite the beating, Dugan was starved. He'd wolfed down the food, slowed only by swollen lips. The empty plate sat on the table as he limped around it.

He looked up as the door opened and read Ward's face.

"Christ, Jesse," Dugan said, "I can't look that bad."

"You OK?" Ward asked.

"Well, a guy who might be a doctor told me I was just peachy."

Ward nodded as Dugan glanced at Carlucci, who stuck out his hand.

"Frank Carlucci," he said. "We almost met at the airport. You look better than I expected. Reyes is tough."

"I cleverly lapsed into unconsciousness," Dugan said. "Even a psycho doesn't get off beating an inert body. What's up with that asshole?"

"A dead wife and injured kids, thanks to *Asian Trader*," Ward said. "Figure it out."

"Son of a bitch," Dugan said softly. "I didn't know."

He listened, subdued, as Carlucci summarized the attack.

"There's more," Ward added when Carlucci finished. "You were set up—fake e-mails, a Cayman account, your authorization on a priority transit slot, all very elaborate."

Dugan nodded and looked thoughtful.

"If Braun went to that much trouble to set me up, that means he's looking to deflect attention and maybe buy a little time. And if he's still in London," Dugan continued, "odds are he has more attacks planned."

"I think so, too," Ward said. "I'm going straight to London."

"What about me?" Dugan asked.

Ward looked at Carlucci.

"We're working on it," he said.

***

Luna sat with his subordinates in a room nearby. He'd promised not to record the earlier conversation but said nothing about future surveillance.

"So, *señores*. What do you think?"

"Their words follow the earlier story," Juan Perez said, "but they may suspect we listen."

"True. Manny?" Luna prompted.

Reyes shrugged. "If Dugan is dirty, he's our only lead."

"Emotion aside," Luna asked, "what does your gut tell you?"

Reyes shrugged again. "Ward's logic seems sound, and this Gardner is an obvious idiot. I think it is possible Dugan is innocent, or at worst, a dupe."

Luna nodded. "We must face facts. We lack resources to operate overseas. Our only real hope lies with the *yanquis* and the English."

Reyes's face clouded. "And so we let Dugan go and hope our kindly Uncle Sam will come back later to pat our heads and tell us what is going on? This is an atrocity against Panama, and we have a suspect in custody. I do not think we should release him so easily."

"And what if Ward is right?" Luna asked. "What if this Dugan's expertise is required not only to prevent more attacks but to bring the perpetrator of this one to justice?"

"I did not say Dugan should not be allowed to go with Ward, *Capitán*," Reyes said, "only that he should not leave our custody."

TOCUMEN INTERNATIONAL AIRPORT
PANAMA CITY, PANAMA

Reyes settled back in the leather seat of the Gulfstream and glared at Dugan in the seat across from him. The man was already snoring, thanks to heavy-duty painkillers courtesy of Carlucci.

"Thank you for releasing him," Ward said from the seat beside him.

"To be clear, Agent Ward," Reyes said, "we did not release him. He is traveling in my custody. I can return with him to Panama at any time. I expect both your government and the British to abide by the terms of our agreement in that regard."

Ward looked as if he were about to speak and then seemed to think better of it. He nodded instead and turned to stare out the window, leaving Reyes to his own thoughts.

His sons were both awake now, and the doctors said there was no great physical injury, but they were confused and frightened. Leaving them had been hard, made possible only by the presence of his parents and in-laws. It had taken all his resolve, but he knew in his heart his sons would want him to bring Maria's murderers to justice.

For all his bluster with Ward, his mission was anything but "official." It was an arrangement hammered out between Ward and Luna, with the Walsh woman on the telephone from UK. Reyes was not even officially assigned to the task. Things were too chaotic in Panama to hope to get such an arrangement approved quickly. Reyes had merely put in for his annual leave, with a promise from Luna that he would clean up the paperwork after the fact.

As the Gulfstream leveled out at cruising altitude, Reyes unbuckled his seat belt and leaned toward Dugan. The man stirred but didn't wake as Reyes unlocked the handcuffs and slipped them into his jacket pocket.

"Thank you," Ward said. "I'm sure he will appreciate that."

Reyes shrugged. "I don't think he's going anywhere."

***

The watchman at Pedro Miguel Lock raised his eyes as the Gulfstream passed overhead. As he watched the lights fade, he heard a muffled screech and then a gigantic groan as the mass in the lock shifted.

"Central Control. This is Pedro Miguel. The plug is shifting. Repeat, the plug is shifting."

CHAPTER TWENTY-THREE

M/T *LUTHER HURD*
GATUN LAKE ANCHORAGE, PANAMA
0325 HOURS LOCAL TIME
5 JULY

Calderon stood at the rail. Deck lights made *Luther Hurd* a bright pool on the dark surface of the lake. Sailors swarmed, rigging hoses and lights into tanks with shouts and curses and rough humor, to the din of impact wrenches loosening tank manholes. A launch scraped against the shipside, and he watched two men climb the accommodation ladder toward him.

The shorter man shook his head. "It is not good," he began.

"Wait, Carlos. The *capitán* should hear," Calderon said, leading the men to where Blake stood with Milam, checking off breached bulkheads on a tank layout.

"Go ahead," Calderon said, nodding at the senior of the two pilots.

"The plug shifted," said Captain Carlos Sanchez. "The current is increasing. And we have only thirty-feet depth before the lock. It will be difficult, even now."

"We need to move then?" Blake asked.

"We should heave anchor in an hour to start into the cut at first light," said the second pilot, Captain Roy McCluskey.

Milam nodded. "I can finish in transit. ETA at the lock?"

"About 0700," Sanchez said. McCluskey nodded agreement.

Milam checked the time. "OK, we can make that."

Sanchez raised a hand. "There's more. We must modify our approach. *Señor Milam*, may I?" Milam passed him the clipboard. The pilot flipped the paper to draw on the back.

"We block the east lock," he said, "with the starboard stern against the center guide wall and the bow against the east bank. The problem is here"—he tapped his sketch—"where the east bank narrows to the lock at this diagonal wall. If we cannot hold the bow against the bank while you ballast, it will be pushed down onto the angled wall and funneled into the lock." He paused. "We must ground the bow fast and hard so it cannot shift. Then the current and tugs will hold the stern to the wall while you ballast down."

Blake nodded. "What's the depth near the bank?"

Sanchez and McCluskey exchanged glances. "Ten feet and falling."

"Christ," Blake said. "Chief, what do we need aft to immerse the prop?"

"Twenty-one feet, minimum," Milam said. "And we lose some power at that draft."

"I can get the bow up to eight feet," Blake said, "but we'll be like a fat man in the stern of an empty canoe. She'll handle—"

"Like a pig," McCluskey finished.

"It will be difficult," Sanchez conceded. "The current is over four knots now. We must go in at speed, two to three knots faster than that."

Blake stared. "You want to put a forty-thousand-ton ship in the worst possible condition, then try to ground at a specific spot at an over-the-ground speed of eight knots?"

Sanchez nodded.

"And if we miss? Or a pressure wave forces the bow to shear? Then we go into the lock 'at speed,' with the weight of the whole lake behind us. This is… this is…" Blake stopped, speechless.

"Total lunacy," Milam finished. "I unvolunteer."

The pilots exchanged looks. "Gentlemen," Sanchez said, "there is no alternative. It is not now a case of slowly losing the lake. If the plug fails, thousands will die downstream. We must attempt this. With or without you."

"You can't do it without us," Blake said. "There is no time."

"Quite a choice," Milam said. "Risk death or spend the rest of our lives looking at news footage of floating corpses. I'll go, god damn it, but I'm not happy about it."

"I agree," Blake said, "but we're only speaking for ourselves."

"Thank you, gentlemen," Sanchez said, his relief evident.

"Tugs?" Blake asked.

"Only room for two," Sanchez said. "One to push the stern into the wall while the other pulls back from our port bow to help turn us into the bank."

"OK," Blake said, "but I'm going to hang off the port anchor. If necessary, we'll drop it to help turn. Warn the bow tug to stay clear."

"Given the depth," McCluskey said, "we might run over it if we drop it."

"If we end up having to use it, that'll be the least of our worries," Blake said.

Calderon looked at the two pilots, who nodded agreement, conceding the point.

"Very well," Calderon said to Blake and Milam, "it is decided. I leave you gentlemen to your work. *Capitáns* Sanchez and McCluskey remain. If you need anything at all, just ask."

Handshakes were exchanged, and the group parted. Milam flipped the paper on his clipboard and studied the diagram.

"Shift ballast anytime," he said to Blake. "I'll be out of the last ballast tank before the water reaches me."

"You sure?" Blake asked. "I don't want to get your feet wet."

"Might be better to drown early and get it over with," Milam growled.

M/T *LUTHER HURD*
NORTH OF CENTENNIAL BRIDGE
PANAMA

Blake gazed at Pedro Miguel, visible in the distance below Centennial Bridge, as the engine labored astern to hold *Luther Hurd* in the current, and the crew descended to the waiting launch. They'd all volunteered, but he kept a minimum, all unmarried except for himself and Milam. Despite his efforts to put her ashore, Arnett had asserted her prerogative as ranking deck officer to man the bow. She was there now, with three seamen to handle lines and run the anchor windlass. Green, Blake's best helmsman, manned the wheel. Milam kept his three engineers.

Blake had refused ACP help. There were enough grieving families in Panama. For the same reason, the pilots had refused offers of their colleagues. The plan would work or fail regardless of the number of pilots aboard.

The second engineer began tugging hoses from the last tank as Milam emerged and flashed a thumbs-up. Blake waved in reply as the engineers started aft.

"I should get forward," McCluskey said, starting for the stairs.

"God be with you, Roy," Sanchez said softly.

"God be with us all, Carlos," McCluskey replied.

The launch with the crew moved away, Blake silently wishing he was aboard. A chopper approached, cameraman perched in the door. Wonderful, he cursed.

M/T *LUTHER HURD*
CENTENNIAL BRIDGE, PANAMA

Blake watched the crew scramble to safety on the west lock wall before stowing the binoculars. Arnett's group passed a line to the bow tug, which moved away, connected and ready to match the tanker's speed. The tug at a safe distance, he saw Arnett signal Alvarez at the windlass, then peer down over the bulwark to watch the port anchor. Alvarez eased the anchor out, the massive chain clunking in the hawse pipe, until Arnett's balled fist shot up and Alvarez stopped the wildcat. She barked an order, and he spun the brake tight and disengaged the wildcat, leaving the anchor dangling, ready for release. Blake felt quiet pride at McCluskey's approving nod.

***

Sanchez spoke into his radio, alerting both tugs.

"Dead slow ahead," he said.

"Dead slow ahead, aye," Blake repeated, at the engine controls.

"Steer one two five," Sanchez ordered.

"One two five, aye," Green said.

"Slow ahead," Sanchez ordered, then after a moment asked, "How's she answering the helm?"

Sweat rolled down Green's dark face. "She wants to do as she pleases, Cap'n."

"Half ahead," Sanchez ordered.

"Half ahead, aye," Blake replied as they increased speed to gain steerage way.

Soon they were moving fast. Too fast. Sanchez felt like a man on his first ski jump, deciding halfway down it was a bad idea. They accelerated as the cross section of the channel decreased and the laws of physics took over. The same volume passing a smaller opening in the same amount of time must move faster. He couldn't control her at this speed. Better to use the tugs.

"Dead slow ahead," he barked.

"Dead slow ahead, aye," Blake confirmed, concern in his voice.

On the bow, McCluskey raised his radio, then lowered it without speaking. There could be only one command pilot.

***

The stern crabbed to port, and Sanchez barked an order to the tugs, overcorrecting into a series of wider and wilder swings as he struggled for control. With the bow pointed dead center at the lock, he ordered an all-out pull to port by the bow tug.

Water frothed as the tug strained. The line snapped taut and parted with a crack, recoiling in both directions, a huge rubber band. It killed one tug hand instantly and knocked a second overboard. On the ship, the other end struck McCluskey and men near him at knee height, slamming them into the steel bulwark, before whipping around a fairlead to strike Alvarez at the windlass controls. Only Arnett was spared, and she stared down at Alavarez's bloody remains.

***

"LET GO THE ANCHOR!" her radio screamed, and she clawed at the brake, panic rising as it didn't budge. She bent to pull a wheel wrench from beneath Alvarez's corpse as she heard Sanchez shouting tug orders into the radio.

***

Sanchez ordered the bow tug back to push the stern to starboard and the stern tug forward to push the bow to port. The stern tug captain hesitated, then dashed forward through the rapidly closing gap between the ship and the guide wall, all too aware of the risk.

***

Arnett had the wrench now, gripped in her left hand and multiplying her leverage. The wheel broke free, and the anchor splashed as the giant chain surged through the spinning wildcat. She closed her eyes as the shower of dirt from the running chain peppered her face. The chain slowed as the anchor hit the bottom, then paid out in jerks as the ship's motion dragged the chain out.

"SNUB IT UP! NOW!" her radio squawked.

She tightened the brake with her good hand. The chain stopped, only to break free again as the ship's motion lifted links off the bottom and the weight overcame the brake. She cursed as the wrench slipped from her hand

175

and bounced under the windlass, then gripped the wheel with both hands and pulled, screaming as bones separated. She collapsed over the wheel with a relieved sob as the brake held at last.

A muffled boom mocked her as the anchor jerked free to crash into the hull, and *Luther Hurd* continued her headlong rush.

***

Carlos Sanchez was a vigorous sixty, respected and near retirement. If unequal to the task at hand, he was by seniority the "least unqualified," and both honor and pride had precluded his refusal when the task arose, despite the dull chest pains he'd suffered for days without complaint. Only a coward would hide behind such trivial discomfort in the face of his responsibilities. But the pain struck again as he started the run at the lock, exploding this time, clouding his judgment during the most stressful minutes of his life. The final sledgehammer blows induced visions of floating bodies, each staring up as if they knew they'd been sacrificed to an old man's pride, as pain stole his breath and speech. He turned apologetically to Blake, sure in his last moments he was the architect of a great failure, shamefully grateful he wouldn't live to see it.

***

Blake knew Sanchez was dead before he reached him.

"Oh shit," Green murmured as Blake searched for a pulse.

Blake moved on instinct, ignoring the tugs as he rushed back to the console and jammed the stick to full ahead. The ship shuddered as the big propeller bit.

"The Lord is my shepherd. I shall not want..." Green prayed, hands tight on the wheel.

"Ten left," Blake barked, praying himself that they had enough speed to steer.

"Ten left, aye." Green spun the wheel. "...lie down in green pastures..."

They turned, Blake timing the rate of swing against a landmark ashore. Too slow, he thought, we're done. But due to luck or Green's fervent prayer, *Luther Hurd* caught a break. The anchor, bouncing through the mud and periodically holing the hull, drove its flukes under a buried boulder. Momentum ripped it free, but not before it jerked the bow, hastening the turn to port. The bulbous bow crumpled and rode up the bank, pushing a huge pile of mud, while the ship pivoted on the bow like a gigantic door in a draft. The starboard stern smashed against the guide wall in a din of screeching steel on concrete and a cascade of sparks, as momentum and current drove *Luther Hurd* tightly into place.

***

Upstream, the channel calmed abruptly, and the captain of the tug now astern cruised in circles, calling Sanchez on the radio. Downstream, unsure what was happening when the ship started to turn, the captain of the second tug had sheltered in the narrow lock entrance. He hovered there now, his bow upstream, holding on his engines as his little boat road atop the dropping water. He made for an escape ladder recessed into the lock wall. The boat was lost, but the crew might escape.

***

Blake rose from where he'd been thrown over the console.

"Thank you, Jesus!" Green cried, clinging to the wheel. "We fuckin' did it, Cap'n!"

The pair were grinning at each other so hard their faces hurt when a terrible screech sounded from the lock. They watched in horror as the changing conditions in the lock disturbed the equilibrium of the debris plug. A creeping crack in the weld between the deckhouse and ruined main deck accelerated through the last few feet of its length, and the mass came undone, tumbling from the lock with a huge splash. Water boiled through the lock, overturning the captive tug just moments before it reached the escape ladder. Then *Luther Hurd* shifted, and the stern screeched against the wall as she settled. Blake rushed to the phone.

"Engine Room. First Engineer," a shaky voice said.

"First. Where's the chief?"

"In the Cargo Control Room," the first said.

Blake heard the hydraulic ballast pumps winding up. Thank you Milam, he thought as he hung up. He started for the stairwell.

"C'mon, Green. Let's get to the bow."

***

Arnett groaned as she struggled upright. Her fingers protruded from the dirty remnants of the cast like painful purple sausages. A moan reached her. Someone's alive, she thought, staggering toward the sound.

The deck forward of the windlass was slick with blood. She stepped over a severed foot laced in a work boot. Thorton and Billingsley were dead against the bulwark, and Roy McCluskey lay moaning between them, his left leg missing below the knee. The stump spurted blood.

She knelt in the gore and removed his belt. He moaned.

"Hang on, Captain," she said.

She wrestled the belt onto his stump with her left hand and twisted. The blood flowed unabated. She held tension with her throbbing right hand and repositioned her left to twist tighter. He was unconscious when she got the blood stopped.

"Don't you fucking die on me!" she screamed, all the pain and horror of the last moments pouring out. She repeated it between sobs as she rocked on her knees in the gore, clutching the twisted belt. They found her there, and it took all Green's strength to pry her fingers away.

M/T *LUTHER HURD*
PEDRO MIGUEL LOCK, PANAMA
1135 HOURS LOCAL TIME
5 JULY

Only Blake and Milam remained aboard. Water leaked by the hull in slackening streams as workers packed earth against the port side. From the bridge, Blake watched trucks on the east bank dumping rocks and broken concrete. The hull rang with repeated clangs as small dozers pushed the rubble out into the water against the ship's side, followed by sand and dirt to fill in the voids and create a solid road against the shipside. The next loads were dumped farther out. They were already fifty or sixty feet along.

Blake winced as rocks and dozer blades scraped new paint and dust billowed over the pristine deck. He shook his head and moved down the stairs. The Engine Control Room was empty, but he saw Milam through the window standing on the walkway looking down into the engine room. His engine room. A spotless place, bright with new paint and full of new equipment. An engineer's wet dream, Blake thought not unkindly.

He moved through the door quietly and stood behind Milam, hesitant to disturb him. The only sounds were the muted drone of the emergency generator and the hollow booms of rocks against the hull. Finally, Blake cleared his throat.

Milam looked back with a sad smile. "What brings a rope choker to the realm of the honest working man?"

"They're burying our ship, Jim. I couldn't watch anymore."

Milam shook his head. "I've been at sea almost twenty-five years. Mostly rust buckets older than me I kept running with duct tape, baling wire, and whatever I could make with a lathe and a welding machine. I finally get the engine room of my dreams"—he sighed—"and it's a friggin' dam." He changed the subject. "We about wrapped up?"

"Yeah," Blake said, "I talked to the office on the satellite, right to Hanley himself. He's chartering a jet to fly us all to Houston, including the injured folks and our... casualties."

Milam nodded. "How's McCluskey?"

"Calderon says he'll make it," Blake said, "thanks to Arnett."

"She's got sand, that one," Milam said, and Blake nodded agreement.

They both stood, reluctant to leave, flinching as a rock boomed against the hull.

"OK," Milam said. "I'll go kill the emergency generator."

Neither moved.

"Look, Vince," Milam said. "You saved our asses. You're a hero."

"I don't feel like a hero," Blake said. "I feel like an asshole who couldn't even get his brand-new ship to the first load port and who got good men killed in the process."

Milam squeezed Blake's shoulder. "Yeah, I guess this hero stuff's over-rated."

CHAPTER TWENTY-FOUR

Dugan drifted toward consciousness, feeling better after a five-hour nap, his headache reduced to a dull throb. He heard voices through the fog and opened his eyes.

"It's motive I can't understand," Ward said to Reyes. "What can Iran and Venezuela possibly gain by targeting Panama and Malacca?"

"Obviously the canal was the prime target," Reyes said.

Ward shook his head. "Not from the allocation of resources. There were ten attackers in Malacca, and they hijacked *Alicia* and stole the boats to set it up. To say nothing of chartering *China Star* and timing her arrival in the straits. All very elaborate. Compare that to the attack on your country. As effective as it was, it seems to be the work of one man, acting alone."

"There may have been others in the crew," Reyes said.

"No way," Dugan interjected. "That crew worked for Phoenix for years. Medina was the only unknown. The regular third mate was due back from vacation but was injured in a car wreck in the Philippines. Medina was a last-minute relief, and the captain was pissed about going through the yard with a green man. He was happy when Medina turned out to be a capable worker." Dugan paused. "Evidently a bit too capable."

"Which brings us right back to why," Ward said. "Closing Malacca would hurt Iran, so a failed attempt there might deflect blame. But destroying the canal wouldn't greatly impact Iran, and I don't see how either act would help Venezuela."

Reyes shrugged. "Oil prices are sure to spike."

"Temporarily, yeah," Dugan said. "But Malacca's still open, and tanker traffic through the canal is minimal. Prices will settle in a week or so. That alone can't be the motive."

Reyes looked pensive. "I do not know about Iran, but Rodriguez is no friend of Panama. He supports the FARC guerrillas in Colombia, who are an increasing problem on our border. Also, it is no secret he is upset our current canal expansion will be insufficient to allow the transit of loaded VLCCs. He openly advocates a second, larger canal in Nicaragua, and there are rumors that he urges the Chinese to pledge to send half their trade though a new canal so that his friends in Nicaragua can secure financing in the international market."

Ward sighed. "That may be part of it, but my gut tells me the worst is yet to come. And we're playing a man down. Tom obviously can't go back into the office. The ship's agent will have reported his arrest by now, so Braun thinks he's in Panama."

"Alex can help Anna inside," Dugan said.

Ward chose his next words with care.

"Alex isn't out of the woods, Tom."

"Bullshit. You know he's being coerced."

"I do. But we have no hard evidence. Closures at either Panama or Malacca increase distances and soak up capacity. Freight rates will skyrocket and Kairouz stands to profit. Money equals motive. A nice, uncomplicated motive. People like things simple, even if they're wrong. And between your relationship with Alex and your own involvement with *Alicia, Asian Trader*, and an offshore bank account, you both look pretty hinky. With Gardner beating that drum in Langley, my support might mean squat. Unless I miss my guess, he's already on the horn, pressing for the Brits to arrest you when we land."

Dugan looked worried. "So how do we play it?"

Ward looked at Reyes and smiled. "Well, since you're officially, or at least semiofficially, in Panamanian custody, it's really out of our hands. That'll throw Gardner a curve, and he'll hesitate to escalate things until he's sure they won't blow up in his face. But make no mistake. This is high profile. The holiday weekend means it'll take a bit longer for a critical mass of political assholes to form, but in forty-eight hours tops, we enter the never-never land of congressional hearings. When the shit hits the fan, I'm the goat and you and Alex are prime suspects. Two days. After that we're toast."

CIA HEADQUARTERS
LANGLEY, VIRGINIA

The *Luther Hurd* at Pedro Miguel dominated the news. Gardner watched on his office television, the graphic gore roiling his stomach. He'd arrived at work at six thirty, sleep denied him by a pounding head and quivering gut. He chased Tylenol with tepid coffee and considered how what he'd learned in the last three hours impacted Larry Gardner. Throwing Dugan to the Panamanians was still promising, presuming Ward hadn't screwed it up. He tried Ward again and hung up at the voice mail. He dialed Panama.

"Carlucci."

"Gardner here," he said. "Ward with you?"

"I'm not at liberty to say."

"Do the Panamanians have Dugan in custody?"

"Who is Dugan, and why do you think he's in custody?"

"Ah… I saw his name in the briefing notes."

"Funny," Carlucci said, "I write those. I didn't mention a Dugan."

"What the hell difference does it make? Where is he?"

"I'm not at liberty to say."

"Look, Carlucci, you're hindering an ongoing operation. If you don't want to end up somewhere even less important than Panama, start being helpful."

"Fuck you."

Gardner burst into obscenities at the dial tone and slammed the phone down. Still cursing, he picked it back up and dialed.

"Flight Operations."

"Gardner here. What do you have on Ward?"

"Let's see, looks like he left Panama for Heathrow this morning at 0215, refueling in Miami. I show his ETA in London as 2015 local; that's 1515 our time."

Hair rose on Gardner's neck. "He alone?"

The man paused. "Nope. Manifest shows Ward, a Thomas Dugan, and a Panamanian national named Manuel Reyes."

Gardner hung up. Son of a bitch. Reyes. With Ward and Dugan. No good could come of this. He needed some cover, just in case. He was parsing the possibilities when Senator Gunther appeared on television, standing at a bank of microphones in front of the Capitol. Gardner raised the volume.

"…will leave no stone unturned in fixing the blame for these intelligence failures. To that end, I've convened a special Senate investigation…."

Gardner smiled. It was about to rain shit, and he'd just found a raincoat.

OFFICES OF PHOENIX SHIPPING

Braun frowned. "Be here, Sutton. That's final."

"But I can upload the virus now and trigger it remotely. I don't need to be here."

"What if it's discovered?" Braun said. "Besides. I want you here tonight to ensure every system is running. Complete destruction. No file remnants on local hard drives."

"You're burning the bloody building. What's the point?"

Braun's stare was ice. "The point, Sutton, is you'll do as told. Now. Back-ups?"

"Held off-site. Only Kairouz and I have decryption keys." Sutton handed Braun a flash drive. "This one works but his doesn't. Without this, the back-ups are useless."

Braun slipped the drive into his pocket. "Good. Is the safe house set up?"

Sutton nodded. "I tested the cable and Internet yesterday."

"And I drove the route," Farley said. "Looked fine."

"Any trouble renting the place with the cover identity?" Braun asked.

"Didn't have to," Sutton said. "It's my aunt's place in Kent."

Braun exploded. "You bloody idiot! A place connected to one of us will be obvious!"

"Bu… but there's no connection," Sutton stammered. "It's in her name. She's in the loony bin. Alzheimer's."

"What's her name?" Braun demanded.

"Married name's Lampkin. Husband's dead. I don't even visit. I got the key when me mum passed last year. It's safer than a rental."

Braun considered it. No time for other arrangements.

"All right," he said. "But Sutton. Don't disappoint me again. Clear?"

Sutton nodded as Braun continued. "Everything ready on your end, Far-ley?"

"Yeah. I checked out the school. Like you figured, it's all girls with no males on staff except a custodian. I slipped in last night to check the setup. One gent's toilet, off a side corridor to a supply storeroom. It's at the back of the building with a window opening on to the alley. It's perfect. We'll be halfway to the safe house before anyone knows she's gone."

Braun nodded. "That's it then," he said, dismissing them. As they left, he moved to his desk and took a pair of pliers from a drawer. He crushed the flash drive beyond recognition and slipped the remains back into his pocket for later disposal, then dialed his phone.

"Sudsbury and Smythe," a pleasant female voice answered.

"Mr. Carrington-Smythe, please. Captain Braun calling."

"He's been expecting your call, Captain. I'll put you right through."

LONDON HEATHROW AIRPORT
2015 HOURS LOCAL TIME
5 JULY

After a great deal of persuasion, Reyes agreed not to cuff Dugan upon landing. However, the big Panamanian kept Dugan close as the pair trailed Ward across the tarmac to Lou Chesterton and Harry Albright. The Panamanian's introduction to the Brits was perfunctory—both men were staring at Dugan.

"Bloody hell, Yank," Harry said. "You hit by a lorry?"

Dugan glanced at Reyes, who remained expressionless.

"You OK, mate?" Lou asked.

"I'm fine," Dugan said. "What's the plan?"

Lou looked at Ward. "A bloke from your embassy called and urged us to detain you. I patiently explained to him that MI5 is intelligence, not law enforcement, and without arrest powers. He then suggested that I convey you, and particularly Dugan here, to the US embassy for 'debriefing.'"

Ward shook his head. "Mr. Dugan is in the custody of Lieutenant Reyes. He will not be going to the embassy, though perhaps the lieutenant and I should go to the embassy and explain the situation while you take Dugan to Anna's building."

"Go where you will, Agent Ward," Reyes said. "I stay with Dugan."

Ward sighed. "All right. Lou, can you take me to the embassy while Harry drives these two to Anna's?"

"My God, Tom," Anna said, "are you all right?"

Dugan's smile faded. "I can't tell you what a confidence builder that was. I'm beginning to feel like the Elephant Man."

"There's a resemblance, mate," Harry said, "but he was quite intelligent."

Reyes smiled, and Dugan laughed, his pain made tolerable by the pills he'd taken on landing.

"They didn't beat the cheekiness out of you I see," Anna said, then turned to Reyes.

"But I'm forgetting my manners. May I offer you something to drink, Lieutenant Reyes?"

"Coffee, if it would not be too much trouble," Reyes said.

"No trouble at all," Anna said. "Tom? Harry?"

Both men nodded and followed Anna into the small kitchen and watched her prepare the coffee. When it was ready, they all moved to the living room.

"Cassie OK?" Dugan asked.

Anna nodded. "Well covered. Two men at all times."

"And Braun?" Dugan asked.

"Quiet. But up to something," she said. "That's my gut anyway."

"Mine as well," Harry agreed.

"Then it's unanimous," Dugan said. "But damned if I can figure his next move."

They fell into frustrated silence, but soon Anna smiled.

"I've seen that look," Harry said. "What are you on to, Anna?"

"We can assume the next attack will be by a Phoenix-owned or -chartered tanker, right?"

"So what?" Dugan said. "We can't check them all without alerting Braun."

"Bear with me," Anna said. "Targets?"

Dugan shrugged. "Suez, the straits of Hormuz and the Bosphorus, maybe the Cape of Good Ho—" He stopped and looked at her.

"Exactly," she said.

Harry and Reyes looked confused.

"Would you two mind sharing?" Harry asked.

"We concentrate on tankers near choke points," Anna said. "That's the short list."

"Braun will only manipulate communications for attack ships," Dugan added. "It'd be noticed if he tried that for every ship in the fleet."

"Tom can call the short-listed ships on a pretext," Anna continued. "Alex can't do it because Braun is watching him closely, and a call from me would seem strange. The captains might call back to see what's going on and alert Braun in the process. But no one in the fleet knows Tom's not in the office."

"And if Tom senses something amiss," Harry finished, understanding, "that's the ship. Bloody brilliant."

"One problem," Anna said. "My computer crashed again, as did Tom's. And Sutton was his usual helpful self. I can't access the position report. Tom, you have a hard copy?"

"Not a current one," Dugan said. "Get word to Alex. He can slip it to you somehow. By the way, does he know I'm here?"

"He thinks you're in custody in Panama. And let's keep it that way. He's reacting as Braun would anticipate. Knowing you're here could change his demeanor and alert Braun."

"But he—"

"You have to trust me on this, Tom," Anna said, ending discussion of the issue.

"Now," she continued, "I have to see him out of the office. I'll call and say I'm worried about Tom and want to talk. I'll suggest we meet tomorrow morning for coffee."

"Wrong motive," Harry said. "Braun thinks you're a tart. Come on to Kairouz—imply you're worried about your position with Dugan gone. Offer to discuss 'serving his needs.'"

"Won't that shock him?"

"He'll get it," Dugan said. "And if he's initially shocked, so much the better."

Anna nodded and called. As predicted, Alex played along and agreed to meet Anna at eight thirty the next morning.

She snapped the phone shut. "My reputation as a slut is secure. Now what?"

Harry yawned. "I'll update Lou and Ward and piss off home to the little woman."

"Do that," Anna said. "Let's all get some sleep."

Harry stood up. "I'll let myself out," he said.

Reyes kept his seat, and Anna shot Harry a surprised look.

Harry shrugged. "Lieutenant Reyes is quite diligent in his custodial duties," Harry said and moved to the door.

The door clicked shut behind Harry, followed by a few seconds of awkward silence.

"Well then," Anna said. "I guess I'll just pop off to bed."

She gave Dugan a rueful look and moved through the kitchen and out the back door to her own apartment.

Dugan glared at Reyes.

"Looks like you're my new roommate, so let's get something straight. There's only one bed, and it's mine. You got the sofa."

***

Twenty minutes later, Dugan stepped out of the bathroom in his boxer shorts, showered and ready for bed. Reyes waited in the bedroom with handcuffs.

"I'm not into that, Reyes," Dugan said, "and you're not really my type."

The Panamanian controlled his temper. "I intend to cuff you to the bed."

"Seriously?" Dugan asked.

"Your colleagues' faith in you is touching, *Señor Dugan*, but I am not a believer just yet. Do you think I would risk waking with my own gun in my face?"

"What if there's a fire?" Dugan asked.

"Unlikely," Reyes said.

"What if I have to piss?"

Reyes shrugged. "Then you will be uncomfortable."

"What if—"

"What if you shut up and extend your hand before I am forced to become unpleasant?"

***

Just before dawn, Reyes rose from the lumpy sofa and moved to a chair by the window. Sleep had been a disjointed series of catnaps, separated mostly by hours of thoughts of Maria and the boys. When he could bear the pain no longer, he had forced his thoughts to the situation at hand.

That was equally troubling. He could hardly contain his disdain for the methods being employed. He had learned enough to be convinced this

Braun was key, and yet the *hijo de puta* was being handled with kid gloves while Ward and the Walsh woman's team gathered "hard evidence."

Where, he wondered, were the secret CIA planes standing by to whisk this Braun to some accommodating country where he could be questioned "aggressively"? Perhaps he should offer the services of his agency? He was sure that after a few hours in the Hole, *El Señor Braun* would be most cooperative.

He sighed. The gringos needed him to keep Dugan at large, just as he needed to remain close to the investigation. He would play their game, as they played his, until he learned who was really behind the death of his Maria and so many others. Then things would be different.

OFFICES OF PHOENIX SHIPPING LTD.
2315 HOURS LOCAL TIME
5 JULY

"That's it. Kairouz's was the last." Sutton looked up from Alex Kairouz's desk.

"Thank you, Sutton," Braun said as he pulled a silenced pistol and shot his surprised underling in the head.

He returned the gun to his waistband and moved to his office, where he opened a small fireproof lockbox and checked the contents: cash, several false passports with Sutton's photo, and the CD of conversations between Rodriguez, Kairouz, and Dugan. He locked the box and carried it to Sutton's office, hiding it in a drawer just as Farley entered.

"All done," Farley said. "I wedged open the stairwell fire doors and set incendiary charges on both the Phoenix Shipping floors. The main sprinkler supply valve is jammed shut. The place will go up in seconds."

"It's all concealed? I want no slipups."

Farley shrugged. "Someone might close the fire doors, but it won't matter. I've rigged both floors. The charges are out of sight."

"And you're sure Sutton's and Kairouz's offices will survive?"

"They should. They're on the outer wall, away from the charges. The fire trucks will pump water through the windows first." He looked around. "Sutton done?"

"Mr. Sutton has, and is, finished," Braun said, "and as promised, his bonus money is now available to augment your own."

Farley smiled. "Right then," he said. "That leaves the timer. When you want to pop?"

Braun had struggled with timing until the Walsh slut's call to Kairouz. Cassie had to be in their control to ensure Kairouz's cooperation, but snatching her at home involved too many witnesses to silence. Authorities might believe Kairouz had the girl snatched, but not that he'd sanctioned the murder of his entire domestic staff. They had to grab the girl at school, and timing was key. It wouldn't do for Kairouz to die in the office fire, but he normally arrived at the office about when Cassie reached school. Kairouz's eight-thirty meeting with the slut was perfect. He'd even have a ringside seat to the destruction of his life's work.

"Set it for eight forty," Braun said.

STERLING ACADEMY
WESTMINSTER, LONDON
6 JULY

Farley accelerated. The retard would dawdle, this of all mornings. If the old bitch had to sign her in as tardy, it would cock things up proper.

"SLOW DOWN, FARLEY," demanded Gillian Farnsworth as he rocketed around a corner. He ignored her, lurching to a stop moments later before Sterling Academy, relieved to see the headmistress still atop of the steps. He leaped out, opening Cassie's door. He grabbed her arm as she scrambled out.

"I gotta use the loo," he said through the open door.

"Get back in this car at once," Gillian Farnsworth said.

"I'll be a while," he grinned. "Don't get your knickers in a knot, luv."

He slammed the door and moved up the long steps, still gripping Cassie's arm. He bobbed his head politely to the surprised headmistress, looking embarrassed as he whispered his need and brushed past before she could object. Inside, he feigned ignorance.

"Where's the loo?"

"Down there," Cassie pointed. "Now let me go. I'll be late."

"Show me first."

"Oh, all right. But hurry." She led him down an empty side hall.

At the toilet door, he clamped a hand over her mouth and pushed her in, her jerks exciting him as he pressed against her. He pinned her head against his chest, fished out a syringe, removed the cap with his teeth, and jabbed her neck. She went limp, and he lowered her to the floor to open the window.

"Right on time," Braun said, framed in the window. Farley passed her out and then grabbed the top of the window frame to swing through the small opening feetfirst. He landed atop a panel truck painted in the livery of the International Parcel Service, backed up to the wall beneath the high window in the deserted alley. Braun was already scrambling to the ground, clad in an IPS uniform. Farley closed the window and lowered Cassie into Braun's waiting arms, then jumped down beside them.

"I'll put her in back," Braun said. "Change and get behind the wheel."

At 8:36, the truck turned onto Victoria Street.

CASTLE LANE
500 YARDS FROM STERLING ACADEMY

"Nanny. Control. Over," squawked the radio.

"We copy, Control. Over."

"Nanny, be advised subject is moving east on Victoria. Over."

The driver pulled around the corner. The two men in the car shared a look of relief at spotting the stationary Kairouz car.

"Negative, Control. Subject's vehicle has not moved. Over."

"I show the subject in motion, Nanny. Eastbound on Victoria. Over."

"Control, I say again. Subject's vehicle is stationary. Check your equipment. Over."

"Nanny, DO YOU HAVE A VISUAL ON SUBJECT? Over."

"Negative, Control. But the vehi—"

The operator abandoned protocol. "The bloody CAR may be there, but the SUBJECT is in motion, now southbound on Artillery Row and getting farther away by the minute. DO YOU COPY?"

"Bloody hell," the driver said.

"Control. We're on it," said the second agent as the driver whipped the car onto Victoria, heading east.

STARBUCKS COFFEE
VAUXHALL, LONDON

Anna and Alex both arrived early and sat now in the Starbucks near the office, empty cups between them. She studied Alex. Panama and Dugan's arrest had taken its toll.

"All those deaths. Thomas arrested," he said. "If I'd just alerted you sooner... maybe you could've prevented it. I was just so afraid for Cassie." His voice broke. "I am still."

Anna took his hand. "She's safe now. I promise."

He sat, eyes downcast, and squeezed her hand before looking up.

"Right then," he said. "Back to business. I'll get you a position report, but how can you contact ships without alerting Braun?"

"We're working on that," Anna said vaguely.

"Well, you're the expert. I'll have Mrs. Coutts slip you a copy."

Anna looked through the window. "You can tell her now."

Alice Coutts was emerging from Vauxhall tube station. They went out to intercept her.

"Why good morning," Mrs. Coutts said. "What a pleasant surp—"

A blast slapped them, followed so closely by a second it seemed like an echo. Shock waves cracked windows. They turned to see smoke billow above a familiar building, and the blood drained from Alex's face as he watched the enterprise he'd built with years of blood, sweat, and tears go up in smoke.

HORSEFERRY ROAD

Braun heard the explosions as they neared Lambeth Bridge. He'd chosen to cross the Thames at Lambeth for visual confirmation of the fire. Once on the bridge, he saw smoke billow on the far bank and heard the distant wail of fire engines. Gawkers jammed the walk south of the burning building.

He jumped at the sound of a horn. Farley was gawking too and almost hit a taxi.

"Keep your eyes on the bloody road," Braun barked.

Farley muttered under his breath as Braun ignored him and dialed his cell phone. Alex Kairouz answered.

"Ah, Kairouz. Enjoying the bonfire?"

"You bastard. I'll see you hang."

Braun laughed. "I think not, Kairouz. But I'll forgive that outburst. I'm sure you'll be more respectful since I'm entertaining Cassie. Remember the videos?"

"Liar! She's at school," Alex said as the "call waiting" tone buzzed.

"Do take that, Kairouz. No doubt it's the Farnsworth bitch. You have ten seconds to deal with her before I disconnect and Cassie disappears. Ready? Go."

"Look, Braun—"

"Nine seconds, Kairouz. Tick. Tick. Tick."

Alex switched calls.

***

"Mr. Kairouz! Thank God!" Gillian Farnsworth said. "That brute Farley has somehow taken Cassie fr—"

"I know. I'll call back," Alex blurted, reconnecting with Braun.

***

"What do you want?" he asked, shaken.

"Much better," Braun said. "Speak to no one. Take the tube to Sudsbury and Smythe on Lombard Street. Do you know the firm?"

"I know of it."

"Ask for Mr. Carrington-Smythe, the managing director. You're expected. He'll give you a case with cash and bearer bonds. Take receipt quickly and leave. Is that clear?"

"Yes."

"Take a cab to Heathrow, the Global Air Charter counter. There's a jet waiting to take you and Cassie to Beirut, your old home. Board and wait."

Alex's hopes rose. To be dashed.

"Cassie, of course, will never arrive," Braun said.

"But, what—"

"Shut up and listen!" Braun said. "When the police arrive, confess you and Dugan conspired to blow up *China Star* and *Asian Trader* to manipulate freight rates, but that when Dugan was arrested in Panama, you panicked and fled. When Sutton discovered your plan to leave him as scapegoat, you killed him and torched the office to cover the murder. You arranged for Farley and me, mere cogs in your evil plan, to collect Cassie as you couldn't trust the upright Mrs. Farnsworth. You will speculate we saw police and, fearing arrest, disappeared with her."

"And if I refuse?" Alex asked.

"Surely you can guess, Kairouz. We've reviewed the video often enough."

A strangled sob told Braun he'd won.

"One more thing, Kairouz," Braun said. "While in custody, kill yourself."

Alex gasped.

"Oh, don't carry on," Braun said. "It's a trade, Kairouz. Your pathetic life in exchange for sparing Cassie."

"You think I trust you?"

"I appeal not to your trust, you fool, but your logic. If Cassie reappears unharmed, it supports what I want believed: that we panicked, dumped the girl, and escaped. They won't waste resources on minor players after they've captured you, the ringleader. But if she disappears or is found dead, she becomes a sympathetic victim and the authorities will keep looking. And if you confess and die, I can release her without fear you'll recant. It's in my interests to do so."

"But how am I supposed to… to…"

"Inmates manage to kill themselves daily, Kairouz. I have every confidence in you. But don't think a halfhearted effort will satisfy me. I need commitment, old boy. Clear?"

"Yes," Alex said, barely audible.

"Excellent. On with it then. And remember, contact no one. In fact, remove your phone battery. I'll know if you don't and might allow Farley a go at darling Cassie."

Braun hung up and smiled. "That went well."

"How are you bugging his phone from here?" Farley asked.

"I'm not, obviously," Braun said with forced patience. "But he's too frightened to do anything but follow orders."

"You think he'll off himself?"

"Of course," Braun said. "But just as importantly, he'll implicate Dugan now. He'll unconsciously compare his own noble sacrifice against a prison term for Dugan. Dugan's fate will seem acceptable." Braun smiled. "Kairouz's suicide will make his confession irrevocable and dovetail nicely with the evidence found in Sutton's desk."

Farley frowned. "So we let the girl go?"

Braun laughed. "Of course not, you idiot. You think I care if some bumbling oafs are looking for me? By the time they suspect anything we'll be long gone."

CHAPTER TWENTY-FIVE

"Bloody hell," Anna said into the phone. "What about the protective detail?"

"On his tail," Lou said, "but quite a ways behind."

She sighed. "All right. Air support?"

"A chopper's en route. Control has Cassie eastbound on Lambeth Bridge, near you. Vehicle unknown."

"I need transport," Anna said.

"It looks like the chase car will be coming right by you," Lou said. "Can you be at the corner of Lambeth Road and Pratt Walk in ten minutes?"

"Affirmative."

"All right," Lou said. "I'll have the chase car call when they near the intersection and start another car en route from HQ as a backup in case the chase moves abruptly in another direction. Harry, Dugan, Reyes, and I are leaving from Askew Road. I'll call Ward, but we've no time to collect him. We'll get her back, Anna."

We better, Anna thought, hanging up and pushing through the crowd to Mrs. Coutts at the mob's edge checking off arriving employees to start a list of missing colleagues. Anna looked around.

"Mr. Kairouz?"

Mrs. Coutts pointed to Alex some distance away, his back turned as he pocketed his phone. He turned as she approached, his face red.

"So much for your bloody promises."

"Alex?… But how—"

"From Mrs. Farnsworth, who is apparently more competent than the whole of Her Majesty's bloody Security Service. Where the hell was the protection?"

"We've a strong signal," Anna said, "and I'm going after her. But you shouldn't be alone now. Wait here while I get Mrs. Coutts."

Anna hurried away. When she returned with Mrs. Coutts, Alex was gone.

***

Alex skirted arriving firefighters to walk north along the river, crossing Westminster Bridge to the tube station. He'd been wrong to entrust Cassie's safety to others. Braun was too smart. He had no choice now but to play Braun's game.

Even now, pursuit endangered Cassie, but he knew he couldn't stop it. Braun was the real target now, whatever Anna said, for only he held the key to the attacks. And if Braun did escape, it would mean he'd found and disabled the implant and knew he was compromised. In that scenario, Alex was Cassie's last chance. Braun the desperate fugitive would kill her and flee. Unless Alex provided an option. Unless his confession and suicide made the news in time for Braun to hear. Braun couldn't even be charged with kidnapping if acting on Alex's orders. Assuming he left Cassie unharmed.

Alex embraced that fragile hope and marched toward a date with death.

BRIDGE STREET
APPROACHING WESTMINSTER BRIDGE

"Any luck?" Lou asked over his shoulder as Dugan dialed again, unaware Alex was entering the tube station only yards away.

"Another 'unavailable' message," Dugan said from the backseat next to Reyes, glaring out at traffic. Assuming Lambeth Bridge would choke first, Lou had diverted to Westminster Bridge, along with most of the rest of London it seemed.

"Try the Farnsworth woman," Harry suggested.

Dugan nodded and dialed. She answered at once.

"Mr. Dugan," she said, "thank God you're here. Farley has kidnapped Cassie. I called Mr. Kairouz straightaway, but he hung up and hasn't rung back. When I call, I get a bloody recording. The headmistress called the police, but Ms. Walsh's 'protection' is nowhere to be seen. What should I do?"

She was coming unwound. Dugan tried to calm her.

"Mrs. Farnsworth—Gillian. You need to be calm for Cassie's sake. Anna's people are tracking her and have a rescue plan." He hoped. "I can't reach Alex either, but I'll keep trying and call you when I do."

"All right," she said, perceptibly calmer.

"We don't want the media involved. Suggest to the headmistress it's likely a kidnapping for ransom. Swear her to silence. Can you do that for me?"

"Of course. You needn't speak to me as if I were a child, Mr. Dugan."

"You're right. Forgive me," he said, relieved at the steel in her voice.

"Anna's guys will deal with the police," Dugan said, looking at Harry, who nodded and dialed his own phone. "You best go home. I'll call when I know anything."

"See that you do," she said, again in control. "Good-bye, Mr. Dugan."

Dugan hung up and waited for Harry to finish his call.

"Cops say they went out the toilet window," Harry said as he hung up. "A two-man job. Braun must be along."

"His plan is in motion," Dugan said. "Burning the office cuts him off from the attack ship or ships and prevents us from searching for it. Which means—"

"We have to take the bastard alive," Lou finished from behind the wheel.

They sat, digesting that. Harry broke the silence.

"You handled the Farnsworth woman well, Yank."

"Maybe in gratitude you can describe the rescue plan I assured her we had," Dugan said.

LAMBETH ROAD EASTBOUND

Farley laid on his horn.

"Are you *trying* to attract attention, you idiot?" Braun said.

Farley sulked. Traffic was worse than anticipated. They had cutout vehicles in multiple locations, but they'd yet to reach the first one. Braun decided to forgo multiple switches and go to the safe house after the first change.

The shadow flickered again, and Braun leaned out to see a helicopter high overhead. He drew in and studied the traffic. The left lane was moving well as cars turned left to escape the accident ahead.

"Turn left on Saint Georges Road."

"But we're almost past the jam."

"Do it."

LAMBETH ROAD AT PRATT WALK

The car pulled to the curb in front of Anna. The agent in the front passenger seat jumped out and got in back, yielding his seat to Anna. Anna got in, and the driver laid on his horn and forced his way back into traffic.

"This is a bloody balls-up," Anna said. "Was watching one young girl too taxing for you two?"

The driver shot a sheepish glance over his shoulder, deferring to his partner in the back. After a long pause the man in back spoke. "Anna—"

"Stow it. There is absolutely nothing you can say to help yourselves. Now give me the damn radio," she said, holding out her hand.

The agent in back passed over the radio, and Anna took charge.

"Control. This is Walsh. I'm now in the chase car at Lambeth Road and Pratt Walk. Do you have the link with all units yet?"

"Affirmative, Walsh. You're Chase One. Chesterton is Chase Two. Chopper is Air One. Target is east of your position on Lambeth, near the War Museum."

"Chase One to Air One. Do you have an ID?"

"Negative, Walsh. I can't separate him yet," the chopper pilot said.

"Chase Two, did you copy? What's your location, Lou?" Anna asked.

"I copy Anna," Lou said. "We're across the bridge, east on Westminster Bridge Road. We'll parallel you in case he breaks north. Where do you want the police?"

"Out of sight," she said. "When the chopper IDs him, we'll fake an accident in his path. When he stops, we'll surprise him."

"Got it," Lou said, then added, "Anna, have you seen Kairouz?"

"Negative. He's disappeared."

"Understood," Lou said.

She wondered briefly about Alex, then cursed traffic. At least Braun was trapped too.

SAINT GEORGES ROAD NORTHBOUND

Traffic moved faster on Saint Georges Road, most turning east on to Westminster Bridge Road back toward Saint Georges Circus.

"Make the right. Stay with the eastbound traffic," Braun said, leaning out again.

As Farley complied, Braun pulled his head in. "Still there," he said.

"Who?"

"The helicopter that's tracking us."

Farley tried to look up through the windshield.

"Eyes on the road," Braun snapped.

Farley shot Braun a glare, then stared ahead.

"Interesting," Braun said. "The police couldn't have found us. Even if someone saw an IPS truck at the school, there are hundreds in the city; that's why I chose it. They're tracking us somehow. It can only be the girl. She must have a tracking device or an implant."

"Christ, the flu jab," Farley said. "It seemed legit. She whined all the way home. Even missed school the next day, which now that I think on seems a bit of a carry-on for a jab."

"Right under your bloody nose," Braun started, then contained himself. First things first.

"All right," he said. "Let's take stock. Our opponents coerced a doctor, have remote surveillance and a helicopter. That says authorities."

"Shit. Cut out the implant and toss it. Better yet, toss her out as a diversion."

"And do what, you idiot? Magically speed through the snarl in this brightly colored shoe box? No, I have plans for our little simpleton. They obviously haven't identified us, or they'd have attempted something. We're still only a signal. Just drive while I think."

It came to him as they neared Saint Georges Circus.

"Take London Road to New Kent," Braun said. "Most of these cars will stay with us, and an IPS van headed to the terminal is normal." He laid out the rest.

Later on New Hope Road, Farley purposely caught the light near a B&Q Super Center.

"OK," Braun said, "the loading dock in ten minutes. And Farley, do act like you belong."

Farley gave an affirmative grunt as Braun left the truck to melt into the crowd.

LᴀᴍʙᴇᴛH Rᴏᴀᴅ
AᴘᴘʀᴏᴀᴄHɪɴɢ Sᴀɪɴᴛ Gᴇᴏʀɢᴇꜱ Cɪʀᴄᴜꜱ

Anna swore. Braun's lead had widened.

"Target is stationary at New Kent Road and Balfour Street," Control said.

"Copy that," the chopper pilot said. "An IPS van and two cars caught the light. It's one of those. Wait; someone is leaving the van. Damn. I lost him in the crowd and—"

"Air One, stay on the signal," Anna said. "We're a mile back. Lou, location?"

"A quarter mile behind you, Anna."

"The cars are turning," the chopper pilot said, "but the van's going straight for the terminal."

"This is Control. Signal is still on New Kent Road."

"Bingo!" the pilot said. "Positive ID on IPS truck."

"Brilliant," Anna said. "Lou, have the police close to two blocks while we work out how to engage."

"Will do, Anna."

She leaned forward as if to speed traffic by force of will just as squealing tires preceded a loud bang ahead, and a wave of flashing brake lights rippled toward her.

Sᴜᴅꜱʙᴜʀʏ ᴀɴᴅ SᴍʏᴛHᴇ
Pʀɪᴠᴀᴛᴇ Bᴀɴᴋᴇʀꜱ
Lᴏᴍʙᴀʀᴅ Sᴛʀᴇᴇᴛ, Lᴏɴᴅᴏɴ

Clive Carrington-Smythe, managing director and majority shareholder of Sudsbury and Smythe, stared at the case uneasily. If generations of Smythes and hyphenated Smythes had learned anything, it was that one's reputation was all, and this felt dodgy. But he couldn't refuse. Thanks to Braun's appearance months ago, Phoenix Shipping was his largest account, and Braun never questioned charges. Almost like halcyon days of old when family fortunes were managed by gentlemen far too polite to question fees. But it was a great deal of money, he thought again, looking at the oversize case.

"Mr. Kairouz, sir," his secretary said, showing a man in.

"Mr. Kairouz, at long last. I've so enjoyed dealing with Captain Braun. I am sorry your own schedule has precluded our meeting."

The man nodded but looked puzzled. The banker was puzzled as well. His visitor was disheveled, with circles under his eyes and a vacant look.

"Coffee or tea?" Carrington-Smythe asked, waving his guest to a sofa.

"Nothing, thank you. I'm pressed, I'm afraid."

"Of course," the banker said, moving the case to the coffee table. "Nasty buggers, these pirates. The Royal Navy should hang the lot, like the old days."

He opened the case. "Had to be creative to fit it all in, I'm afraid. Dollars, pounds, and bearer bonds." He offered a paper. "If you'll verify and sign, we're done."

"I'm sure it's all in order." Kairouz scrawled his signature.

"But… but… my God, sir, that's twelve million doll—"

"I'm sure it's fine." Kairouz closed the case and rose, hefting it in his left hand and extending his right. "Do forgive my rush, but as I said, I am pressed."

"Of course," the banker said. "Is there anything else?"

"No, I… Actually, yes. My phone battery is flat. Could you call a cab?"

"Absolutely. Where to?"

"Heathrow. The private terminal."

B&Q SUPER CENTER
NEW KENT ROAD
NEAR IPS MAIN TERMINAL, LONDON

Braun left the B&Q with a long box on his shoulder. He dashed for the terminal, slowing as he reached the gate to wave to a bored guard and get a nod in return. He spotted Farley at the far end of the covered loading dock next to another truck, both backed in with only their fronts visible from above. He crossed the distance and climbed in, motioning Farley to follow him to the back.

"Tape her up so she can't flail about," Braun said, tossing Farley a roll of duct tape.

Farley worked quickly, glancing over as Braun opened the box.

"Data Shield—Window Film," he read aloud. "What the bloody hell is that?"

"This, Farley, will make our guest invisible. Help me wrap her."

Minutes later, Cassie was encased in a silvery cocoon.

"OK," Braun said, "when you hear my tap, be ready to carry her to the next truck."

"But why—"

"JUST DO IT," Braun said, raising the rear door to exit, then closing it after himself.

He moved into the back of the next truck. The driver was stacking boxes, his back turned. He turned as the van shifted with Braun's weight and got a bullet in the forehead, the soft pop of the silenced pistol lost in the dock noise. Braun moved boxes to the dock, building a wall behind the two trucks, then tapped the back of his own truck and ripped up the roller door. Farley carried Cassie into the next truck unseen.

Braun looked in, nodding at the dead driver. "Get the keys and be ready."

"Where are you going?"

Braun smiled. "To arrange a little distraction," he said and rolled the door down.

The break room was empty, its worn furniture littered with newspaper. Vending machines lined a wall across from a counter holding small appliances. In a corner, Braun found a utility closet with a gas water heater. He moved to the counter and stuffed newspaper into a toaster oven, leaving the oven door ajar before returning to the utility closet. Gas hissed as he unscrewed the connection. He turned the oven on and left.

NEW KENT ROAD
HALF MILE WEST OF IPS TERMINAL

"Control. This is Chase One. We're moving again on New Kent Road," Anna said.

"I copy, Chase One. Target is... wait... no signal, repeat, no signal."

"Air One," Anna said, "do you have visual?"

"I can see the front of the truck," the pilot said. "He hasn't moved."

"Control, is your equipment OK?" Anna asked.

"We're fine, Chase One. The transmitter has been disabled."

The bastard's made us, Anna thought. "Lou. Status?"

"A half mile back," Lou said, "Harry's on with the police. They're hamstrung by jams; they need more time to close."

"Chase One," the chopper broke in, "movement in the terminal."

"Braun's van?" Anna asked.

"Negative. But four others are queuing to leave."

Braun was taking Cassie, Anna realized, else he would've left the signal as a decoy. He was moving, but not his van, and men afoot dragging a girl could hardly escape notice.

"All units," Anna said, "Cassie's in one of those trucks."

"This is Air One. All four are eastbound on New Kent. Whom do I tail?"

"Air One," Anna said, "they have to take the Great Dover roundabout. That leaves four trucks with three possible exits. Stay over the largest group. Chase Two and I will tail trucks that split off. Keep as many in sight as long as possible to vector in police cars. All units confirm."

"Understood, Chase One," the pilot said, doubt in his voice.

"We copy," Lou said. "Harry's called a second chopper, and the police are ordering IPS to ring all of their drivers to stop. Even if he slips us, he'll be the only truck moving."

"Brilliant, Lou," Anna said. "I see the back of the last truck ahead of us now."

"We have you in sight as well," Lou said. "We'll get the bastards, Anna."

Your lips to God's ears, Anna thought, focusing on the truck ahead.

NEW KENT ROAD EASTBOUND

Farley drove third of four.

"Which way?" he asked.

"One chopper can't follow us all. We'll go wherever the others don't," Braun said, watching the trucks ahead and glancing in the side mirror at the truck behind.

The lead truck and the last truck moved left as the second truck edged right.

"Good," Braun said. "Two look to be heading northbound on Great Dover, and the one behind us is going south on Old Kent Road. We'll take Tower Bridge Road. Odds are the chopper will follow the two northbound trucks. And"—he peered back at the terminal in the side mirror—"we should get a little help right about... now."

He grinned as flame bloomed behind them, followed by a low rumble.

Tower Bridge Road

"We've lost them," Braun said. "Time to dump the truck."

Farley nodded. "Our closest cutout is in the car park on Saint Thomas."

"Think, Farley. We stick out like a sore thumb. Duck into the next covered parking. I'll sit on the girl while you change and take a cab to bring the car from Saint Thomas."

Farley nodded, and minutes later, was pulling into a space on the second floor of a parking garage. He changed into street clothes. As he left, Braun dialed his phone.

"Mr. Carrington-Smythe, please. Captain Braun calling," he said.

A moment later, Carrington-Smythe was on the line.

"Good morning ,Captain Braun. How may I—"

"Please," Braun whispered, "you must help me. Has he been there yet?"

"Who? Kairouz? Why yes, some time ago. I did just as you asked."

"Only under duress. Kairouz threatened my family. Poor Sutton resisted, and the monster shot him and torched the office to cover it. He's looting the company and fleeing."

"Good Lord, man! You must go to—"

"I can't. His goons are watching. Notify the authorities, but please, please, leave my name out of it for the sake of my children. Wait! Someone's coming. I must—"

Braun hung up, smiling. That should do it.

CHAPTER TWENTY-SIX

"I'm fine, Tom," Anna repeated.

The IPS terminal had exploded just before her car passed it, wreaking havoc and bringing traffic to an immediate halt. Caught accelerating into the melee, her driver had rear-ended a taxi despite his best efforts. Double black eyes from the exploding air bag left her with a racoonish look, prompting Dugan's unwanted solicitude. She'd insisted on returning to HQ, and the paramedics hadn't argued, having had more serious injuries to attend.

Destruction of the terminal halted efforts to stop the trucks. The police were searching, but she knew they'd find an abandoned truck and cold trail.

"Harry, where's Lou?" she asked. "He and Ward should be here by now."

"He called. They stopped by New Scotland Yard. Didn't say why. I'll give him a call." He was raising his phone when Lou walked in with Ward.

"Christ," Ward said. "Anna, are you—"

"I'm fine."

"Welcome to the Elephant Man Club," Dugan said, earning a glare from Anna.

Dugan ignored the glare and turned to Ward. "So, Jesse. Did the police have something?"

Ward glanced at Lou.

"Metro arrested Alex Kairouz at Heathrow with $12 million in cash and negotiables," Lou said. "He confessed to engineering the attacks. Says he panicked at your arrest and decided to escape."

"Bullshit. How can anyone believ—"

Lou held up a hand. "There's more. He also confessed to killing Sutton and setting the firebombs in the office to cover it. Metro confirmed Sutton's death." Lou paused. "And he named you as coconspirator, Tom."

"Braun coerced him. He's trying to save Cassie. Who can blame him when we screwed up by the numbers? Did you tell that to Scotland Yard?"

"I did," Lou said. "But his story's tight. Says he ordered Braun to grab Cassie for fear Mrs. Farnsworth wouldn't play along. He speculates Braun didn't bring her to the plane because he had an observer who saw the police and warned him off. Rubbish, but credible."

"We need to talk to him," Dugan said.

"We did, Tom," Ward said. "When he learned we'd lost Cassie, he said, 'It's always been up to me—tell Thomas I'm sorry,' and asked to return to his cell."

"Christ on a crutch. Am I under arrest, Jesse?"

"Of course," Ward said, nodding toward Reyes, "you're in Panamanian custody. And Agent Chesterton was most creative in explaining to the Financial Crimes folks at New Scotland Yard both the arcane aspects of international law that allowed you to be in Panamanian custody on British soil and just how they should go about requesting transfer of custody."

Lou Chesterton smiled. "I also assured our law-enforcement colleagues we're keeping close tabs on you and that you had information that is key to our operation. How much time that buys us, I don't know."

Dugan shot Lou a grateful look.

"All right, let's get cracking," Anna said. "Parallel objectives—thwart the attacks and find Braun and Cassie. Tom, you're our ship expert. Thoughts?"

"I'll have Mrs. Coutts check the off-site backups, but I'm sure they're compromised. That leaves my week-old position report and some educated guessing.

"Braun's departure," he continued, "suggests imminent attacks, say within two days. If I exclude Panama and Malacca and draw circles around other choke points with a radius equal to two days' steaming time, we have probable attack-ship envelopes. With the old report, I'll try to weed out tankers that can't possibly have reached these areas."

Anna nodded. "A short list, like before."

"More like a 'much-longer-than-I-want list.' Working with week-old data will complicate things." He sighed. "But I don't have a clue what else to do."

Anna nodded. "Get started straightaway. Tell Harry what you need. This will be our ops center. The IT people will have us up and running within the hour. Braun's escape was improvised, and he's probably reassessing. We'll keep pressure on. I released his photo, along with Farley's and Cassie's, to the media. Moving will be difficult.

"He'll be close," she went on. "We'll check rentals and utility hookups in a fifty-mile radius and cross those against known aliases and family and associates for Farley and Sutton."

Anna saw skepticism. Ward voiced it.

"That's a big area, Anna. There must be a thousand possibilities."

She sighed. "Several thousand. We best get started."

17 SAXON WAY
GRAVESEND, KENT

Braun opened the pantry. "Bloody fuck all."

"Here either," Farley said, standing in front of the open refrigerator.

Braun cursed Sutton as an incompetent fool. First the balls-up about renting the safe house and now this. How difficult could it be to lay in food and supplies? He now understood Sutton's sudden insistence on sabotaging Kairouz's computers via phone link. He'd put off stocking the safe house and intended to do it while Braun and Farley were in the office. He must have been sweating bullets while he sabotaged the computers, rushing to finish so he could get away and stock the place before they arrived. He died before he had the chance, and now Braun regretted not killing the fool slowly.

Braun sighed. "I'll go to the market we passed. But let's check the news first. Assuming that bloody idiot actually got the cable connected."

They moved to the living room and turned on the television.

"...Alexander Kairouz was taken into custody at Heathrow."

Braun smiled.

"Kairouz's daughter is missing, abductors thought to be Karl Braun and Ian Farley, whose photos are shown here along with the girl's. Anyone seeing..."

"Bloody hell," Farley said as Braun's smile faded.

"We'll adapt," Braun said. "You stay here. I'll disguise myself and go. But first, let's take care of the girl."

***

Cassie lay in her silver cocoon on the bedroom floor as they transformed the big closet, taping film to the walls and ceiling and spreading it on the floor, covering that with a rug. Finally they lined the door and hung a film curtain inside, a barrier when the door opened.

Farley carried Cassie in, and Braun squatted on the closet floor beside her as Farley unwrapped the girl. A bloody implant. He fingered her scar. It was deep, but he could get it. No need to rush. They'd be here a while. If she became a great liability, he'd have his fun and slit her throat. He ripped the tape off her mouth and rose, leaving her bound and unconscious.

"I'm going to get ready. Stay in the bedroom and call me if she wakes."

"There ain't a telly in the bedroom. I'll hear her fine in the living room."

"So might the neighbors, you bloody fool," Braun said.

"Oh, all right, but at least let me watch the porn on your laptop."

***

"Just at the best part," muttered Farley as Cassie whimpered.

"Wher... where am I?" she asked as he pushed through the silver curtain.

"In the bosom of your new family."

She lowered her voice. "I have to pee."

"Go ahead," he whispered back, laughing as he left.

He exited the closet to come face-to-face with a stranger, and his hand flew to his shoulder holster.

"It's me, you idiot."

Farley stared. Black hair, not blond. Gray at the temples with a salt-and-pepper mustache. Oral inserts made Braun's face fuller.

"Bloody magic."

"I'll bask in your admiration later, Farley. Is she awake?"

"Yeah." He smirked. "Said she had to piss. I told her go ahead."

"Brilliant. Did you tell her you'd clean it up? She'll be in there several days. Get a pot from the kitchen and a toilet roll from the bathroom."

Chastened, Farley started off as Braun entered the closet.

"Who are you?" Cassie asked.

"Call me 'Uncle Karl.'"

"Please. I have to go to the bathroom really, really bad."

Braun fished out a pocketknife to slice her restraints. He helped her stand as Farley entered and set the pot and toilet paper in the corner.

"I can't use *that*," Cassie whined.

Braun twisted her arm.

"You're hurting me. OK, I'll do it," she said, staggering to the pot.

"Go on," Braun said as she hesitated.

"No. You both leave."

Braun suppressed his anger and motioned for Farley to follow him.

"Goin' soft, are we?" Farley asked outside.

"Slapping a retard with a full bladder is ill-advised, Farley. I'll attend to her before I go."

"I'll do it, guv." Farley rubbed his groin. "I need some fun."

"Forget it, Farley. If you're randy, have a wank."

"But you said—"

"I lied. Live with it."

Farley's nostrils flared. Braun mollified him. He needed Farley. For now.

"Look, Farley, she wasn't part of your original deal. I went along later because your interest terrified Kairouz, but the wogs will pay a fortune for a blond virgin. We'll split it. And if she gets too hot to move, we'll both have a go, then kill her. Fair enough?"

Farley nodded, and Braun beat on the closet door.

"Get a bloody move on, princess. Sixty seconds."

***

Cassie swayed as she rose on stiff legs. She steadied herself on the wall, shifting a strip of film. She watched, terrified, as it curled down from the ceiling in a growing triangle. They'd hurt her again even though it was an accident. She pushed at the tape, smoothing it as far up as she could reach. It looked OK, then the unattached corner resumed its slow crawl downward.

She jumped at the pounding on the door, then calmed herself. A proper young lady did not go flibbertigibbet at setbacks. A young lady rose above difficulties. She slipped out of one shoe, grasped it by the toe, and squatted to explode upward, stretching to push the errant corner in place with the shoe heel. She was slipping back into the shoe as the door opened.

***

Braun pushed her down.

"Tape wrists and ankles again, Farley, wrists in front," Braun said, nodding as Farley complied.

"That's good. Now stand her up and hold her from behind. And pay attention, Farley. You might learn something."

Braun got in her face. "You did a very bad thing, Cassie."

She shook her head, wide-eyed. How did he know?

"You defied me, Cassie. Told me to leave. Now I must punish you."

She was trembling. Farley chuckled.

"Now Farley," Braun said, "with market value a factor, avoid knuckle damage. Use a flatty." He slapped her with his open hand, snapping her head to the side. He went on, ignoring her sobs. "An alternative is the backhand flatty, but it requires care. Jewelry that might leave scars should be removed and nails well trimmed." He pocketed a ring and wiggled manicured fingers.

"The backhand flatty is delivered thus."

He snapped Cassie's head to the opposite side, then pinched her chin between thumb and forefinger, turning her face from side to side.

"Observe, Farley. Only soft-tissue damage. Painful but fast healing. The only scars are mental. The most useful sort."

"Now Cassie," Braun said, "do you understand you must never be bad again?"

She squeezed her eyes shut and nodded.

"Say it."

"I… I wo… won't b… be ba… bad."

"Good, Cassie. But"—he feigned regret—"I'm not sure you're sincere." He slapped her again, twice to each side of her face, and signaled Farley to drop her.

"I'll be back in an hour or so. Leave her in the dark and stay in the bedroom."

SECURITY SERVICE (MI5) HQ
THAMES HOUSE, LONDON

"How's it coming?" Ward asked, passing Dugan a cup of coffee.

"Just peachy. Too many prospects already."

Dugan sighed and looked around. Reyes sat nearby, sipping coffee and watching. Technicians manned terminals. Harry was on the phone with London Metro's Specialist Fire Arms Command, also known as CO19, the hostage rescue unit. Anna and Lou sat, heads together, in the corner.

His phone rang, and Dugan saw Gillian Farnsworth's number on the caller ID. He considered letting it go to voice mail again. He answered on the fifth ring.

"Mr. Dugan. At last. What news?"

"Ahh, there have been… setbacks."

"Setbacks?"

"We lost her signal. We… we've lost her."

Anna hurried over and motioned Dugan to put the call on speaker.

Gillian's voice exploded into the room. "… failed to keep me informed, and those fools with whom you're associated lost Cassie as well. This on top of the lies about Mr. Kairouz in the media—"

"Gillian, this is Anna Walsh. Where are you?"

"On my way to New Scotland Yard. I am—"

"Gillian, I think—"

"I bloody well don't care what you think. I've had quite enough of you all. After I speak with the police, I'm going to the media. With everything in the open, Braun may see there's no advantage in—"

"Gillian, stop behaving like a bloody twit. Your anger's justified, but don't be rash. Come here to Thames House. See what we're doing. Then go to the media if you wish."

"Very well. Daniel is driving me. I'll be there in fifteen minutes."

"I'll have you met in the lobby."

"See that you do." The speaker hummed with a dial tone.

"Anna, you can't be serious?" Ward said.

"Hopefully she'll understand," Anna said. "But if not, we'll have to detain her."

***

"I'm here, Ms. Walsh. Just what am I to see?" Gillian Farnsworth asked.

"The resources we're devoting to Cassie's recovery. Suggestions are appreciated."

"Really? After you ignored my suggestion to move Cassie out of harm's way?"

Anna's response was cut off by a loud beeping.

"Hit on the implant!" a technician screamed.

Anna rushed to his side.

"East. In Kent," he continued. "Yes, North Kent. Let's zero in."

The screen refreshed with agonizing slowness.

"There. Gravesend. Now the address... damn... lost it."

Anna turned. "Sarah. Filter rentals and hookups. Gravesend only. John. Search on Sutton and Farley with Gravesend as primary filter."

"Over a hundred recent hookups," Sarah said quickly.

"Damn. Still too many," Anna said as John hooted.

"Bingo. An obit, two years ago." He read, "'Margaret Sutton. Survived by son, Joel Sutton, of London, and sister, Mary Lampkin, seventy-eight, of Gravesend, Kent.'"

"Address?"

"Checking... got it," John said. "Seventeen Saxon Way, Gravesend. Taxes current. But National Health shows her widowed and resident at a nursing home with senile dementia."

"But planning a recovery," Sarah added. "A new cable hookup at that address was paid for by Joel Sutton."

"Brilliant," Anna said. "Nearest police station?"

Sarah pulled up a map. "There. The North Kent Station."

"Helipad?" Anna asked.

"No," Sarah said. "But there's a car park."

"Lou," Anna said. "Ring North Kent Police to cordon off their car park. They should expect a landing in fifteen minutes."

"On it," Lou said.

"Harry. Ring the CO19 lads with the site. Request a chopper for us as well."

Anna turned back to the technicians. "Sarah, send the—"

"Maps and photos to your phone. Done," Sarah said. "I sent it to the CO19 lads as well."

Anna nodded thanks and turned. "All right, people, let's get to the roof."

They raced out the door. As they rushed down the hall, Anna turned to speak to Ward and stopped in her tracks.

"Gillian, what are you doing?"

"Following you, obviously."

"Out of the question."

"Now you listen—"

"I'm sorry, but this isn't negotiable, and I've no time for argument. You're staying here."

Anna turned and called to a young man walking down the hall. He hurried over.

"Wentworth," Anna said, "escort Mrs. Farnsworth back to the command center and place her in Sarah's care. Tell Sarah Mrs. Farnsworth is to stay there until she hears otherwise from me."

The young agent nodded as Anna turned back to Mrs. Farnsworth.

"Gillian, the command center will be in touch with us at all times, so you'll know what's going on. That's the best I can do," Anna said, then turned and led the team away.

Gillian stood enraged, watching their backs. They'd bungled things and now had the cheek to suggest she wait patiently to be "informed," as if they hadn't bungled that as well. Sod that.

"Ma'am? Mrs. Farnsworth?"

Gillian roused and stared at the young man.

"Please come with me," he said, taking her arm.

Gillian saw a door marked Women nearby. She faked a stumble, then bent slightly at the waist and clutched her midsection.

"Ma'am? What's wrong?" Wentworth asked.

"All the… stress and exci… excitement…" Gillian gasped, moving toward the toilet. "I… I'm ill."

Wentworth allowed Gillian to lead him through the door and stood uncomfortably in the center of the women's restroom as Gillian stumbled into a stall and let the door swing shut behind her. She made horrible retching sounds.

"Ma'am? Are you all right?" Wentworth asked.

"I… I… think you better get… get help. Ge… get… Sarah. Ple… please hurry."

Wentworth raced to the door of the toilet and looked out at the closed door of the command center, down the corridor. He looked about for help, but it was lunch hour, and the hallway was deserted. He called Sarah's name several times, then reached for his cell phone just as another strangled cry came from the stall. The command center was only fifty feet away. He pocketed his phone and raced for the door.

***

Gillian was on her feet and out of the stall as soon as she heard the toilet door swinging closed. She caught it just before it closed and held it open a crack, watching Wentworth's back as he rushed away. She timed her exit as he reached the control room door, bursting from the toilet and across the hall to the stairwell. The stairwell door opened with a loud clunk, and Gillian heard Wentworth's angry shout through the closing stairwell door as she rushed down the single flight to the ground floor.

The ground-level exit was prominently marked EMERGENCY EXIT ONLY—ALARMED DOOR. Gillian burst through it without slowing, and the piercing wail sent her already racing pulse even higher. She raced around the building to find Daniel in the waiting area where she had left him only minutes before.

"How far to Gravesend?" she gasped, out of breath as she slid into the rear seat.

"Are you all right, mum?" Daniel asked, his concern obvious.

"I'm fine, Daniel. But quickly. Gravesend?"

"Do you have an address?"

"Seventeen Saxon Way, Gravesend."

The old driver nodded. "Me wife used to visit a friend out that way before she passed. It's maybe three-quarters of an hour. A bit less if I push."

"See that you do. We're off to get our Cassie."

He turned to the wheel, and she was thrown back in her seat as tires squealed.

17 SAXON WAY
GRAVESEND, KENT

Farley watched porn, pants bulging as he debated a wank. Bloody Kraut. Leading a bloke on. He got up and stalked to the living room, parting the drapes. Slip a taste and slap her quiet? If Braun twigged, what would he do? Cut his bloody bonus, that's what. Bugger. He let the curtains fall and moved back to his porn.

***

"We can't worry about her now, Sarah," Anna said into the phone as she peered between the blinds at the house across the street. "And I don't think she'll go to the media given that she knows we're closing on Cassie's kidnappers."

Anna's radio crackled. "One to Walsh. Positive ID on Farley."

"I have to go, Sarah," Anna said into the phone, hanging up to key the radio mike.

"I saw him, One. Anyone else?"

"Negative. Infrared shows one heat signature. Our lads have a good angle on the window in the back of the garage. There is no vehicle."

"Hold positions; I will advise."

The front door and attached garage of Braun's safe house faced the street, with the backyard enclosed by a fence. Throughout the neighborhood, service alleys separated residents' backyards from those of their neighbors on adjacent streets. Fourteen Saxon Way, diagonally across from the safe house, was vacant, and Anna's team had entered unseen from the service alley. She stood now in the living room, a sniper in the bedroom above and an assault team in the alley directly behind number seventeen.

Anna stepped back from the window as Lou moved to take her place.

"They must have shielded the implant," she said. "We got the flicker when that was somehow compromised. But if they shielded a whole room, Cassie and Braun might be inside. But where's their car?"

"Farley stared one way," Ward said. "He's expecting someone. My bet's Braun."

Standing nearby, Reyes grunted agreement.

"Take Farley out," Dugan said. "Save Cassie and wait for Braun."

Anna looked doubtful. "Braun may have some sort of prearranged "all clear" signal before he returns. If Cassie's with him, we risk losing them both. Taking out Farley's not worth the risk of losing both Cassie and any chance of sweating Braun."

"I don't think we have to worry about Farnsworth going to the media," Lou said from the window.

"Bloody hell," Anna said as she joined him to see a poorly disguised Gillian Farnsworth approach a nearby bus stop.

"What can we do now?" Dugan asked.

"Nothing," Anna said. "If we try to pull her in, Farley will spot us for sure, especially if she makes a fuss. All we can do is pray Braun develops myopia. Harry," Anna said over her shoulder, "when it hits the fan, go collect Mrs. Bloody Farnsworth."

***

Gillian Farnsworth sat at the bus stop in a head scarf and dark glasses. Sufficient, she was sure. She'd be the last person Braun expected.

They'd arrived before Daniel's projection, and it had taken all her persuasive powers to get the driver to agree to drop her and park well away to await her call. She was unsure what to do but trusted it would become obvious. She peeked over her shades. She could hardly do worse than the "professionals," after all. It was obvious their priority was Braun, not Cassie.

***

Braun returned the clerk's smile, though he hardly felt cordial. The selection was abysmal, and his cart was piled with food he detested. He rolled it out to the van, parked between the supermarket and the chemist shop where he earlier bought supplies for removing the implant.

Braun loaded the supplies and pulled out of the parking lot, turning away from the safe house to trace a meandering path through the surrounding neighborhood, alert to anyone following. Good tradecraft was always necessary, even when one was sure of no surveillance. He smiled. Or perhaps especially when one was sure of no surveillance.

He completed a series of random turns and was just about to head for the safe house when he passed Kairouz's car. It was parked in plain sight on the side of the road, the driver leaning against the side and smoking his pipe. What the hell was the old kike doing here? Coincidence? He didn't believe in coincidence. But if it was some sort of trap, why was he parked in the open? Braun continued, scanning his surroundings with even more care than usual.

***

Farley rubbed himself through his pants. Braun would likely dawdle, picking wine and other Frenchified crap. Not like a proper bloke who'd grab a few cases of Guinness and some grub. Farley had time. And he'd thought on the virgin thing. No problem. She could give him a gobble, then take it up the bum.

She blinked up at the light.

"You need a stretch." He smiled as he cut the tape on her wrists and ankles.

"Th… thank you."

"We should be friends, Cassie. Nice to each other, like."

215

"I... I guess so."

"Good," he said, unbuckling.

She drew away, but he grabbed a fistful of hair with one hand and pushed down his pants with the other.

"Here's a new friend then. Come on. Give him a kiss."

***

Braun continued his circuitous route, confidence returning as each unnecessary detour failed to reveal a tail. Then he spotted Gillian Farnsworth at the bus stop. How'd she find them? That idiot Sutton must have let something slip to the Coutts hag, who then told Farnsworth. Sitting in plain sight in that ridiculous disguise was proof enough she was acting alone. Even the police weren't that incompetent.

However she'd found him, she was a complication, bound to call the police when she spotted him. But he had to get the laptop and take care of Farley and the girl. She turned toward him, then looked away without recognition. Good. She'd be confused when he turned into the drive and likely delay calling the police. He'd finish his business inside and be gone, two minutes tops. He'd put a bullet in her head on the way out. Even if she'd already called, he'd have plenty of time before the cops showed up.

He turned into the drive, his plan in place, to be undone by an earsplitting scream from 17 Saxon Way.

CHAPTER TWENTY-SEVEN

Cassie tried to stay calm, remembering the secret things Mrs. Farnsworth taught her. She chanted to herself in the dark, comforted by the words and the rigid sliver concealed between cupped palms. Then he was there—all kind words and a mean smile. She felt a sharp pain as he yanked her by the hair and shoved her face toward his ugly, swollen thing. She fought down her terror and lived the rhyme:

Jab it in deep
Right to the end
Knickers to knees
Then run like the wind

Farley screamed when she drove the needle through his penis. He groped himself with both hands, and Cassie jerked his pants down and scooted away. Farley lunged and fell forward, his clawing fingers just brushing her as the needle snagged the carpet, tethering him in place by his member.

Cassie burst from the closet and raced through the house. She found the front door locked tight with a keyed dead bolt and retraced her steps, racing past the bedroom where Farley bellowed. She rushed through the kitchen toward the door to the garage, but the sound of the garage-door opener brought her up short. She darted into the pantry, making herself small against shelves to squeeze the door closed to a crack just as Uncle Karl burst in from the garage, gun drawn, rushing toward Farley's voice.

As Uncle Karl disappeared into the hallway, Cassie bolted through the open kitchen door just as the big garage door kissed the concrete. The windowed back door was also locked with a keyed lock. Heart pounding, Cassie mashed the wall control and raced to the big garage door. She fell to her hands and knees as the door inched upward, intent on the widening opening.

***

Farley held up bloody pants with one hand and gripped his Glock with the other.

"You get her?" he asked.

"You lost her? You bloody imbecile."

"She stabbed me. You must—"

Braun heard the garage-door opener and cursed as he raced back through the kitchen and around the van. The rising door was eighteen inches off the concrete, and Cassie's feet disappeared beneath it. He thought quickly. The Farnsworth bitch would rush to the girl. He'd drop them both and drag the bodies inside. Then he'd deal with Farley and be away before the cops arrived. There was time still. He dropped to one knee, waiting for the rising door to reveal his targets.

TWO MINUTES EARLIER
ACROSS THE STREET AT 14 SAXON WAY
GRAVESEND, KENT

"One. Can your man wound him?" Anna asked into her throat mike as the van turned in.

"If he gets out before the door closes. And the house?"

"Have your lads crash it on your shot."

"Roger," he said.

A scream split the air, and Anna watched Gillian Farnsworth stand and rush forward.

"God damn it," Anna said. "Stand down, One."

Anna turned, but Harry was already moving.

***

Harry overtook her in the drive as the garage door closed. He grabbed her arm.

"Come along, luv. Off the street."

Gillian turned. "Let me go, you bloody fool. Cassie's in there."

"And we'll save her if you don't muck it up," Harry said, pulling her along.

They both turned at the sound of the rising door to see a blond head appear. Cassie wriggled free, and Gillian flattened Harry's nose with an elbow worthy of an NBA point guard and bolted. He rushed after, blood pulsing from his nose as he drew his gun and focused on the door, alert to pursuit.

"Get her across the street!" Harry yelled to Gillian, moving to shield them. He saw Braun's feet and fired, cursing as the feet disappeared and the big garage door reversed course. He backed after his charges, gun trained toward the threat.

***

Mrs. Farnsworth held Cassie, whispering reassurance. Despite her outward calm, Gillian Farnsworth simmered. Anna saw it in her eyes as she touched the girl's bruised face. Only Cassie's need was containing that rage. Anna turned back to the task at hand.

"Good work, Harry," Anna said. "They've no leverage now, and they'll be rattled."

"What's the plan?" Ward asked.

"We'll let them stew a bit until they're ready to deal," Anna said. "With any luck, they'll surrender, and we can separate them—play one against the other."

The men nodded, then everyone looked toward the windows at the sound of gunfire from Braun's hideout.

"Bloody hell," Anna said. "Now what?"

"I think, Agent Walsh," Reyes said, "someone is securing a monopoly on marketable information."

"Crash the house," Anna yelled into her mike.

***

Braun was angry but not rattled. He fully intended to surrender—after he'd taken care of things. The laptop was on the living-room coffee table, with the programmed destruction of the hard drive in progress.

"I finally got it out," Farley said as he limped in. "Where is that little bitch?"

Farley was oblivious, having left Cassie's pursuit to Braun to sequester himself in the bathroom, preoccupied with his punctured dick.

"She escaped, you idiot. And we're surrounded."

"What?" Farley limped to the window as Braun mulled options.

With the girl free, he had only information to trade. He had a bit of negotiating time, perhaps as much as twenty-four hours before the next attack, then the value of his information would plummet as the body bags were stacked. Farley knew little, but the authorities wouldn't know that. They might waste valuable time on the idiot, a costly delay for Braun. He drew his gun. He had to clarify the situation for them.

Farley peered out, his back turned. "I don't see—"

He dropped as he saw Braun's reflection in the windowpane, just before the *sphut*, *sphut* of the silenced pistol and the sound of breaking glass. Farley scrambled, popping up behind the sofa to return fire, his Glock booming. Braun crawled unseen behind an armchair and covered the only door just as Farley fired at Braun's last position and ran. He was framed in the doorway when Braun's bullet shattered his spine. He pitched forward, his Glock clattering on the hardwood as Braun stepped into the hall and shot him twice in the head.

Braun returned to find the computer done, the screen black, just as projectiles crashed through the windows. How unnecessary, he thought, tossing his gun to the floor and flopping down on the sofa, hands over his ears, eyes shut. The flash bangs were followed by splintering wood. So bloody predictable it was hardly a challenge.

"I'm unarmed. I surrender," he called.

***

"What now?" Dugan asked.

Farley sprawled in a bloody pool. Braun was perched on a straight-back chair in the dining room, bound hand and foot and under guard.

"With a firearm-related fatality," Anna said, "the locals will document the scene. Our request for Braun will go through channels, but we can question him now, while we wait."

Ward walked in. "Where's Harry?"

"With Cassie and Mrs. Farnsworth," Anna said. "He'll see them home."

Ward nodded as she turned to the uniformed officer guarding Braun.

"You can go, Constable," Anna said. "Thank you."

"Glad to help, Agent Walsh," said the cop as he left.

"*Agent* Walsh is it?" Braun said. "And you played the slut so well. Experience? And Dugan's an agent as well? Bravo. I've never been outfoxed before."

Anna smiled. "Yet here you sit, trussed up like a bloody Christmas goose."

"A temporary setback."

"Oh really?" she asked.

"Don't be tedious, Anna. You know you need my help, and I'm not unwilling to give it."

220

"In exchange for what?"

"Immunity and a private jet, of course."

"Not bloody likely," Anna said.

Braun shrugged.

"Let's just beat it out of him," suggested Dugan.

Braun laughed. "You pathetic amateur. I'm trained to tolerate harsher methods than you lot are allowed. By the way, when can I see a lawyer?"

Ward grabbed Dugan as he lunged, and tugged him into the hall.

***

Reyes thought Dugan's suggestion was eminently sensible, and he followed as Ward wrestled Dugan into the hallway. Ward gave Reyes a look over his shoulder and then ignored him to concentrate on Dugan.

"Tom. Control yourself or leave," Ward said.

"That son of—"

"Like it or not, we play by the rules," Ward said. "We don't beat suspects or hook jumper cables to their balls. Remember that."

"Suspect? He's not a suspect. We know the bastard's behind this, and people—more people—are gonna die if he doesn't talk, so maybe we just need to remember red is positive and black is negative."

"God damn it, Tom. We don't—"

Dugan held up his hands in surrender. "All right. All right. I'll control myself," he said.

Ward gave him an appraising look, then nodded, leading Dugan back into the room. Reyes followed. He was beginning to like this Dugan.

***

The three men returned to the dining room, trailed by a local policeman.

"Harry Albright?" asked the cop, directing his query at the group.

"Across the street," Anna said.

The cop keyed his mike. "Colin. George here. Is Albright, the MI5 bloke, near you?"

"Right here," came the reply.

"A friend of his at Metro called," the cop said into his radio. "He hasn't been able to get through on his cell but asked us to pass the word that some bugger named Kairouge hung himself. Said he figured Albright would want to know."

"He heard, George."

"OK. Thanks, mate." As George left the room, a peal of laughter shattered the silence.

"Now this makes the cheese more binding," Braun said. "Kairouz dead. In a fit of remorse, no doubt. I'm sure my lawyer—"

Dugan was faster than Ward this time. He knocked Braun to the floor and was over him in a flash, cocking his fist again as Ward and Lou wrestled him away. Dugan screamed abuse and kicked at Braun with adrenaline-fueled rage as he struggled in the men's grasp. Lou pressed a hard knuckle behind Dugan's ear, and he slumped.

"Wha… what the hell was that?" Dugan asked a moment later as Ward helped Braun to the chair.

"Subjection pressure point," Lou said. "We need the bastard conscious, Tom."

Braun grinned up with bloody teeth. "Enjoy that, Dugan? It changes nothing. Kairouz hung himself up like a fat, rotten Christmas ornament, and now I'm untouchable. And the price of information has risen. Take a few minutes to consider a reasonable offer, why don't you all? But not too long. Tick. Tick. Tick."

14 Saxon Way
Gravesend, Kent

Cassie clutched Gillian's hands. "Is Poppa all right?"

"I'm sure he is, dear. I'll just go straighten this out," Gillian said, gently freeing her hands. "Agent Albright," she called.

Harry entered tentatively, unsure if they'd overheard the radio.

"Agent Albright. Stay with Cassie. I need a word with Agent Walsh."

"Ah… I don't know—"

"Thank you," Gillian said.

She maintained her composure until she got outside, then tears blurred her vision as she crossed the street in a stumbling run, praying she'd misunderstood. She walked into number seventeen and stopped, staring at Farley's body in a pool of blood, his gun nearby on the hardwood floor beside a numbered marker as technicians photographed the scene. Then she heard

Braun's odious, mocking voice from a doorway down the hall, so like another she'd silenced long ago.

"...changes nothing. Kairouz hung himself up like a fat, rotten Christmas ornament, and now I'm untouchable. And..."

In that horrible moment, she knew it was true that Braun had somehow killed the noblest man she'd ever known. Suddenly she knew what she must do, drawn to the door like a mongoose to a cobra, scooping up Farley's gun from the floor on the way.

"You bloody arsehole!" she screamed as she rushed into the room.

She was Daisy now, firing point-blank, the round punching into him. Recoil spoiled her aim, and the next shot went wild as the slide popped open, the Glock empty. She charged, the gun a club, and it took both Ward and Lou to restrain her.

The next thing Daisy remembered was Anna's voice in her ear.

"Cassie needs you now," said the voice, and rage abated, replaced with a strange emptiness. Daisy searched for Gillian as she was led away between two constables, afraid her wonderful life was lost forever.

***

Braun lay faceup, frothy blood bubbling from his bare chest. He was blue.

"Sucking chest wound," Lou said. "No exit. Hit a rib maybe. Gotta seal it."

"Tom," Ward said. "The bedroom. I saw some duct tape there."

Dugan rushed out as Anna called medevac. When he returned, Ward taped the wound, and they sat Braun up against the wall. He quickly improved—and sneered.

"Bravo," Braun said. "Is this where I'm overcome by gratitude and tell all?"

Lou looked at the others and jerked his head toward the door.

"ETA on the chopper?" he asked in the hall.

"Fifteen minutes," Anna said. "Will he make it?"

"Probably," Lou said. "Not that it matters much now."

She nodded. "By the time he gets out of surgery, we'll be up to our bums in lawyers. And it may be too late anyway."

"Unless he has a change of heart," Lou said, "near-death experience and all. Pity we can't ask, seeing as how we must help the locals prepare a landing area for the chopper."

Lou turned to Dugan. "Can you ask him, Tom? Now mind you, he's not to be mistreated—though he may well claim you did, there being no witnesses and all."

Anna objected. "It should be one of us. Tom's not a trained interrogator."

Ward shook his head. "No, Anna. Lou's right. Braun's not worried about us, but Tom's a credible threat."

Anna looked at Dugan. "Can you do it?"

Dugan's eyes left no doubt. "Oh yeah," he said softly.

Reyes spoke for the first time. "May I suggest that it may seem more credible to Braun if it appears that *Señor Dugan* has slipped away to question Braun on his own?"

Moments later, Anna cleared the house by requesting all the local police to help cordon off the landing zone. As people trooped into the street, Ward hung back a bit, his hand on Dugan's shoulder. They locked eyes.

"I guess sometimes maybe it has to be red is positive and black is negative," Ward said.

Dugan nodded, and Ward moved off with the others.

***

"Where did everyone go, and what are you doing here?" Braun demanded.

Dugan locked the door and squatted by Braun, forearms across his knees. He smiled.

"I slipped back for a chat about the next attacks. It'll help at your trial."

"What trial? Kairouz confessed. Worry about your own trial, you idiot."

Dugan changed tacks. "Think of the thousands that will die."

Braun's laugh finished in a bloody cough.

"They mean nothing to me," he said as he recovered. "You look ridiculous, squatting there like some movie cowboy. Say something appropriate. Yippee tie yie yay, perhaps?"

Dugan rose and grabbed Braun's ankles, jerking the man from the wall so fast his head bounced on the hardwood. Dugan ripped the tape off the wound and got in Braun's face.

"Yee haa," he said, spraying spittle. "How's that, asshole?

"You've fucked me all right," Dugan continued. "Maybe a little too hard. I got nothing left to lose. You think I give two shits about your evil masters or your motives. News flash. I don't. I can use info about the attacks to save my own ass. If you won't provide it, I've no reason to keep you alive. I'll watch you drown in your own blood, then slap the tape back and sit you up. There's no downside, Karl. I can't be any worse off than I am."

Braun gasped, and Dugan patted his shoulder.

"I know it hurts. And I want you to know, I'm still open to a trade. But don't take too long, because you're looking a little blue." He paused. "What was that phrase you like? Oh yeah. Tick. Tick. Tick."

Braun's lips moved. "O… OK," he said.

"Great, Karl. Let's start easy. How many more attacks? I'll say numbers, and you nod or shake your head. OK?"

Braun nodded.

"Here we go. Three or more?"

Braun shook his head.

"Good," Dugan said. "Two more attacks?"

Again, Braun shook his head.

"Great, Karl. So there's one more attack?"

Braun nodded. Eyes closed. Face a blue mask. Dugan slapped his cheeks.

"Stay with me, Karl. Where?"

Braun's lips moved, and Dugan put his ear close. "Is… Is… Ista…"

"Istanbul? The Bosphorus Straits?"

Braun managed a nod.

Dugan slapped him harder. "What ship? What load port? Talk to me."

Braun opened his eyes and tried to speak as frothy blood whistled from his wound. "O… o…" he began. His head fell to one side.

Dugan slapped the tape back and dragged Braun upright just as paramedics entered the house. Dugan ran outside.

"One more attack," Dugan shouted over chopper noise. "Istanbul."

Anna shouted back. "We've good news too. Alex survived, but he's in serious condition."

Dugan closed his eyes and nodded as Ward gripped his shoulder. He opened them to see paramedics rush Braun to the chopper.

Anna had called in their own chopper, and as they flew back to Thames House, Dugan's thoughts turned eastward to Istanbul, city of thirteen million astride the winding Bosphorus.

CHAPTER TWENTY-EIGHT

Dugan looked up as Anna entered the waiting room.

"How's Braun?" he asked.

"Still under from the surgery," Anna said. "And Alex? What's the doctor say?"

"That he's lucky to be alive," Dugan said. "The activation bulb in the sprinkler head he rigged the rope to fractured and set off the sprinklers. They got to him fast, but we won't know about brain damage unless... until... he wakes up."

"Have you been in?"

Dugan shook his head. "Visitation's limited. I didn't want to deprive Cassie and Mrs. Farnsworth of any time in case..."

Anna nodded, and Dugan fell silent, composing himself before continuing.

"Thank you for Gillian. She couldn't bear being locked away now."

Anna shrugged. "She was bringing the gun to us, and it accidentally discharged."

"You're OK with that?"

"When the law is at odds with justice, I'll take justice."

"Thank you," he said again. Then added, "I have to get to Russia."

"Why? It's up to the Russians and Turks now."

A known target had cut Dugan's list to six ships, and he'd called each with news of the office fire and updated their positions in the process. Only the M/T *Phoenix Orion*, loading crude at Novorossiysk, Russia, was close enough. Braun's "'O... o...'" had meant "Orion."

"Someone has to protect Alex's interests. Liability from the *Asian Trader* alone could ruin him, and you can count on the underwriters denying claims on the premise of criminal activity."

"But what's that have to do with the next attack?"

"Because he'll need all his assets to survive this. *Orion* is a profitable ship, and I need to be on the ground to persuade the Russians not to impound her after they stop the attack. And there's the crew. Remember that school incident? The Russians killed half the kids along with the terrorists. You think they care about our crew?"

"But what can—"

"Ingratiate myself. Offer advice. Whatever. I'll play it by ear."

Ward walked in during Dugan's discourse and was nodding.

"Can you even get there in time?" Anna asked.

"I need help," Dugan admitted. "Commercial flights are via Moscow with long layovers, but it's only five hours by business jet. The airport is daylight only, but if I leave by eleven, I'll be there at dawn."

Anna stared. "Aren't you forgetting something? You're still in 'Panamanian custody,' and even if you weren't, with Alex's confession, Scotland Yard considers you a suspect. We can look the other way, but neither Jesse nor I can openly provide transport."

Ward cleared his throat. "I don't think the Panamanian custody thing will be too big a problem. Being a good cop, Reyes has figured out where the bodies are buried. He's sticking to Braun like glue. He seems to have lost interest in Tom."

"And I don't expect either of you to provide transport, Anna," Dugan said. "I'm betting Braun prepaid that charter outfit to take Alex to Beirut. How would they react to a call from MI5 questioning their involvement?"

"Nervously, at the very least," Anna said.

Dugan smiled. "Now suppose you implied Her Majesty's Government would be grateful if the forfeited payment were used to take me to Russia?"

She nodded. "Devious, Dugan, but it might work."

She pulled out her phone, then noticed a No Mobile Phone sign and moved to an exit.

Dugan turned to Ward.

"So Jesse, how are things at the Langley Puzzle Palace?"

"Shaky. With these latest developments, Gardner's back up on the fence ready to hammer us or take credit, depending on the outcome. But he hates your guts. I'm concerned about you going to Russia solo."

"Come with me."

Ward shook his head. "I need to stick near Braun. He's still the key. But I'll try to watch your back. With Gardner involved, anything could happen."

Dugan nodded as Anna returned.

"Air Dugan departs tonight at ten thirty," she announced.

AIRBORNE EN ROUTE TO RUSSIA

Dugan jerked awake.

"Dugan," he said into the phone.

"Tom. Jesse."

"Is Alex—"

"No change there, but Braun talked. But we had to cut a deal—"

"We've got the ship. Why rush to cut a deal with that—"

"No, we don't. He was saying 'Odessa,' not 'Orion.'"

"We got nothing loading in Odessa. I couldn't—"

"An unrecorded charter. Not your fault, Tom."

Dugan sighed. "OK. Let's hear it."

"*Contessa di Mare*, owned by Fratelli Barbiero Compagnia di Navigazione, loading gasoline in Odessa for Genoa. Four Chechen terrorists aboard."

"I'll divert."

"Too late. She sailed yesterday. ETA at the Bosphorus pilot station is 1100 local today. Langley notified everyone, but the Turks seem skeptical. Our earlier misstep didn't reassure them. And the Russians are still involved. They won't ignore a threat to the Bosphorus."

"Christ. What should I do?"

"Nothing. Things are too unstable. Langley, Moscow, Ankara, and God knows who else are in the act. Land, refuel, and leave before the shit hits the fan. If you're met, give what advice you can and leave."

"Got it," Dugan said. "By the way, what's the target? The strait's pretty long."

"Unknown. Braun was having problems. The docs made us stop. We'll try later."

"OK, pal. See you soon," Dugan said.

M/T *Contessa di Mare*
Black Sea Due North of Istanbul
0130 Hours Local Time
7 July

Khassan Basaev's gut knotted from weeks of stress, but it was almost over. The Chechens and their weapons, boxed as "ship spares in transit," sped through the airport behind liberal bribes. The midnight boarding had gone equally well.

Awakened from his attempt at a few hours rest before a predawn sailing, the chief engineer was predictably confused by the forged work order. He'd ordered no riding gang. On cue, Basaev suggested riding to Istanbul, a day away, confirming the orders in transit. If there was a mistake, he promised his team would disembark at no cost. Happy to avoid spending the rest of the night on the phone to Genoa, the captain and chief engineer agreed.

They seized the bridge just after departure, Basaev holding the captain at gunpoint as his comrades corralled the crew in the aft rope locker. The Chechens freed a few crewmen at a time to raise cargo-tank covers and remove the steel blanks from the manifold discharge flanges as Doku and Shamil rigged charges along deck.

Then they used their recent training, and fumes boiled from the hatches as they ventilated the cargo tanks with fresh air. Inert gas hung above the deck in a cloud, changing to an explosive mix of air and gasoline as the inert gas was purged. Finally, they concealed their work, stopping the fans and moving the hatch covers almost, but not quite, closed. The wind dissipated the explosive cloud, but the fans would force it from the tanks again when the time was right.

Basaev touched the detonator in his pocket. He'd increased speed to claim the first morning transit slot. Soon he would be in Paradise, and the Russian scum would be choking on their oil. He thought of his loved ones' deaths and wrapped himself in hate like an old, familiar blanket. A poor substitute for love, but it was all he had.

Vityazevo Airport
Anapa, Russian Federation

"Welcome to Mother Russia," the copilot said from the cockpit door as the plane rolled to a stop. "We'll refuel and stand by, but I think you'll have a welcoming committee. They asked for you by name when we requested clearance."

Not good, Dugan thought.

Three men waited on the tarmac: two in black behind a short man in a baggy brown uniform. Shorty glanced over his shoulder before turning back to Dugan and extending his hand.

"Passport," he said, exhausting his English. Dugan surrendered his passport, and Shorty passed it to the larger of the men behind him.

Mr. In Charge studied the passport and Dugan's battered face as Dugan reciprocated, ignoring Shorty. The others were tall, midthirties, with old faces. They wore tailored combat utilities with the Russian tricolor on the shoulder.

Mr. In Charge pocketed the passport and barked at Shorty in Russian, and the little bureaucrat scurried away without a backward glance.

"You come," Mr. In Charge said as he and his subordinate turned.

"Wait," Dugan said, "I'm returning to London."

"Nyet," the Russian called back, walking away.

Dugan hustled past them to stop in their path, his arm extended palm outward. Soon it pressed against Mr. In Charge's chest.

"OK, let's try that again. Give me my damned passport and tell me who the hell you are. If I like your answer, we'll talk."

The Russian glared at the hand until Dugan removed it. Then he nodded.

"I am Major Andrei Borgdanov, and this is Sergeant Ilya Denosovich. We belong to Federal Security Service, Special Operations Detachment, Krasnodar, Directorate V, Counterterrorism Unit." He paused. "And your plane leaves when I say. So if you want me to authorize this, you come. Or plane will be here long, long time."

The Russians resumed their walk toward a Humvee-like vehicle. Left with no choice, Dugan followed. The sergeant pointed to the rear seat before crawling behind the wheel, as Borgdanov took shotgun. They roared away, Dugan groping for a nonexistent seat belt, up the taxiway to a service area and a helicopter surrounded by men in the same black uniforms.

The sergeant braked hard, dumping Dugan on the floorboard to jeers from the waiting Russians. The major yelled something, stifling the jeers if not the smirks. The sergeant grinned over the seat at Dugan.

Eight of the Russians were dressed like the sergeant, but three had different uniforms, Dugan saw as he got out. Aircrew, he thought, not full members of the Crazy Commando Club. Borgdanov wrapped a big hand around Dugan's bicep and steered him toward the chopper.

"We must get ready," he said.

Dugan jerked his arm free. "So what can I tell you?"

"What? Nyet. Get ready." The major nodded toward black utilities and body armor the sergeant was unloading.

"Whoa. I'm an advisor. I'm not going with you."

"You are Agent Thomas Dugan of American CIA, here to help us as agreed." Borgdanov nodded, and the sergeant approached, intent on undressing Dugan, by force if necessary.

Dugan backed away, alarms clanging at "Agent Dugan."

"Look. I'll just be in the way."

"*Da*, but you are American. We go to extreme range and must land in Turkey after, but Turks deny permission because we are Russians. So, we become multinational force, *da*? Turks are in NATO and will accept American-led force. You are only American close enough, so"—he smiled —"you are leader."

"I'm not CIA," Dugan insisted.

"Gardner explained you have to say this, but do not worry, Dugan. Now you work with us. This man Gardner agreed on conference call. Is his idea. He is your CIA superior, *da*?"

"Shit," Dugan said, pulling out his phone. The sergeant snatched it, smirking. Dugan swallowed his anger, his judgment improved since Panama.

"Communications blackout," Borgdanov said, adding, "Dugan, is safe. You are here for show. You stay with chopper."

"I am not getting on that fucking chopper."

Borgdanov's face clouded as he drew his pistol. "Understand, Dugan. Body of CIA man and American passport is enough I think, maybe easier. Our American leader maybe killed during attack on ship. You decide."

Dugan swallowed his heart and nodded.

Borgdanov smiled, holstering his gun and unleashing a burst of Russian that had Sergeant Denosovich and another Russian tugging off Dugan's jacket.

"But why do I have to wear this shit?"

"Must look good for Turks, and armor is in case terrorist bastard shoots at chopper."

So much for safe, Dugan thought as he struggled with the unfamiliar gear and the sergeant's running commentary drew chuckles from the others.

"I'd feel better if Sarge here didn't say 'dead' every second sentence."

"Not 'dead,' Dugan. '*Dyed.*' Short for '*dyedushka*,' or grandfather."

Dugan glared at the sergeant, who grinned back and spit out a stream of Russian.

"What did he say?" Dugan asked, still glaring.

"He says that from looks of grandfather's face, he has seen recent combat, but he doesn't think you win this fight."

Borgdanov struggled to keep a straight face.

"Actually, Dugan," he added, "*dyed* is term of great respect."

I guess that explains the shit-eating grins, Dugan thought.

The sergeant looked him over. Satisfied, he ripped the Russian Federation tricolor from Dugan's shoulder and pressed an American flag patch onto the Velcro. He moved beside Borgdanov, and to Dugan's amazement, both came to attention and saluted.

"Agent Thomas Dugan of American CIA. I greet you as American component and Commander of Multinational Strike Force One." Borgdanov snapped his hand down.

"Now get in chopper."

***

Dugan sat beside the major, facing backward at the others. A man pointed, and Dugan saw another helicopter. He looked quizzically at Borgdanov, who produced a headset, miming for Dugan to put it on as he did the same with another.

"Is Captain Petrov's team. They assault. We are support and backup. Always we send two teams. How you say? Redundancy?"

Dugan nodded. "What's the plan?"

"We attack at sea. Both choppers come in high, then drop and sweep bridge with Gatling guns. Then we circle while Petrov closes. They use ropes. How you say..."

"Rappel?"

"*Da*, rappel. Then Petrov kills fanatics and stops ship. Your CIA says four fanatics on board. We should kill one or two on bridge. Should not take so long for others."

"What about the bridge crew?"

Borgdanov seemed confused. "They die. Of course."

Dugan stared. "That's the plan?"

"*Da.* We have fuel to stay a few minutes only. If ship gets to Bosphorus, many people die, including all crew. We save many people, maybe even some crew. Is better, *da*?"

Brutal, but logical. Dugan nodded without speaking, listening to exchanges in Russian between the choppers. Then came a lengthy burst, the voice strained. Borgdanov responded, triggering an argument. Borgdanov screamed a final "nyet" and a short sentence that ended it.

"What's up?" Dugan asked when his headset grew quiet.

"Other pilot complains of very high headwinds. It means increased fuel consumption, and he claims no way to reach target with such winds. He wants to abort. Always these flyers look for tricks to escape duty. I refuse."

Their pilot glared over his shoulder, obviously an English speaker. Borgdanov glared back, and the man looked away.

"But how can you stop him from aborting?" Dugan asked.

"If he aborts, I say to Petrov to shoot flight crew as soon as chopper lands."

Christ, Dugan thought, this is one scary bastard.

***

An hour and a half later, Dugan roused to the pilot's voice in his headphones. Borgdanov acknowledged the pilot and returned Dugan's passport, motioning the sergeant to return his sat phone as well.

"Point of no return," Borgdanov said, "now we continue to Turkey no matter what. But I need your help. The terrorists have disabled GPS on ship so she is not so easy to find. My plan was to fly to Bosphorus entrance, then north on course for Odessa to find ship, but now pilot says because of wind, fuel is too low for this. He exaggerates, of course, but even so, I think we do not have fuel to waste. With good position, we go straight to ship. I need CIA satellites."

"What about your own satellites?"

"We have not so many now, and they watch US and China, not Black Sea." He smiled. "I think your satellites already look Black Sea, so no need to retask, *da*?"

Dugan nodded, then shed his headset and called Ward, phone jammed against one ear and his finger in the other against the noise of the chopper.

"God damn it, Tom, where the hell are you? The charter plane pilot said th—"

"In a Russian chopper over the Black Sea thanks to your asshole boss."

"Gardner? Son of a bitch. He's screwed this up by the numbers. OK, look. Have the Russians—"

"Too late. We're low on fuel. You have a position on the ship?"

"Christ. Langley was to have updated the Russians an hour ago. I guess Gardner screwed that up too." He paused. "She'll reach the pilot station four hours early. Your best bet is to intercept just before arrival."

"Not good, Jesse. We've got strong headwinds. What about the Turks?"

"Langley's in contact with Ankara, but it's a cluster fuck. I have no clue what's actually filtering down to the locals in Istanbul or to the Bosphorus pilots. We're dancing in the dark."

Dugan sighed. "OK. Got a specific target yet?"

"We're still waiting to resume questioning Braun."

"Ship info?"

"Yeah, Anna's tech wizards converted the vessel particulars sheet to a text message. We'll send it to your phone."

"Thanks, Jesse. Keep me posted."

"Will do, Tom. Watch yourself."

"Like I have a choice," Dugan said.

CHAPTER TWENTY-NINE

M/T CONTESSA DI MARE
BLACK SEA
NORTH OF TURKELI LIGHTHOUSE

Day dawned as Basaev watched radar dots become ships, converging on the Bosphorus. He moved to the bridge wing, his stomach knot tightening at the sight of the tanker overtaking him, a competitor for the first southbound slot. A slot he had to have to arrive when his target crawled with infidel tourists and fawning Turks.

Passage through the Bosphorus "without delay or regulation" had been guaranteed by treaty for decades when the Turks moved unilaterally in 1994 to regulate burgeoning tanker traffic. Her northern neighbors protested still, while many Turks pressed for a total ban. Western Europe, hungry for Russian oil, stayed neutral, and a compromise developed. The Black Sea states refused to accept Turkey's actions, even as they complied, and the Turks let compliant tankers pass. A compromise Basaev would end, God willing. He moved to the radio.

"Turkeli Control, this is the tanker *Contessa di Mare*. Over."

"Go ahead, *Contessa di Mare*."

"Our ETA is oh seven hundred. We request clearance, over."

"You are early, *Contessa*," came the reply, "from your twenty-four hour rep—"

"Control, this is tanker *Svirstroy*," said a Russian voice. "*Contessa* is not at reporting point. I will arrive first and claim first slot. Over."

"*Contessa*, this is Control. You are cleared for transit. Call the Kavak Pilots on channel seventy-one. Use twelve in the strait, but report on thirteen at Anadolu Light. Over."

"Control, this is *Contessa di Mare*. I copy and will—"

"*Svirstroy* to Control. I protest. I was clearl—"

"Control to *Svirstroy*. Go to anchor. You are next in queue. Presuming you comply."

Basaev smiled. "Thank you, Control. *Contessa di Mare*, out."

"Safe transit, Captain. Turkeli Control, out."

***

Basaev watched from the bridge wing as the pilot climbed aboard, then moved back into the wheelhouse to wait as Shamil, uniformed as the third mate, escorted the pilot up. He glanced at the helmsman. The young Italian was behaving like the chief engineer in the Engine Control Room, aware the slightest transgression would mean death for their shipmates.

The pilot arrived and introduced himself, giving cards to both Basaev and Shamil. Shamil went into the chart room, ostensibly to record the man's name in the logbook. Basaev stayed with the pilot to review a transit check-list.

In the chart room, Shamil entered the pilot's name into an Iranian-supplied laptop and smiled. He printed out the information, pulling a pistol from a drawer as the printer whirred, then collected the output and stepped onto the bridge behind the pilot. He jammed the gun to the back of the man's head.

"That's a gun, Captain," Shamil said. "Raise your hands. Slowly."

The pilot complied as Basaev relieved him of his radio and cell phone. Then Shamil handed Basaev the information.

"Very good, Captain… Akkaya," Basaev said, glancing through the pages. "And your wife and daughter are beautiful," he said, displaying photos.

"Shamil here made a call," Basaev lied, "and our colleagues ashore are going to visit them. Their safety is in your hands. Will you cooperate?"

The pilot nodded, ashen faced. Basaev gestured he could lower his hands.

"All right," Basaev continued in Turkish. "Proceed and report as usual. No tricks. I speak your language." The man nodded.

"Good. Captain Akkaya. You have the bridge."

The pilot took over, and Basaev lifted the console phone.

"Engine Room," Aslan said.

"Aslan. Start the fans."

Dugan looked toward the Turkish coast as a burst of excited Russian sounded in his headphones, precipitating a three-way exchange between Borgdanov and the pilots of both choppers. Finally, Borgdanov shot a worried look across at the other chopper and gave a resigned "*da*" as the other chopper peeled away and headed away from the coast out to sea.

"What's up?" Dugan asked when he was sure the Russians were finished speaking.

"Low-fuel alarm on other chopper," Borgdanov said. "He has twenty minutes air time, no more. Is no way he will reach Bosphorus with us."

Dugan looked at the nearby coast, confused. "But why is he going out to sea?"

"He has no American aboard," the Russian said, "and would be big problem if he lands in Turkey. I tell him to go well to sea to be sure he is clearly in international waters. He has enough time to get there and hover while crew deploys raft. Then he will ditch. One of our naval vessels is already on way to pick up men."

Dugan was still confused. "Why was he lower on fuel than us?"

"Because he hovers a few minutes at rendezvous point while we collect you," Borgdanov said, "and also as primary strike force he has heavier load—five more men and their weapons. Under most conditions, would make little difference, but with this wind…" The Russian shrugged, leaving the thought unfinished.

Borgdanov spoke in Russian into his mike, and Dugan saw an answering nod from the chopper pilot. The chopper dropped to skim the surface of the water and moved closer to the Turkish coast.

"I think Turkish radar will pick us up soon," the Russian said, "but we will stay as low as possible to delay that. We have you aboard, so we can land if necessary." He smiled. "Assuming Turks don't shoot us down first and ask questions later."

***

Ten minutes later, as Dugan watched the Turkish coast flash past the left side of the chopper, a raucous alarm brought another burst of Russian in his headset.

"Fuel alarm," Borgdanov said. "Pilot says twenty minutes, no more."

"Do we land?" Dugan asked.

"Nyet," the Russian said. "We are close now. We will complete mission."

He smiled at the worried look on Dugan's face.

"Do not worry so, *Dyed*," he said. "Always these pilots exaggerate the danger."

Dugan was about to debate the point when his phone vibrated.

"Jesse. Thank God. Talk to me."

"I called the Turks direct. The Bosphorus pilot boarded an hour ago. A Turkish Coast Guard boat is closing, but chopper response will take time. I informed the Turks the Russians are in route. They want your help."

"An hour ago? She must be halfway through the strait. What's the damn target?"

"Braun just talked. Sultanahmet, between Attaturk Plaza and Eminönü ferry terminal."

Sultanahmet, a dense square of attractions—Topkapi Palace, the Attaturk statue, the Grand Bazaar, Sultanahmet Mosque, all clustered around the bustling ferry terminal, sure to be thronged on a beautiful summer morning.

"The Russians have a plan?" Ward asked.

"Yeah. For an open-sea intercept. Now? Who the hell knows?" Dugan said as the fuel alarm buzzed again.

AIRBORNE
OVER UPPER BOSPHORUS STRAITS

Dugan stared forward as they cleared Fatih Mehmet Bridge.

"There," Dugan pointed. "Stay high and hover."

Southward, almost to First Bosphorus Bridge, was a tanker with a distinctive green hull and BARBIERO in white letters on her side. A boat sped toward a pilot ladder rigged on the ship's starboard side. As the boat neared, a figure appeared on the starboard bridge wing, carrying something.

"RPG," Borgdanov said as the boat disappeared in a fireball. Dugan watched, stunned. The Russian shook his arm.

"Dugan. I said how long to target?"

Dugan looked beyond First Bosphorus Bridge to Topkapi Palace in the distance and did a quick mental calculation.

"Assuming full harbor speed of eight knots, she'll pass the bridge in about ten minutes. Then maybe twenty-five more to target. You have a plan?"

Borgdanov shook his head. "Only that we rappel aboard and try to kill fanatics. If we cannot kill them, we set charges and jump in water. Some people die, but maybe not so many."

"What about RPGs?"

"I think no problem. How far from wheelhouse to bow of ship?"

"Four hundred fifty, maybe four hundred sixty feet, give or take—"

"Nyet. In meters, Dugan. In meters."

"Sorry," Dugan said. "About a hundred and forty meters. Why?"

"Because RPGs accurate to only eighty meters. This we learn in Afghanistan where our choppers have no problem until Americans give savages Stinger missiles."

He glared, then continued. "I know these savages. They will not risk blowing up ship with wild RPG shot over deck this near complete success. We circle wide, hide behind bridge, and drop near front of ship by surprise. After that?" He shrugged.

Hell of a plan, thought Dugan as the fuel alarm buzzed again.

HOVERING
SOUTH OF FIRST BOSPHORUS BRIDGE

The alarm was constant as they hovered behind the span.

"Will they attack when you board?" Dugan asked.

Borgdanov looked up from his preparations. "Nyet. They know we must come to them. Two will probably defend engine room with two on bridge. Maybe some booby traps." He raised his eyebrows. "You have some idea, *Dyed*?"

"Sultanahmet's at the south entrance of the strait. You could override the bridge at the emergency steering station and change course into the Sea of Marmara."

Borgdanov looked doubtful. "Fanatics stop engine," he said.

"But you'll be on a new course. A loaded tanker doesn't stop quickly."

Borgdanov hesitated. "We know nothing of these controls, *Dyed*. For this, you must come. You do this?"

Dugan envisioned charred bodies in the ruins of Sultanahmet as the buzzing fuel alarm defined the limits of his options. May as well go down swinging. He swallowed and nodded.

Borgdanov grinned. "Good. So is unnecessary to have Ilya shoot you in painful but unimportant place. You come with me. How you say... tandem jump."

Oh goody, Dugan thought.

M/T CONTESSA DI MARE
SOUTHBOUND
NORTH OF FIRST BOSPHORUS BRIDGE

"You are certain, Shamil?"

"I saw him after I fired the RPG but lost him. You think I cannot recognize a Russian?"

"Forgive me," Basaev said, "I was surprised. If the Turks now ally themselves with Russian scum, I strike them with a song in my heart."

Shamil nodded as Basaev lifted binoculars and looked ahead.

He handed Shamil the glasses. "The surface just beyond the bridge."

"I see only ripples," Shamil said, peering through the binoculars.

"Or a downdraft," Basaev said.

Shamil trailed him to the bridge wing. Barely audible through ambient noise was the thump of blades.

"He hides behind the span," Shamil said.

Basaev nodded. "An ambush."

"What now?"

Basaev smiled. "Praise Allah for Russian targets. Get on the wheelhouse with the Stinger. Shoot the tail like the Iranians showed us. He will spin away."

Shamil grinned and rushed inside as Basaev moved in to call the engine room.

"Doku," Basaev said, "we will be attacked. I will transfer engine control to you. They know of us, so we no longer need to follow rules. Go to sea speed, send Aslan to the Cargo Control Room to prepare to discharge, and arm booby traps on all the engine-room doors."

"At once," Doku said and hung up.

Basaev called to Shamil as he hurried past.

"Take time to aim well. A few of them on deck are less a threat than a flaming chopper."

Shamil nodded, annoyed.

Basaev grinned. "Besides, why should you have all the fun?"

Shamil returned his grin and hurried out.

***

Dugan stood terrified as wind and noise blasted him. The major yelled in his ear.

"On 'set,' wrap arms around my neck and legs around my body like lover. On 'go,' I jump. Don't worry. I control everything." Dugan nodded mutely as the Russian continued. "Ilya goes first and will hold rope. When we land, I unclip here"—he put Dugan's hand on the carabiner clip—"and we separate. Fast. Understand?"

Dugan nodded again and was still pondering his lunacy when the sergeant disappeared. Seconds later he was hurtling downward, a death grip on Borgdanov.

"Release my arm, idiot! I cannot control speed," the Russian screamed.

He made his point by smashing his helmet into Dugan's battered face. Dugan's hands flew to his nose, and Borgdanov stopped their plunge abruptly, just above deck. Dugan's legs jerked free, leaving the pair joined by their web gear and spinning. They hit the deck hard, Borgdanov on top. Dugan lay gasping as the Russians clawed at the snarled rope.

FLYING BRIDGE
M/T CONTESSA DI MARE
PASSING FIRST BOSPHORUS BRIDGE

Shamil sat, elbows on knees and the Stinger on his shoulder as the bridge loomed. A man dropped into view as the bow cleared the span, the chopper still shielded. The man landed cleanly in a clear area of the main deck just aft of the raised forecastle deck and pulled the rope taut for a pair of men that followed, faster and without grace, landing in a jumble of flailing limbs.

Shamil could see the chopper skids now and waited impatiently. Then it was there, and he locked on to the tail rotor and fired. A fireball bloomed, and he panicked momentarily as a flaming chunk plunged, narrowly missing the bow to splash into the sea. The chopper corkscrewed away, slinging black-clad Russians to their deaths.

"*Allahu Akbar!*" he screamed.

The sergeant released the rappelling rope and leaped back as the two men slammed to the deck. He watched the rope jerk taut as an explosion rocked the chopper and it twisted away, dragging the mass of tangled limbs and twisted rope toward the ship's rail. He grabbed the rope one-handed, dragged along as he reached into his boot with his free hand and pulled a knife to saw at the rope. Ten feet from the rail, the rope parted, and the men collapsed in a heap.

He recovered first to cut the men apart and hook a hand in Borgdanov's armor and drag him under the protection of the centerline pipe rack. He turned to see the American limping to join them.

***

Dugan was unsure whether his nose or rope-burned leg hurt worse. The Russians seemed indestructible. They conferred, heads together, looking aft with undisguised hatred.

"OK," Borgdanov said. "We go back. Ilya first, then you Dugan, while I give cover fire. Then Ilya covers me. Then repeat."

"Cover fire? Smell that gasoline! A muzzle flash will blow us all to hell."

"But fanatics shot RPG and Stinger."

"Yeah," Dugan said, "up high. Fumes hug the deck. A flash on the bridge won't ignite them. The boat exploded away from the ship, and the chopper was high, plus its downdraft dissipated the fumes."

"You tell me this now? How we kill fanatics?"

"You can't fire here, but you can inside. Air intakes are high, and fans maintain a positive pressure inside so no fumes leak in." Dugan looked at ripples on the water. "And there's a good breeze, so the open deck aft is probably OK as long as you don't shoot forward. A ricochet spark here in the cargo area could be deadly."

"So. We go fast and hope fanatics also do not want sparks."

Borgdanov spoke in Russian, and the sergeant darted aft.

"Wait," Dugan cried. Too late.

NAVIGATION BRIDGE
M/T CONTESSA DI MARE

Basaev raised the binoculars and watched the chopper careen across the summer sky toward Sultanahmet, leaking Russians. He laughed as it splashed down just offshore, and he saw tiny figures ashore rushing to the water's edge to point and gawk like moths to a flame. All the more people in the kill zone.

"Well done," he said as Shamil returned. "Only three got down, one injured. They cringe beneath the pipes."

"I saw. What now?"

"We give them something to think about," Basaev said as he called the Cargo Control Room.

"Aslan," Basaev asked, "ready?"

"I need only start the pumps," Aslan said.

"Defenses?"

"The outside doors on this deck are jammed. They can only get to me by entering the deckhouse on the main deck and coming up the central stairwell, and I have the door from the stairwell on this deck booby-trapped. It will explode in their faces. I will finish any survivors."

"Draw them to you then," Basaev said. "Start the petrol early. They may try to stop it."

"But it will trail us like a fuse."

"Let it cover the strait and increase the destruction," Basaev said. "Nothing is likely to ignite it before we are upon the target, and if then, momentum will complete our task whether we live or not."

"Very well, Khassan," Aslan said, sounding unsure.

"Watch from the window, Aslan. Time the start to catch them between the manifold and the rail. Try to wash them overboard."

"It will be done, my brother," Aslan said.

Shamil yelled a warning.

"Aslan," Basaev said, "be ready. They are coming. Port side."

MAIN DECK
M/T *CONTESSA DI MARE*

Dugan peeked around the deck locker at the sergeant crouched behind a tank hatch farther aft, then he looked back at Borgdanov sheltering behind a winch. In the interest of speed, the Russians chose the less cluttered route near the rail, over the piping maze inboard. But as Dugan had anticipated, the sergeant had run out of cover, leaving him a long sprint down the rail past the cargo manifold.

The sergeant made his move just as Dugan's neck hair rose at the whine of hydraulics and the rumble of pipelines filling. His warning cry was lost in the growing din of the cargo pumps, and Dugan started after the sergeant in a limping run, screaming. The Russian was even with the manifold when a fluke of acoustics allowed Dugan's screams to reach him. He stopped and turned as Dugan arrived, oblivious to gasoline trickling into the drip pan beside him heralding torrents to come. Dugan grabbed the Russian and heaved himself backward. They hit the deck hard, the sergeant on top, as an eight-inch jet of gasoline rocketed through the space they'd occupied.

"Get off me, you dumb asshole!" Dugan yelled, keeping low as he dragged himself from under the Russian. He struggled backward on his elbows to clear the stream of gasoline that shot above them, splashing the rails and deck on its way overboard. When he was clear, he stood and surveyed the situation. He was looking to starboard as Borgdanov arrived.

"We should've gone inboard in the first place. Now let's try it my way," Dugan said, limping to the cover of the centerline piping without looking back. He plunged aft through the maze, squeezing over and around pipes, scraping his shins and banging his helmet in his rush as the larger Russians struggled to keep up.

NAVIGATION BRIDGE

"I cannot see them."

"Do not worry, Shamil," Basaev said. "Our defenses are good. They are few with little time." He paused. "Depending on their target, you help Aslan or Doku. For now, guard the outside stairways and watch for boats or aircraft. Take a radio. The Turks know we are here, and I doubt they speak Chechen."

He pointed toward Sultanahmet. "We meet in Paradise."

MAIN DECK
PORT SIDE OF DECKHOUSE

Dugan stood by the side of the deckhouse, watching the gasoline spread in the ship's wake.

"Dugan! We must get to the steering place. Now," Borgdanov yelled over the hydraulics.

"We have to stop that gasoline," Dugan yelled back.

"Nyet. Is fanatic delaying trick."

"Look, asshole. They'll cover the strait, and one spark will ignite it. There are hundreds of people out there on ferryboats. We deal with this."

Without waiting, Dugan entered the deckhouse, the Russians trailing. He paused at the central stairwell and motioned the sergeant to guard the stairwell door, then followed his ears down a nearby corridor, Borgdanov in tow. The din in the power-pack room was deafening. Dugan yelled into Borgdanov's ear.

"You booby-trap the door. I stop the power packs. We leave. OK?"

Borgdanov nodded and began taping a grenade above the door. He finished and nodded, and the space fell silent as Dugan pressed buttons and rushed out. Borgdanov followed, looping a string from the grenade over the inside doorknob as he closed the door.

They retraced their steps, the sergeant falling in behind as they passed, walking backward, gun trained on the stairwell door. Outside, gas barely trickled from the manifold.

"That'll distract 'em," Dugan said. "Which is good since we have to run aft in the open. They won't be slow to shoot down at us back here." He started astern in a limping run before the Russians overtook him on either side, lifting him under the armpits to dash aft.

NAVIGATION BRIDGE

Basaev debated killing his two captives. The Turkish pilot at least understood their intentions by now and might take desperate action. His thoughts were interrupted by the plaintive moan of dying hydraulics. He rushed to the window as the gasoline streams slackened to dribbles.

"Aslan," he said into his radio, "why have you stopped?"

"I did not. They must have stopped the power packs."

"Restart them. We must maximize the fire."

"I tried, but they switched the power packs to local control. They can only be restarted from the power-pack room. Perhaps they try to draw me into an ambush," Aslan said.

Shamil broke in. "All the Russians run aft."

Basaev processed that. Why would the Russians go to the stern?

"Doku," he barked, "you heard?"

"Yes, Khassan," Doku said from the engine room.

"Is the infidel engineer secure?" Basaev asked.

"He is handcuffed to the console."

"Leave him. The Russians will attack you from the Steering Gear Room. Take cover with a clear field of fire to kill any that survive the booby-trapped door. Warn the infidel to keep the engine full ahead, or we kill his shipmates slowly before his eyes."

"Understood," Doku said.

"Aslan," Basaev said, "stopping the power packs was merely a diversion to distract us while the Russians went aft. Get the gasoline going again, then go aft and toss grenades down into the steering gear room. Our Russian friends will be trapped between you above and Doku in the engine room."

"At once," Aslan said.

As Basaev turned, the pilot met his eyes.

"You are fortunate," Basaev said, "to witness the work of Allah."

"The work of Allah is not murder. The god you serve is your own twisted hatred."

Basaev staggered him with a fist, but the Turk straightened. Basaev hocked and spit. "Spoken like a woman, Whore of the Crusaders."

The pilot was calm. "Better that than to be ruled by fanatics. I would prefer death."

"A wish I can grant," Basaev said, drawing his pistol. The Turk smiled.

"Death amuses you?" Basaev asked.

"Your arrogance amuses me. These Russians are smarter than you think."

"What do you mean?"

He smiled again, and Basaev pistol-whipped him, knocking him down. He aimed at the Turk's head, finger quivering, but stayed his hand. Something felt wrong, and he might yet need this Turkish whore.

CHAPTER THIRTY

Main Deck Aft
Entrance to Steering Gear Room

"Let me go, you asshol—" Dugan stumbled as they released him.

"Careful, Dugan," Borgdanov said, "and do not call me asshole."

Dugan bit off a response, startled by the view ashore over Borgdanov's shoulder. They'd increased speed.

"This is door to steering place?" Borgdanov asked.

Dugan nodded. "There'll be another from the engine room."

"Ilya goes down first," Borgdanov said, nodding to the sergeant. Descending between the Russians, Dugan reflected. At this speed, he'd have no time with the controls, likely in Italian, and if he got control, he'd be steering blind. He'd just concluded this was one of his dumber ideas when the sergeant jerked to a stop at voices below.

Italian voices.

Dugan pushed him down the last few steps and rushed past, around a corner to a wire-cage locker. The crew stood atop piles of mooring lines, cheering his arrival.

"We have to free them," Dugan said. "They can help."

Borgdanov aimed at the padlock, but Dugan pushed the gun down, pointing at the steel bulkheads surrounding them. "Ricochets," he said.

A man pointed through the chain link. "*Martello*—hammer—there."

Dugan limped to a workbench to return with a short-handled sledge. He raised the hammer, but Borgdanov jerked it away and destroyed the lock with one blow. Italians boiled out, laughing and shouting as the captain pumped Dugan's hand, thwarting explanation. The major improvised, grabbing a crewman.

"Silence, or I kill him!" he yelled to instant quiet.

"Captain," Dugan said, "the terrorists will ground the ship and explode her in less than ten minutes, killing thousands. If they succeed, none of us can escape in time. You must help us prevent the grounding."

Pandemonium broke out anew as English speakers translated.

"*Zitto!*" the captain shouted, restoring calm and turning back to Dugan.

"How can we help, *signore*?"

Dugan nodded to the steering gear. "Have the chief engage emergency steering."

"The chief engineer is captive. The first engineer is here." He turned and spoke to the man who'd pointed out the hammer.

"*Si, Commandante,*" the man said and rushed to the steering gear.

"What more?" the captain asked.

"Change course to port. And"—Dugan nodded at the engine-room door—"block that door. Maybe wedge it. They might use explosives—"

The captain held up a hand. "*Signore.* May I suggest you let us solve these problems while you concentrate on keeping us alive to do so?"

Dugan nodded, impressed.

"*Grazi,*" the captain said, turning to bark orders. In moments, the crew formed a line from the rope locker, passing heavy mooring lines hand over hand and piling them against the door.

Damn smart, Dugan thought. This might work.

"A DECK"
NEAR CARGO CONTROL ROOM

Aslan disarmed his booby trap and descended the stairwell. At the bottom, he crept into the passageway and hurried toward the power-pack room. He was almost inside when the grenade handle clanged against the far bulkhead. He ducked down in the open doorway and looked around, unsure. The grenade took his head off.

STEERING GEAR ROOM

The pile of mooring lines formed a huge Gordian knot from the deck to above the door and ten feet at its base, an impenetrable barrier. Borgdanov nodded approval.

"Fanatics must come over deck now. But we must kill them without big fight." Borgdanov's face clouded. "I worry if, as you say, bullets go forward to make sparks."

Dugan nodded. "Me too, but I have an idea."

They jerked at the thump of the explosion in the power-pack room.

"Now there are three," Dugan said with grim satisfaction.

Borgdanov shot him an appraising look.

"You are not such dumb fellow, *Dyed*." No derision now. "Tell me your idea."

NAVIGATION BRIDGE

"What was that explosion?" Basaev demanded into the radio.

"Nothing in the engine room," Doku reported.

"Understood, Doku," Basaev said. "Aslan, report."

After repeated failures, Basaev addressed the others. "I think Aslan has preceded us to Paradise. Doku, what is your situation?"

"No change. But the door moves a bit, like they push against it."

"Understood, Doku. Shamil. Approaching threats?"

"Nothing," Shamil said, "but what are the infidels doing?"

"Playing foolish games as time slips away," Basaev said. "Soon Allah will vomit on their souls."

ENGINE CONTROL ROOM
M/T *CONTESSA DI MARE*

Sweat dripped off the chief engineer's nose as he hesitated, concerned the *beduino* would return. They didn't resemble Arabs, but who else would blow themselves up? He turned back to working at a screw with the steel ruler from his pocket overlooked by the terrorists and now his makeshift screwdriver. He gripped it tight, willing the screw to turn before the ruler edge bent. If he could remove the rail support, he could free himself.

He had no qualms, despite their threats. Any *cretino* could see the *beduini* intended to blow them all up anyway, and the chief engineer was no idiot.

The oxygen meter showed 21 percent in the cargo tanks with the fans running in fresh-air mode. No one would place a loaded tanker in such a condition unless planning an explosion.

The screw yielded, and as he moved to the next, he heard a muffled thump. Would that, whatever it was, draw them back? He swallowed his fear and worked on.

MAIN DECK AT STERN

Dugan looked down at the captain supervising two burly sailors wrestling a square of steel plate up the stairs. That damn thing weighs over two hundred pounds, he thought, hoping this wasn't a waste of valuable time.

The Russians stood behind opposite corners of the machinery casing, watching forward with hand mirrors, as volunteers from the crew found cover on the stern. There were eleven Italians plus Dugan divided into six pairs, holding things from tools to fist-size bolts. Dugan nodded to his partner, the second mate, crouched behind a mooring bitt.

Dugan jerked at the shriek of steel on steel as the sailors heaved the plate on deck, skidding it edgewise to the starboard rail. They leaned it against a gooseneck vent, and one dashed back to the shelter of the machinery casing, and the other dropped behind the plate as bullets whined off the steel. The man behind the plate unwound a rope from his waist and, exposing only his arms, flipped a loop over the plate to settle six inches above the deck. He cinched the rope behind the upright vent pipe, securing the plate from slipping.

"*Tutto pronto, Commandante,*" the man shouted.

"*Bravo, Mario,*" the captain replied from the shelter of the machinery casing. "*Uno... Due... Tre... Ora!*"

On three, they exchanged places in a rush. The captain squatted behind the plate and peeked down the starboard side. He nodded back to Dugan.

How the hell is he going to conn the ship from there? Dugan wondered.

Reading Dugan's expression, the captain pointed to the chief mate squatting behind the machinery casing at the small rope hatch. Dugan smiled.

NAVIGATION BRIDGE

"Shamil. Why did you fire?" Basaev asked.

"The Italians are up to something on the stern."

"Fire occasionally. Keep them timid. And do not worry so. Success is near."

MAIN DECK AT STERN

Alarms buzzed up through the rope hatch as the first engineer changed over the steering.

"*Tutti pronti, Commandante!*" yelled the chief mate, squatting at the hatch.

The captain replied with a helm order, relayed by the chief mate to the man in the rope store below, who shouted it through the wire cage to the first engineer.

Dugan smiled at changing vibrations underfoot as the rudder bit.

NAVIGATION BRIDGE

"I... I... do nothing," the terrified helmsman said as the steering alarm buzzed and Basaev jammed the Beretta under his chin.

"Leave the boy alone," the pilot said, silencing the alarm.

Basaev turned on the Turk. "What's happening?"

"Obviously, they activated emergency steering."

"Transfer it back, or you die," Basaev said, "as will your family."

The Turk shrugged. "My family is away on holiday in Cyprus, so I soon realized your threats were empty. And the Russians control steering at the source. I cannot override, even if I wanted to."

Basaev watched the bow creep to port, weighing the Russians' chances of success. Something moved in his peripheral vision.

"Stop!" He froze the fleeing helmsman with raised pistol as the man eyed the door. Then Basaev's arms were pinned.

"Run, boy!" the Turk screamed, bear-hugging Basaev as the sailor fled out the door to vault off the bridge wing.

***

On the bridge wing, Shamil turned at shouts from the wheelhouse and footsteps behind him. He had no time to act as the young sailor raced past him and vaulted the rail. He rushed to the rail and looked down at a widening circle of ripples, the only evidence of the sailor's passing. Shots drew him back inside the wheelhouse, to see Basaev push the gut-shot Turk to the deck.

"A slow and painful death, Whore of the Infidels," Basaev said. "Unfortunately our departure for Paradise will shorten your agony. In the time remaining, petition Allah for enlightenment."

Basaev spit on the dying Turk and moved to the bridge wing.

Shamil followed Basaev outside. "Who's steering?" he asked.

"The Russians." Basaev pointed at the improvised conning station, then looked toward Sultanahmet ahead, the bow now aimed at Attaturk's statue.

"But why so timidly?" he mused aloud, then smiled. "They cannot see well and fear a drastic turn will leave us slipping on the original course. So, we have time to deal with them yet."

"Shamil," Basaev said. "Take the extra grenades. Doku will meet you. You will attack down both sides, coordinating on the radios. They cannot hide from a grenade barrage, and when they retreat down into the Steering Gear Room, we make it their coffin. Multiple grenades down into a closed steel box will finish them.

"Doku can secure the infidel engineer on deck," Basaev continued. "After the attack, we will force the infidel to transfer steering, or time lacking, steer from there. I will lay covering fire to occupy the infidels while you and Doku position yourselves."

"Grenades and bullets at main-deck level will ignite the fumes too soon," Shamil said.

"God willing, wind keeps the stern clear," Basaev said. "And we have no option."

Shamil nodded and moved to collect grenades as Basaev raised his radio.

"Doku," Basaev said. "Meet Shamil on deck. Bring the infidel engineer. Shamil will explain."

"Yes, Khassan," Doku said.

Basaev moved inside for an assault rifle to be met with more buzzing alarms and flashing lights.

"Beard of the Prophet. What now?"

ENGINE CONTROL ROOM

The chief engineer pulled the rail free and slipped the ring of the handcuff off the end just as the buzz of the steering-failure alarm sent his heart into his throat. The alarm fell silent, and status lights on the console blinked to local control. His shipmates.

He stopped, unsure now how his initial plan to black out the ship would impact his shipmates. But he still needed a diversion, something to draw the *beduini* here so he could slip by them.

He stopped the fans to the cargo tanks and smashed the controls with a fire extinguisher snatched from the bulkhead. At the console, he stopped the engine and swung the extinguisher in a roundhouse arc against the upright lever, bending it badly and smashing the housing. Seconds later, he crouched in the engine room, watching the control-room windows.

MAIN DECK AT STERN

The captain was squinting down the starboard side, longing for a glimpse of open sea, when the helmsman hit the water cleanly. Seconds later a head broke the surface, even with the stern.

"*Bravo, Salvatore!*" he yelled, rewarded by an upraised fist.

"*Martucci è sfuggito!*" the captain called to the crew's cheers.

***

"What's that about?" Dugan asked as Borgdanov watched forward with his mirror.

The Russian didn't turn. "Their comrade on bridge escaped."

"Good," Dugan said absently. "When will they come?"

"Soon, *Dyed*. You should get in position." Dugan didn't move.

"Remember. Leave the pins in."

"It may be your plan, *Dyed*, but I am not idiot," Borgdanov said, eyes on the mirror. "You should take cover," the Russian repeated.

Dugan nodded and moved starboard to dart behind the minimal shelter of a tank vent. He squatted there, feeling the throb of the great engine through the deck and willing the terrorists to come soon. He was rubbing his injured leg when the vibration stopped.

"Midships!" yelled the captain, adjusting to the engine stoppage with a stream of orders, alternating between midships and slight left rudder, coaxing the bow to port without killing speed. This guy's good, Dugan thought.

NAVIGATION BRIDGE
M/T *CONTESSA DI MARE*
A HALF MILE FROM SULTANAHMET

"He's gone," Doku said. "He stopped everything and destroyed the controls!"

Basaev watched the bow creep to port. The speed log read six knots and dropping.

"What shall I do?" Doku asked.

"Forget him. Join Shamil on main deck. Disarm all the engine-room booby traps except the steering-gear door and bring the grenades."

"Khassan," Shamil's voice interrupted, "how can we change the steering now without the infidel engineer?"

"Kill the others and put the rudder hard right; it cannot be complicated. Allah provides a target we cannot miss. Call me when you are ready to start aft."

MAIN DECK AT STERN
M/T *CONTESSA DI MARE*
0.4 MILES NORTH OF SULTANAHMET

Dugan cowered behind his cover as automatic fire raked the starboard stern. The fire ceased abruptly, and he tensed at the two-note "get ready" whistle from Borgdanov.

***

Borgdanov was elated. The fanatics' attack route was obvious. External stairways jutted from both sides of the machinery casing, shielding the portion of the bulkheads forward of the stairways from the Russians' view. The fanatics would use that, creeping close along each bulkhead and stopping just forward of the stairs to coordinate the attack. He counted on that. Depended on it, in fact. His nagging concern had been when. Now he knew.

The fire to starboard was obviously meant to keep heads down while a fanatic approached. The third fanatic would provide cover fire for the attacker to port as well, and when that stopped, both fanatics would be in place. Borgdanov smiled. Then the surprise.

As fire stopped to starboard, Borgdanov looked over at the sergeant, who nodded, their thoughts identical. Borgdanov whistled softly to the others and leaned back against the casing, grenade ready.

Starboard Side of Bridge Deck Aft

"Doku," Basaev said. "Shamil is in place. I am coming to cover you."

"Yes, Khassan," Doku said as he prepared to rush aft.

MAIN DECK AT STERN
M/T *CONTESSA DI MARE*
0.35 MILES NORTH OF SULTANAHMET

"GO!" shouted Borgdanov as the gunfire died to port. The Russians lobbed grenades, pins in place, to clang on deck beside the terrorists' hiding places. Death at their feet and unable to retreat, the Chechens broke cover just as Dugan and the crew also burst forth, each man screaming as they dashed into the open to trade hiding places with their partners, hurling their missiles as they ran.

The attackers were paralyzed by multiple targets and the clang of what they took for grenades on the deck all around them. From semi-concealment, the Russians dispatched the confused Chechens with single three-round bursts. When Basaev emerged on the starboard bridge wing a moment later, a burst from Borgdanov staggered him and drove him back.

The Italians reemerged cautiously, then cheered before being silenced by the captain, who stood smiling at a growing patch of open sea to starboard.

"*Paolo*," he yelled to the second mate, " *La zattera! Subito!*—The life raft—quickly."

As the man moved to comply, the captain called orders to the chief mate and moved to Dugan's side.

"We will miss the headland, I think," he said, "but the current is tricky, and we can do no more. I ordered the rudder locked amidships and—"

"*Commandante*," the chief mate said, "*il Capo Macchinista viene.*"

The chief engineer rounded the corner, handcuffs dangling from his wrist.

"*Bravo, Directore*," the captain said, embracing the engineer before pointing him aft where the chief mate kept a tally as men leaped overboard to swim toward the bobbing raft.

The captain turned back to Dugan. "If the *beduino* lives, he will explode the ship. We should go, *signori*." Dugan nodded and watched enviously as the captain moved to the rail to follow his men overboard.

Dugan turned to Borgdanov. "You think he's alive?"

Borgdanov shrugged. "I know I hit him. How bad, I cannot say."

Dugan darted from the shelter of the machinery casing to squat behind the Italian's makeshift conning station. He looked down the starboard side toward Sultanahmet and tried to gauge the ship's speed before dashing back to the Russians.

"I can't tell how close we'll pass to the headland," Dugan said, "but my best guess is we'll be as close as we're going to get in five minutes. If the asshole's alive and able to detonate, that's when he'll do it." Dugan added, "My guess is he'll stay on the starboard bridge wing where he can best judge the distance."

"Good, *Dyed*," Borgdanov said, starting up the starboard side, "we go."

"Hold on," Dugan said. "We'll be exposed if you approach up the starboard stairway. Best go to port stairway to the bridge-deck level. You can attack through or around the wheelhouse."

Borgdanov nodded and spoke to the sergeant in Russian. The sergeant started forward along the port side in a crouching run, Dugan close behind.

STARBOARD SIDE OF BRIDGE DECK AFT
M/T *CONTESSA DI MARE*
0.20 MILES NORTH OF SULTANAHMET

Basaev's head ached where the Russian's bullet creased his scalp. He wiped blood from his eyes and crawled on his belly to the back of the bridge wing to peer down over the edge. The deck was empty save for Shamil's body. Streaks of foam marked the wake, and a raft bobbed astern, Italians pulling themselves aboard. Where were the Russians?

He knew. They were coming. They always came.

Basaev studied the now-straight line of foam marking the wake, then rose cautiously and turned toward Sultanahmet, mentally extending the track. The bow pointed to sea, but the current set the ship to starboard, and she might yet graze the shore. God willing, he would succeed. If he could hold off the Russians.

He put his assault rifle in single-shot mode and ran to the catwalk behind the wheelhouse. He rushed to port on the catwalk and then quickly walked backward, his gun pointed down, as he blasted the metal clips securing the aluminum grating. He retraced his route, ripping up sections of grating as he walked backward this time, tossing them over the rail to clatter on the deck far below. In less than a minute he had created a gaping chasm behind the wheelhouse, blocking the access to both the starboard bridge wing and the single ladder to the top of the wheelhouse.

Next he ran through the wheelhouse to the port side and slammed the heavy sliding door and locked it. They couldn't come through, over, or around the wheelhouse now to get at him on the starboard bridge wing. The exterior doors into the deckhouse and the doors of the central stairwell were still booby-trapped on the upper levels, and if they tried to come up the starboard exterior stairway, they would be sitting ducks as he fired down at them through the open treads of the stairway. He could hold them off for an hour here. He needed only minutes.

Basaev positioned himself at the top of the stairway, facing ashore with his back to the wheelhouse. His eyes flickered between the stairwell and the crowded shore as Sultanahmet drew closer.

MAIN DECK
PORT SIDE OF DECKHOUSE
M/T CONTESSA DI MARE
0.10 MILES NORTH OF SULTANAHMET

Dugan jumped at the sound of firing followed by metallic clanging from behind the deckhouse. "OK, I guess he's not dead," Dugan said.

"What is fanatic doing?" Borgdanov asked as the sliding door crashed shut two decks above them.

"I think he's getting ready for us," Dugan said. "Maybe it's time for Plan B. Let's try the stairs inside."

Borgdanov nodded and spit out a stream of Russian. The sergeant moved to the deckhouse door and began to ease it open.

He froze and pointed to a thin wire visible through the narrow crack of the open door.

Borgdanov cursed. "Booby trap."

"Can't you cut the wire? Disarm it?" Dugan asked.

"*Da*," Borgdanov said, "but it must be done carefully, and if there is one, I think there are others, and there is no time. We must go up. Now," he said and started up the exterior stairs.

STARBOARD BRIDGE WING
M/T *CONTESSA DI MARE*
SULTANAHMET 100 FEET FROM SHORE

The crowd milled and pointed as the ship approached, the locals long accustomed to the nearness of ships, and the tourists following their lead. Basaev's hopes of grounding died, stillborn, as water trapped between the bank and boxy hull cushioned the ship and she began to sheer away. He raised the detonator, and some in the crowd mistook it for a wave, but those nearest saw the bloody face and rifle and turned to claw through the crowd as his cry pierced the air.

"*Aallaaahuuu Aak...*"

Basaev's wrist smashed the rail, and the detonator flew overboard. The pilot rolled off his arm and sank to the deck, back against the rail, smiling as he finished the cry, "*Akbar*."

"What have you done, Excrement of Satan!"

"As you... advised... petitioned Allah. For... for... strength to stop murder... in His Name."

Enraged, Basaev fired into the Turk's face until no face remained. He looked back landward and watched the gap widen as ashore the fleeing clashed with the ignorant that were pressing forward for a better look. He reached for a grenade, then remembered Shamil took them all. He rushed forward and leaned over the wind dodger to spray the main deck with bullets, smiling as the rounds sparked through the maze of pipes, until his gun fell silent, magazine depleted on the Turk.

PORT BRIDGE WING

Dugan reached the port bridge wing on the Russians' heels just as a burst of automatic fire rose from the starboard wing. They caught a glimpse of the terrorist through the side windows of the wheelhouse, firing wildly at something at his feet. They ducked down before he saw them, and the sergeant raced forward, keeping low. He tried the sliding door into the wheelhouse, then turned to Borgdanov and shook his head.

Borgdanov nodded and rushed aft, the others at his heels. They turned the corner of the wheelhouse and stopped, brought up short by the gaping chasm where the catwalk had been. They returned to their starting point as gunfire erupted again to see the terrorist leaning forward over the wind dodger, spraying the main deck with bullets.

"Christ. He'll detonate the fumes. Shoot the bastard through the windows!" Dugan yelled.

Dugan backed up from the window with the Russians as the pair opened fire at the terrorist in full auto. The bridge windows were laminated double thicknesses of toughened, tempered glass, designed to withstand hurricane-force winds. The port-side glass spiderwebbed with cracks as the bullets penetrated, then whipped across the wheelhouse and through the starboard-side glass with the same result. Deflected by the double impact, the Russians' fire was wildly inaccurate, and the bullet-riddled glass clung tenaciously in place, obscuring their target.

STARBOARD BRIDGE WING
M/T CONTESSA DI MARE
SEA OF MARMARA
1,000 FEET SOUTH OF SULTANAHMET

Basaev reached in his pocket for a fresh magazine and found none, then pulled his Beretta, cursing the infidel engineer for stopping the fans. Wind dissipated the fumes, and igniting the invisible pockets remaining was hit or miss. He fired methodically now, placing shots around the nearest cargo-tank hatch in hopes of igniting the fumes.

Basaev jerked as bullets sprayed through the bridge window, and bits of glass peppered his neck and the side of his face. But no bullets hit him, and he resumed his measured fire, oblivious to the Russian threat.

PORT BRIDGE WING

"I need clear target," Borgdanov said, and he and the sergeant slapped in fresh magazines as the fire continued unabated from the starboard wing.

Borgdanov yelled instructions to the sergeant, who turned his gun to stitch the window perimeter while Borgdanov held his fire. In seconds the glass toppled from the port window, and the sergeant started on the starboard. The glass crashed from the starboard window, and Borgdanov fired a three-round burst. The terrorist jerked and fell out of sight below the window opening.

Relief washed over Dugan, then quickly evaporated as he glanced forward. They were out of the strait, clear of the approach channel and still moving at three knots toward an anchorage crowded with ships awaiting a pilot. He looked astern. They were well clear of Sultanahmet now, with its hordes of tourists. He turned at a babble of Russian as the sergeant started through the ruined window.

"Wait," he called. "Where the hell is he going?"

"Ilya goes to check fanatic," Borgdanov said.

"No time," Dugan said, pointing. "In two minutes, we'll crash into one of those ships, and there'll be plenty of sparks. In this condition, there's no way she won't blow. We need to be as far away as possible."

"But fanatic—"

"Leave him. We missed Sultanahmet and stopped massive casualties. Even if she blows now, she won't block the channel. We've got no engine, no steering, and no time. If we stay here, we're dead," Dugan said. "It's that simple."

The Russian hesitated as Dugan looked over the rail at the long drop to the water. He thought better of that idea and moved toward the stairs.

"But we must do something," Borgdanov said.

"Yeah," Dugan said as he started down the stairway, his injured leg forgotten as adrenalin dulled the pain, "run like hell."

He rushed downward as fast as his legs would carry him, and behind him he heard the Russians' voices raised in argument. He was halfway down to main deck when he heard the Russians' boots clanging on the steel treads above him, coming down fast.

STARBOARD BRIDGE WING
M/T *CONTESSA DI MARE*

Basaev lay on his back in a pool of blood, his feet toward the wheelhouse and the Beretta in a two-hand grip and pointed at the shattered window. The

Russian scum would come soon, and he thanked Allah the Merciful for the opportunity to send another of them to Hell before he died.

But they did not come, and he heard shouting through the shattered windows and then the sound of heavy boots on steel stair treads, loud at first, then growing faint. He smiled. The scum was fleeing. He shoved the pistol into his waistband and reached up to grab the wind-dodger handrail. He bit back the pain as he hauled himself to his feet.

MAIN DECK PORT SIDE

Dugan was already crawling over the rail when the Russians got to main deck. He paused and screamed encouragement.

"Wait, *Dyed*!" Borgdanov screamed back as he rushed toward the rail.

Wait my ass, Ivan, my enlistment is up, Dugan thought, going over the rail.

He hit the water feetfirst and plunged deep, spreading his arms to slow descent, then kicking upward. He rose slowly, sinking if he slacked at all. The armor. Kicking hard, he tore off the helmet and clawed at the vest for straps. He found one and parted the Velcro to free the vest at his waist as he sank, despite his frantic kicking. No time, he thought and dove downward to slip the vest like a tee shirt, with a gravity assist. Hope surged as it slipped, yielding to panic when it trapped his arms.

His lungs were near bursting, and ice picks drove into his ears when he finally fought free to stroke hard for the surface. But he was too deep, too tired, and too old. Unable to suppress the breathing reflex, he sucked in water like life itself, and his larynx spasmed and clamped shut. His panic subsided, almost as if he watched from a safe place, disinterested. He didn't see his life pass before his eyes or a white light, only growing dimness broken by his last conscious thought.

Christ, Dugan. What a dumb-ass way to die.

STARBOARD BRIDGE WING

Basaev leaned against the wind dodger and stared back at Sultanahmet astern, a multicolored tapestry, details indistinct. He was calm now, accepting the Will of Allah. Had the Turk been correct? he wondered. Was hatred now his faith? He felt weary, the Beretta leaden in his hand as he turned and aimed down over the wind dodger at the hatch of the nearest cargo tank.

"*Allahu Akbar,*" he said softly and fired. The gun bucked in his hand, and he dropped it and watched it tumble toward the deck, almost in slow motion. He never saw it land because his aim was true at last, and a great explosion rocked the ship, throwing his mangled body skyward and releasing him from the pain in his heart. Was that not indeed Paradise?

CHAPTER THIRTY-ONE

"Always a pleasure, Mr. President. See you soon."

Motaki hung up, elated. What a difference a day made. Knowing the Iranians were pinched, only last week the Russians were cool to the idea of a crude-for-gasoline swap except on outrageously favorable terms, even hinting they might vote in favor of sanctions at the UN. But now, with the cork in the bottle at Istanbul, the Russian president was calling him, seeking an audience. God willing, Iran would be awash in cheap petrol.

He smiled to himself. It was an ingenious plan indeed and succeeded even when it failed. Intelligence was limited, especially since Braun had been apprehended, but it seemed clear the Chechens had failed. How ironic that the Turks, shaken by the near miss, had only to look to the unintended devastation in Panama for a reminder of just how catastrophic the attack could have been. The message was clear, and the Turks had unilaterally closed the strait to all tanker traffic until further notice. With Russian oil off the market, crude prices had doubled overnight, other producers enjoying a windfall as Russian foreign exchange plummeted.

Now the Russians were pinched, and when the Russian gasoline flowed freely into Iran, calm would be restored. Motaki's political opposition would evaporate, along with the foolish calls for the dismantling of his nuclear program and rapprochement with the West.

His single regret was Braun. He could have used the German for future projects. But then again, Motaki always assumed Braun might be captured. That's why he employed a freelancer with no connection to Iran in the first place and hired him through Rodriguez. Any trail would stop in Caracas. He smiled again. The Americans may have invented the term "plausible deniability," but it had taken a Persian to perfect it.

Braun was the single loose end, and he lifted his phone to snip it.

Dugan drifted awake, unable to understand his inability to touch his throbbing nose. He blinked in the fluorescent glare at a man rising from a bedside chair.

"Easy," the man said. "You're in the hospital." He stepped back, replaced by a man in a white coat.

"Mr. Dugan," the doctor said, "you survived a near drowning. We left you intubated as a precaution. I'll remove the tube now. I apologize for the restraints," he continued, freeing Dugan's wrists, "but you kept pulling at the tube. You also," he added, talking as he removed the tube, "have a nasal fracture, aggravated by CPR. I realigned and splinted it. You will feel discomfort for several days."

"Thanks," Dugan croaked when the tube was out.

The doctor nodded. "You're welcome, but in truth you should thank your Russian friends." He checked the time. "I'm due on rounds. Call if you need anything."

His visitor smiled as the doctor left. "Discomfort is doc speak for 'hurt like hell.'"

"Do I know you?" Dugan rasped.

"Wheeler, Jim Wheeler." He extended his hand. "Cultural attaché."

Friend or foe? Dugan wondered as he regarded the hand and thought of Gardner.

"Also a friend of Ward's. I think you got a shitty deal."

"That makes two of us," Dugan said, taking the hand. "What's this about the Russians?"

"They jumped in after you. You were all underwater a hundred yards from the ship when it blew. They got you clear of the burning gasoline and were burned in the process, but not badly. A Turkish chopper brought you all here."

"What's the situation?"

"You've been out two days, and it's bad, but not like Panama. There are thirty dead, counting the Turk pilot and Coast Guard boat and the Russians. The rest were passengers on a ferry that ignited the patch of dumped gas. More were burned, so the death toll's rising."

"The Italians?"

"They all made it," Wheeler said. "Now everything's political. What's left of the ship is still afloat. They've contained the fire and are waiting for it to burn out so they can tow it. The Turks reopened the strait, but they've banned tankers. Globally, radical environmentalists support them, though no one seems to know how Europe is going to run without oil. Russia's vowing intervention, which puts NATO on the spot. It's total chaos."

Dugan nodded. "Where's all this leave me?"

"With a jet standing by. Gardner wants you in Langley for debriefing." Wheeler smiled. "But you refuel in London."

Dugan smiled back. "When?"

"The doc said tomorrow or the next day, but I'll see what I can do," Wheeler said, moving for the door.

"Thanks, Jim. Can I see the Russians?"

"I'll let 'em know you're awake," Wheeler said as he left.

They arrived in minutes, wearing hospital pajamas and grins. Their hands were bandaged, and angry red skin, shiny with ointment, marked patches of their scalps.

"So, *Dyed*, just when I think you are clever fellow you leap into sea with kilos of armor. If Ilya here was not number-one swimmer, I think you are now very dead."

"You're right," Dugan said. He looked at the sergeant. "Thank you."

The sergeant looked embarrassed and said something in Russian.

"Ilya says you save him from washing into sea by petrol, so is even," Borgdanov translated.

Dugan nodded. "Your burns?"

"They are nothing, though Ilya is hoping for a scar to impress ladies when he tells of bravely defeating fanatics," Borgdanov said.

The sergeant grinned.

"What will you do now?" Dugan asked.

The Russian's face clouded. "I do not know. I failed, so nothing good I think."

"But you saved thousands of lives."

Borgdanov shook his head. "The Turks close strait to tankers. I failed at what matters, *Dyed*. There is talk of war."

SURGICAL STEP-DOWN UNIT
SAINT IGNATIUS HOSPITAL
LONDON

The soft whir of the floor buffer whispered down the corridor, lulling the guard toward sleep. He jerked upright and rose to pace as the buffer operator felt the syringe in his pocket and cursed the cop's diligence. The more heavily staffed day shift would begin soon, making it even harder to get at the German.

A piercing alarm sounded, and the cop stepped aside as medical personnel rushed into the room. The killer edged the buffer closer, straining to hear.

"Time of death 5:23 a.m.," he heard at last.

***

"So he's dead then?" the cop asked as a nurse emerged from the room.

She nodded.

"Christ. Couldn't wait now, could he. The brass'll have their knickers in a knot on this one right enough. They wanted to sweat this bugger proper."

The nurse shrugged. "Not your fault."

"Aye, but try telling that to my sergeant." He sighed. "Oh well, I best grab a cuppa tea and get to the bloody paperwork."

***

The killer kept buffing, watching for an opportunity. He was just past the door when a nurse rolled the corpse out, leaving the gurney unattended to go to the nurses' station. He swung close, holding the buffer one-handed and lifting the sheet with the other to compare the pasty face with the photo he'd memorized.

He grinned. Easiest hit ever. His secret, of course, to preclude any quibbling about the remaining fee. He eased the buffer down the hallway and abandoned it near the stairwell door. He raced down the stairs, shucking his coveralls as he descended to reveal street clothes. He jammed the wadded coveralls in a trash bin as he left. Several blocks away, he called to report Braun's death, then tossed the throwaway phone down a storm drain.

When the CIA Gulfstream plane touched down at Heathrow at eight the previous evening, Anna had marched aboard and officially detained Dugan "for debriefing on orders of Her Majesty's Government." She'd then taken him home and "debriefed" him so enjoyably he'd had difficulty getting out of bed this morning. Beat the hell out of water boarding, thought Dugan as they walked toward Alex's room.

"He's doing well, Tom. No brain damage. They say the vocal chords will mend in time, though he'll be hoarse." Anna paused. "Gillian's my concern. She's hasn't left his bedside. She even eats there—when she eats at all. Mrs. Hogan is looking after Cassie. Gillian needs rest, but she acts like he's at death's door."

Dugan saw for himself as they found an unkempt Gillian dozing in a chair under Alex's worried gaze. Alex frowned up at Dugan's nose splint, then relaxed as Dugan smiled.

"Thomas," he croaked.

"The pad, Alex," Anna reminded him, nodding toward a pad and pen on the side table. Gillian roused and jumped up like a soldier caught sleeping on guard duty.

"Mr. Dugan…" She stopped, befuddled.

"Gillian," Anna said, "please go home and rest. Harry's waiting to drive you."

She shook her head. "I can't possibly. He may need something."

"He'll be discharged soon," Anna said, "and when he really needs you, you'll be exhausted. I insist you go rest."

"Oh, *you* insist, do you…" Gillian started, then she sagged, on the verge of tears. "May… maybe you're right. I'm just so confused…."

Alex held up his pad, a message scrawled in block letters.

ANNA'S RIGHT, LUV. GO REST. I'M FINE.

Mrs. Farnsworth nodded, and Anna embraced her. "Don't worry. We'll look after him," she whispered as she walked Gillian to the elevator.

"Alex," Dugan said as they left, "I'm responsible for this. If we'd leveled with you sooner, you wouldn't be in that bed. And if we hadn't let the bastards grab Cassie—"

Alex scribbled furiously and held up the pad.

DID YOUR BEST. CASSIE SAFE. ALL THAT MATTERS.

Before Dugan could reply, Anna returned, Ward at her side.

"Look whom I found getting off the lift." She smiled as Ward advanced with outstretched hand, shaking first Alex's hand, then pumping Dugan's.

Ward cocked an eye. "How the hell do you break your nose drowning?"

"I had help. Russian this time. I'm an equal-opportunity punching bag."

Ward chuckled, then turned serious. "You know about Braun?"

Dugan nodded. "Can't say it breaks my heart, but where do we stand?"

"If by 'we' you mean you and Alex," Ward said, "I'd say you're in good shape. We got enough out of Braun before he passed to combine with what we knew from other sources to piece together the plot." Ward smiled at Anna. "And using a rather liberal interpretation, we classified the info from Braun as a deathbed confession, which carries legal weight. The Panamanians have dropped the charges against you, and no charges will be filed against either you or Alex in the UK or the US."

"Anna told me," Dugan said, "but is Gardner really signing off on that?"

Ward smiled again. "A lot of folks up the food chain are looking now. Larry Boy wants to take a bow. Given your results in Turkey, he can hardly throw you under the bus again without looking like the asshole he is."

Ward's smile faded. "If only everything had worked out as well."

"What do you mean?" Dugan asked. "You got it figured out. Can't you go public or to the UN or the World Court or someplace?"

"Knowing and proving are not the same, Tom," Anna said. "And for all our efforts, the plotters succeeded."

"Well, not Venezuela," Ward said. "Best we figure there, Rodriguez wasn't trying to destroy the canal, merely spook China into backing a second canal through Nicaragua. One big enough for VLCCs to get his crude to Asian markets without a competitive disadvantage. That literally blew up in his face. Ironically, the disaster in Panama worked to his buddy Motaki's advantage. When the Turks dodged the bullet, it didn't take too much imagination to figure out just how bad it could have been."

"So you can't prove it in court," Dugan said, "so what? Surely you have enough to share with the Russians and the Chinese? I can't believe they'll sit still for this."

"What choice do they have even if we convince them?" Ward asked. "The Chinese won't even openly admit they were victims, because to them, it would be a big loss of face. They'll likely internalize it and make the plotters pay, but it may be years from now. And Motaki's got Russia by the balls. He needs Russia as a safe, overland supplier of fuel—a source we can't use our naval presence to interdict, but now Russia needs Iran's crude even more."

"I don't see how that necessarily makes Iran any more secure," Dugan said. "If our navy can cut off gasoline going into Iran by tanker, surely we can do the same for crude coming out by tank—" He stopped. "Oh yeah."

"Right," Ward said, "no one in the West is going to get too upset if we embargo gasoline into Iran, but the crude coming out to fulfill Russian supply contracts is going to our European allies. The idea of stopping Iranian crude exports is unlikely to get much traction, not with Russian crude off the market."

Dugan looked thoughtful. "Then maybe we should concentrate on getting Russian crude back on the market," he said.

SECURITY SERVICE (MI5) HQ
THAMES HOUSE, LONDON

"That should just about do it," Dugan said, nodding at the pile of maps and intelligence briefing reports piled on the table in front of him. "This was terrific—a hell of a lot more information than I'm used to working with."

Beside him, Harry scratched his head. "So tell me, Yank, how is it a ship bloke knows so bloody much about overland pipelines?"

Dugan smiled. "I'm a graduate of Tanker Trade 101 at the prestigious Alex Kairouz School of Economics. At some point or another, almost all pipelines end at a marine terminal where ships pump something in or take something out. Alex figured that out a long time ago. Pay attention to new pipelines—get a leg up on future trade patterns."

"This is first-rate, Tom," Anna said. "It will take some work on the diplomatic front, but the Russians should go for it. Motaki will be right back to square one—short of fuel and facing domestic unrest."

"Actually," Dugan said, "I've been thinking about that. I think maybe our Russian friends should give Mr. Motaki all the fuel he wants."

"What do you mean?" Ward asked.

"I mean sometimes you should be careful what you wish for," Dugan said.

"Thank you once again, Agent Ward," Reyes said, shaking Ward's hand.

"The pleasure was mine, Lieutenant," Ward said. "Have a safe trip home."

Reyes nodded. "I wonder if I might have a word alone with *Señor* Dugan."

Ward shot Dugan a puzzled frown. Dugan shrugged. "OK by me," he said.

"Ah… fine," Ward said. "I'll just go get the car and meet you at the passenger pickup point, Tom." Ward turned back to Reyes. "I'll be in touch about our joint operation in your area, Lieutenant."

Reyes nodded, and Ward walked away, leaving Dugan alone with the big Panamanian. Reyes waited until he was sure Ward was out of earshot.

"First, *Señor* Dugan, let me apologize for my regrettable behavior during our first meeting," he said.

"Understandable," Dugan said, "given the circumstances."

"Thank you," Reyes said. "I wished to speak to you alone because I have some concerns to which I believe you will be more sympathetic than your colleagues."

"Ah… how's that?"

"I do not know quite how to phrase this," Reyes said, "but I am not completely comfortable with the way things stand. Up to the point of the bastard Braun's death, I was fully involved in the operation. I was napping in the hospital lounge, to be notified immediately when he regained consciousness so that we could resume interrogation, and the next thing I knew he was dead. Since that time, I have been kept a bit at arm's length."

"I'm sure Jesse—"

Reyes held up his hand. "Please, *Señor* Dugan. Do not feel the need to defend Agent Ward. I know he is your friend, and I'm sure he is merely doing his job. But that is my problem."

Dugan looked confused, and Reyes continued.

"You see," Reyes said, "I am a simple policeman, not an intelligence agent. Agent Ward promises a "joint operation" against Rodriguez and assures me I will "participate." However, I suspect my definition of participation will be quite different from his."

"Go on," Dugan said.

Reyes continued. "I want to be present when we deal with Rodriguez, but I strongly suspect that because of my personal loss Agent Ward considers me too emotionally involved—in short, a liability. I believe that the operation timetable might be arranged so that I am otherwise engaged and unable to participate in the main mission."

"Even if that's true," Dugan said, "how can I change that?"

Reyes took a business card from his shirt pocket and handed it to Dugan.

"Not change, *señor*," he said, "merely inform. I know that you are… shall we say "quite close" to Agent Walsh. I need only know the real date and time of the operation. If you learn of this and call me, I will be forever in your debt."

Dugan was noncommittal. "I probably won't know, but if I do, I'll think about it."

Reyes extended his hand. "I can ask no more. Thank you, *señor*."

"So what did Reyes want?" Ward asked as Dugan got in the car.

"He apologized for kicking my ass," Dugan said. "I told him I understood. And the thing is, I really do. When Ginny died, I was ready to find someone to pin it on and kill them on the spot. I can't imagine how much harder it must be to really know who was responsible and have to bottle up your rage. It must be eating the poor guy alive."

Ward nodded. "Well, hopefully the Venezuelan op will bring him some closure."

CHAPTER THIRTY-TWO

"Landing in ten, ma'am."

The secretary of state smiled her thanks up at the steward before stuffing a file into her briefcase and fastening her seat belt. It had been a whirlwind seventy-two hours, with stops in Ankara, Turkey, and Baku, Azerbaijan. She still couldn't quite believe what she'd managed to accomplish in such a short time. She looked at the file and smiled. She was no great admirer of the intelligence community, but the spooks had outdone themselves this time. The plan was masterful.

She thought again about leaving the Chinese out of the plan and again reluctantly concluded it was for the best. She had provided her Chinese counterpart the basic intelligence, enough to assuage any concerns about US duplicity in the Malacca attack. But there were enough moving parts in the spooks' plan as it was; Chinese involvement would just complicate things unnecessarily. Russia was the key.

The Kremlin

The secretary sat with the Russian president and Russian foreign minister, watching their faces as they, in turn, watched the video, their rage barely contained. When it was over, the foreign minister turned to face her.

"This is obviously most disturbing, Madam Secretary," he said, glancing at the Russian president. "We will analyze this and act on it accordingly, but I think it is obvious that nothing can be done in the short term. And as much as we appreciate you bringing it in person, we are puzzled as to your intention in doing so."

The secretary of state looked at the Russians. "I came to seek your cooperation in, to use a Russian proverb, killing the wolf closest to the door."

The Russian president spoke for the first time. "It will be difficult to hide our outrage, but until the strait reopens to tanker traffic, we must play Motaki's game. The first cargoes of Iranian oil to fill our European contracts are in transit to Rotterdam, and payment in Russian fuel is arriving in Iran even now."

"And if the strait does not reopen to tanker traffic?"

His face colored. "Unacceptable! That threatens our entire economy. International law and long-established precedent are on our side. If the Turks persist, military response is inevitable."

"Your points are sound, but the Treaty of Montrose was signed over seventy years ago. Given current world public opinion, I doubt the Turks will respond to ultimatums."

"What would you propose? The Black Sea Straits"—he used the Russian name—"are open to all by treaty. Failure to defend that right puts control of our only warm-water ports in foreign hands. Would the US accept a Cuban blockade of the Florida Strait? And we cannot deal with Iran until our oil flows again."

"Must it flow through the straits?"

The Russian president snorted. "How then? Pipelines? All are inadequate and cross Turkey or Georgia, involving contracts of dubious enforceability. You ask us to abandon legal rights of free passage to place ourselves at the mercy of other countries?"

"Not abandon, Mr. President, merely assert more strategically." She spread a map.

"If I may," she said. "Five percent of Black Sea exports can be moved north to Baltic ports through your own pipelines. Correct?" He nodded.

"As you know," she continued, "Western interests are in constructing a pipeline across Turkey, from Samsun on the Black Sea to Ceyhan on the Mediterranean, projected operational in six months. Completion can be accelerated to six weeks or less, allowing tankers to shuttle between your ports and Samsun. From there the oil can be pumped across Turkey to Ceyhan, bypassing the straits. That can handle half your exports." The Russian listened, nodding.

Her finger moved east. "At Baku in Azerbaijan, the Baku-Novorossiysk line, formerly carrying Azeri oil to your oil port, lies idle as the Azeris now prefer the Baku-Tbilisi-Ceyhan line."

The Russian grunted at the reference to yet another incidence of Western companies undermining Russian influence. "What has that to do with anything?"

"The terminals for the Baku-Novorossiysk and the Baku-Tbilisi-Ceyhan lines are two kilometers apart. There is spare capacity on the Baku-Tbilisi-Ceyhan line, and a connection could be built in days, allowing you to reverse the direction of the Baku-Novorossiysk line and pump your oil from Novorossiysk to the Mediterranean via Baku. These steps combined could see 95 percent of your exports flowing to Western markets in weeks."

"And the remaining 5 percent?"

"Will transit the Bosphorus via tanker, maintaining your right of free passage."

The Russian looked skeptical. "The Turks and Azerbaijanis accept this?"

"They do, pending negotiation of pipeline tariffs. The Turks will accept the tankers with increased security against accidents and terrorism. They want joint inspection teams to include a Russian, a Turk, and a neutral-country observer on a rotating basis. Ships will be inspected before departure from Russian ports, by 'invitation' of your government. No one will be seen as 'conceding.' This arrangement can be publicized as a cooperative international effort to deal with a difficult issue. Mutual cooperation and diplomacy at its best."

The Russian scoffed. "Except, of course, the tariffs. We pay ransom to transport oil that is now moving freely. This is behind the Turks' fine talk of safety and environment."

"The tariff they've agreed to barely recoups their operational costs."

"But it increases our own. And why a low tariff? That alone is suspicious."

"Because, Mr. President," the secretary said, "the Turks know a 95 percent traffic reduction achieved peacefully is a bargain." She paused. "And the tariffs are a pittance compared to the cost of military action against Turkey, which will draw NATO in on Turkey's side."

The Russian glared. "This leaves Turkish hands on our jugular."

"With respect, sir, history and geography placed those hands long ago." Her voice hardened. "Will you fare as well in the grip of Iranian fanatics?"

He sighed, then gave a wan smile. "Points well-taken, Madam Secretary. You are disturbingly familiar with our oil distribution network."

She smiled back. "I take it you concur with our analysis?"

He nodded, his brow furrowed in thought. "Fifty percent in days and full resumption in six weeks seems possible. But perhaps we can be secure much sooner. The Iranians are being quite accommodating. If we press them, I believe we can convince them to export heavily now, and put a six-week reserve on the water beyond their control. We will use the excuse that the recent disruption has us nervous, and that we are renting extra storage capacity in European ports. I think we'll be back to business as usual in a week, or perhaps ten days." He smiled a hard smile. "And then we will see about choking off their fuel."

The secretary of state smiled back.

"Again with respect, Mr. President," she said, "perhaps you might wish to supply them even more."

The Russians looked at each other.

"Another 'suggestion,' Madam Secretary?" the foreign minister asked.

She nodded and presented the rest of the plan.

Borqei limped along on a leg full of Iraqi shrapnel, troubled after a meeting with Yousif's adoptive parents. The couple had been shocked beyond belief when the boy's bullet-riddled corpse was found on the street outside their home, the apparent victim of a drive by shooting. How Yousif got there remained a mystery, and the boy's parents were hardly comforted when Borqei shared with them Motaki's message describing Yousif's death as heroic. He doubted they believed it any more than he did.

The press had lionized "Joe Hamad," all-American boy, and linked his death to a Latino gang, prompting a reprisal. The Defenders of Islam was a motley collection of delinquents of Arab descent, none devout, but nonetheless determined to uphold the honor of Islam. Their single foray into southwest Detroit wounded a member of Los Pumas, the dominant gang, and tensions rose, with calls for calm from all sides. Borqei had been on television twice and received death threats, but that didn't bother him like the loss of his protégé for doubtful ends. He trudged along, thinking of Yousif, praying he was enjoying the rewards of Paradise.

***

Lieutenant Manuel Reyes sat in the front passenger seat. He had suspected Dugan was an honorable man and was thus unsurprised at last evening's phone call. He was equally unsurprised that the little "favor" he was undertaking now for Agent Ward seemed to be planned so that it would be impossible for him to take part in the Venezuelan operations. That is, it *would* have been impossible if he performed the favor tomorrow as requested. That's why he was performing the little favor a day early.

"This is embarrassing, Manny," Perez said from the driver's seat of the lowrider, shouting over the Spanish rap. "If I have to listen to this *pinche* 'music' much longer, the only one I'm going to kill is myself."

Reyes nodded. Both wore blue bandannas of Los Pumas with faded jeans and tank tops exposing garish, but temporary, gang tattoos. They dripped gold chains.

"That him?" Reyes asked, pointing across a vacant lot to a cross street.

Perez followed the finger. "That's him. He looks just like the picture."

"Move into the street," Reyes said, "and raise the front."

Perez nodded. The car lifted with a whine as Reyes silenced the throbbing music. They crept forward, a malevolent predator, high in front with the rear almost dragging.

Borqei was well into the street when they struck him waist high, trapping his body between the pavement and the rear bumper. They striped the street with gore to the end of the block, where Perez raised the rear and sped away, leaving just another gang-related death.

F.A.R.C. TRAINING CAMP
SANTA MARIA DE BARRINOS
VENEZUELA
20 JULY

Manuel Reyes and Juan Perez stood before a crude shack, dressed in sweaty camouflage, eyeing a group of similar buildings. A paved runway lay in contrast to the dirt track providing access to the camp from the Venezuelan interior to the east and the Colombian border ten kilometers west. A man emerged from a building and trotted over.

"The gringos finished, *Teniente*," said Corporal Vicente Diaz, "the camp is secure."

"*Bueno, Vicente*,"—Reyes checked the time—"eat and rest. You too, Juan." He nodded at Perez. "I'll join you in a moment."

As they moved away, Reyes watched with approval. For two years, young Diaz had played a disaffected Panamanian in FARC, the Revolutionary Armed Forces of Colombia. He'd been invaluable, monitoring activity in the Darien, the jungle sprawl between Panama and Colombia used by FARC as safe haven. He wouldn't be able to return undercover, but Reyes and Captain Luna agreed this mission justified the loss.

Reyes turned as the leader of the "gringos" approached and smiled at the term. Sergeant Carlos Garza, US Army Special Forces, and his five men were hardly gringos. Natives of places from Puerto Rico to Texas, they shared Hispanic heritage and a desire to be the best soldiers on the planet. Special Forces had seen to that, then immersed them in language training. Now, whether their native dialect was East LA slang, Puerto Rican Spanglish, or Tex-Mex, they could pass as native in any Spanish-speaking place on earth.

Reyes and Perez had had to scramble to meet "Garza's Gringos" the night before to crash the Venezuelan border with Colombian forces in hot pursuit, bolstering the illusion with a hail of intentionally inaccurate gunfire. The FARC commander had been waiting at the training camp, alerted by the Venezuelans at the border. He saw a truckload of new recruits led by Diaz, a man known to him and trained in that very camp. Such arrivals were not unprecedented, and the FARC leader decided to bed them down and deal with it all in the morning. A day that never dawned for the twenty narco-terrorists in the camp.

"The camp is secure, Lieutenant," Garza said as he reached the shack's porch.

"Diaz told me. What now?"

"We take their places and wait. After the hit we'll place bodies to mimic a firefight, dressing a few with no tattoos or other marks in Colombian uniforms and mangling them with grenades. Make it look like a cross-border action."

"Need help?"

"No, sir," Garza said, "my men are more convincing FARC if we get visitors. Diaz gave us passwords." He paused. "A good man, Diaz."

Reyes smiled. "I agree, *Sargento*, though it is nice to hear from another professional."

Garza hesitated. "Sir, can I ask something, one professional to another?"

"Ask away, *Sargento*."

"I expected Diaz, but not you and Perez." He paused. "Your presence is unplanned, and unplanned is risky. I don't know what numb nut OK'd this, but if it ends up costing casualties, I assure you that individual and I are going to have a discussion."

"Apologies, *Sargento*. There is no 'numb nut' involved, and I suspect your superiors may be equally upset when they learn of our presence. Now that we can't be sent back, I will tell you the truth. We invited ourselves, knowing that you were observing radio silence and gambling that if we just appeared, you would accept us at face value." He shrugged. "I will face any consequences when we return."

Garza stifled a curse, then said, "All right. You're here now, but you're strictly observers. Got that?"

Reyes looked the American in the eye. "I may have to disappoint you there, *Sargento*. I have a promise to keep."

Garza studied the ground. "It's your wife, isn't it?"

Reyes stiffened. "How do you know that?"

"I overheard your men. I can't let your hard-on for Rodriguez compromise the plan."

"The plan is to kill Rodriguez, no? Who has more right to shoot the bastard than myself?"

"Shit," Garza said as he sat on the porch step. "I suspected as much. You only know part of the plan. Sit yourself down, Lieutenant. No one is going to shoot Rodriguez."

***

Rodriguez gazed down as the King Air circled, glad the FARC men were waiting in formation. A quick tirade against the *yanquis* while his people checked the warehouses and he'd be off. His men did the checking, of course, so he could honestly say he saw nothing. Honesty was important.

He sighed. Not everyone was so honest. His deal with FARC called for payment of 10 percent of the value of the cocaine transiting. Amazing how revenue increased after he began these impromptu visits to the camps.

Even without the drug money, the camps were assets, placed to terrorize his opposition. Initially FARC had traded muscle for havens to rest and re-arm, but as US aid allowed Colombia greater resources to disrupt drug traffic, FARC moved distribution under Rodriguez's protection. For a fee, of course. Free muscle and cash to boot.

His mood was transformed in the anxious weeks since Panama, with the media diverted by the Bosphorus attack and news of Braun's death bringing the welcome realization that the lone thread linking him to the attacks was severed. Confident now, he was on the offensive, his speeches condemning the attacks as an American plot, a pretext to exert control of global choke points with the ultimate aim of reclaiming the Panama Canal. He ended his speeches with a pledge of "the honor and treasure of the Bolivarian Republic of Venezuela to resisting to the death American hegemony."

Rodriguez scowled, his mood dampened by the close confines of the King Air. Runway length precluded the use of his jet and reduced his security detail to six. But they were his best, and, he thought, smiling back at the last row, there was the sacrificial lamb.

"Navarro," he taunted, "are you ready to take a bullet for your *presidente*?"

The sullen face staring back was a copy of his own, down to the smallest scar. The men were dressed identically in chinos and bright-red open-collared shirts.

"Really, Navarro," Rodriguez said, "so morose. You have a handsome face that required little surgery; I provide a fine life and ask only that you smile and wave. Yet you sulk. Perhaps your daughter would be better company. She is what? Fifteen now?"

"Forgive me, Excellency. I would be honored to fall in your service."

"Much better, Navarro," Rodriguez said, then grinned at the bodyguard next to him.

The man grinned back. "As usual, *Señor Presidente*, Navarro goes first. When we're sure all is secure, he'll reboard and you deplane in his place."

Rodriguez sighed. "If the fool could speak, I wouldn't take these tedious trips at all."

***

Reyes stood at attention as the door opened and six men deplaned, forming a circle into which a red-shirted man emerged. The bogus guerrillas stood at present arms, safeties off their weapons. A shot inside the plane drew the bodyguards' attention as the man in their midst dove to the tarmac. The Americans' guns came up as one, and the six bodyguards were dead before they hit the ground.

Garza and his men circled the plane as Red Shirt's twin stumbled down the steps, followed by the copilot with a pistol.

"The pilot?" Garza asked the copilot.

"Dead," the man replied. "He was loyal to Rodriguez."

"I am not Rodriguez," said the man beside the copilot. "I am Victor Navarro. *He* is Rodriguez," he pointed to his approaching double.

"Really?" Garza asked. "What is the countersign?" The man looked panicked as Garza continued. "The rain in Spain—" Garza stopped. "Complete the phrase."

Rodriguez smiled. "Falls mainly on the plain."

"Actually, I made that up." Garza turned to the second Red Shirt. "Pass phrase, *Señor?*"

Navarro smiled. "Rodriguez is an asshole."

"*Mucho gusto, Señor Navarro,*" Garza said, nodding for his men to bind Rodriguez.

"Now," Garza said to the copilot, "I suggest you and"—he smiled at Navarro—"*Señor Presidente* here coordinate your stories. We'll add authenticity with bullet holes in noncritical areas of the plane."

"*Un momento, Sargento,*" said Navarro before Garza turned away, "perhaps you should also shoot me in some 'noncritical' area."

"Hardly necessary, *Señor Navarro.*"

"To the contrary. I can blame a difference in my voice or gestures on the stress of being shot. In this case, I am only too happy to 'take a bullet' for the president."

Garza shrugged. "OK, then. A grazing wound to the arm. Just before you leave." Navarro nodded, and Garza moved to Rodriguez, kneeling on the tarmac, encircled by two Americans, Reyes, and Perez as the rest of the force staged the bodies.

"What now?" Reyes asked Garza.

"Presidente Rodriguez/Navarro returns, plane shot up. He is enraged, so everyone keeps their heads down. Suspicion will fall on the vice president, who will be allowed to resign and be replaced by an obscure member of Rodriguez's clique, a secret member of the opposition.

"Then," Garza went on, "Navarro will undo the worst abuses: restore term limits, ease press controls, et cetera. In a few months, he'll have a fatal heart attack, and the vice president will take over. Navarro and his family will be smuggled to the US for plastic surgery and new identities. And Rodriguez here"—Garza looked down—"will have a state funeral."

Muffled protests came from Rodriguez's taped mouth as he struggled.

"Good," Reyes nodded. "No assassination. No conspiracy theories."

"An embalming table and cold storage await in Colombia," Garza said.

Rodriguez struggled harder as a soldier produced a syringe. Garza nodded to Reyes.

"You want to do the honors, Lieutenant?"

Reyes hesitated. "For days, I've dreamed of little else but putting a bullet between his eyes, but this… this pathetic piece of shit sickens me. I had not envisioned putting him down like a rabid dog."

"Just remember Miraflores," Perez said softly, "and the many more has he killed just with the filth in these warehouses. He is worse than a rabid dog, Manny, for the dog has no choice in the matter."

Maria's agony filled Reyes's mind, and in seconds, he was over Rodriguez, the needle deep in the man's neck. Long after the body stopped twitching, Perez pried his fingers away.

TEHRAN, IRAN
25 JULY

Motaki smiled as he read. The Russian fuel was flowing, with the state press trumpeting the news, and there was optimism in the streets for the first time in recent memory. He put down the report and pressed the intercom.

"Ahmad," he said, "please have the car brought around."

"At once, Mr. President. May I know your destination to alert security?"

"No place in particular, Ahmad. I just want to go among the people. And no security detail. They intimidate people."

"Are you… are you sure that is altogether… wise, Mr. President?"

Motaki stifled a rebuke. "I'll be fine, my young friend. Like the early days, when I roamed freely. The driver is all I need."

"Very well, Mr. President," Ahmad said.

***

Boron carbide was the perfect contaminant—virtually indestructible, inert, the third-hardest material known to man, and available commercially as a fine powder. Mixed into the paint used on the interiors of the tank trucks and railcars, the hard, tiny crystals were initially harmless and fuel quality hardly compromised during inspection and custody transfer at the border. After all, no one was testing for boron carbide.

As Russian fuel surged through the Iranian distribution system, the impact was cumulative, felt first in smaller towns near the border. Here and there, ancient cars coughed to a halt, and country mechanics scratched their heads, the scattered failures prompting no concern.

The cancer spread to the population centers, reaching critical mass in Tehran in the wee hours of morning as cars coughed and died in increasing numbers. Their drivers shrugged off this latest hardship and pushed their cars to the nearest garage. By dawn, every shop had a line; the drivers clustered in groups, smoking and musing on the cause of the serial breakdowns.

Fuel was the obvious culprit, and admiration of Motaki's Russian coup changed to anger as motorists waited for the bill for his stupidity. The verdict came midmorning as mechanics removed cylinder heads to peer at seized and blackened pistons. Like doctors pronouncing a terminal illness, they folded greasy hands and gave the news: engine replacement required, a diagnosis that doomed most of the stricken cars to the scrap yard.

News spread as waiting drivers crowded round and thumbs flew, sending texts to warn family and friends against refueling. Warnings already too late, as across the city vehicles bucked to a stop, an unmoving mass of blaring horns and angry voices. The battered cars were mobility, one of few remaining freedoms, and a loss not easily endured.

Voices gained purpose and coherence as they coalesced into a chant.

"Death, Death, Death to Motaki!"

***

Motaki stared out the car window, bemused. Cheap fuel meant crushing traffic, but he was enjoying the ride as people did double takes. He wanted to be among people to bask in their approval. He might get out and walk, he thought, since they weren't moving.

The driver stood outside, craning his neck. He got in, shaking his head.

"What is it, Rahim?"

"Bonnets raised everywhere, sir. And distant chanting. 'Death to America,' I think."

Motaki smiled. "Praise Allah for providing our people a target for frustration, though I am not sure the Great Satan creates traffic jams."

Rahim chuckled as Motaki watched a motorist peer under his hood. The man pulled a cell phone from his pocket and stared at the display, scrolling through a text. He grimaced and raised his eyes, recognizing Motaki, then pointing at him as he shouted. A mob surged around the car, tugging at locked doors and pressing angry faces to the windows, picking up the faraway chant: "Death, Death, Death to Motaki!"

The car rocked with the chant as Motaki fumbled for his phone, and was lifted off the ground, crashing back to throw its occupants about like rag dolls. On the next heave, the car rolled over. Motaki dropped the phone, and Rahim was knocked unconscious, a blessing he'd never appreciate. Motaki lay on the ceiling, gazing out at feet and taunting, upside-down faces. He heard glass break and smelled gasoline as the remains of a bottle hit the pavement and clear liquid ran down the outside of the bulletproof window.

"Here's your Russian petrol, Excrement of Satan," a voice screamed. "Drink it. It will not run our cars!"

More gasoline splashed over the car from nearby stations overrun by the mob. They descended with anything that would hold liquid, hurling the tainted fuel and screaming abuse. The fuel pooled around the car, finally igniting from a stray spark and setting a dozen rioters alight with it to run screaming through the mob like human torches.

A warning was transmitted by text message as motorcycle police wound their way through unmoving cars, and the mob scattered. The police rushed to the charred limo, the more foolhardy burning their hands on locked doors or trying to force bulletproof windows. Pointless efforts—the driver was dead from head trauma, and Motaki was curled in the fetal position on the smoldering headliner, baked to a turn.

CHAPTER THIRTY-THREE

Dugan lay in bed, arm around Anna as she dozed, her head on his chest. She stirred and lifted her head to smile at him sleepily, then put her head back down.

"Penny?" she said against his chest.

"Just thinking about the Russians and Iran," he said.

"Hmmm. Just what a girl wants to hear after fantastic sex."

"Sorry," Dugan said, to which Anna mumbled something inaudible, patted his chest, and rolled on her side.

"I'm just really surprised the Russians accepted our plan so readily," Dugan said a few minutes later.

"Hmmm…" Anna muttered. "…Braun's smirking face on video must have… done the trick…" Her voice trailed off into the steady breathing of sleep.

***

Dugan sat alone in the dark living room, a half-finished beer on the coffee table in a puddle of condensation. He looked up at a sound from the bedroom door.

"Tom?" Anna said.

He heard her move through the dark and shut his eyes against the glare as she turned on a lamp. He opened them again as she wrapped the thin silk robe around herself and sat down across from him.

"What's the matter, Tom?"

"How many people do you know that smirk on their deathbed? And if there was a video of Braun, why didn't I see it?"

"Tom… I…"

"The bastard's alive, isn't he." It wasn't a question.

"Tom… please… you don't under—"

"Don't what? Don't understand? Oh, I understand all right. It's all professional spook 'need to know' bullshit. Some sort of 'the end justifies the means' deal with the Devil. What could possibly motivate you and Jesse to cut any sort of deal with this murdering bastard?"

Anna was calm now, her voice ice. "Your bloody freedom, for one thing, and Alex's as well. Has it occurred to you that, despite everything that happened, we had not a scintilla of hard evidence against Braun? Alex had confessed and implicated you, and at the time we made the deal, we didn't even know if he would survive to recant. And even if he did, it was essentially his word against Braun's."

She continued before Dugan could interrupt.

"Just how do you think we got the name of the ship out of Braun?" Anna asked. "Did you think Jesse water boarded him in the recovery room? Despite your disdain for 'professional spooks,' on occasion we do have a better appreciation for the realities. We did what we had to do, and you and Alex are free men because of it."

"OK," Dugan said, somewhat mollified, "but why not tell me?"

"Because we concluded you were incapable of keeping the truth from Alex," she said. "Given what he and his family endured, we feel it better if he never knows Braun is free."

"Free? What do you mean free?" Dugan said. "I assumed you promised the bastard some sort of sentence reduction, but this is… this is…"

Anna sighed and reached for her phone. "I'm calling Ward over," she said. "I don't want to go over this with you more than once."

***

"Full immunity," Ward repeated two hours later. "All jurisdictions—UK, US, Turkey, Singapore, Panama, Indonesia, and Malaysia—and upon recovery, a private jet with a five thousand-mile range to take him anywhere he wants to go."

"Where is he now?" Dugan asked.

"In an apartment in Kensington," Anna said, "set up as a private hospital. The doctors specified a three-week convalescence. He'll be released day after tomorrow."

"So that's it then," Dugan said, "you just kiss him bye-bye at the airport, and you're done. Karl Braun no longer exists. You don't keep track of him?"

"He didn't even bother to put that in the agreement," Ward said, "because he knows we'll try to track him. But he's a slippery bastard, and somewhere there'll be another plane waiting, or maybe a whole series of planes. When he hits the ground the first time, chances are we've lost him. If there's a third cutout plane, or maybe two waiting at the same airport that go in different directions, we're toast. I think losing him is a near certainty."

"If he's officially dead anyway," Dugan asked, "why not just grease the bastard now?"

Ward looked at Anna, then back to Dugan. "Because it doesn't work that way, Tom. The heads of state of seven countries have signed off on this. If it somehow leaked that either the US or UK reneged on a deal we ourselves brokered, it could have severe adverse consequences on future diplomatic efforts, even if the deal in question is with a murdering thug."

Dugan sighed and picked up the written agreement from the coffee table.

"Tom," Ward said, "you're wasting your time with that. The State Department and Anna's folks have had a dozen lawyers going over that agreement with a fine-tooth comb. Braun's no fool. The agreement is very specific and airtight."

Dugan ignored Ward and kept reading. After a while, he looked up, a slow smile spreading across his face.

"Now let me get this straight," Dugan said to Ward. "You and Anna put him on the plane, and you're done, right?"

"Essentially. But Tom," Ward warned, "whatever you're thinking won't work. Our orders are to follow this agreement to the letter."

"I wouldn't have it any other way, pal," Dugan said.

Heathrow Airport
London
28 July

"Off," Braun said, extending cuffed wrists to Lou and Harry.

"Not yet," Lou said as they rolled through security. Harry just glared.

"Idiotic," Braun said, "but have your petty victory."

Braun brightened as the limo rolled across the tarmac toward the plane, and he spied familiar figures. "Agent Ward. Agent Walsh. How nice of you to see me off," he gushed as he was dragged from the car.

"Cut the crap, Braun," Ward said.

"I suggest you lot cut the crap as well," Braun said, holding up cuffed wrists. "You can start by telling these baboons to uncuff me."

Anna nodded, and Lou uncuffed the German, none too gently.

"Much better," Braun said, rubbing his wrists. "But now, if there's nothing further, I'll just be on my way."

"Bon voyage," Ward said.

Braun laughed and bounded up the short steps into the plane. As soon as he entered the plane, two large black men grabbed him by the arms, forced him into a seat, and cuffed his wrists to the armrests.

"What the bloody hell—"

A much-smaller, well-tailored black man stood looking down at him and spoke.

"Karl Enrique Braun," he intoned. "You are under arrest for terrorist acts committed against the Liberian flag vessels M/T *China Star* and M/T *Asian Trader* on 4 July of this year. Under Liberian law, statements you make or have made can and will be used against you."

"What is this nonsense?" Braun said. "I have immunity, you idiot. Now remo—"

"Actually, you don't," said a voice behind him, and Braun twisted his head to see Dugan walking up the aisle, rolled papers in his right hand tapping the open palm of his left.

"Meet Mr. Ernest Dolo Macabee," Dugan said, nodding at the smaller black man, "Foreign minister of the Republic of Liberia."

"I don't give a damn who he is," Braun said. "I have full immunity. Now —"

Dugan held up the papers. "Turns out you aren't quite as bulletproof as you thought, Braun. There's no mention of Liberia in this agreement."

Braun sneered. "Your games don't fool me, Dugan. The intent of the agreement was global immunity. I don't believe for a moment your government will allow you to turn me over to these monkeys."

Macabee stiffened. Smooth move, Karl, thought Dugan as he smiled down at Braun.

"The governments involved *are* following the agreement, Braun. To the letter, in fact. What's happening isn't covered by the agreement."

"I HAVE FULL IMMUNITY!" Braun shouted.

"Alas, Mr. Braun, not in Liberia," Macabee said as if lecturing a dull student. "But it's not surprising we were overlooked. We have many ships under our flag and limited administrative resources. We invariably cede jurisdiction to the country where crimes occur or, if at sea, authorities in the next port. But we always retain the right to prosecute, if necessary. Justice must be served, Mr. Braun." He paused. "Even 'monkeys' know that."

"This is preposterous," Braun said. "This will never hold up, Dugan. I was promised freedom and a plane to take me anywhere I wanted to go."

"And you walked aboard this plane a free man," Dugan said, "whereupon you were arrested by different authorities. And as far as the plane goes," he continued, tapping the paper in his palm, "it says absolutely nothing about the ownership of the plane. It merely specifies range capability and that you will be transported to a destination of your choice."

Dugan turned to Macabee.

"Mr. Minister," he asked, "are you prepared to transport Mr. Braun from here to the destination of his choice before you return with him to Liberia?"

Macabee nodded. "Most assuredly, Mr. Dugan, though I regret he will be unable to deplane at his chosen destination."

Dugan made a show of studying the agreement, enjoying himself.

"Hmm... nothing in here about deplaning," he said.

Braun strained at the cuffs and screamed abuse. Macabee nodded to one of his men, who stifled the tirade with a piece of duct tape over Braun's mouth.

"I will discuss Mr. Braun's desired itinerary with him once we become airborne," said Macabee. "May I have a word with you on the tarmac, Mr. Dugan?"

Dugan nodded and followed the dapper African down the short steps. As agreed, Ward and the Brits were long gone, having fulfilled their part of the agreement and left. On the tarmac, Macabee turned to face Dugan.

"Well, justice delayed is justice denied, so I'll get Mr. Braun home," he said, extending his hand. "However, I did not want to leave before thanking you and your government for the generous gift."

Dugan gripped the man's hand. "My pleasure, Mr. Minister, though please be discreet regarding the plane. Agent Ward had to call in a few favors from friends in the Drug Enforcement Agency. The transfer wasn't completely according to Hoyle, but I'm sure you'll make much better use of it than the drug smugglers from whom it was confiscated."

Macabee smiled. "I understand," he said and bounded up the short steps into the plane.

Ten minutes later, Dugan watched the jet roar skyward, at ease for the first time since he'd met Ward and Gardner in Singapore two months and a lifetime ago.

EPILOGUE

"Great, Jesse," Gardner said, "please go on."

"That's it for Panama. In Iran, the situation is confused since Motaki's death. The unrest is being brutally suppressed, but the student-led opposition is winning. The regime is collapsing, and Ayatollah Rahmani has requested asylum in France."

Gardner scowled. "Why wasn't I told?"

"I just got it. I'm telling you now."

Gardner bit off a reply and smiled. "I understand, Jesse. Sorry to interrupt. Prognosis?"

What's with this asshole? Ward thought as he continued.

"Unknown," he said. "The likely beneficiary is the Council of Resistance. They pay lip service to democracy but have Marxist roots, even though most of the world knows that ship has sailed. They'll dominate any coalition. Not so bad, really. Sometimes"—he sighed—"a rational and predictable enemy is the best one can hope for."

Gardner filed that away.

"Great job, Jesse." He paused as if embarrassed. "I... I want to apologize for past behavior. I should have listened to you."

Ward gave a wary nod as Gardner extended his hand.

"Friends?" Gardner asked with a hopeful smile.

"Ah, sure," Ward said as he shook.

"Good man." Gardner walked Ward to the door with a hand on his shoulder.

Ward walked back to his own office, ill at ease and counting his fingers.

OFFICE OF THE DDO
(DEPUTY DIRECTOR FOR OPERATIONS)
CIA HEADQUARTERS
LANGLEY, VIRGINIA

"At times," Gardner said with a practiced sigh, "a rational and predictable enemy is the best one can hope for."

The deputy director looked puzzled.

"Yes, well, all in all a great briefing," he said, recovering.

"Just doing my job, Mr. Director."

"And quite well. But where's Ward?"

"Off today." Gardner lowered his voice. "Personal problems."

"I'm sorry to hear that," the DDO said. "Ward's a good man."

Gardner's silence spoke volumes.

"If you've something to say, son, say it."

"Sir, I think he's a burnout. The fitness report I just finished reflects that."

The DDO nodded. "Sad, but it happens. I don't second-guess supervisors."

"Yes, sir. Thank you, sir."

"And you've impressed me. How'd you like to work directly for me?"

"In what capacity, sir?"

"Something I've considered for years," the Old Man said. "We use tons of support, an effort decentralized across many groups. I want a sort of 'czar' to take charge. You've done operations. A staff position will enhance your résumé. How does assistant deputy director for administrative services sound?"

"It... it sounds fine, sir," Gardner stammered, "ah... when..."

"Right now. We'll get you moved over. Any loose ends?"

"No, sir." Gardner stopped. "Well, yes. I have to review Ward's fitness report with him."

"Leave that for his next supervisor."

"I better do it, sir. He'll be upset. He may even make groundless accusations."

"He's not the first burnout we've dealt with," sighed the DDO. "We'll handle it."

***

Ward fidgeted. He'd arrived at work to find Gardner's office empty and an e-mail that his performance review would be done by "his next supervisor," whatever that meant. Then this summons to the DDO's office.

"Jesse. Sorry for the wait," the DDO said, emerging from his office. "Come on in."

He pointed Ward toward a sofa, and as he sat, the Old Man retrieved a file from his desk before sitting opposite, a coffee table between them.

"Damned impressive." The DDO tapped Ward's personnel file. "A string of superior ratings and a Director's Citation. The only negative—a repeated refusal to accept advancement. Don't you like hanging around the office, Jesse?"

Ward squirmed. "I'm better in the field and—"

"And you hate office politics. Believe me, Jesse, I know the downside of advancement."

"Yes, sir, I suspect you do."

"More on that later. First, tell me how you became a fuckup."

"Sir?"

"Your latest fitness report." The DDO passed him a single sheet of paper.

Ward read with building anger. "This is… this is complete horseshit!"

"I take it you dispute the evaluation?"

"You're goddamned right I dispute—" Ward looked up to see the Old Man grinning.

"Good enough." The DDO snatched the report and crossed to his desk. A shredder whirred.

"This," the Old Man said, returning with a form, "says a disputed report was reviewed by senior management, that's me, and voided. This"—he laid a report in front of Ward—"is a fitness report from your new supervisor, also me, full of praise. Some of it might even be true. Sign."

"But, but… you're not… I'm way down the food chain."

"We'll get to that. Sign," ordered the Old Man, smiling as Ward complied.

"Now a question," the DDO said. "Think before answering. An American citizen named Borqei died recently. What do you know about it?"

"Just what the FBI told us, sir. We suspect a hit by foreign nationals of unknown origin. The trail disappears in Mexico City."

"Good answer," the Old Man said. "Now, the next issue. Recent events showed everyone, including the president, the potential of maritime threats.

At his order, I'm forming a Maritime Threat Assessment Section reporting to me. You're gonna run it."

"Sir, I'm just a field spook. I don't—"

"Don't give me that crap. I'm a field spook too, but here I sit, long past retirement. Because the country needs me, just like it needs you." His face softened. "Jesse, it's a good deal. You get a chunk of the black budget, and I'll keep the politicians off your ass."

"I don't know what to say."

"'Yes, sir, thank you, sir,' would be appropriate."

They locked eyes. "Yes, sir, thank you, sir," Ward said.

"Fantastic." The Old Man thrust out his hand. "The paperwork's ready. Start forming a team. And get that Dugan guy. He knows the industry, and I like his instincts."

"I'm all over that."

"Good. You and Dee Dee ever been to the White House?"

Ward looked confused. "Uh… we took a tour when the kids were little…."

The Old Man laughed. "Well, you and Dee Dee are dining there next week. Just a quiet private dinner where you'll receive a Presidential Commendation."

"I… I don't know what to say."

"For a smart fellow, Ward, you sure have a limited vocabulary."

"But what about Gardner?"

The Old Man's smile faded. "Yeah, we need to cover that, but what I'm about to say never leaves this room. Understood?" Ward nodded.

"You know Gardner's being groomed for office. Intelligence work enhances the résumé, and his family leaned on enough senators to get him forced on me. It had to be a "leadership position." Since you'd refused the top job in your group, I figured he could sit at that desk a while, and you'd keep him from stepping on his dick. I was prepared to step in if required, but Gardner's idiotic actions caught me flat-footed. Thankfully you salvaged things."

"So where's he going now?"

"I was gonna fire him regardless, but then I realized that wasn't enough. He might eventually end up somewhere he can do some real harm. I made him office-supply czar with a big title. Now he can't cause any disasters except maybe a stapler shortage."

"But won't he just move on in a year or so?"

"That's all I need. Like everyone else, he signed a privacy waiver. He's been under surveillance a month and already documented with underage prostitutes and buying cocaine. Soon, I'll have more than enough to leak to the press if he runs for so much as dog catcher."

"The surveillance is legal but leaking it isn't. Why tell me this, sir?"

"Because he'll be around long after I'm dead. I'll give you a copy of his file and rest easy knowing his balls are in the palm of your very capable hand. Can you live with that?"

"Yes, sir, I can."

"Good, then we're done." He started to rise but stopped. "By the way, Gardner tried to snow me with some bullshit about 'a rational and predictable enemy.' Sounded familiar."

Ward grinned. "It's from a speech you gave. I knew he'd use it sooner or later."

TEMPORARY OFFICES
PHOENIX SHIPPING LTD.
LAMBETH ROAD, LONDON
19 AUGUST

Like its legendary namesake, Phoenix Shipping rose from the ashes in temporary space with rented equipment, the hum of voices punctuated by ringing phones as monitors flashed atop a sea of cheap metal desks. Mrs. Coutts sat as gatekeeper to the closet-size cubicle of Mr. Thomas Dugan, acting managing director of Phoenix Shipping Ltd.

Dugan smiled out at the scene. Business was booming, and an able assist from MI5 hadn't hurt, providing quiet assurance in the right ears that Alex had performed exemplary service to the Crown and that Her Majesty's Government would take a dim view of allegations to the contrary. Claims on M/T *Asian Trader* were paid promptly and in full, and lines of credit were restored, and in most cases, increased.

Dugan left each night tired but happy, usually to meet Anna for dinner. They'd taken an apartment in Belgravia, and nothing had felt so right since that long-ago time when life was full of promise and he'd return from sea to find Ginny on the dock, laughing as she held up a sign reading HEY SAILOR. LOOKING FOR A GOOD TIME? Ginny would approve, he thought.

"Mr. Ward on line one, sir," Mrs. Coutts said.

Dugan lifted the phone. "Jesse. How's it going?"

"Good," Ward said. "Better than good. We've formed a dedicated maritime-threat section. They're letting me run it until I screw up."

"Fantastic, Jesse, and well deserved." Dugan paused. "What about that asshole Gardner?"

"Managing paper clips. He's no longer a factor."

"Well, that's good. At least you won't have to watch your back."

"And speaking of watching things, you know how badly we need—"

"Stop right there, pal. I like what I'm doing."

"Great," Ward persisted. "Stay there. It's perfect cover. We'll make it worth Alex's while financially, and you just keep your eyes and ears open. Piece of cake."

"Let's recap, shall we? The last time you said that, I was beaten by a crazy Panamanian, forced to jump out of a helicopter onto a moving ship, nearly washed overboard by gasoline, shot at, just escaped being blown up, and almost drowned. Oh yeah, I forgot the broken nose."

"Nothing like that's likely to happen again."

"Damn right, because I'm not playing."

"Just think about it, Tom. That's all I ask."

"Listen closely, Jesse. I—DO—NOT—WANT—TO—DO—THIS. Understood?"

"Just think about it. Talk to Anna. I'll call back. Sorry, but the DDO is calling. Bye."

Dugan stared at the receiver. Some friggin' nerve, he thought as he hung up.

Five time zones away, Ward smiled. He'll come around, he thought.

KAIROUZ RESIDENCE

Dugan and Anna held hands under the table. Dinner had been pleasant, and Gillian seemed a different person from the hollow-eyed wraith that had haunted Alex's bedside a month earlier. For that matter, she seemed a different person than she'd ever been. She had on a modest but stylish dress, obviously new, and most of the white had disappeared from her hair. Both she and Alex fairly glowed, trading sly smiles as Cassie seemed near bursting with some great secret. As they all finished coffee, Alex asked Mrs. Hogan and Daniel to join them and addressed the table, his voice raspy.

"We want you all to share a special moment. Recent events have been life changing, and they've led me to count my blessings"—he beamed at Cassie and Gillian—"and take some long-overdue action. I asked, and Gillian has done me the great honor of—"

"Mrs. Farnsworth's gonna be my new mom," Cassie blurted.

Alex sat bemused as Gillian struggled in vain to suppress a peal of laughter. "Well, yes, I suppose that's what I was taking rather too long to say," Alex said with a broad smile.

Dugan and Daniel rose and pumped Alex's hand, while Anna and Mrs. Hogan beamed approval.

"Out with it," Anna said, "the juicy details. When did this happen?"

Alex took Gillian's hand. "When I realized what I'd overlooked for many years."

"It caught me a bit off guard," Gillian said, actually blushing.

"But to quote a very wise woman," Dugan said, "'a lady is prepared for any eventuality.' And you, Gillian, are, and always have been, a great lady to the bone."

"Hear, hear." Alex squeezed Gillian's hand as Cassie held the other, and Gillian blinked back happy tears.

"Right, then," she said, "there's champagne chilling. Mrs. Hogan,"—she started to rise—"I'll help with the glasses."

She had to wipe away more tears as Cassie jumped up. "I'll do it, Mom."

***

After toasts, the ladies slipped away to discuss the wedding, and Alex led Dugan to the library. They sipped brandy in amicable silence until Alex spoke.

"Thomas, I'll be spending more time at home. I need you here. As managing director and an equal partner. In addition to salary, of course."

"Alex, that's extremely generous. I don't know what to say."

"'Yes' comes to mind."

"If I agree, how do you see things structured?"

"You handle operational matters; I look after finances. A perfect team, really."

Dugan stared into his glass. "Ward wants us to help the CIA. I said no, but I'm waffling."

Alex chuckled. "He is persistent. As is Anna. They've both pressed me, you know."

"How do you feel about it?"

"Positively, as long as it places neither you nor my family at risk."

"Agreed. Having the gratitude of the US and British governments is mighty helpful."

"So you're accepting my offer?"

Dugan smiled as he offered his hand. "I guess I am, partner."

CENTRAL PRISON
MONROVIA, REPUBLIC OF LIBERIA
8 SEPTEMBER

Concrete grated Braun's knees as he lapped at the puddle, grateful for the leaky roof; rain water was cleaner than the murky liquid his jailers dispensed. Mold thickened the walls over his rotten, sodden mattress, and he'd long ago sacrificed his shirt and underwear as rags to keep himself as clean as possible. His ragged pants hung loose, a legacy of the gruel ladled into his bowl with indifferent frequency. He devoured the sludge, saving some to attract cockroaches and other protein, and saving some of those to bait up geckos and rats. His thin face, framed by a beard and greasy hair, smiled back from the puddle. He was a survivor.

But he was concerned. He'd sent word to Macabee weeks ago, yet here he rotted. He was considering the likelihood of a double cross when a key rattled in the lock and Macabee entered, impeccably dressed and nose wrinkled, taking pains to avoid touching anything.

"Well, Mr. Braun, here I am."

"Where the hell have you been, Macabee? Why the delay?"

Macabee shrugged. "I felt time would make you more fully appreciative of the benefits of my assistance. Then there was the matter of a trial. The court docket is quite full."

"And when is my trial?"

Macabee smiled. "Last week. You pled guilty and were sentenced to hang."

"What—"

"Don't be tedious, Mr. Braun. A timely 'death' is perfect. Unless you want to stay?"

"No, no. I'm quite ready to leave."

Macabee nodded. "Let's hear your offer."

"It hasn't changed from what I offered on the plane, Macabee. Two million dollars."

"Method of payment?"

"I'll give you the number of my solicitor in London along with a code word. He, in turn, will give you account numbers and authorize the bank to verify availability of funds to you directly. I text you the authorization code to withdraw funds once I'm safely away."

Macabee laughed. "And I'm to trust you? That's as idiotic as your offer. Let's settle that first. Ten million US dollars."

"Preposterous," Braun said. Macabee turned to go.

"Wait! Ten million leaves me nothing. Make it five."

"Your ultimate solvency is both unknowable and irrelevant, Mr. Braun." Macabee smiled at a gnawed rat carcass in the corner. "Ten million—final offer."

Braun hid his elation. "Very well. Ten million."

"Good," Macabee said. "How is the money held?"

"Three accounts. Approximately two, three, and five million, respectively. Why?"

"You'll give me the account number and authorization code to withdraw the two million now as a deposit," Macabee said. "I'll confirm the existence of the rest with your solicitor, in the manner you indicated. I'll fly you under guard to wherever you want, but you won't be released from the plane until the remaining eight million is in my account. Agreed?"

"Agreed," Braun said, mulling plans to outwit the Liberian.

Macabee pulled out a notebook and pen. "Details, please."

***

Four hours later, Macabee sat at his desk, undecided and regretful he hadn't squeezed more from the German. He'd realized his mistake later as he mulled how easy it had been. He'd expected Braun to up the ante, especially after he'd tasted weeks of Central Prison hospitality, but still, it had been a bit too easy.

He sighed; perhaps he shouldn't be too greedy. He hesitated a moment more, then made his decision. He picked up the phone and dialed a London number.

CENTRAL PRISON
MONROVIA, REPUBLIC OF LIBERIA
10 SEPTEMBER

Braun trudged, wrists tied behind him and sandwiched between ragged guards with feet bare as his own, as the trio picked their way between puddles to the gallows. The ragged shirt provided by Macabee hid a wide belt around his torso. At the back of the belt, accessible through a rip in the shirt, was a strong eyelet. A thin wire braided into the rope above the noose would be hooked into the eyelet, transferring the force of the drop into the belt. The death certificate was signed, and the space below the trapdoor was shielded from prying eyes by plywood, concealing men waiting to help Braun down and into a coffin for his ride to freedom.

"Ah, Macabee," he said, topping the crude stairs, "good of you to see me off."

Macabee nodded as Braun was moved onto the trapdoor and hooded. Braun smiled under the hood as the noose was snugged and a metal tape unrolled to touch him at the heel and back of the head, measuring to set slack in the rope. Good showmanship.

Hands released him, and the trapdoor shifted as the others stepped off. Braun turned his hooded head toward Macabee. "The wire," he whispered.

"Alas, Mr. Braun. There will be no wire. I'm afraid you've been outbid."

"What? You can't do this, Macabee!"

"Actually, I can."

"Wait, Macabee! We can work this out. There's more money, much more. I lied."

"I know, Mr. Bruan," Macabee said, "and it's such a pity you waited until this late date to be forthcoming. And by the way, I've a message from Alex Kairouz. He asked me to tell you to enjoy your trip to Hell."

Macabee nodded, and the hangman pulled the lever.

Milam clung to the ladder and looked down into the tank, bright with work lights, the crackle of the welding arcs mixing with the clang of steel on steel—the din of progress. He grabbed the top rung and pushed his head through the manhole to find himself gazing at worn boots and an out-stretched palm.

"Need a hand, old timer?" Captain Vince Blake asked, grinning down at Milam.

Milam smiled back and gripped Blake's hand to haul himself up onto main deck. He tugged sweat-drenched coveralls away from his skin as he moved to the rail in search of a breeze. "Christ. And the sun's barely up. Calderon was right about more productivity on the night shift. By noon it'll be tough to work down there."

Blake nodded, watching a line of passing ships. "Good to see the canal at full capacity," he said. "I can't wait to get in that line."

The ship had been refloated two days earlier, Blake and Milam dogging the salvage master's steps until he threatened to put them ashore. They'd maintained silence with difficulty and shared relieved grins when *Luther Hurd* was finally towed sternforemost to the lake for temporary repairs.

They had debated taking other assignments, but leaving *Luther Hurd* to others didn't seem right. Arnett had rejoined them, promoted to chief mate at Blake's behest. A new first engineer completed the group, a man Milam recruited. They'd ride on the tow north, inspecting and making repair lists.

Blake looked around and shook his head. Generator sets and welding rigs crowded the deck amid debris of ongoing repair work. Clean decks and bright paint had fallen victim to blowing sand and dirt from dam construction, and rains had washed the filth into hard-to-reach places or carried it to leach down the sides in dirty streaks. The port side and starboard stern were masses of rust, twin legacies of rocks and equipment that laid the steel bare and impact with the guide wall. The ship rode deep at the stern, exposing the mangled bulbous bow.

"God, she's a shit house."

"Yep," Milam agreed, "damn sand went everywhere: glands, seals, you name it."

Blake nodded. "How's the engine room?"

"Not as bad," Milam said. "I closed the dampers, so not much got below. Crankshaft deflections are in limits. We'll recheck when the engine is warm, but there's no bottom damage aft; at least none that carried to the engine. Prop and rudder are OK. Except for the tank holed by the anchor and the forepeak tank, the hull's tight. Divers are plugging those outside so we can make temporary repairs inside. When she's tight and we patch the holes between tanks, we can go. Two days maybe." His eyes narrowed. "If Little Dutch Boy gets his head out of his ass."

Blake suppressed a groan as he saw Pedro Calderon approach with Captain Frans Brinkerhoff, the salvage master's face flushed bright red. The Dutchman zeroed in on Milam.

"Vat is this nonsense about running the main engine, Milam?"

"I need to test it. I figure we leave on the main engine and make up tow outside."

"Oh, you do? I must remind you that it is not your decision to make."

Here we go, Blake thought as Milam reddened. By agreement, the Panamanians were responsible for returning the ship to service, including the return to the builder's yard in San Diego for repairs. They had in turn contracted a Dutch salvage company, relegating Blake and Milam to observers, a part neither liked but which Blake handled better than Milam.

"Actually, Captain Brinkerhoff," Blake said, "the chief is right. I'm sure you won't break tow at sea to let us test the engine. This will be our only chance."

"Nee. This is not my problem. We lock down with tugs and make up tow at Miraflores guide wall and tow straight to sea. This is most efficient, ja?"

"Look, asshole," Milam said, "no ship I'm chief on leaves port on a rope, so—"

"Ahhh… so this is about saving the pride of the chief engineer, ja? And who is to pay?"

"Pay for what?" Milam asked.

"Extra cost for harbor tugs to stand by, launch to return line handlers to shore, time lost, all costs not in our quoted price," Brinkerhoff said. "We follow my plan."

Milam glared as Calderon spoke. "Perhaps I can help, Capitán Brinkerhoff. The ACP will provide the needed services at no charge. Is that satisfactory?"

Brinkerhoff glared at Milam. "Ja," he said at last before stalking away in disgust.

"Thank you, Señor," Blake said as Milam nodded.

"It is nothing, Capitán," Calderon said. "I can at least ensure your departure is dignified."

M/T *LUTHER HURD*
GATUN LAKE ANCHORAGE, PANAMA
18 SEPTEMBER

Chief Mate Lynda Arnett stood at the main-deck rail, peering straight down as the pilot boat inched closer to the ship's side. The pilot stepped off the boat onto the rope ladder and began his climb toward her, showing her only the top of his head as he concentrated on the swaying ladder and the task at hand. As he neared the deck, Arnett stepped back to give him room to come aboard.

"Captain McCluskey," Arnett said as a smiling face appeared.

"You didn't think I'd let anyone else take you out, did you?" Roy McCluskey asked as he ignored Arnett's outstretched hand to fold her in a hug.

"I have to say, this is the first time I've ever hugged a second mate," McCluskey said, releasing her.

"Chief mate," Arnett corrected him.

His smile widened. "Fantastic. And well deserved."

Arnett tried not to glance at McCluskey's feet and failed.

"How's the... how are you?" she asked, her eyes back on his face.

"Right as rain." McCluskey stamped his prosthetic foot on the deck for emphasis. "They were able to save the knee, and that made a huge difference."

Arnett nodded, smiling back, and they stood for a moment in awkward silence.

"Lynda. If it wasn't for you—"

"Just doing my job, Captain," Arnett cut him off.

"Well, thank you just the same," McCluskey said.

Arnett nodded again, thankful he'd sensed her discomfort and cut his thanks short.

"Now," McCluskey said, "let's go see Captain Blake and start you on your way."

BRIDGE OF THE AMERICAS
BALBOA, PANAMA

No event save the opening of the canal itself had impacted Panama like the attack of July 4. It was named by consensus, but unlike 9/11, date alone was unsuitable, the people instinctively rejecting a name that relegated their tragedy to second place behind the birthday of their huge northern neighbor. Instead, it became simply "Pedro Miguel," a division in time. Things occurred "before Pedro Miguel" or "a week after Pedro Miguel," spoken with sadness and growing pride as the story unfolded.

Many stories, actually: the pilot who delayed the flames, quick-thinking tug captains who herded burning gasoline with their propeller wash, firefighters who abandoned traffic-snarled vehicles to run kilometers in the heat in a heroic but unsuccessful bid to save children at Miraflores; the list was long. But in a visual age, none was quite like the plunge of the *Luther Hurd*.

The video was viewed globally, but as the Bosphorus, then Iran and a dozen fresh stories dominated the news, it faded. But not in Panama, where it was shown repeatedly, and the *yanqui* ship with the strange name became, regardless of her flag, a Panamanian icon. Her repair progress was widely reported, unnoticed by the four Americans, lacking the time to watch the news and the Spanish to understand it if they had. But the people of Panama had no intention of letting *Luther Hurd* slip away quietly.

***

Manuel Reyes stood on the walkway, peering through the chain-link barrier, a hand on the shoulder of each of his boys. His sons held flags, Panamanian in one hand and American in the other. He'd been uneasy with the gringo flag, but the old plea of "But Papa, all the other kids…" had stolen his resolve. And, he thought, the *yanquis* helped him avenge Maria. He gave each shoulder a gentle squeeze. They were beginning to show signs of their old spirit.

"Look, Papa." Miguelito pointed. "There. Where the little boat is shooting water."

"Hah. A lot you know, Miguel," scoffed Paco, irritated his twin had spotted the ship first. "That is a fireboat. You should use the right name."

Reyes smiled. Much improved. "You are both right. Yes, Paco, that is a fireboat, and yes, Miguelito, I do believe the ship is *Luther Hurd*."

His words were drowned out as the people of Panama bid farewell to *Luther Hurd*.

M/T *LUTHER HURD*
PASSING BALBOA DOCKS, PANAMA

Blake paced the bridge as McCluskey conned the ship. Arnett was at the console, and the ACP had provided a helmsman, leaving Blake no real duties and edgy. And, he admitted, gazing down at his filthy, rust-streaked ship, embarrassed. It was like walking around with your fly open, hoping no one noticed. He wished again they'd departed at night.

McCluskey smiled. "Don't worry, Captain Blake. I won't run into anything."

Probably wouldn't matter much, Blake thought as Balboa docks loomed to port. "What the hell's that?" he asked as berthed ships all began to sound their horns.

"Ships in port wishing *Luther Hurd* Godspeed," said McCluskey, puzzled at the reaction.

Blake gave a tight-lipped nod. So much for slipping away, he thought as they negotiated the waters of the port and turned south. "What the hell—"

"Dead slow ahead," McCluskey ordered.

"Dead slow ahead, aye," Arnett confirmed.

McCluskey grinned. "This may be a bit tricky, Captain, but I think we'll get through OK."

***

"Slowing down," said the first engineer. "Wonder what's up?"

Milam shrugged. "Who knows? We gave up sightseeing when we decided to push her rather than point her." The phone buzzed before the first could reply.

"Engine Room. Chief."

"Jim. Come up. You've got to see this."

"I've seen Balboa before, Cap. I need—"

"Just come, Chief! Now." Blake hung up.

"Shit," Milam said. "You got it, First? The Old Man has a bug up his ass."

The first engineer nodded, and Milam started the long climb, muttering about rope chokers with no regard for people who worked for a living.

As he exited the machinery space into the quarters, he heard a strange noise outside. Concerned, he raced up the central stairwell, two steps at a time, and burst onto the bridge to join Blake at the forward windows. The harbor was jammed with boats of all descriptions, stretching under the

Bridge of the Americas to the sea. *Luther Hurd* moved slowly seaward through a narrow lane marked with temporary buoys and patrolled by police boats, tugs bow and stern to see her safely through, and a fireboat preceded her, throwing arcs of water skyward. The air rang with handheld air horns and whistles and sirens and bells, the less well equipped beating pots with large spoons. Flags were everywhere, most Panamanian, but also a liberal sprinkling of US flags among them. People were cheering and waving signs saying Thank You and *Muchas Gracias*.

"Christ," Milam said as they moved toward the Bridge of the Americas, where a banner hung reading *Muchas Gracias, Luther Hurd*, and in smaller letters below *De parte de los niños de Panamá*. The bridge walkway shimmered with flags in thousands of small hands.

"Who's that on the bridge?" Milam managed as Blake raised his binoculars.

"It's… it's kids," Blake said, "a lot of 'em."

As they moved under the span, McCluskey shot them a knowing smile, and a large net hidden by the banner released thousands of tropical flowers and handwritten well-wishes to cascade on the ship, covering *Luther Hurd* like a float in the *Carnival* parade. Milam lost it.

"Damned allergies," he growled, wiping his eyes with the back of his hand. "Christ, these fucking petunias are gonna clog the ventilation intakes. I gotta go reverse the fans." He fled to the sanctuary of his engine room as Blake and Arnett smiled at his retreating back.

***

Later under tow, Milam stood with Blake on the bridge wing as the coast receded.

"What do you figure, Jim," Blake asked, "three months?"

Milam shrugged. "Should take two, but it'll probably be four, depending on the priority they give us. And you know everybody has a warm and fuzzy feeling now, but as soon as I start insisting we tear into things and somebody has to pay, the honeymoon's over." He sighed theatrically. "Everybody wants to save a buck, but when it goes tits up at sea, I'm the guy stuck with it. I see nothing but arguments, long hours, and midnight inspections ahead."

Blake couldn't contain his laughter. "Who're you bullshitting? You love it."

Milam failed miserably in an attempt to look indignant. "Well anyway, we should start our second 'maiden voyage' in four months."

"Maybe this time I can get her to the load port," Blake said.

Milam chuckled and leaned back against the wind dodger as the battered bow of *Luther Hurd* plowed slowly through the swell behind the tug. Blake watched scattered flowers blow along her dirty deck and drift down her rust-streaked sides, but somehow, he didn't feel the slightest bit ashamed.

Thank You

Time is a precious commodity. None of us truly knows quite how much we'll have, and most of us are compelled to spend large blocks of it earning a living, making our leisure time more precious still. I am honored that you've chosen to spend some of your precious leisure time reading my work, and sincerely hope you found it enjoyable.

If you enjoyed this book, I do hope you'll spread the word to friends and family. I also hope you'll consider writing a review on Amazon, Goodreads, or one of the many sites dedicated to book reviews. A review need not be lengthy, and it will be most appreciated. Honest reader reviews are the single most effective means for a new author to build a following, and I need all I can get.

I invite you to try the other books of the Dugan series listed on the following page, and if you're a fan of post-apocalyptic fiction, I hope you'll also consider my *Disruption* series, beginning with *Under a Tell-Tale Sky* and available on Amazon.

And finally, on a more personal note, I'd love to hear your feedback on my books, good or bad. If you're interested, I'd also like to add you to my notification list, so I can alert you when each new book is available. You can reach me on my website at **www.remcdermott.com**. I respond personally to all emails and would really like to hear from you.

Fair Winds and Following Seas,

R.E. (Bob) McDermott

More Books by R.E. McDermott

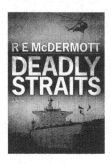

Deadly Straits - When marine engineer and very part-time spook Tom Dugan becomes collateral damage in the War on Terror, he's not about to take it lying down. Falsely implicated in a hijacking, he's offered a chance to clear himself by helping the CIA snare their real prey, Dugan's best friend, London ship owner Alex Kairouz. But Dugan has some plans of his own. Available in paperback on both Amazon and Barnes & Noble.

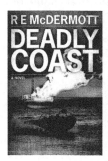

Deadly Coast - Dugan thought Somali pirates were bad news, then it got worse. As Tom Dugan and Alex Kairouz, his partner and best friend, struggle to ransom their ship and crew from murderous Somali pirates, things take a turn for the worse. A US Navy contracted tanker with a full load of jet fuel is also hijacked, not by garden variety pirates, but by terrorists with links to Al Qaeda, changing the playing field completely. Available in paperback on both Amazon and Barnes & Noble.

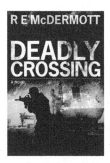

Deadly Crossing - Dugan's attempts to help his friends rescue an innocent girl from the Russian mob plunge him into a world he'd scarcely imagined, endangering him and everyone he holds dear. A world of modern day slavery and unspeakable cruelty, from which no one will escape, unless Dugan can weather a Deadly Crossing. Available in paperback on both Amazon and Barnes & Noble.

Made in the USA
Monee, IL
05 April 2021